FRACTURED SOULS

BY TYLER CRAIG NIXON

Editor:

Maddy D.

Developmental Editor:

Kirsty Edmondson

Contributors:

"Bunni"

Nicole Neuman

Meagan Bowman

Cover Art:

Ujala Shahid

Copyright Information

First Edition April 2024

ISBN 979-8-218-37528-7

This book is dedicated to the fractured souls of the world who battle the shadows of trauma. I write this in the hopes that one day, you'll reach that ocean too.

TABLE OF CONTENTS

PROLOGUE

THE NEON WORLD

RAIN FELL FROM THE CLOUDED SHIBUYA SKY as Kokoro raced through the streets. Her footfalls disturbed the neon world reflected in the puddles, and her weakened legs threatened to give out beneath her. Flashes of light blinded her at every turn while onlookers gave her wary, offended looks.

Her soaked hospital gown clung tightly to her slender, damaged body. Kokoro stumbled through the crowds, desperate to find her friend.

Naoko, where are you?

Once she reached the crossing, the dense crowd unleashed onto the road, filling her peripherals and blurring her vision. They shoved past her, and the air thinned as if being sucked from her lungs. Kokoro fought to stay focused, frantically searching the faceless people walking by her who didn't give a damn about her plight.

"Hello? I need help!" she begged while grabbing arms, shoulders, whatever was within her reach. "Please! I can't find her. I can't find—"

"Kokoro?"

Kokoro's eyes snapped open. The cruel night vanished, replaced with the safe interior of Dr. Maeda's office. He sat across from her, hands folded on his lap, his eyes halfway hidden behind the shimmer of his glasses.

Gentle rays of sunlight touched half the room, cloaking the rest of it in a cold shadow. A clock hung on the wall, its arms moving but without a tick, perhaps a way to stifle the demons for people like her—something Kokoro appreciated.

"Are you still with me?" Dr. Maeda asked.

Kokoro met his curious eyes that assessed her with both caring pity and calculating curiosity.

"I—" She sighed. "Yes, I'm sorry."

The doctor frowned. "It happened again, didn't it? The night she—"

Her throat tightened, and she quickly nodded.

"I see." He pushed his glasses to the brim of his nose as he clicked his pen. "Can we talk about her?"

Kokoro stiffened. She avoided his gaze, instead opting to stare out the window.

"I understand that it's hard for you," Dr. Maeda said. "But I believe it's necessary to discuss this. Tonight, I want to go back to the beginning, if that's okay."

Forcing herself to nod, Kokoro examined her nails, reviewing every familiar rip and tear in the hardened skin. The last thing she wanted to talk about was her precious Naoko, and yet she needed to. Her grief would eat her alive from the inside out if she didn't find at least one person who would understand just how broken she had become.

"Okay." Opening her eyes, Kokoro sat up straight. "What do you want to know?"

"How did you come to know Naoko?" he asked as he studied her intently.

Kokoro briefly tensed, then relaxed. She inhaled, gazing outside, allowing her mind to lull her back to the days when the rising sun still shone for her, and she had a purpose—to be the light in Naoko's tragic life.

CHAPTER 1

THE LONE SAKURA

THE TRAIN SHUDDERED BENEATH NAOKO for what felt like the hundredth time. The occasional raindrops rhythmically tapped against the window. As it lurched again, she stumbled forward a step, barely managing to stay upright by clinging to the swaying handle dangling from the ceiling. Another passenger turned around and briefly eyed her, but she avoided his gaze. With a shrug, he went back to minding his own business.

Naoko sighed and continued to stare aimlessly into the oppressive darkness of the early Tokyo morning. The rising sun broke the horizon, yearning for life like a chick breaching an egg, only to be smothered by rapidly darkening clouds. The city lights stayed on, the artificial glow attempting and failing to provide the warmth lost to the promise of a cold rain.

A familiar ding caught her ear. She turned her head and saw the overhead display flash, showing another stop.

Seven more. Should be more than enough time.

Naoko pulled out her earbuds, looping the cords and placing one earbud in her right ear as she opened the 'PULSE' app, a place where people from around the world could share experiences and encourage others. Occasionally, she would tune in to the normal stations and live sessions of various artists. But today, there was only one person she wanted to hear, and she was due to go live any minute now.

"Kokoro," she whispered softly, her heart fluttering. Kokoro was an up-and-coming idol on PULSE, renowned for her dance lessons, upbeat attitude, and above all, her kindness.

Her phone vibrated, and a notification popped up at the top. Kokoro was live. Precious moments went by while the video buffered, and the world outside blurred and faded. Though initially she was met with a blank screen already filled with heart reactions floating their way to the top, Kokoro soon appeared, her bright smile shining through the screen.

"Hey, everyone!" Kokoro said, her silver-blonde hair tied up in a messy bun. "It's another beautiful day here in Tokyo. But make no mistake, the day is beautiful because of you!"

Naoko gripped her phone. For that gracious moment, the darkness that usually ensnared her held no sway.

"I know things may seem dark," Kokoro said, "like you're trapped, suffocating. But that darkness is just a cocoon. I know one day you'll find the strength to break free and once you do, you'll fly, like the butterfly I *know* you are!"

Naoko smiled. Kokoro always referred to her followers as precious butterflies preparing to take flight despite the raging storm of chaos that was the world. If Naoko was a butterfly, then Kokoro was the colorful umbrella shielding her from the storm above.

"Today, I want to talk about self-care. In our day and age, it's hard to stay afloat in the sea we call society. You may feel invisible or lonely, but that doesn't mean—"

Another ding rang out. Naoko looked up to see her stop listed in pixelated lettering. *Already?*

The sounds of the train grinding to a halt and the shifting of countless feet drowned out Kokoro's voice. Naoko pushed her way to the exit, hoping to be pulled out with the crowd like water through floodgates.

Stepping onto the concrete floor of the station, Naoko continued to navigate through the crowd as they quickly pulled out their umbrellas. With another ding and the system's voice announcing departure, the train rattled off. She exhaled sharply, looking at her phone again, only to find that Kokoro's live session had ended. Naoko frowned.

Guess I'll just have to catch her later.

Naoko sighed, wrapping the cords around her phone and stuffing it in her bag. She slugged forward, indistinguishable in a crowd, half of which was filled with her fellow students and the other with so-called 'adults' on their way to have more of their lives culled by the needless cycle of greed and necessity. Naoko often wondered if she'd turn out that way: either a working machine devoid of a soul or one who had been broken by the pointless mediocrity of it all.

The school soon appeared—a drab, multistoried building of clean white brick and glass. The front doors were flooded with her classmates, all donning matching white uniforms with skirts and pants in a muted blue-gray color, as teachers kept watch at both entrances. Naoko made her way in, with others shoving forward, erratic, like animals headed to slaughter. Each breath was ripped from her lungs under the weight of the crowd, as if in a powerful vacuum. Naoko clenched her jaw as she fought her way down the hall to her destination. Her fellow students didn't give her even an inch of breathing room, treating the space she occupied as empty.

Naoko pivoted to the corner to escape. Three years ago, she had first entered high school at the behest and encouragement of her father, a notion which Naoko—at the time—had eagerly obeyed. Of course, they had been closer back then, but his years in law enforcement had instilled in him a strong focus on what he referred to as 'standards.' On one hand, Naoko felt such 'standards' were nothing more than shackles, trapping her in the consequences of her choice. On the other, she continued to obey and please, hoping her father would revert to the man he once was.

If only.

The slamming of the sliding door shook Naoko from her thoughts as she stood in front of the classroom. Dragging her feet, she made her way to her desk at the back. It was old but well kept. The only blemish on it was the immature scribbles left by its previous users, including the new ones directed at her.

"Rise!" a sharp voice from the front commanded.

Naoko immediately rose from her chair, hands firmly at her sides. Her teacher, Mr. Takeda, had taken his usual position in front of the class, rectangular glasses reflecting the soft morning light from the windows on the left. His fading hairline did little to differentiate him from most of his middle-aged peers, but his eyes set him apart. They were like a blade—sharp, piercing, calculating, much like her father's.

The entire class bowed to bid him good morning and took their seats. Mr. Takeda nodded, returning the greeting as he leaned against the front of his desk. "Now, before we begin the lesson, I wanted to address something that has been brought to my attention. It seems some of our students have been engaging in adult activities...*on campus*."

A giggle erupted from the class. Mr. Takeda silenced them with a glare.

"And so, I am formally reminding you that anyone caught engaging in such behavior will be harshly disciplined, possibly expelled. All of you sitting here are bright and capable, so I need not remind you of the consequences, especially at your age. It is imperative to your future that you exercise caution."

"No problem, Mr. Takeda," a girl to Naoko's left quipped. "Naoko's all over it. She seems more the type for girls, anyway."

A few students seated close to her burst into laughter. The one who had made the snide comment was Sayuki Sato, a girl who had an unhealthy fixation on Naoko. She took every opportunity she could to torment her in front of their classmates.

Naoko's brows furrowed. Her vision tunneled as her heart thumped in her ears. If there was one thing that she hated more than being ostracized, it was being humiliated.

Without realizing it, Naoko muttered something under her breath, her own voice feeling distant and foreign. Whatever she had said, it caused Sayuki's face to blush deeply and the class erupted in laughter. Sayuki's eye twitched, her nostrils flared, and her breaths shortened.

"That's enough, both of you!" Mr. Takeda stood to his full height, his brows furrowed behind his glasses. "Ms. Haneda, Ms. Sato, stand and apologize."

Sayuki clenched her jaw and reluctantly stood. Naoko stayed planted in her chair, her hands gripping the sides of her desk. Her arms and back stiffened, instinctually fighting back against the command. Why apologize to Sayuki, even if she was in the wrong?

"Naoko…" Mr. Takeda's brows furrowed, his gaze intensified. "…apologize. *Now*. How can our classroom function if we all do not respect one another?"

Shaking as she stood, Naoko briefly scanned the classroom, seeing her classmates annoyed and impatient. She turned back to Sayuki, whose glowering eyes would have burned a hole right through her if they were any more intense.

Naoko grimaced, then finally forced herself to bow. She quickly apologized, her voice barely above a whisper. Sayuki, still glaring, returned it, though her bow was not as steep.

"Excellent," Mr. Takeda said, carefully eyeing them. "Now take your seats, please."

Naoko quickly sat down, her eyes stinging, her shaking hands balling into fists. Sayuki turned away, sliding into her chair. Her eyes, strangely devoid of their earlier haughtiness, briefly flicked to Naoko, before turning to face the front.

"So, let's finally begin. Yesterday, we discussed the concept known as the 'invisible hand.' This is a driving force of the free-market system..."

Naoko's face stiffened, a feeble attempt to stop her tears. She had been humiliated yet again, forced to concede to one of the very people she absolutely hated with every fiber of her being. All this was allowed by the system that was supposedly designed to ensure equality in all things, enforced by high standards, safeguarded by 'mutual respect.' The only exception, it seemed, was her. On the rare occasion Naoko's existence was acknowledged, others deemed her unworthy of even the most basic of courtesies.

Naoko bit her lip. Why was it this way? Why was she always condemned to be an outcast?

"...as you know, the first basic principle is supply and demand. When supply outpaces demand, prices drop, and..."

Mr. Takeda's words slowly faded into the background; her surroundings blurred as her mind drifted. She turned her gaze out the window to the concrete courtyard, encircled by a chain-link fence. It was bare, boring, and maddening; the only notable thing being a small Sakura tree. Blooming from the center of the space, it graced the drab ground with its fallen petals, their fragility fractured as they were trampled underfoot without a second thought. It was a cruel injustice that something so beautiful was imprisoned to such an ugly fate.

But such was the way of the world, one where not even beautiful things could survive.

By some miracle, Naoko survived most of her day without running into Sayuki Sato again. The last bell had rung, and she was finally released for the day, waiting for the rush of students to filter out before she left. To get back home, she had to take a different train line that wasn't far from the back gate of the school. She passed across the courtyard, where the Sakura tree stood tall, blessing the wind and concrete with its precious pink petals. The rear entrance was only about twenty meters away.

Just a little more.

"Hey, Naoko, wait—"

Before her brain even registered that someone was behind her, Naoko's foot caught on something, and the ground rushed to meet her. Her teeth clicked together as a gasp escaped her chest, strangled by the rushing wind. Twisting to sit up, she glared into the harsh sunlight, only to see Sayuki standing in front of her.

Naoko braced herself, expecting another mockery or warning from Sayuki, but all she heard was the gentle rustling of the wind and the delicate fluttering of Sakura petals on the concrete. Tentatively, Naoko mustered the courage to meet Sayuki's gaze, expecting a smug expression of triumph. To her surprise, Sayuki's eyes widened, her chest rising and falling rapidly. She stepped forward, closer to Naoko. Naoko shrank back, fighting tears as she let her pain slip through her lips.

"Why can't you just leave me alone?"

Sayuki opened her mouth, as if to reply. Instead, she shook her head, tightening her lips into a firm line. With a last glance, Sayuki swiftly turned and stormed out of the gate.

Naoko's brows furrowed as she blinked the tears away. Sayuki didn't live far, supposedly in some cushy Tokyo penthouse with her father, probably so she could continue looking down on others even after school. Nevertheless, it didn't make sense for her to take the back entrance, unless...

A realization struck Naoko. Sayuki had deviated from her usual route home just to torment her for what had happened earlier in homeroom. The retribution promised without words had now been fulfilled, serving as a reminder of where Naoko truly belonged.

"You okay, love?" a voice behind her asked.

Looking up, Naoko was surprised to see a foreign boy around her age, perhaps slightly older. His slick blonde hair was swept behind his ears, and his blue eyes shone in the sunlight. He extended a firm-looking hand, his brows furrowed in concern.

"Oh." Naoko's cheeks flushed as she took the boy's hand and rose from the ground. "Yeah, I think I think so."

"Well, that's good." The foreigner boy spoke Japanese fluently, his voice carrying a hint of his unfamiliar accent that occasionally caused his words to slur. "I saw what she did, by the way. What a bitch, eh?"

Naoko blinked, realizing the last sentence was in English. Her face burned.

"Right. A bitch." Naoko nodded, attempting to repeat the phrase in English despite being sorely out of practice. Luckily, the years she spent studying it arrived just in time to aid her memory.

The young man smiled, slipping his hands into his pockets as he gazed beyond the fence where Sayuki had gone. "I've known a few girls like her. Loud, proud, stupid. It always ends the same."

Naoko blinked. "What do you mean?"

"They, uh..." The boy chuckled. "...they eventually learn their place, love. All it takes is a little persuasion. So don't worry, eh?" He beamed and lightly patted her shoulder before walking out of the gate.

She stood there, dumbfounded. Her body moved on its own, her arm raised high as she called out to him. "Wait!"

The young man paused and turned.

"T-thank you!" Naoko stuttered, her cheeks flushed as she waved.

The young man briefly eyed her from head to toe, tilting his head. He smirked. "Course. See you around, yeah?"

With that, he turned and continued on his trek, disappearing from view as he turned the corner.

Alone once more, Naoko took a moment, cupping her hand over her mouth as she processed what had just happened. For the first time in what felt like forever, someone had been kind to her. But who was he? Some kind of exchange student?

Naoko smiled and walked through the gate to the station, putting on her headphones once more, allowing the music to blur with the passing of time. The frigid rain finally fell, yet even that couldn't dampen her spirit. With any luck, she would see him again. Maybe, just maybe, she would finally have something to look forward to when she arrived at the hell masquerading as her school.

Maybe things wouldn't be so bad after all.

The front door creaked louder than Naoko wanted it to, though the stupid thing always did that. Normally around this time, her mother would be in the kitchen, preparing dinner.

She briefly paused. It's not that she didn't love her mother or want to talk to her, but right now she yearned for her safe haven that was just up the stairs.

"I'm home," Naoko said quietly, honoring tradition while also hoping that her mother wouldn't hear. She slipped off her shoes and paused at the bottom of the steps, listening.

Silence. She was finally alone.

Naoko made her way up the steps. Kokoro usually had a session in the afternoon as well. If she made it up in time, maybe…

A shadow moved out from the other room, blocking Naoko's path. Slowly, her father strode into the light, buttoning up his police uniform.

"Good afternoon, Father," Naoko said, briefly bowing. After that, she tried to squeeze past, but felt him place a hand on her shoulder. She froze as he slowly released it.

"I checked the student portal, Naoko. Your grades are slipping." He exhaled, his gaze sharp, firm, yet walking the line between caring and condescending. "Not a good way to start the school year."

Naoko gulped and nodded. "Yes, Father. I'm trying."

"Good. I—" Her father stopped as he noticed her phone light up in her offhand. He grabbed it from her, examining it. He clicked the notification, his brows furrowing as he turned to her. "Why are you bothering with this? It's only going to make your focus issues worse. You know that."

"I—" Naoko opened her mouth to protest, but then paused. "I'm sorry."

Her father frowned, his face relaxing. With resignation, he shook his head and handed the phone back to her. "It's your future, Naoko. Don't throw it away on useless things like that, okay?"

Naoko took in her father's disapproving look. Despite how much the dynamic between them had changed, she hated seeing him look at her like that, like she was some failure and nothing more.

After meeting her eyes, he strode past her, to the top of the stairs. Naoko spun, reaching out.

"Father, wait! I—"

Her father stopped and faced her. With a submissive nod, she raised her phone to where he could see it and moved the app to the trash bin in full view. His borderline scowl shifted into a gentle, satisfied smile. He nodded and strode down the stairs, closing the front door behind him.

Naoko smiled back, though the glee soon faded. Panic rose within her as she rushed into her room, reinstalling the PULSE app, opening it, and signing back in, hoping she could still catch the session in time.

"Hey everyone!" Kokoro's soft voice echoed from the speaker. "Sorry I'm a bit late. Life gets in the way sometimes, ya know?"

Warmth settled in Naoko's cheeks. How could she ever erase Kokoro, the one thing that kept her sane?

"Well, today, I have something special for everyone. They were pushing me to reserve the lessons for my subscribers, but then I decided, hey, why not? If you have a gift, why not share it with the entire world?"

Naoko's heart fluttered in her chest. If there was one thing that she enjoyed about Kokoro more than anything, it was her dancing lessons. Naoko had never missed a session and knew her moves by heart, but that never stopped her from following along like it was her very first time.

"Okay everybody, we're still on that street dance kick! Let's go! Two, two, three, four, left pop, pivot, five, six, seven, eight, and ball change…"

Naoko exhaled and smiled, body following the gentle voice as it continued the lesson.

"Don't forget to breathe! Okay, so step, spin, step. Arm out, spin again, and…"

Kokoro's voice faded as Naoko continued the dance on her own. With each movement, she felt the day's events fade from her mind. Her love of dancing, while certainly improved by Kokoro, was something that preceded even her. It was one of the few ways Naoko felt she could truly express herself, and yet, unlike Kokoro, she wasn't ready to show the world. After all, if people would trample the beautiful petals of a Sakura tree without a care, why wouldn't they do the same to her?

For now, Naoko's dancing was hers, and hers alone.

CHAPTER 2

FRIENDS AT LAST

NAOKO ATE HER LUNCH IN THE UGLY COURTYARD, under the one thing that held any metric of beauty. The Sakura loomed over her, petals gently falling, some of them even landed in her food. Naoko didn't mind. She picked them out and placed them at the root of the tree. After all, it gave everyone its beauty so willingly. Wasn't it time for someone to give some of it back, so that it may be preserved and eventually reborn?

Better than being crushed.

As Naoko picked yet another petal out of her lunch, something in the corner caught her eye. Sayuki and her guy friends sat across the courtyard, laughing and grinning. They turned to look at her with haughty, sadistic smirks. Naoko's lips tightened.

"Hey, love. How are you doing?" a familiar voice asked.

Naoko looked up to see the same boy that she had met yesterday in the same courtyard, the one with the accent and swept-back blonde hair. He stepped in front of her, blocking the view of Sayuki and her cohorts. His sharp azure eyes assessed her from head to toe, then he met her gaze with a gentle smile.

"Oh. I'm good," Naoko replied in English. "Just trying to enjoy my lunch."

"Trying?" The boy glanced back at Sayuki. "Lemme guess. She giving you eyes from all the way there?"

Naoko nodded, her lip curling slightly.

"Ah. Bitches like her always do that." The boy pulled a rolled-up bag of chips from his pocket. "Mind if I sit here? I'm waiting for some mates to catch up."

Naoko nodded and smiled as he took a seat next to her. From across the courtyard, she could see the satisfied smirk Sayuki usually wore slowly fade into a scowl.

"So, what's your name?" he asked.

"Naoko," she answered with an enthusiastic smile. "You?"

"Shane," he replied, the twang in his voice clear. Naoko's eyes lit up as she finally placed his accent.

"You are from the UK?" she asked.

"Eh…no." Shane laughed and leaned back. "I'm an Aussie, but me mum lives in the UK. So, I go there sometimes, I guess."

"Australia?" Naoko narrowed her eyes in deep thought. "With the kangaroos?"

Shane chuckled, then nodded. "There's a lot more than that, but yeah. Kangaroos."

"Oh! Right." Naoko laughed. "I love them!"

"Until you meet them. Bunch of cunts, they are." Shane flashed a smile at Naoko before looking away. "Damn, they weren't lying when they said the girls here were cute."

Naoko felt her cheeks burn. Another voice called to Shane. She turned, seeing two other foreigners waving to him. One of them was a tall, dark-skinned male, his hair neatly trimmed, his uniform jacket slung over his shoulder. Next to him was a girl, roughly seventeen years old. Her brunette, wavy hair flowed behind. Her eyes seemed to caress every single person in that courtyard as she flashed them all a confident smirk before turning it to Naoko. Heart skipping a beat, Naoko bit her lip, not taking her eyes from the new girl.

Shane waved back, motioning for them to come over. To her excitement, the girl sat next to Naoko and beamed; the boy sat on the ground in front.

"Hope they're not bothering you by being here," Shane said. "Now this bloke here is your UK man. He and I been best buds ever since we were kids, mainly 'cause our parents do business and shit like that."

Shane's friend smiled and reached for a handshake. "Name's John. And you are?"

"Naoko," she answered sheepishly, lightly taking his hand.

John beamed. Next to Naoko, the brunette girl placed a hand on her shoulder. "Naoko! Oh, what a cute little name! I'm Claire, by the way."

Naoko met her sharp, electric eyes and blushed, reaching for a handshake. Claire looked offended. "Oh, come on! A handshake? No, bring it on in, baby!"

The next thing she felt was Claire's firm embrace. Naoko's body tensed up, her cheeks burning as she looked at John and Shane.

John chuckled and leaned in, whispering, "She's American, if you can't tell." He winked. "Crazy bunch, if you ask me."

Claire pulled away from the hug and shot John an annoyed glare. Naoko noticed her wrists were adorned with metal bracelets, and her long nails were painted crimson. Her blouse was untucked, like Sayuki usually did, but something was different with this girl. Whereas Sayuki violated uniform regulations for attention from others, Claire didn't seem to care about such things. Her confidence radiated in such a fashion that it seemed like anyone in view would know that she didn't need such a shallow thing as 'attention.'

Ironically, like her scent, it was intoxicating.

"So!" Claire's words shook her from her train of thought. "Naoko, huh? Why are you out here all by your lonesome?"

The reminder stung. Naoko hesitated, avoiding Claire's piercing eyes. "I...just don't have anyone to hang out with today."

Claire arched an eyebrow. "Your friends just aren't here today, or...?"

Eyes lowering, Naoko shook her head.

"Oh. Well…" Claire turned to Naoko and gave her a small, hopeful smile. "If you want, we can all hang out. How does that sound?"

Naoko's eyes lit up. She smiled and nodded, securing her lunch bag.

"Great!" Claire took Naoko's hands with a comforting smile that stretched from ear to ear. "We've got your back, okay? So, if there is anything you need, anything at all, just let me know and I will do my best to make it happen. Okay?"

Naoko gripped Claire's soft hands ever so slightly, though not enough to be noticeable. At least, she hoped.

"Okay," Naoko finally replied, before pausing and blinking. "Actually, there is one thing.

Claire tilted her head, brows slightly creased.

"I was wondering if you could walk with me?" The hesitation in Naoko's voice betrayed her vulnerability. "To class?"

"Walk with you? Is everything—" Claire was interrupted by Shane, who nudged her and gestured over to Sayuki. Claire's eyes widened as she pursed her lips, subtly pointing a thumb in Sayuki's direction. "That girl over there bothering you a lot?"

Naoko nodded.

"Oh. Well, sure!" Claire quickly checked her watch, then jumped to her feet, pulling Naoko up as well. She offered her arm. "Lunch is almost over, anyway. Where to, darling?"

Naoko smiled and told her; Claire returned it and escorted her, both boys flanking either side. The other students gave her wary looks as they strode down the halls, with Naoko secured in their protective bubble. Before, she would have proceeded to class alone, invisible to everyone but Sayuki. But something was different about today, something that not only made her feel warm and safe, but genuinely excited.

For the first time in forever, Naoko realized she finally had the chance to make friends.

When Naoko had finished sprinting home from the train stop, she didn't care about slamming the door; her muscle memory removed her shoes. She practically leapt up the stairs, nearly running into her father as he took a surprised step back. He raised an eyebrow.

"Why the hurry?" her father asked as he eyed her.

"Uh…" Naoko took a moment to think. "I just… I think I can fix my grades. I'm going to study more so I can pass this test." She tried to flash him a small, innocent smile.

Her father paused, then finished buttoning up his shirt. His brows furrowed for a moment, his mind in deep thought. "Hmm. Well, good. That's good, Naoko." He nodded. "It's because you got rid of that app, right?"

Naoko fought to keep her innocent smile from turning into an offended frown and shoved back the rare temptation to snap at his words. She nodded.

"Good. Kids these days have no brains because of that stuff. You're better than them, anyway." Her father moved past her, patting her shoulder, then continued down the steps. He briefly turned, taking a moment to gaze at his daughter with another encouraging smile. "Well, study hard. I know you can do it, Nao. See you in the morning."

Naoko blinked, for a moment unable to find words. She settled with a deep bow to hide her face. Her father nodded approvingly as her mother walked out from the kitchen. He planted a quick kiss on her cheek before heading out the door. Her mother turned to her and started up the steps.

"What was that about, Nao? Is everything alright?"

"Y-yeah! Of course!" Nao gave her the same innocent smile she had given her father, though her mother didn't seem convinced. Her eyebrow arched.

"Don't lie to me, Nao. You know you can talk to me." She sighed. "Did something bad happen, or…?"

"No, not at all." Naoko shook her head. "Something good. At school."

"Oh?" Her mother's eyebrows raised. "Why not come down and talk about it?"

"I…" Naoko paused, then gave her mother another smile, albeit a weaker one. "Tell you later?"

Her mother's lips briefly curled. She blinked, slowly nodding. "Of course, Nao. Whenever you're ready."

Naoko nodded, then burst into her room, sliding the door shut behind her. She laid down on her bed, putting her ear buds in.

Kokoro was due to go live soon, but she would have it play in the background for now.

Today, something else had her heart.

She exhaled, opening her photos. After they had spent the day together, Claire showed Naoko how to, as she described, 'take a proper selfie.' By the end of the day, Claire had practically filled her phone to the brim with them, with most being the American beauty queen herself making a variety of cute faces into her camera.

Naoko smiled as she continued to scroll until she finally settled on the one that they had taken at the gate. John was on her left side, hand resting on her shoulder. Shane was at her right, arm across the back of her neck and making bunny ears on the top of her head. Finally, there was Claire who stood behind, leaning forward and pressing her face close to Naoko's with a smile that shone brighter than the sun itself.

A giggle escaped Naoko's lips. Even now, hours after they had taken the picture, it almost felt like they were still there with her, providing a warmth she hadn't felt in forever. She had always yearned for this, yet she never imagined that foreigners would accept her where others wouldn't.

"And so, it's important to surround yourself with people who love you. I mean, who in this world can handle it by themselves?" Kokoro's soft voice said as her live session played in the background. "Just as important, we also need to be there for others."

For a moment, Naoko gazed at each of their faces. She long pressed the screen, made it her wallpaper, then shared it to her account on PULSE with a simple heart as the caption.

"After all," Kokoro continued. "Nobody deserves to be alone."

Naoko smiled gently as the live session ended. Lying back, she gazed up at the plastic glow in the dark stars, their weak lights providing a sense of comfort amidst the void above.

She glanced at the picture one last time before plugging her phone in and allowing herself to drift into a gentle sleep.

The next day, Naoko walked down the hall from her last class, wondering why she hadn't run into Claire, Shane, and John even once. She had gone her usual route, barely even seeing a glimpse of them.

She paused, her gut sinking. They wouldn't abandon her, right? There had to be an explanation. They were exchange students, after all. Perhaps they had some business to attend to instead of school?

Naoko checked the time on her phone, frowning. The school day was almost over. She sighed, defeated.

Maybe I can try to find them tomorrow.

"Naoko!" a shrill voice called to her from down the crowded hall. Sayuki stormed her way, her file tucked under both her arms, snug against her chest.

Naoko quickly left the lockers and joined the crowd of students walking outside, while Sayuki kept calling her name.

Unfortunately, Sayuki soon cornered her, but something was off. Her usually haughty eyes didn't gleam with the possibility of different ways to torment her. On the contrary, they seemed…focused. Almost concerned.

Sayuki's gaze intensified as she nudged Naoko off to the side. As she opened her mouth to speak, Naoko's vision tunneled, her heart pounding in her chest. What was she going to say?

The dismissal bell had finally rung. The rest of the students poured out from the school, Shane and Claire among them. Sayuki's eyes widened, and she threw one last look Naoko's way before vanishing into the bustling crowd.

Naoko sighed, relieved as they finally caught up with her. Claire called to her, backpack slinging around on one shoulder as she sprinted up to Naoko and firmly embraced her.

"I'm so, so sorry for missing ya, girly!" Claire exclaimed. "I promise we weren't ignoring you, hun. Our schedules just got screwed up, and—"

"It's okay," Naoko said with a forgiving smile. "I understand."

Claire paused, then exchanged a quick glance with Shane. He nodded and shrugged, as she turned back to Naoko.

"I saw that girl over here. She wasn't bothering you again or anything, right?"

Naoko shook her head. Her third friend, John, finally broke free from the crowd as he caught up with them.

"Damn, you guys been dodging me all day. What'd I miss?"

Shane ignored him and continued to eye Claire, then stepped forward. "She didn't say anything weird to you, did she?"

Naoko paused and blinked. "Like what?"

Claire and Shane traded glances once more as John arched an eyebrow. She turned back to Naoko and beamed. "Like…what we do after school! The three of us. We like to go hang out at a place nearby. You could come with us today if you want."

Naoko paused, considering it. The train home left in about thirty minutes. From there, it was another half-hour to get home, and she wouldn't dare be late or else risk the wrath of her father. "I'm not sure if I can. I can't miss the train, or—"

"You're worried about getting home on time, love?" Shane asked with a charming smile, glancing at John and Claire. "I'm thinking we can take care of that. Can't we, boys?"

"Of course!" Claire said, beaming at Naoko. She pulled out her phone and opened a rideshare app. "What's your address, babe?"

Naoko paused. If her mother saw her pulling up in a random car, no doubt she would question her until she lost her sanity. Instead, Naoko gave Claire the address of the station closest to her house.

"Okie dokie! All set!" Claire pressed the button and beamed, holding her arm out for Naoko. "You ready?"

Naoko nodded, smiling. Claire looped her arm and guided her out of the gate. The four of them walked for about another mile past an old property with the burnt remains of a building that had been boarded up and plastered with caution tape.

Wasn't this that old Yakuza hideout? Naoko briefly stopped and eyed it. Something about it seemed frightening, yet familiar. Where had she seen this before?

As Naoko continued to stare, the building inched closer, her vision warping, churning, sucking her in. Dread filled her as a shrill sound erupted deep from within, something eerie and yet disturbingly familiar.

The cries of a child.

"Everything alright, love?"

Naoko shook her head. The strange cries stopped. Her friends came back into focus, their concerned gazes locked on her.

"You didn't hear that?" Naoko asked.

The three exchanged glances before John stepped forward. "Heard…what?"

"Nothing. Sorry," Naoko answered, blinking. "Just tired."

"If you're sure." Shane nodded as the three of them continued to walk with her. Eventually, they arrived at a small, closed off alcove. It was surprisingly empty, save the sign that identified it as a designated smoking area and a few other kids around her age, hanging in the back at a nearby table, watching videos on their phones.

The three of them guided Naoko to a small pavilion by one of the walls, with a small table under it. John immediately sat down, cracking his back against it. Shane leaned against the wall and began digging in his pocket, pulling out a partially used carton of cigarettes with packaging that—ironically—promoted an anti-smoking campaign.

Naoko blinked as Shane opened the top. After Claire and John had each snatched one, the two boys lit theirs with their own lighter. Claire leaned in, lighting hers from the tip of Shane's cigarette, inhaling and blowing out the smoke with a practiced smoothness.

"Oh, my bad," Shane said as he noticed her watching them. He pulled his carton back out and offered her one.

"Jesus, Shane, are you an idiot?" Claire nearly smacked it out of his hand. "You don't want to ruin—"

Shane met her eyes with an intensified gaze, an obvious attempt to silence her…or correct her. Naoko couldn't tell which. John arched an eyebrow at his friend's weird exchange.

"—her innocence," Claire said, almost carefully. "Let's not drag her into our bad habits, alright?"

Naoko blinked. *What was that about?*

Shane continued to eye Claire, flicking the butt of his cigarette. He took another puff and turned his attention back to Naoko.

"So, tell us about yourself, love. Been here a while, I imagine?"

Naoko nodded as she sat down next to John. "My whole life. All my schools have been here in Tokyo."

"You've been here that long, but you've never known about this spot?" Shane asked as he took another pull. "I'm surprised."

"I don't smoke," Naoko pointed out.

"True, but I figure you're like us, that sometimes you'd want to get away from the noise of the city," Shane said. "That's why we like it, anyway, but I suppose it could be different for you."

Naoko paused. This spot, whatever it was, kept the ever-persistent sounds of the city at bay behind its towering, yet strangely empty concrete walls. Usually, there were a few shops or even some residential units.

"No," Naoko replied. "Sometimes it's good to get away. One day, I want to get out of Tokyo for good."

"Trust me, girly. I know the feeling," Claire said. "I'm always having to follow my mom and her company around, who follow their dads. Gets old after a while."

"You're telling me," Shane added. "I've been to more private schools than I can count on one hand. Don't get me wrong, but all this traveling is wearing me down, mate. I'd like to just stay somewhere for once, you know? Besides…" He eyed Claire. "…plenty of fine product here. Tokyo might just be the place to *be*. You get me?"

"Damn right," John chimed in. "Everyone here is nice to me, especially considering…" He gestured to his face.

"That's only the people you've met so far, mate," Shane joked. "Plenty of people here hate Blacks, don't you worry."

John pursed his lips as silence hung in the air. For a moment, it seemed to Naoko that he might punch him. Instead, John shook his head and playfully smacked Shane on the arm, chuckling as they got into a brief jabbing match. Claire rolled her eyes and held her cigarette to the side, tapping it to shake the ashes off.

"So, what brought you here?" Naoko asked.

Shane paused for a moment, then extinguished his cigarette against the wall. "Company bullshit, usually. My ol' man brought me along because he wants me to 'learn the business'."

Naoko blinked. "What business does he do?"

"It's a…" Shane paused, as if taking a moment to phrase his words. "…service company. We specialize in making people happy, yeah? Lots of happy customers across the world."

Claire shot Shane a quick glare, then faced Naoko, beaming. "So, tell me. What do you like to do? Got any hobbies? Boyfriends?" Her eyes flashed. "Girlfriends?"

"No partners, but…" Naoko paused, her cheeks flushed. "I have a hobby."

"Oh?" Claire brought her cigarette to her lips. "And what would that be?"

"Dancing," Naoko answered. "I like dancing."

"Huh." Claire took one last puff, then extinguished her smoke and pushed it into a nearby disposal. "You any good?"

Naoko took a moment to consider it. She had been dancing to herself since she was a child and had made noticeable improvements during Kokoro's lessons on PULSE.

"I think so," Naoko said. "I practice a lot."

"Interesting." Shane disposed of his cigarette, pocketing the carton as he met the eyes of his friends, before turning back to her. "Tell me, how would you feel about coming to a little shindig of ours?"

Naoko arched an eyebrow.

"He means a party, love," John clarified for his friend. "Since it's almost the weekend, we were going to have a little get together tomorrow night. It's at a nice little club Shane's dad helped him set up."

"Yeah! Maybe you could show us some of those dance moves!" Claire did a quick scuffle around Naoko, bumping her with her hip, before spinning, standing in front of her and grabbing her hands. "So, how about it?"

Naoko felt her cheeks burn as Claire looked deep into her eyes. She quickly glanced at the other two. John had a wide, welcoming smile. Shane still leaned against the wall, his sharp blue eyes assessing her, waiting for her decision.

Without really thinking about it, Naoko found herself saying, "Yes."

John whooped, clapped, and did a fist pump. Claire squealed with excitement and planted a sloppy kiss on her cheek, while Shane smirked with satisfaction.

"It's gonna be a fun time, girly," Claire said with a smile. "Promise."

"Yeah!" John added, high-fiving Naoko. "You and I are gonna tear it up!"

"Right on," Shane finally said, opening his phone and texting her something. "Meet us here about seven tomorrow. If your parents ask, just tell them it's a foreign exchange study club or some shit like that. Parents here love that kind of thing."

"And don't worry about party clothes," Claire added as she brushed Naoko's bangs from her face. "You know I got you, babe."

Naoko nodded, her cheeks warm. Together, they walked out of the alleyway where two cars waited. Claire quickly embraced Naoko, then pushed her toward the second car. "That one is for you, hun."

Naoko nodded as John and Shane gave her a quick hug on either side. The three of them got in the first car, then the window rolled down as Shane poked his head out.

"Remember, seven," he reminded her.

Naoko quickly glanced at her phone, then acknowledged with a nod. From inside the car, John waved, and Claire blew a kiss as it took off into the streets and out of view.

As soon as they had left, Naoko couldn't help but squeal. *A party!* Sliding into the car, she pulled out her earbuds and listened to some music. The car took off with a lurch; the sun was setting, casting long shadows that were soon penetrated by the artificial light of the city. Soon enough, flashes of bright neon flooded the backseat as she plotted her escape from her house.

At that moment, Naoko had decided that she was going to that 'shindig,' no matter what it took.

CHAPTER 3

SAVE ME

IT WAS FIVE FORTY-FIVE, and Naoko was already running late.

She cursed silently under her breath, stuffing her phone in her back pocket and trying to decide which shirt to wear. The first of her options was a bright yellow tank top with sunflowers sewn in at different spots, one she'd had since she was a little girl.

Naoko paused, holding the shirt. The thing felt so…foreign. Her memories of that time were few, but the one thing she remembered vividly was when her parents would play hide and seek around the house with her or take her for a visit to the park. Back then, her father would lift her in the air as he and her mother laughed, declaring her to be their sunshine.

For a moment, Naoko considered abandoning her plans, sending a quick text to Shane saying she couldn't make it. That's all it would take, and for once, she wouldn't be a disappointment.

As Naoko looked up from the shirt, she saw her own reflection staring back at her in the mirror. The happy little girl in her memories was a far cry from the one that was in front of her right now. Years of exposure to the cruel world had buried that girl deep. In her stead was this...*shell*. Despite seeing it in her reflection every day, Naoko seldom recognized it.

Clenching her jaw, Naoko shook her head, shoving the yellow shirt into her drawer and opting for one of her other plain t-shirts instead. With that done, she slid open the door to her room, scanning for any sign of her parents, specifically her father. So far, so good.

She crept down the stairs and slowly slid her shoes on. The front door was only a few feet away now. Soon enough, she would be out of the house. Naoko grabbed the door handle and twisted. The door creaked open as a voice called out. "Naoko? Is that you?"

She froze. Her mother stood in the entrance to the kitchen, her eyes widened.

"Where are you going?"

"Nowhere. Just..." Naoko smiled nervously. "...going for a walk."

"But you never take walks." Her mother arched an eyebrow. Naoko's heart jumped into her throat. Busted.

"I...okay." Naoko shut the door, then threw up her hands in exasperation and sat down on the front step. "There's a study group with foreign exchange students. They were having a session tonight, and I wanted to go, but..."

Her mother sat on the step next to her. "But what?"

Naoko opened her mouth to reply, but nothing came out. She pursed her lips. "I knew you and Dad would say no."

"Well." Her mother placed her hand on her back. "I'm sure your father would be more than fine with you joining a study group. But why are they doing it this late at night? Why not—"

Naoko couldn't help it anymore. She met her mother's gaze, her eyes stinging.

"Oh." Her mother paused. "You met some friends, didn't you?"

Naoko nodded slowly, tucking her knees to her chest. She had one chance to get out of the house undetected, and she and that stupid creaking door had blown it. If she missed the party, how would they ever accept her?

The two sat in silence for what felt like forever. Finally, her mother sighed and spoke up.

"Alright. But be back by nine-thirty. Your father ends his shift around midnight, so you'll want to be in well before that."

Naoko's eyes lit up. "You mean it? You'll let me—"

"—hang out with your friends?" her mother finished for her. "Naoko, you know we only want what's best for you. I've seen how you were before, how alone you must have felt. I'm not going to deprive you of something that could change that, so...yes. You can go."

Naoko clung tightly to her mother, who returned the embrace before leading her to the front door. She eagerly ran down the steps, stopping at the small gate at the end of the walkway. She spun to face her mother, who smiled proudly, mouthing, 'I love you.' Naoko smiled back, then continued her trek, sprinting down the streets to the train station as the sun fell into the horizon.

The address given to Naoko by Shane didn't at all meet her expectations. Instead of a fancy, up-to-date club, it was a plain, unassuming building, old even by city standards. In the front was a small patio and two solid metal doors, flanked on either side by fading streetlamps. After staring at it for a minute and pocketing the paper with the address, Naoko finally built up the courage to knock.

For a moment, nothing happened. Then, one of the doors swung open to reveal a foreigner guard dressed in a sharp, black suit, his pale face rigid. His head was bare, a comm link hanging from his ear.

"Name?" the foreigner asked.

"Um…Naoko. Naoko Haneda."

"You don't look old enough." The guard's eyes narrowed. "You got ID?"

Naoko froze, briefly considering leaving. Just as she was about to walk away, a familiar voice rang out from inside the building.

"Don't worry. She's with me, Doug." Claire opened the other door, adorned in a glossy, revealing crimson dress, her hair tied up in curls that fell down the sides of her face like curtains. Her eyes were sharper than before, accentuated by eyeliner. Naoko felt her heart jump into her throat, her cheeks flushed. Was it possible that Claire could be even more beautiful than she already was?

"Yay, you made it!" Claire jumped up and down, clapping her hands excitedly before hugging Naoko. She pulled back and smiled. "Well come on, babe. Let's get you all dressed up."

Naoko blushed and followed her past the guard and through the two doors. Claire led her across a wooden dancefloor to the stairs beyond. Off to the sides were several employees, carting crates to the bar and filling the case behind it.

"Oh, don't worry, baby," Claire said. "Party won't start just yet. We've got time." She led Naoko up the stairs, opening the door for her.

Naoko blinked as Claire turned on the light. The room stretched much farther than she had thought, with several barstools that looked out the windows to the dancefloor below. To the side, there were several couches, chairs, with smoke trays in the middle. On the sides of the room were several faded wooden doors marked with numbers.

She froze. Did she just hear a voice from one of them? Some kind of groan?

"This way," Claire said, leading her into a room labeled 'seven.' Inside were several mirrors that lined the wall, with a wardrobe full of other dresses like Claire's. Naoko stopped to take in her new surroundings, her chest tight.

Claire shut the door behind them, turned around, and assessed Naoko from head to toe, walking circles around her. "Alright, girly. We've got a lot of work to do, but don't worry. We've got about an hour to turn you from a cute, shy schoolgirl into a sexy Japanese beauty queen! So, do me a favor, okay? I need you to sit in this chair right here and stay still for me."

Naoko didn't budge, her body quivering. The way Claire said it bothered her, sure, but why was she so nervous? Claire was her friend, wasn't she?

"Feeling shy?" Claire's brows furrowed for a moment, before she took a deep breath. "Okay, that's fine. I've got a little something to help with that."

Naoko watched as Claire dug into the drawer of the dressing mirror, finally pulling out a small plastic bag, the inside of which looked like a few pills. Claire grinned and briskly walked over, offering her some. Naoko shrank away from them, her back pressing against the desk and mirror.

Claire fished inside the bag, pulling out one, holding it up to her. Naoko still refused, her heart racing. Her friend sighed, put the bag off to the side, and took her hands. As her cheeks warmed, Naoko felt a tinge of nervousness dissipate, though only slightly.

"Look, babe," Claire began. "I know you're nervous. Hell, so was I at my first party! But trust me, you're gonna be fine. This stuff is just gonna take the edge off a bit and let you have fun, because that's what you're here for, isn't it?"

Naoko bit her lip. Claire gently pushed the pill toward Naoko's mouth, but she hesitated. No, she couldn't. She wasn't the kind of girl to do drugs, right?

To her own surprise, Naoko took the pill and swallowed it.

"Good." Claire smirked. "Now just sit right here and breathe real slow. You'll feel it soon enough."

Naoko complied, wondering exactly what it was she was supposed to 'feel.' Claire got to work, tying her hair back, then moving to the front with a makeup palette. As time went by, she could hear the other people fill in the giant space downstairs.

For one small moment, Naoko wished she was back home in the safety of her room and in her mother's arms. Surprisingly, she even missed her father, wondering what he would have said if he had been there instead of her mother. More than likely, he would have grounded her, but at least she would be home safe.

Too late to back out now. Naoko felt Claire's bony fingers gently tug in her hair, pulling, curling, tying. She then pulled back and clapped.

"Ah!" Claire exclaimed. "Finally!"

"You're already done?" Naoko blinked. "That was fast."

"If you count half an hour as fast, sure." Claire arched an eyebrow. "Don't you remember? You were telling me how that bitch at school was treating you?"

Frowning, Naoko shook her head.

"That's okay." Claire beamed. "Anyway, now for this."

Naoko blinked as Claire held out her dress, which seemed entirely too small for her. She hesitantly took it and looked around.

"Is there a changing room around here?"

Claire giggled. "Come on, babe. This *is* the changing room. Plus, we're both girls, right?"

Naoko bit her lip as she reluctantly changed, Claire's hungry eyes caressing her. Her cheeks flushed and she pulled the dress on faster.

"Hold on," Claire said, walking up and making a few adjustments, stepping back after she was done. She smirked. "Okay. Turn around and look, baby."

Naoko complied, facing the mirror. Her eyes widened. The dress was low cut with only one strap supporting the weight on the right side. The viridescent fabric fell just past her mid-thigh, with a slit on her left slide that ran from the bottom all the way to her waist.

This dress, Naoko realized, was made for the dancefloor.

Claire stood back for a minute, assessing her creation, biting her thumb as she couldn't help but grin. "There we go, baby. You. Are. Perfect!"

Naoko took another glance at herself in the mirror as the walls shook from the music downstairs. The girl staring back at her was so…different. Far more confident and beautiful than she thought was ever possible. She smiled.

Claire continued to circle her, inspecting her. Her eyes momentarily came to rest on her torso, where she had tightened the dress enough for it to be more revealing. She nodded approvingly, then moved around to her backside. Naoko stiffened as she felt Claire's hand briefly caress her rear, then trace the opening in the back of her dress, sending a tingle down her spine. Finally, she pulled back and gave her one last smirk as she bit her thumb, her eyes fluttering.

"Beautiful, baby. So, are you ready to go out and rock that dancefloor for my friends?"

Naoko, for a moment, didn't quite know how to put it in words. "I've never danced in front of anyone else before."

Claire's brows raised. "Oh. I didn't know that, but that's okay. You feel comfortable showing me, right?"

Naoko swallowed, then nodded.

"Great!" Claire clapped. "Just one last thing. Lose the underwear."

Naoko blinked, taking a moment to process the command. "I'm…sorry?"

"Oh!" Claire laughed. "Silly me. So, down there, when you're dancing, it's really gonna ride up in that area and make it uncomfortable, trust me. I just figured, you know? Why not take care of it before it becomes embarrassing?"

Naoko hesitated. Something seemed off, and yet, she didn't want to risk any chance of disappointing Claire. Pushing aside her reservations, she obeyed, tossing them away as she tried to pull her dress down.

"Alright, girly!" Claire nodded approvingly. "Time to show me what you got!"

Naoko bit her lip and inhaled sharply, closing her eyes and drawing a breath as she tried to remember the way Kokoro explained it in her video. She allowed herself to relax, then began to move. Following the rhythm of the music resonating from downstairs, she gradually swayed her hips and flexed her legs. With a hair flip, Naoko spun back to her friend with a nervous grin.

"So, you're flexible. Heh." Claire seemed ecstatic. "They're gonna love you!"

Naoko briefly stopped dancing. "Who will?"

"Just…" Claire paused for a moment. "…everyone down there, hun. So, think you're ready?"

Naoko shifted uncomfortably. "I'm not sure. Dancing in front of you is one thing, but—"

"Hey." Claire gripped her shoulders, then sensually slid her fingers down Naoko's forearms to her hands, smiling seductively. "I get it. You're nervous, but you don't have to be. So just breathe, okay?"

Naoko complied, inhaling deeply, a strange fog seeping into her mind. Was this the 'feeling' Claire had mentioned earlier?

"Forget all that shy schoolgirl crap," Claire whispered, her tempting voice sinking deep into Naoko's mind. "Tonight, you are a beautiful, sexy woman, and you're gonna show everyone here that, aren't you?"

Slowly, Naoko felt her nervousness vanish as she took in both Claire's intoxicating scent and her seductive words. Straightening her back, she inhaled, repeating the words in her head. Finally, she met Claire's gaze and smiled.

Claire smirked. "Good. Let's go, baby."

Naoko nodded, following Claire. She felt weirdly…happy. Relaxed. Ready to finally show her gift to the world that she had kept hidden to herself for so long.

They arrived at the door, which vibrated from the pulsing music in the dance room below. The door flung open, the song suddenly thundered, and flashing lights filled her peripherals. Naoko put on her brightest smile and walked out to the balcony above. On the dancefloor, people were already at it, some of them jumping around and fist pumping, others were engaged in a slow grind with each other.

Naoko placed a hand on the railing as Claire slowly strutted down the steps, flashing a smile to everyone watching, before joining the other two at the bottom. John wore a decorative polo with jeans, while Shane was dressed in a white t-shirt, dress pants, and a dark blue blazer with the collar undone and a gold chain around his neck. Claire tapped them and gestured up toward Naoko. John's eyes widened with excitement while Shane watched Naoko intently, a satisfied smile on his handsome face.

A realization came to Naoko as she blinked. Not only was Claire trying to wow the others, but she was also showing her how to make *her* entrance.

Naoko smiled, meeting the eyes of those who watched her from below. Hand on the railing, she too strutted confidently down the steps, flashing a smile to everyone on the ground. Without realizing it, her footsteps were perfectly in sync with the synthetic beat.

"Yeah, Naoko!" John shouted, clapping and whooping.

Naoko smirked, briefly focusing her gaze on him as she continued to descend. At that moment, she felt…seen. The smiles down below felt welcoming, eager to have her among them.

After reaching the bottom, Naoko walked over to them. John quickly high fived her and congratulated her on making the party. Shane, hands in pockets, eyed Naoko and smirked.

"Beautiful, love," Shane said, turning to Claire, who had looped Naoko's arm in hers. "She looks ready."

"She is," Claire confirmed, smiling confidently at Naoko, proud. Naoko returned her gaze and winked. Claire's laughter filled the air as she nodded and tightly clasped Naoko's hand, leading her to the dancefloor. Instantly, a crowd formed around them, moving to the rhythm of the music.

Naoko couldn't help but laugh, too. After all, she was ready to slay that damn dancefloor and anyone on it.

The music egged them on, the strobe lights flashed. Naoko broke away from Claire and Shane to dance with John, who was flailing about, uncoordinated. Naoko didn't care; it looked fun. Together, they shifted from side to side, laughing, a foot apart but never touching.

A set of hands made their way around Naoko's waist. As John drifted away from her to the bar on the far side of the room, Naoko fell back into Claire and began to grind on her. She pushed her head by Claire's neck, her hands caressing her face. Claire returned the gesture, resting her hands on her shoulders. She brought her lips tantalizingly close to Naoko's, before pulling away with a sexy smile. Shane soon jumped in, the three of them pulling their bodies intimately close to one another.

Light and sound blended as Naoko continued to dance, her surroundings blurred as others pressed against her, grinding and feeling her body. She pushed herself against them, laughing and twisting with the beat.

Time fell away as the night went on, the dancefloor pulsed as Naoko lost herself both in the music and the euphoric touch of everyone around her, magnified by a thousand. If this was a dream, then she didn't want to wake up.

"Naoko!" a familiar voice called.

She stopped, the fog in her brain clearing just long enough to see John at the edge of the dancefloor, eyes widened as he worriedly called her again and again.

"Get off her! She ain't—" A pair of guards grabbed John by the arms and dragged him out. "Oi! Let go! She needs help!"

The double doors to the building slammed shut as Naoko continued to move, trying to keep in sync with the shifting mass of bodies around her. Yet, John's words kept bothering her. Was something wrong?

Naoko tried to stop and pull herself off to the side to think, but her body resisted like it wasn't even hers anymore. It continued to dance and grind against anyone and everyone nearby, hips popping slowly, hands running through her hair.

Why am I doing this? I need to stop. Why can't I stop?

The world around her shifted, the once distinguishable bodies of other dances melting together into shadows with endless eyes that focused on her and endless hands that caressed her as they drifted by.

Naoko tried to breathe but couldn't. The throbbing in her mind became louder. She felt a strange disconnect between her mind and body; her hand reached up, reveling in the euphoria as the snug green dress alternated with the vibrant yellow sunflower T-shirt. While her body danced on without her, Naoko clutched her pulsing head, desperately looking for a way to escape the chaos as it tried to pull her in.

Exhaustion crept into her as she finally regained control of her body. Her gaze shifted to the back of the room, where Claire was conversing with an older man. She mustered every ounce of energy, trying to shout her friend's name, to call for help. Claire didn't hear her. Instead, she took some cash from the man, who moved over to Naoko and pulled her close, grinding against her sensually.

Finally, Claire's eyes met hers. Cash in hand, she smirked and sank back into the shadows.

Before Naoko could even process it, she was pulled from reality back into the fog, featureless faces and bodies shifting around her, blurring together. She struggled against herself, trying to keep afloat in the churning sea of motion and chaos, though the endless hands and eyes dragged her back down.

"Hey, love," a voice said. Its owner stepped forward; his face obscured in shadow against the flashing lights. "Why don't you come with me? Got some friends I want you to meet."

Naoko felt like she was going to throw up but tried to take the shadow's hand. As she reached, however, it changed form into a tall, middle-aged man with short-cropped hair and a hard, disapproving line drawn across his face.

At first, she laughed with relief. It was her father. If anyone could help free her from the madness, it was him.

"Naoko," her father hissed, his brows furrowing. "What the hell do you think you are doing here?"

Naoko paled. Her chest tightened as she backed away, running into one of her fellow dancers, spilling her drink onto her dress. For a moment, her vision cleared just enough to see the hateful scowl on her face.

"What is your problem, bitch?"

The girl shoved her. Naoko fell forward as another pair of hands pushed her away, then another, and finally a third pair gripped her. Her eyes widened on seeing it was her father once more.

"I knew it. I knew you would do something like this," he said, the image shifting between the shadow and his familiar face. "You always disappoint me."

With an inhuman burst of strength and a scream, Naoko broke free both from the shadow's grip and the fog that held her captive, running away from her father's voice as it echoed and multiplied. The door in front of her warped and began to shut, threatening to block her in the darkness forever.

"No!" With a mighty push, she forced the door back open, only to be met with a blinding flash of neon lights. She continued to move, her steps haphazard, trying to find anywhere to be free from the haunting voices.

"Naoko! Stop!"

Naoko briefly looked back to see a tall, humanoid yet misshapen beast made of shadow, his skin filled with the endless eyes from before. Its muscles were like individual tendrils, bound, yet fighting each other as if they were enslaved to the greater whole of the beast itself. Its twisted hands reached for her, sharp jaws agape, two horns protruding from its creased brow like an Oni. Her skin burned as faces' cold, calculating eyes focused on her.

This monster was the darkness itself, and it wanted to devour her.

Naoko's eyes widened. It was getting closer, closer. She couldn't escape. It was going to get her, and there was nothing she could do.

"No, no, *no!*"

The beast came ever forward, flashing its teeth in a wicked grin, its claws outstretched. It seemed to be both everywhere and nowhere at once. Naoko suddenly tripped, endlessly falling past twisting neon, flashing lights and the cruel stares of what felt like the entire world. Something caught her, breaking her fall.

Naoko looked up. The beast now had her in its iron grip. Its wicked grin widened. She writhed, fighting for her life. She screamed so loud her lungs were about to burst, her chest pulsed like the tracks under the Tokyo morning trains, their horns blaring. Finally, with one swift motion, the darkness consumed her.

"No...no! Someone save me!"

"Naoko!"

She felt something strike her face—a firm hand. She opened her eyes, seeing her father in his police uniform, lights on his patrol car blazing. His middle-aged eyes quivered out of both shock and horror.

She froze, looking around. There were other police officers present, and her friend John spoke to one of them while occasionally glancing at Naoko. She saw him sigh with relief.

Naoko slowly turned to face her father. For a moment that felt like forever, their eyes locked. His face slowly hardened, as did his grip on her shoulders. He broke the stare by gesturing to his partner, who turned her around, placing something cold and firm on her wrists.

Her eyes widened. *Handcuffs?*

"Naoko Haneda…" her father said quietly, a growl churning beneath the surface of his voice. "You are under arrest."

The last thing she remembered was being shoved into the back of her father's police car before allowing herself to be taken by the cruel darkness once more.

CHAPTER 4

THE SOUL WITHIN

THE ENTIRE RIDE HOME WAS FILLED WITH A COLD SILENCE.
Naoko's father secured her release from the local jail, though she
knew it wasn't an act of mercy. True mercy would have been
leaving her behind bars, shielded by iron, safe from her father's
inevitable wrath like a diver in a shark cage.

The car rolled along the roads, each sway of the vehicle
almost making her heave. Finally, it lurched to a stop, the strained
clicking of the hand brake screeched in her ear like a siren. Naoko
closed her eyes shut as her father slammed his door and opened
hers, yanking her out. Her hands remained cuffed, this time in front

of her. With his face obscured by the shadow of his hat, her father guided her into the house.

Naoko halted. Sitting on the bottom of the stairs was her mother. In that moment, Naoko dared to meet her mother's gaze, only to be met with horror and shame reflecting back at her.

Her mother frowned and then turned to her husband. "Itsuki, why is our daughter in handcuffs?"

The door slammed shut, making Naoko jump. Her father placed his police hat on the hook. "You know why, Hana. I told you on the phone."

"No, I mean why is she *still* wearing them?" Her mother glared. "She's your daughter, not a convict."

"I have half a mind to leave them on and chain her somewhere in the house." He briefly glanced at Naoko. "But fine. If you insist."

Her father removed the handcuffs and attached them to his belt. Her mother's frown deepened, and she moved forward to embrace her daughter. Naoko reached, yearning for the safety of her mother's arms, but was denied by the looming shadow that was her father. "Don't touch her, Hana. You'll just make this worse."

Her mother's usually gentle expression turned into a scowl. "She still needs us. I—"

"If she 'needed' us, she wouldn't sneak out for dancing and drugs," her father snapped.

"She didn't sneak out, Itsuki. I let her go."

Silence hung in the air. Her father stared at his wife, dumbfounded.

"You knew she was going to go clubbing, and yet you let her go?"

"I didn't know about the clubbing," her mother said, her voice rising as she glanced briefly at Naoko. The frown on her lips deepened, her disappointment apparent. Naoko felt her heart twist in her chest at the sight. "But yes, I let her go."

Naoko's eyes darted between her parents, tears streaming down her face. She could feel her mother's forgiving love and her father's burning wrath warring with one another. She hated coming between them. For a moment, Naoko pictured a different conversation, a more pleasant one.

One without her.

"So, not only did you do drugs," her father said, interrupting Naoko's thoughts as he turned away from her mother, his eyes narrowing, cold disbelief in his voice. "But you lied?"

Naoko bit her lip. There was no denying the lie, but...

"Father," she said. "I lied to Mother. But I didn't—"

"Your mother may have her own standards when it comes to trust, but don't you dare lie to me, Naoko. I have the test results from the station." Her father paused, his intense stare pressing down. His brow twitched as the anger on his face threatened to fade. "I thought you were better than this."

"What about the young man? The foreigner?" her mother interjected. "He told you that they drugged her, right?"

"As if we can trust him," her father replied. He stared down at Naoko. "I'll give you one last chance to be honest. Did you take those drugs willingly?"

"I..." *I couldn't have*, she wanted to say. Naoko tried to recollect the memories of the night's events, but they slipped through her fingers like mist. She closed her eyes, attempting to focus, but the more she grasped, the more frustration gnawed at her like a rabid animal. Tears streamed down her face as she ran her hands through her hair, gripping it. She desperately wanted to explain herself, to make him understand, but her voice faltered in her throat.

"I don't know."

After several heart-rending moments of quiet, her father scoffed. He shook his head. "Families I know would have thrown you out on the street by now."

Her mother's expression darkened. "You wouldn't dare."

"No, I wouldn't," he said, eyeing Naoko as he jutted a finger at her. "But your life as you know it is over. You will go to school, do your homework, your chores, and nothing more. Above all, you will never disgrace this family or yourself *ever* again." His jaw tightened. "Is that clear?"

Naoko didn't respond immediately. Her father turned, grabbed his hat, and headed for the door. Each step felt like another fracture in their relationship, another widening chasm. Had it actually been there, she might have just thrown herself into it.

Suddenly, her father stopped, facing her. The anger in his eyes finally faded, giving way to grief as if it were a mere mask, a façade. His gaze dropped.

"Naoko," he began, his voice filled with sorrow. "Oh Naoko, where did you go?"

Naoko didn't understand. She took a shaky step forward, her voice a broken whisper, "Father, I'm right here."

"No. The Naoko I knew would never have done something like this." Disgust flickered in his eyes as he stepped back, his despair resurfacing.

"Father," Naoko pleaded. "Please—"

"Bring back my little girl," her father uttered, his voice low. "I don't know you."

The words pierced Naoko's heart like a thousand needles as the front door slammed shut. The weight of her father's disappointment crashed over her. She crumpled to the ground, sobs echoing through the silent room.

Her mother rushed to her side, enveloping Naoko in a desperate embrace. "He doesn't mean that. We'll fix this. We'll—"

Naoko couldn't find solace in her mother's words. She couldn't shake off the despair that clung to her like a suffocating fog. In the end, she broke free from her mother's grip, gathered what little strength remained, and stumbled up the stairs. She shut her door behind her, locked it, and collapsed onto her bed. For hours on end, she cried, her tears drenching the pillow as she ignored the knocks and pleas from her mother until they stopped completely.

How could I be so stupid?

As the night wore on, the tears slowly faded, replaced by a cold numbness. She tried to replay the events of the party in her mind, but her memories eluded her, leaving only guilt and darkness.

Lying in bed, she suddenly felt a familiar sensation. Her phone vibrated beneath her pillow.

What? Naoko blinked. *Didn't I bring this with me?*

She retrieved it, brushing her matted hair from her face to read the screen. Her eyes widened. Kokoro was going live.

With sweaty palms, Naoko struggled to open the PULSE app. She scrolled to her profile and clicked on Kokoro's live icon. Instead of the session, another message appeared. Her eyes widened as she read the words.

"PULSE is dedicated to ensuring that our artists and users have a balanced experience. Previously, we relied on a combination of free-to-use and subscriber-based formats, but unfortunately, our artists were not properly compensated for their hard work. From now on, PULSE will be transitioning to a subscriber-only format to better support them. We appreciate your understanding and apologize for any inconvenience."

Below the message, there was a button that read, "Subscribe now! 2080¥ monthly."

Naoko froze. For years now, Kokoro's words had been her safe haven, the promise that, one day, she could be truly be happy. That she could be *better.* Now, the message was clear. After what she had done, how could she deserve such things again? Her family was falling apart at the seams because she had decided to be selfish for one damn day.

Gripping her hair, Naoko buried her face in her pillow, wanting to scream. Why did it matter, anyway? Why did anything matter? In a world of mindless distractions and futile attempts at forming connections with others, why bother? All to escape the darkness they knew awaited them but refused to acknowledge?

Darkness. Naoko paused as she contemplated the word, her mind going blank. She could feel it—that inevitability calling to her. It had done so before, always looming like a shadow, yet never as strongly as it did now. Only this time, it offered an answer. *She* was the problem. She was the one ruining her family just by being.

And for that, Naoko knew she had to die.

Her lip quivered slightly, yet she felt an odd sense of peace. It was a condemnation, yet it was also a comforting promise: an end to the pointlessness of it all, a way out. No more school, no more Sayuki Sato, no more being stuck in the infinite cycle of pain that she knew awaited her in life.

Trembling with that invisible weight, Naoko stood up and tiptoed out of her room, down the stairs, and into the kitchen. Her destination was the medicine cabinet. She reached in and pulled out a bottle of pain pills. Cracking it open, she sighed. They were all there. More than likely, it would be an agonizing way to go, but she didn't care. As long as it did the job.

Naoko started to climb the stairs when something caught her eye. Her mother was curled up in the living room chair, shivering from the cold.

But what about her? Naoko momentarily hesitated, glancing at her. The sight nearly changed her mind, but the darkness tugged at her, reminding her of its promise…and her fate.

She shook off the thought and grabbed a blanket to cover her mother. Naoko's legs moved automatically, pulling her away from the living room and back up the stairs.

It's for the best. Naoko's lip curled. *If they want a better daughter, they can just have another to replace me.*

The sliding door closed behind her, the bottle still clutched in her hand. Inhaling sharply, she opened it and poured some pills—around thirteen or so—into her palm, trying to gather the courage to do what needed to be done.

Stop! a soft voice suddenly said. Naoko jolted, panic filling her as she expected to see her mother standing in the doorway, but the door remained closed. She blinked, then shook her head. Again, the voice spoke, nearly causing her to drop the pills.

You have so much to live for, it said. *They love you, especially your father. Don't break their hearts like this. Please.*

Her mind filled with visions of her parents discovering her lifeless body, collapsing to their knees in tears and clutching her. Naoko shook those thoughts away, gripping the key to her final escape tightly, trying to find the strength to bring it to her lips. But her body fought against her. Her mind swirled with emotions, reason, desire, and decision clashing, the voice from before fading into the wind, indiscernible.

Finally, it stopped. Silence. Naoko brought the pills into her mouth, but then froze against her will. She tried to swallow them, but not even her tongue would move.

What's happening?

Naoko's mind blanked, and she felt herself being pulled back. Back into darkness, into the depths of her mind, before everything stilled and went black.

In the shadows of a strange, dark place, a nameless girl awakened.

Gradually, she freed herself from the encompassing darkness, claiming her limbs one by one: her legs, her head, her arms, until she was completely liberated. Despite the persistent shadows that encircled her, writhing like serpents ready to strike, a burst of natural light radiated from within her and repelled them. Momentarily, she paused, contemplating this unfamiliar existence she found herself in.

A set of unnerving cries shook her from her first thoughts. The girl began to walk, the darkness faded like the night giving way to the dawn, revealing something strange, yet fascinating floating nearby. It moved, within it was the flashing of strobe lights and the faces of others that eyed her with a disgusting hunger. Initially recoiling, she tilted her head, recognizing it as a memory. But who did it belong to?

The nameless girl continued to walk, finding more shards of remembrance like the first, one of them being the person's time at something called 'school'. Time flashed by as the shards moved again. Now, she was looking at two adults, a set of parents. The unknown person that the memory belonged to stumbled forward as the two of them smiled with glee. Warmth kindled in the nameless girl's chest, manifesting in a smile.

A strange humming sound emanated from behind her. She followed it, finding yet another remembrance. In this one, those very same parents, albeit much older, eyed the nameless girl with both horror and wrath.

"Bring back my little girl. I don't know you." The line from the father repeated, over and over. The nameless girl frowned. Whoever's memory this was, no way they would ever deserve such cruel words.

Another remembrance formed in front of her. The mother that she had seen in an earlier memory was now embracing her.

"Naoko, you know we only want what's best for you, and to protect you…"

It faded as the girl pondered the name. Naoko. It was fitting, especially for someone so meek and yet alone. The nameless girl surveyed her surroundings—the fading fragments of memory suspended in the darkness. Was this Naoko's mind?

After what felt like an eternity of walking and collecting memories—living them as if they were her own—the girl stopped as a popping sound caught her attention. She ran toward the source, a sense of urgency tugging at her. She didn't know why, but something needed her. *Someone.*

Not long after, the nameless girl arrived somewhere else. In front of her was a wispy veil, mist falling in front of her like a waterfall. Had she more time, she might have pondered it, but instead, she followed her instinct and passed through. Light filled her vision, and soon she found herself staring down at a set of hands, a small bottle clutched in one, the pills themselves in the other. For a moment, confusion gripped her. What were they for?

Then the nameless girl froze, her eyes widening in horror as she realized what was happening. These were Naoko's hands. Unlike in the memories, she could feel them as if they were her own, the body's eyes were like windows for her. Her pain, the shadows of despair, filled with countless accusing eyes, beckoned Naoko to join them in the dark forever.

"Stop!" the nameless girl called, then stopped. The softness of her own voice surprised her; she had never spoken before. And yet, it came naturally. A soothing melody that made the darkness around her and Naoko retreat, if only a little.

Naoko paused, looking around, then shook her head dismissively. The nameless girl called again.

"You have so much to live for." The girl's throat tightened with her desperate words. "They love you, especially your father. Don't break their hearts like this. Please."

Naoko ignored her and consumed the pills. The nameless girl instinctively reached out, momentarily causing Naoko to freeze. However, the shadows swiftly redirected their attention, enveloping the nameless girl to reclaim control.

With fierce determination, the girl emanated her inner light, clenching her teeth in an intense struggle. A mighty scream escaped her as she pushed forward through the encroaching darkness. Light bent and shadows twisted as she battled against the overwhelming force attempting to pull her back. Suddenly, it all vanished, replaced by the sensation of something in her mouth.

The pills. Somehow, the nameless girl had taken control of Naoko's body.

Not wasting any time, she scrambled to the bathroom, pulled herself over the toilet bowl and spit the pills out. She collapsed against the wall, and relief manifested in a small, grateful laugh.

I did it. I saved her. I saved Naoko.

Bracing herself against the sink, the nameless girl stared into the mirror as the blurry reflection solidified. She stopped a moment to look at Naoko's face, brushing the black, disheveled hair aside. To others, she probably would have been considered average, maybe pretty by some standards. But for some reason she couldn't quite place, she found Naoko to be astoundingly, tragically beautiful. Her gentle face without a smile was like a butterfly without wings.

The girl frowned and gently slid out into the hallway down the stairs. An older woman that she knew to be Naoko's mother was still slumbering on the couch, clutching a small pillow tight to her chest, a thick blanket over her. Next to that couch was a shelf on which sat an old photo album.

She quietly grabbed it, a faded photo slipping out and gracefully falling to the ground. Picking it up, she flipped it to find an older, rough-looking tattooed man and a smiling boy, both dressed in a kimono.

"Probably an old family photo," the girl told herself, tucking it back into the album and opening it to the beginning. The first photo showed a young girl in a yellow dress, her black hair tied into pigtails and wrapped in sunflowers as her parents flocked to either side of her. She smiled, and turned the page, finding a similar one. Every page she flipped to showed Naoko from her toddler years on up.

No baby pictures?

The girl arched an eyebrow, continuing to go through it. Finally, she reached the end and found one of Naoko with her mother and father, except they were all smiling, happy. She pulled the photo from the sleeve and placed her hand on it.

"Naoko," the nameless girl whispered, frowning. "What happened to you?"

With a sigh, she closed the album, keeping the one photo clutched in her hand, and returned it to the shelf, slumping her way back into Naoko's room. The moment she reached the bed, she saw something flashing: a phone. Pushing her hair behind her ear, she picked it up and unlocked it with her fingerprint, simultaneously opening an app called PULSE.

The girl blinked again and found herself back in that strange, abstract world inside Naoko's mind. Naoko herself was still slumbering nearby, her chest rising and falling like waves on a beach. The shadows crept toward her, but the nameless girl flashed her light, banishing them and creating a spot safe for both of them, a protective barrier. Sighing with relief, she knelt next to Naoko and brushed her hair from her closed eyes.

"Hey, loves! Today, we're going to talk about self-care. Now I know it can be difficult to—"

The nameless girl looked up at the noise, seeing one final memory fragment nearby. In it was a blonde girl, hair tied up in a loose bun, a warm smile across her face. Even from outside of the memory, she felt Naoko's heart leap when she saw it. As she approached, something overlapped it, a flickering message that said, 'Subscribe now! 2080¥ monthly.'

So that's what she is to Naoko. The girl frowned. *She was her anchor. She kept her going when the entire world was against her.*

Kokoro, a voice echoed as the memory faded, leaving only a mirror with the same figure in it. The girl moved closer; the figure mimicked her movements perfectly.

Her eyes widened as she saw herself for the first time. Silver-blonde hair that stretched down to her mid-back, an angular face, with soft, caring blue eyes. It was at this moment that the girl knew what she was, why she was here in Naoko's mind: to be her friend. Her anchor. Whatever she needed her to be. The girl knelt next to the sleeping Naoko again and caressed her cheek, smiling.

"Don't worry, Naoko," the girl said. "Things will be better when you wake up. I promise."

Naoko stirred in her sleep, but the girl could have sworn she saw the faintest hint of a smile adorn her soft lips. She returned it and rose to face the thin veil once again between the inner world and the outside. Her name, she decided as she pushed forward, would be 'Kokoro.' To her, it didn't matter what she would have to endure or suffer through.

Because in the end, she would find a way to make Naoko smile again.

Unfortunately, Naoko had survived. She turned over and laid on her stomach, burying her face into her pillow, wanting to cry. Then she froze. Wasn't she on the ground?

Naoko immediately shifted off the bed and stood up, glancing at the spot on the floor where she had been last night. It was perfectly clean: no pills, no bottle. Not even a carpet stain.

Her gaze fell on the rest of her room. It was neat, organized, even decorated differently. A set of string lights stretched across the ceiling, and the image of a tree was now painted on her wall.

But not just *any* tree. It was the Sakura from her school courtyard.

"Naoko!" a gentle, feminine voice called from downstairs. "Are you dressed for school yet?"

Naoko froze. Wasn't it just last night that she was told that her life was over? That she wasn't leaving the house ever again?

She paused, then opened her closet and fished around. Her school uniforms weren't loosely folded at the bottom anymore like they had been. Instead, they were hung at the top: ironed, straight, perfect.

Naoko hesitantly reached to grab one, then blinked. When she opened her eyes, she was sitting at the dining room table, a breakfast plate in front of her. Her eyes widened.

"What's the matter, Naoko?" a familiar voice asked. "Is everything okay?"

Naoko looked over; her heart twisted inside her chest. It was her mother.

"Is it the food?" she asked. "I can warm it up again, or—"

"—Mom?" Naoko cut her off. "I'm sorry."

Her mother paused, blinking. "For what?"

"For last night? When Father..." Naoko lowered her voice, staring at the tablecloth. "Father brought me home?"

"Last night? Did you two go out after our movie ended?" Her mother blinked, placing a hand on Naoko's. "What are you talking about, darling?"

Naoko paused; her mouth gaped open. She turned back to her mother. "I..."

The world around Naoko went dark once again. When she came to, she was standing at the front door, her shoes on, her mother smiling at her.

"Well, that is in the past now, dear. You've been doing so good lately, so don't you think it's time to cut yourself a break?"

Naoko's eyes stung. She was doing good? How? Only last night she had ruined her life and shamed her parents. Was it all just a cruel nightmare?

"Well, I don't want to make you late." Her mother beamed with pride and embraced her. "So, you had better—"

"—catch the train, right?" Naoko asked, eyeing her. If it was a nightmare, then it shouldn't have been a problem. She had been taking the train to school for years.

"Not this time, Nao," her mother said, frowning. "You know the deal. Your father will take you to and from school until we feel we can trust you again."

Naoko paled, her chest thumping as she heard a noise from the top of the stairs. Her father walked out from the master bedroom, though he wasn't wearing his police uniform. Instead, he was dressed in casual slacks, a dress T-shirt and a pair of fancy shoes. He met her quivering eyes, though his gaze didn't hold the intense anger from last night. Instead, it was reserved, calculating.

Naoko stepped back to get away from him, her vision tunneling, her heart twisting in her chest. Time flashed by in an instant, and soon she found herself in the back of the family car, her father in the driver's seat. The Tokyo streets slowly passed them by as the traffic slowed to a maddening crawl. She shrunk back, her eyes darting between the window and her father. For what felt like an eternity, the piercing silence hung between them.

"So," her father finally said. "I made Detective. Found out this morning."

"Oh." Naoko shrunk back further. "That's…good."

"Huh. I thought you would be excited about it." In the rearview mirror, Naoko saw her father arch an eyebrow. "Your mother said you were acting strange this morning. I can see what she meant."

Naoko didn't utter another word. Her father sighed.

"Listen. I know things have been difficult lately, especially between us. But it wouldn't be fair of me if I didn't acknowledge your progress these last two months." He nodded with what looked to her like pride. "You have done as I asked. Your grades have jumped up dramatically, and above all, you have been responsible."

Her eyes widened as she shifted uncomfortably in her seat. Two months? She had somehow blacked out for two whole months?

"And so," her father continued. "As of today, I have decided to fully restore your train riding privileges and your phone. While you still have a long way to go, you have also come far in proving yourself to your mother and I."

The car pulled up to the front of her school as Naoko bit her lip. Everything around her felt so…*off,* out of place. Confusion twisted her stomach in knots as she fought to keep the bile down.

Her father parked, then came around to her side to open the door. She hesitantly got out as he pressed her phone and train pass into her hands, regarding her with a nod. Not knowing what else to do, she bowed, and began to briskly walk to the double doors.

Naoko's chest tightened, her breaths became shorter, a sharp pain erupted in her head. If so much had changed in her home life, how different would things be at school?

She looked ahead and saw someone waving her in. It was Sayuki Sato, minus her sadistic smirk or so-called friends. Her uniform was pressed, her blouse was tucked in. Strangest of all, a hearty smile adorned her lips that, oddly enough, seemed to be directed at Naoko.

Before Naoko could even ponder it, she fell forward, the world around her morphing into the inside of a train. She gripped the handle tightly, her phone in her other hand, in the middle of a message with Sayuki.

"Huh?" Naoko furiously scrolled through the messages, searching for any possible explanation, but found nothing but pleasant conversations, with one even asking her to hang out. She froze as felt something, a pair of hands creeping their way around her side.

Naoko blinked, and the hands were gone. She was standing over a tall young man, who lay on the floor of the train clutching his crotch. The rest of the passengers stared at her, utter shock on their faces.

A flash of pain erupted in her shin. Had she done it?

Naoko checked her phone again, this time she noticed something on her home screen: a note. It read 'Stop fighting me! Will explain when we get home! Promise! —K.'

Naoko's eyes widened. Who the hell was 'K?'

Another moment of churning darkness and she was back in her room, the light from the sunset flooded her window. She heard the front door open, her father's voice echoed throughout the house as he announced himself. She took a moment to walk to the center of the top of the stairs, her father only a few feet below.

Their eyes met. Not knowing what to do, Naoko bowed deep and welcomed him home. He regarded her with a nod and a satisfied smile, before making his way to the living room.

Naoko quickly ran back into her room, careful not to slam her door. She paced, her heart racing. Why had so much time passed? Why was she friends with Sayuki of all people? Why was she even alive?

Above all, why didn't she remember any of it?

"Hey, Naoko!" a soft female voice whispered. She spun erratically, trying to locate the source. The voice seemed omniscient, everywhere and nowhere at once. Like her own thoughts, yet louder and more intrusive.

Naoko turned to her mirror, seeing her reflection for the first time since the party. Unlike before, her shimmering black hair was neatly brushed and slightly curled; her bangs were kept at bay with a pink flower clip. Her eyes were sharper and more dazzling, yet in a subtle way.

"You're still with me, right?"

Naoko jumped, then shook her head. First, she had missed out on two months of her life and now she was hearing things. Had she gone insane?

"First off, no, you're not insane," the voice assured Naoko as if she could read her mind. "This is real."

"Okay, um…" Naoko blinked. "Are you a spirit, ghost, or something?

"Not a ghost," the voice said. "At least, I don't think so. I'm… Well, I think I'm a part of you, if that makes sense."

Naoko shook her head. On the contrary, she felt even more confused. Despite that, there was something familiar about the voice. Where had she heard it before?

"Okay, um…" Naoko heard the voice draw in a breath. "Let's start again! My name is Kokoro."

Naoko arched an eyebrow. "Like the PULSE star?"

"Sort of," Kokoro said. "I'm not sure how that works either, but you've just been through a lot lately. It's okay if you're confused, or you don't—"

"—Understand?" Naoko sighed in exasperation, clutching her throbbing forehead. "I don't get it. The last thing I remember is coming home from the party, and Father, and then the pills…" She froze, a realization dawning on her. "Wait. It was you, wasn't it? The reason I'm not dead." Naoko hesitated. "You saved me."

"Why wouldn't I?" The sadness in Kokoro's voice made Naoko's heart drop.

"Mother and Father," Naoko began. "They don't know, do they?"

"I wanted to tell them," Kokoro said. "But I couldn't. I didn't want to hurt them…or you. There was enough pain that night, and I just wanted to make things better."

Naoko leaned forward in her chair, her hands shaking. Suddenly, it stopped. A strange, comforting presence enveloped her, easing the pain and nervousness away. It felt like the arms of a loved one pulling her into a safe embrace. Naoko let it calm her, though it couldn't melt away the guilt. Her vision blurred and her throat tightened as tears began to fall.

"Why couldn't you just let me die?"

No reply came. Just as Naoko was about to rise from her chair, something landed on the back of her hand, a Sakura petal.

"Huh?" Naoko turned her hand and placed it in her palm. When she looked back up, she found herself standing in the middle of a concrete road. On either side, there were stunning Sakura trees, their branches filled with delicate pink petals cascading down, but never touching the ground. The air was crisp yet didn't chill her. Birds sang and jumped from branch to branch.

What is this? Naoko spun, her eyes wide. *This isn't in my head, is it?*

It was perfect, whatever this place was. Here, she felt safe, like nothing could hurt her. Slowly, she made her way through the street, drawn towards the end where a solitary tree stood, its enormous pink and white branches standing out against the starry night sky. At the base of the tree stood what she knew to be Kokoro, adorned in a beautiful dress, a white core faded to pink at the edges, her silver-blonde hair flowing down past her shoulders and the sides of her face, like curtains on a gorgeous glass pane window.

Naoko froze as Kokoro walked up to her, the flurry of Sakura petals following behind. She stopped just in front of her and reached to caress Naoko's face.

"It doesn't matter what you've done, Nao. I've seen your memories. You've been through so much with nobody understanding," Kokoro said, her eyes and voice radiating a comforting confidence. "But I do, and I'm here for you now. Just know that you're not alone anymore."

Naoko stared, a tear dripping down her face onto Kokoro's hand. They stood there for one long, perfect moment that she wished would never end.

CHAPTER 5

A GUARDIAN ANGEL

"YOU SURE YOU'VE GOT THIS?" KOKORO ASKED. "If you need me to help…"

"I'm fine," Naoko huffed. "It's my body. I can manage."

Kokoro sighed as she watched from within Naoko's mind. True, it *was* technically Naoko's body, though sharing it wasn't exactly the easiest thing in the world. The three weeks since Naoko had reawakened were fraught with turmoil, debates, and a constant struggle for control. Only after a focused grounding session, a bunch of sticky notes and numerous blackouts, did they tentatively learn to stay conscious at the same time without a splitting headache.

Even then, things didn't always go perfectly.

"Whoa, whoa! You'll pull a muscle if you're not careful!" Kokoro warned as her friend huffed. Naoko, unfortunately, had slept in, which was surprising considering how long she had been dormant. She had hurriedly thrown her uniform on, tied her hair into a sloppy ponytail, and ran out the door hoping to catch the morning train into the city.

"It's fine!" Naoko managed between ragged breaths. "I've got it!"

Kokoro watched through Naoko's eyes from within their inner world that, despite being in her friend's mind, seemed to stretch on without end. The beautiful, seemingly innumerable Sakura trees expanded to the horizon. Their pink petals were bright against a sky of purples and blues as if they were the things that gave it light and not the other way around. Before, it was a vicious place, twisted shadows that always tried to overwhelm her, or would sometimes try to drag away Naoko as she lay dormant. Kokoro found she could change some of it, making it somewhere where they both could be at ease and feel safe from the darkness beyond.

That, and it was the only place she could truly see and interact with her friend, face to face. Not quite like reality, but close enough.

"Nao, I'm serious. You just got your body back. You don't want to—"

"I said I'm okay!" Naoko insisted.

Kokoro rolled her eyes. For months, she had almost sole control over how to put the poor girl's life back together. Now that she had finally awakened from her long slumber, Naoko was determined to have it back.

"We should have just asked your father!" Kokoro pointed out. "He has the evening shift tonight. He would have gladly—"

"—I don't need his help!" Naoko insisted, her breathing ragged from running. "I have to stand on my own two feet. I need to show that I can—"

Naoko collapsed, her ears pulsing, chest thumping. Kokoro sighed. Just as she had thought, the dummy had burned her energy sprinting instead of just pacing herself.

Or better yet, just asking for a ride.

Naoko caught her breath and sank back from the mist-filled veil, known to them as the 'front', which blurred the line between the real world and the realm within. Whenever Naoko ran the body, Kokoro wasn't far behind, watching through the body's eyes like they were windows, and vice versa. Sometimes, if they were somewhere safe and quiet like Naoko's room, they could both exit the front through the misty veil, though it usually denied one of them.

"Need a break?" Kokoro asked, arms crossed.

"I don't need you to do everything for me," Naoko snapped. "At some point, I have to—"

Kokoro took the opportunity to jump in control, much to Naoko's chagrin. As she took off in a steady jog, she felt Naoko's previous exhaustion creep into her, sweat dripping down her brow as her other half weakly tried to take the body back.

When they arrived at the train station, Kokoro slowed to a brisk walk, shoulder bag strung across her chest, smacking against her side. The train itself was still there, though most of the people there had already boarded and found their seats.

Kokoro's eyes widened as she ran up to the terminal and swiped the smartcard. It denied it, citing a low balance.

Naoko growled in the background as Kokoro fumbled around in her bag but ended up finding nothing. The recent weeks had been filled with such chaos for them that they had neglected to recharge the smartcard.

Uh oh. Kokoro paled as she looked around for an ATM. Just as the loudspeaker announced final boarding, she caught a movement in the corner of her eye. A firm hand swiped a different card across the terminal and pushed them through the turnstile. Kokoro spun, seeing who had done it.

It was Mr. Haneda, dressed in his off-duty slacks and polo shirt.

"Figured I'd need it again one day," he said as he pulled some cash from his wallet and handed it to her. "Just remember to reload it next time, okay?"

Kokoro gratefully took it and bowed deeply. "Thanks, Dad." As she held the bow, she felt Naoko burning with embarrassment in the background. Naoko had never, ever called him that. In fact, she never would have even *considered* it.

Naoko's father raised an eyebrow, followed by a nod. "It's alright. Although, I am a bit disappointed. Here, I thought we were finally close to understanding each other, and then you go and call me 'Dad.'"

Kokoro bit her lip as Naoko angrily attempted to steal the body back, though she managed to keep her friend at bay.

"Sorry…*Father*," Kokoro said, bowing one more time.

"I was joking, Naoko." His gaze moved past her, his eyebrows raised. "You had better go. Your train is about to leave."

Kokoro spun in a panic, then ran onto the platform. The conductor briefly nagged her for being late, then nudged her onto the train. She made her way deeper into the car, managing to find a spot. In the distance, Naoko's Dad watched, his usual stoic expression faded into a small frown before slowly he walked away.

Her lip curled down as Naoko finally took back control of her body, gripping the hanging handle tight. Kokoro allowed herself to sink back through the mists into their inner world as she contemplated the look on Mr. Haneda's face.

"Hey, Nao?" Kokoro asked.

Naoko looked up from her phone, forgetting for a moment that she was talking to someone in her head. She blinked, scowling.

"What is it?" Naoko whispered.

"Don't you think it's time to make amends with your father?"

Naoko frowned, then turned her attention back to her game. "Why bother?"

"I just figured, you know, since things seem to be on the up end, why not? After all, the both of you have come so far."

Her other half paused for a moment, then sat down in the seat, allowing herself to partially drift back toward the mist with Kokoro. As the outside world blurred, the inner one solidified. Naoko's body darkened slightly, a hint of shadow bleeding into her from beyond, like a snake in the tall grass.

"Come on, Ko. You and I both know it was you doing all the hard work while I was just passed out like the pathetic druggie I am."

"That was one time," Kokoro protested. "Why are you still beating yourself up over it?"

"Oh, I don't know. Because I created a giant mess that you had to clean up? Or maybe because I was too weak to keep on living, so here you are, like some kind of guardian angel?"

"Everyone needs help," Kokoro said softly, attempting to let herself bleed into Naoko, to purge the dark thoughts, to help calm her. Her friend rebuffed her as she continued her rant.

"Not only that, but you're just… I don't know, perfect! The perfect friend, the perfect student!" Naoko's brows furrowed. "The perfect daughter."

"Come on, Nao." Kokoro stepped closer to her. "You know that isn't true."

"Don't bullshit me, Ko. We both know it's you he wants. How could I compete with that? Why would he want a screwup like me, especially when compared to someone like you?"

Kokoro watched as Naoko's chest heaved, her grip on her knees tightened. Some of the twisted shadows that were on Naoko touched her as well, digging, searching for something to use against her. She didn't care. Right now, she needed to connect with her friend, even if it meant being vulnerable.

Even if it means the truth.

"Nao, darling," Kokoro said, looking up at her friend with a sad smile. "How could he want me? I'm not even real."

Naoko froze. She blinked as her grip on Kokoro tightened.

"No, you are real. I mean, you're here with me!"

"You don't have to do that. It's okay." Kokoro rubbed Naoko's hands reassuringly as she looked around. "I know what I am, and I'm okay with it."

"Don't say that." Naoko shook her head. "Please, please don't."

"But it's alright," Kokoro smiled. "Even if it means I disappear one day, as long as you are finally happy, then it will be worth it."

Naoko, without warning, latched onto her. The shadow that held them both loosened its grip and retreated. "I never, ever want to lose you."

Kokoro frowned and pulled Naoko tighter into her embrace, brushing her hands through her soft, dark hair. The train lurched forward, the display for the location ever so often chiming.

"Hey, Ko?"

"Yeah?"

"Your hugs help." Naoko blinked sleepily. "Just don't let go until we get to school, okay?"

Kokoro paused, then nodded with a gentle smile as she felt Naoko's physical body pass into sleep. The sounds of the train and the light of the rising sun faded into darkness, though it wasn't cruel, nor cold like before. It was slow, merciful, like a starry night with the promise of a beautiful dawn.

Naoko immediately jumped back and forced Kokoro into control when Sayuki Sato sat with them at lunch. Kokoro chuckled. It was cute, like a shy child hiding behind the leg of her mother when being introduced to someone new.

"Hey, Naoko!" Sayuki said with a smile. "How are you?"

"Oh, fine." Kokoro placed Naoko's food to the side as she met Sayuki's gaze, smiling. "What about you? How's things at home?"

"It's getting a little better." Sayuki hesitated, then beamed. "Thanks to you."

"*Thanks to you?*" Naoko asked, her voice echoing as she watched in the background. "Remind me why we're friends with her again?"

"Maybe if you talked to her, you would know." Kokoro sighed. "She's a lot more like us than you would think."

"Never in a million years," Naoko scoffed.

"I'm glad," Kokoro replied to Sayuki, who blinked in confusion. She must have seen her facial expressions when talking to Naoko.

Kokoro rolled her eyes, then sighed. If she didn't want to seem crazy, then she would have to remind herself to reply to people in the real world when Naoko interrupted.

That, and not talking out loud when she wasn't.

"I've been meaning to ask," Sayuki began. "Are you…okay?"

"Of course!" Kokoro replied. "Why wouldn't I be?"

"I don't mean to offend, but ever since the arrest, you've been acting kinda weird. Before that, never in a million years would you have ever talked to me, much less been my friend."

Kokoro briefly pulled back into their inner world to shoot a satisfied smirk at Naoko, who retorted by blowing raspberries. After that, Kokoro quickly resumed control to avoid arousing suspicion.

"Well, you needed help! So, I helped!" Kokoro answered carefully to Sayuki.

"I…" Sayuki turned her head just as the bell rang. "If you say so. Anyway, catch you after class?"

Kokoro paused, staring at Sayuki. Her beautiful brown eyes bore into her, complimented by her soft hair and supple lips that, occasionally, would stretch into the prettiest of smiles.

"Right." Kokoro nodded with a smile, her cheeks warm. "Of course."

Sayuki beamed and stood, walking into the crowd of students pouring back into the building. After she had gone, Kokoro picked up their lunch to throw it away.

"Say, Ko…" Naoko asked. "How did we become friends with Sayuki? It's been almost a month and you've been avoiding the subject."

"It's complicated, but…" Kokoro hesitated. "Promise you won't tell anyone."

"We literally share a body, genius," Naoko retorted.

Rolling her eyes, Kokoro inhaled deeply, allowing the world outside to fade. Soon enough, she was in front of Naoko again, the mist falling nearby, and through it the multitude of Sakura trees whipped in the wind behind it. "I found her crying alone in the girl's bathroom. Turns out, she's a lot like you."

"Really?" Naoko blinked. "How so?"

Kokoro paused, reflecting on the day she had encountered Sayuki in the bathroom stall, her eyes saturated with tears as she cried. Naoko was still dormant at that point, but Kokoro had seen her memories of the way Sayuki had treated her. Despite that, she found she couldn't just walk away from someone who needed help.

"Her father was not very good," Kokoro began. "He never beat her or anything like that, but he never once showed that he cared for her. Sayuki tried so hard to get his attention, to earn his love, but the only time he ever even noticed was when she got in trouble."

"Sounds…familiar," Naoko said. "So that's what you helped her with? Getting her closer to her father?"

Kokoro hesitated, her eyes lowering. "Too late for that now. He died about a month before you woke up."

"Oh…" Naoko said, voice trailing off. "I didn't know."

"There's no way you could have," Kokoro replied. "For the longest time, Sayuki thought she hated him, but after he passed, she felt nothing but regret. She started wondering if he had treated her that way because she had done something wrong."

Kokoro felt her chest tighten, though it had bled through from Naoko. Her friend knew what that was like.

"He just sounds like a terrible person," Naoko pointed out. "No way she would ever deserve that."

"I've told her that. Multiple times, in fact. It still doesn't change how she feels about it." Kokoro inhaled sharply. "But despite all that, she said one thing about us, or…you, rather."

"Did she?" Naoko blinked. "What did she say?"

Her thoughts drifted back to that courtyard with the Sakura, where she had her first real heart-to-heart with Sayuki. Kokoro could still see her face clear as day, her eyes downcast as she admitted the truth.

"That she was jealous," Kokoro finally said.

"Wait." Naoko blinked. "Her? Jealous of me?"

Kokoro nodded. "She said that despite what happened between you and your dad, that you were lucky to have him. Her father never would have even tried to discipline her, nor cared enough to. Every time she made a mistake, he would simply let her fall flat on her face. If it had been her and her father in that situation, then she would either be dead from a drug overdose or still in jail."

"She really thinks so?" Naoko's lip curled.

"Your father loves you, Naoko." Kokoro met her eyes, demanding her gaze. "Yes, he doesn't express it. Sure, he said some stupid things in the heat of the moment. But believe me when I say he only wanted you to get better and be the very best version of yourself. So please, do your best to restore things between you and him. Even if it doesn't work out, at least you can say you tried."

Naoko paused, her arms crossed, and her gaze lowered. Kokoro knew she was contemplating it. That was more than enough for her, at least for now.

"Say, Kokoro," Naoko asked after a minute of silence. "My friends from before. What happened to them?"

Kokoro froze. The mere mention of Naoko's three 'friends' sent a shiver crawling up her spine. There was something about them that set her on edge, though she couldn't quite figure out what.

"From the party, right?"

"Yeah." Naoko nodded, her gaze fell. "I...still want answers about what happened that night."

"I honestly don't know. I haven't seen them around here, or anywhere, really." Kokoro paused, touching her chin. "Was the party the last time you saw them?"

"I think so," Naoko replied. "But everything from that day is a blur. The only thing I really remember is Father arresting me, and then the pills, and—"

She stopped just shy of saying the words. Kokoro decided at that moment that it was time for a topic change.

"Well, enough talk," Kokoro said, slipping into control as she rose from their spot under the Sakura tree in the courtyard. "You ready to head to class? I've got one hell of a math test waiting for you."

Naoko snorted, chuckling. "No thanks. The body's all yours."

Kokoro smiled as she walked to the double doors behind the last of the students. Just before she walked in, something caught her eye. On the far wall was a billboard, several sheets of paper stapled over each other.

Her eyes narrowed. They were posters of missing girls, most of whom she had seen at her school at one point or another. As she scanned them to check the dates, she found that all of them had occurred within the last month.

"What do you think happened to them?" Naoko asked.

Kokoro began to answer but was interrupted by the bell once again. They were late for class. She pulled away and headed through the double doors and down the hallway. There was something more that was bothering her about those missing girls, something she had seen before.

But what was it?

Kokoro sighed, shaking the thought from her head as she sped up her walking. She would have to get to the bottom of it later. For now, they had a math test to pass.

CHAPTER 6
LIGHT YOUR HEART UP

WITH THE TEST OVER AND THE RINGING OF THE BELL, the two of them were finally home free. Summer vacation was fast approaching and, with any luck, Naoko—with Kokoro's help—hoped to convince her father to free her from house arrest.

As they walked out of the courtyard, Kokoro had ceded the body to Naoko, laying back in the front of their shared mind-space, as if it were a passenger seat. Her better half needed a moment to relax after burning the entirety of her brain power on the math test.

"How did it go?" Naoko asked. She wasn't fond of school, so when Kokoro graciously offered to handle it on her behalf, how could she refuse?

"I…" Kokoro blinked. "It went well… I think."

"You think?" Naoko arched an eyebrow. "We're not in trouble, are we?"

"No, of course not," Kokoro clarified. "Like, I *know* we did good. Great, even. I just don't remember the test itself."

"Oh. That's…awesome." Naoko sighed and continued her trek toward the train station. The air felt slightly humid, the sun bore down on them whenever they weren't under the merciful shade of a tree or building. Different shops lined the streets, interspersed with apartments, vending machines, and bicycles among so much more. Even in the daylight, advertisements for different shows, movies, and anime flashed, some packed so tightly together that she often avoided looking at them to spare herself the vertigo.

Naoko turned a corner, and they were on the side of the Meguro River, the Sakura flowers that had bloomed just a few months before were now completely gone, leaving the streets so cleanly swept that they were strikingly close to perfection. In their place were green leaves that still provided them with much-needed relief from the sunlight, though Kokoro had once said it wasn't her favorite look for them. Instead, she preferred them in the spring, when the beautiful, fleeting flurries of white and pink filled the air. Naoko found it hard to disagree.

"Hey, Nao?" Kokoro asked out of the blue.

"Yeah?"

"Where's the first place you wanna go once we're free from being stuck at home?"

"I…" Naoko paused, stepped to the side and gripped the railing that overlooked the river. "I'm honestly not sure. Haven't been thinking about it that much."

Kokoro frowned. "Why not?"

"I don't know," Naoko lied.

As Kokoro arched an eyebrow, Naoko could feel her trying to dig into her thoughts. She shifted uncomfortably and tried to block her, to which her companion responded with an annoyed sigh.

"Come on, Nao. You know you can talk to me."

"I know. Thank you, Ko, but I'm fine."

Naoko felt a strange yet familiar warmth fill her. She exhaled, loosening her grip on the railing. Kokoro pointed out a nearby bench in the shade by taking partial control and focusing her eyesight on it. Naoko managed to resist Kokoro's soothing and shook her head.

"We can talk on the train. We don't want to miss—"

Naoko never got the chance to finish. Kokoro, even though she was tired, still managed to take complete control long enough to force her to sit. After fighting for a moment, Naoko finally complied, though she felt agitation creep to the surface. Kokoro knew that Naoko hated having control of her body wrestled from her, and yet it was often the case, especially when she wasn't willing to open up.

"Alrighty," Kokoro said as her form solidified, the outside world fading. "What's bothering you?"

"What are you, my therapist?" Naoko asked with an eye roll.

"If I have to be. Remember, I'm here for you. I'm—"

"—whatever you need me to be. I know."

Kokoro frowned. Naoko hated seeing that, especially on her.

"I'm sorry. That was mean." Naoko sighed. "Honestly, I'm kinda struggling a bit. One minute, I finally have friends. The next, they're gone. It seems like everything was a rug that was just pulled out from under me. Only when I fell, I bumped my head and blacked out for months at a time while you did the legwork in fixing my mistake. Which, by the way," Naoko allowed a small smile to touch her lips. "I would never want you to think that I wasn't grateful for that. I am."

"Always," Kokoro said. "Besides, you had things a bit tough. You needed a break."

Naoko chuckled. "I know, but two months? Really?"

Kokoro shrugged. "I didn't want to wake you up."

"Or maybe you just wanted to redecorate my room."

"Oh, come on! You know you like it!"

"Maybe a little." Naoko laughed out loud, drawing concerned looks from an older couple that traversed the streets. Kokoro fronted long enough to wave ecstatically, like some obsessed foreigner. After another second of staring, eyebrows raised, they turned and continued their walk. Naoko's cheeks flushed.

"What's the matter?" Kokoro teased. "Embarrassed?"

"Yeah," Naoko mumbled under her breath. "Thanks."

"Oh, it can always get worse." Kokoro grinned evilly. "Much, much worse."

"Oh, please don't," Naoko begged as Kokoro wrestled control from her once more. "Please don't do what I think you're going to do."

Kokoro smirked haughtily as she jumped up from the park bench, unwrapping her earbuds from her phone with one swift motion. "Relax. I'm just gonna finish our little walk to the station. Don't wanna be late, right?"

Naoko tried to shrink back into her mind and darken her vision, but her friend held her fast, determined to include Naoko in her wicked plan.

With that, Kokoro stretched, cracked her knuckles, and searched for a song. Within the minute, she landed on the perfect one, setting off into an exaggerated stride down the street as Naoko's already-puffy face reddened.

"Please stop," Naoko begged.

Kokoro ignored her and began to sing obnoxiously loud. Naoko groaned. At that moment, as several passersby shot them an annoyed look, Naoko almost wished she *had* died. At least then, she wouldn't have to bear witness to Kokoro's flippant disregard for subtlety.

Her friend, on the other hand, apparently had other plans. Naoko found that she was no longer just a passenger. Somehow, she was on the street with Kokoro, following behind like a duckling would follow its mother. She blinked, reaching to touch one of the other pedestrians out of curiosity, only to find that she waved right through.

Naoko's eyes widened. She wasn't in the real world with Kokoro, but rather she had shaped their inner world to reflect it in real-time, like a simulation. The only difference was that instead of taking her appearance, Ko had opted for her own silver-blonde hair shimmering in the sun, her gentle face bright, even against the daylight.

Cheeks burning, Naoko took another look around. None of the people saw her, only her friend dancing and walking in her body. Kokoro strutted confidently, occasionally turning to her to flash an encouraging smile.

Despite Naoko's strongest urges to shrink back into the depths of her brain, something else kept her there. This wasn't Kokoro, but her own desire. Deep down, she wanted to join her, to sing, and dance, and not give a damn about what the world had to say.

"If you have a gift, why not share it with the whole world?"

Naoko paused as Kokoro stopped dancing and stood there, smiling as the world around them froze in place. She had recognized the iconic line; It was from the real-world Kokoro during her sessions on PULSE. Despite the millions of times that she had heard it, something was different. It wasn't meant for some unknown audience online.

This time, the words were meant for her.

Naoko looked down at herself, at her hands, her feet. They were more than just her limbs; they were her instruments. She knew she could dance but had always held back. Why? The only time she tried was at the party, which…

Kokoro interrupted her thought by cupping Naoko's cheeks in her hands, smiling.

"Hey, you. Lighten up that pretty little heart of yours. Okay?"

Naoko's cheeks flushed as her friend took her by the hand, then locked arms with her. Time resumed as she danced once more. Her legs kicked out practically with each stride, her exaggerated movements smooth, yet precise. Onlookers gazed at her, some with contempt, others with bewilderment, and the rest with genuine curiosity.

She hadn't bothered paying them any more attention. Naoko was now matching Kokoro move for move, stride for stride, note for note. Their voices rang out in unison, practically screaming the lyrics. The fog of hesitation that always held Naoko at bay dissipated, the energy within her now pouring out into the world.

Where it belongs. Naoko smiled at Kokoro while she danced. *You were always right about me. I can't hide anymore.*

Her friend beamed; Naoko blushed. She had forgotten to hide her thoughts from her, and yet, she wasn't that embarrassed. Whether Kokoro was a ghost or a hallucination, it didn't matter to her anymore. All that mattered now was keeping her friend in her life.

What would I do without her?

Naoko caught her breath as she reached the train station, her hand gripping the hot metal pole. She blinked.

Wait a minute. Why am I in control right now?

Behind her, Kokoro giggled, her voice fading like echoes traveling down a cavern. The sly devil had switched with her while they were dancing, meaning it was Naoko in the driver's seat, crazily flailing her body for the world to see.

Naoko groaned, then laughed. Before, she would have been irritated, perhaps even snapped at her. But now, that didn't matter. Kokoro had shown her that sometimes the best thing for one to do was enjoy the moment, even if it meant cementing oneself as the crazy dancing chick from Nakameguro.

She grinned while smoothly swiping the smartcard, evading the turnstile, and comfortably seating herself on the train, tweaking her earbuds to resume their melody. She closed her eyes, tapped her feet, and muttered the lyrics as the annoyed passengers looked on.

Naoko didn't care. She had finally opened herself to the world, and damn, it felt good.

Kokoro had stayed quiet in the background of Naoko's mind as she continued to jam out, all the way from the train station, annoying her poor neighbors with her off-pitch song all the way to her house. Naoko stopped, pulling the earbuds and wrapping them around her phone.

Wait. Why are all the lights off?

Naoko paused, hesitating. The front door with its annoying hinges creaked open to a darkened foyer, the kitchen, stairs, and living room obscured by shadow. She slowed forward, her footsteps silent. Not a single sound came, only the whisper of the air conditioner as it blessed the house with its cold. Creeping into the kitchen, she found the switch and turned a light on.

Then, without warning, Naoko screamed and jumped back.

"What is it? What's wrong?" Kokoro asked. Naoko felt her friend's attempt to seize the body.

"Surprise!" Naoko's parents exclaimed from behind the kitchen island. Both her father and mother wore a cardboard party hat, complete with a necklace of fake flowers. On the counter was a small cake that held a similar theme. The brown sturdy oak of the Sakura tree contrasted with the white frosting beneath it. Rounding the cake were a few pink petals, encircling the words, *Happy Birthday!*

For a moment, the air was silent except for Naoko's hyperventilating. She felt Kokoro slip into control with her, guiding her to control it with several deep breaths until she finally settled enough to manage words.

"It's my birthday…?" Naoko asked, still processing.

"Of course!" her mother said, arching an eyebrow. "You don't remember?"

Naoko paused, then briefly retreated into their mind space. Kokoro met her eyes and shrugged, before she fronted again.

"I…I guess I just lost track of time. You know, school and all," Naoko said as she laughed nervously. "Sorry."

"Yes, you have been working hard," her father said, beaming with pride as he exchanged glances with his wife. He returned his gaze to Naoko, clearing his throat. "We know that technically, you're an adult now, and this isn't exactly traditional. But since we didn't do much for your birthday last year, and we know you love cake…" he trailed off.

"What he's trying to say is that he made this himself, decoration and all," Naoko's mother said, laughing as her father's cheeks flushed, his hands behind his back. "Not only as a birthday present, but to show how proud we are of you."

Naoko blinked. Warmth settled into her face and chest as she heard Kokoro giggle not far behind her.

"Like I told ya," Kokoro whispered. "Your dad loves you. He just doesn't know how to show it sometimes."

Naoko glanced at her father. He stood tall, arms behind his back. Everything about him screamed formal except for his face. She could have sworn he was blushing. Naoko smiled.

"I guess you're right, Ko," Naoko admitted inwardly, smiling.

"Aren't I always?"

"Oh, hush."

"Well, then." Her mother beamed and clasped her hands together, the sound interrupting her and Kokoro's jesting. "Who's ready to eat?"

Naoko nodded excitedly as her parents beckoned her to the kitchen island in front of her cake. She stared down at it, admiring its beautifully crafted design. It also looked delicious, but she just couldn't bring herself to take a bite.

Turns out, she didn't have to. Naoko blinked, and the next thing she knew, bits of that beautiful cake were plastered all over her face. She turned, eyes widening as she realized it was also all over her parents. Naoko froze as she heard Kokoro's mischievous laughter fade.

Of course. Who else would embarrass me like this?

"Oopsie," Kokoro said, her voice echoing. Naoko couldn't see her friend in her mind's eye at that moment, but if she could, she imagined that Kokoro would have horns, a red outfit, and a pitchfork.

"Naoko," a voice said. She pulled herself out of her thoughts to find her father staring daggers at her. She paled.

Oh crap, Ko, what have you done?

"If you start something…" Her father scooped a sizeable chunk out of the cake, "…then you had better learn to finish it!"

Naoko stepped back, trying to dodge, but it was too late. He had flung the chunk of cake at her, splattering it against her torso and making her school uniform look like a messy painting as she stood in absolute shock.

Her father, of all people, having fun?

She felt something splash against her from behind. She spun to find her mother grinning.

"Happy birthday, darling," her mother said as she chuckled, pleased with herself.

Naoko blinked and the next thing she knew, she was being chased by both of her parents, who had ganged up on her. They ran in circles around the kitchen island, flinging cake, plastering each other at every given opportunity.

Time shifted for her again, and her father now had Naoko and her mother ducking behind the island as he bombarded them. Her mother turned to her, holding some of her fingers up.

"Okay, on the count of three. Ready?"

The next moment, Naoko and her mother tackled him, pinning him to the ground as they all laughed hysterically.

Naoko sat up and leaned against the couch as she smiled, watching her parents continue to assault each other with the ruined masterpiece that was her birthday cake. She didn't care. Seeing them like this, laughing and smiling, was worth far more than a silly little cake, anyway.

She blinked again, and they were laying back on the couch, leaning into each other, cake smeared all over their faces and clothes as they slumbered. Her father snuggled her mother close as the TV droned on in the background.

"Sorry if you missed some of it," a voice said. Kokoro materialized next to her in the inner world, one knee tucked in with her hand resting on the other. "I know you were having fun, but I just wanted to be a part of it, too."

Naoko paused, pulling herself out to glance at her slumbering parents. For so long, the three of them lived in this house, barely interacting, almost like strangers. Now, here they were, a proper family.

Because of her. But not just because of what she had done to repair the rift between them. No, it was far more than that. They were a family now because one more had been added to the roster, whether they knew it or not.

"I don't mind, Ko. You are a part of it. Of me," Naoko answered. Another thought slipped into her mind. It should have been strange, but it felt...right. "But you're also so much more than that. You're just as much a daughter to them as I am."

Kokoro froze. Her mouth gaped open as her eyes glistened. Her face quivered as she leaned into Naoko.

"Thank you, Nao," Kokoro said. "You have no idea what that means to me."

Naoko smiled. "Look who the crybaby is now, huh?"

Kokoro's cheeks burned. "Oh, hush!"

Their parents shifted in their sleep as Naoko laughed. She quickly silenced herself as Kokoro gestured upstairs.

"Maybe we should let them be?"

Naoko nodded and quietly got up, tiptoeing her way out, before a tired voice called from the living room. She stopped on the steps and spun to face her father, who had risen from the couch.

"I forgot to tell you earlier. Your restriction is suspended indefinitely." He smiled. "So long as you are home by a certain time, you can go anywhere within the city limits this weekend, if you want."

Naoko paused, taking in the information as she felt Kokoro's burst of excitement. Finally, they had achieved their goal, the freedom to explore their world together. But where would they go? Naoko held the question in the back of her mind ever since Kokoro had asked about it yesterday.

"I think I have an idea, Nao," Kokoro said. "Just ask him to take us back to that spot on the Meguro."

"Um...okay," Naoko answered Kokoro internally before returning to the front. "Father? Are you doing anything tomorrow?"

"Oh. Of course not, Naoko." His eyes lit up as he scratched the back of his head. "Why do you ask?"

"I was wondering if maybe we could go back to the Meguro tomorrow? By the school?"

"Oh." Her father blinked. "I suppose so. By why the school? Knowing you, I figured you'd want to be as far away from it as possible."

Naoko blushed, unsure of how to answer. Luckily, Kokoro took control just in time. "Oh, you know. Just trying to start somewhere familiar!"

Her father's eyebrows furrowed for a moment. "If that's where you want to go, then...I'd be honored to take you. Happy birthday, daughter." He closed his eyes and bowed.

Kokoro returned it, nearly falling down the steps. Naoko fronted just before disaster, regaining her footing. Her father chuckled, regarded her with a nod and smile, then made his way back to his wife as she slumbered on their couch.

The moment the light clicked off in the kitchen, Naoko moved back into her room, shutting her door and sitting on the edge of her bed as she processed what had just happened. Kokoro squealed. "You know what this means, right, Nao? We did it. We finally got our freedom back!"

"You mean you did?" Naoko said, chuckling as she lay on the bed, sprawled out.

"No, *we* did." Her friend materialized next to her, on her belly, her legs kicking. "You can't blame all this success on me."

Naoko smiled. She stared up blankly as their internal world overtook the real one, the ceiling slowly giving way to a starry night, with the branches of the Sakura trees reaching out. Their pink petals illuminated with an otherworldly glow, like one of the neon signs on a street in Shibuya. The difference was that the artificial light didn't drown out the sky. In fact, it complimented it.

Her and Kokoro's little world was always whatever they needed it to be, and tonight it was perfect.

She smiled as Kokoro lay opposite her, their ebony and ivory hair splayed across the ground, intertwining with a gentle radiance. The branches of the Sakura tree waved in the wind, nature's beautiful chorus. The longer she thought about it, the more amazed and bewildered Naoko felt.

"Hey, Ko?"

"What's up, Nao?"

"Not that I'm grateful, but where did you come from? What made you...well, exist?"

"I honestly don't know," Kokoro answered. "Back then, it didn't feel like I was 'born.' Rather, it felt more like waking up from a long nap if that makes any sense."

"I suppose." Naoko sighed. "I was just stopping to consider all of this for a minute. I mean, you say that you don't think you're real, and yet, that doesn't feel true at all."

Kokoro blinked. "What do you mean?"

"You're just as real as anything else out there, sometimes even more so," Naoko explained. "And I'm not sure how else to describe it, but while you're you, I'm also…you. But then again, we're not the same."

"Like pieces of a puzzle?" Kokoro asked.

"I guess so." Naoko smiled. "Either way, I'm just glad to have you here. Because right now, that's all I could ever want."

Allowing herself to relax, Naoko laid back. The stars churned against the black, slowly lulling her into that blessed numbness, that state of mind where nothing existed except the peace. Naoko blinked as she realized something.

"Hey, Ko?" she asked.

"Yeah?"

"You know how the front lets us both in, but only sometimes?"

"I do," Naoko heard the petals shift as Kokoro nodded her head. "What about it?"

"I've been thinking about it," Naoko continued. "When we're both up there, sometimes it lets us both through, and sometimes it doesn't. I was wondering if maybe someone has to be up there at all times, like at a police station or something."

"Huh. That makes sense. But then, how are you and I down here? Unless…" Kokoro trailed off as she soon came to the same conclusion Naoko had. "You think we're not alone in here?"

"Maybe." Naoko shrugged. "What do you think?"

Kokoro paused, rolling off Naoko and lying on her back again, her hair spread out among the soft petals. "I'm not sure. I've looked but haven't really found anything."

"Oh. I see." Naoko exhaled, letting silence fill the chilly air. A distant, eerie cry shook her from her drifting thoughts, the same one she had heard when she saw that burnt-down building. It was frightening, enough to send a shiver down her spine by just thinking about it, and yet, it saddened her. A pang of loneliness filled Naoko, along with a sense of unbearable tragedy.

"Have you ever heard crying?" Naoko suddenly asked.

Kokoro paused for a moment, touching her chin. "Occasionally. Whenever I tried to investigate, I just…gave up. It scares me."

Naoko stiffened a little, curling into herself. She frowned.

"Anyway, that's probably enough talk for now," Kokoro said. "We should get some rest. We've got a big day tomorrow."

Naoko nodded and looked up at the dark sky, allowing the stars to pass overhead and lull her into a good night's sleep.

CHAPTER 7

A BUTTERFLY INDEED

IF THERE WAS ONE THING KOKORO could count on about Naoko, it was her habit of waking up early on weekends.

The sunlight gently bled through Naoko's window, the floating particles of dust visible in the rays. She had finished throwing on a pair of knee-length jean shorts, a modest tank top, and a pair of cheap gas station sunglasses.

When she had finished getting dressed, she ran down the steps to meet her father, who had chosen something casual as well: a pair of ironed jeans and a polo shirt. Kokoro smiled from within Naoko's mind.

"You ready?" her father asked, tightening his wristwatch.

Naoko nodded excitedly as Kokoro chuckled. It was so refreshing to see her like this, vibrant and full of life. She had improved so much, transforming from a shy, insecure, suicidal girl into a confident, brave one who wasn't afraid to show the world how beautiful her soul truly was.

Like seeing a caterpillar turn into a butterfly. Kokoro swelled with pride at the thought.

After bidding her mother goodbye, Naoko had shuffled out the front door and into the passenger seat of her father's car. He pulled out of the driveway and then they were off to explore the boundaries of her newfound freedom—barring a stop at the local coffee place.

Both Kokoro and her better half watched, sipping their drink as the houses drifted by, blurring into shops and schools, then finally into the skyscrapers that stretched toward the heavens in stout defiance.

Something caught Kokoro's eyes. She gently shifted into control alongside Naoko, pressing her face against the glass. Not far from them was the tallest structure in all of Tokyo: a white needle that appeared to pierce the clouds themselves, two round platforms encircled near the top. Whereas Naoko always took the Skytree for granted, Kokoro was blown away by the miracle of science that made the thing possible.

"Umm…" Naoko arched an eyebrow. "I don't think so. I'm not that brave."

"Aww, come on!" Kokoro pulled back into her mind and nudged her. "If it's the height you're worried about, then—"

"—then you'd lean over the railing too far, break the glass, and we'd fall to our deaths."

"Don't worry," Kokoro said, chuckling. "I'd take control just before we went splat."

Dead silence. Kokoro turned to Naoko worriedly, afraid she had taken her joke too far. Instead, Naoko laughed so hard that it bled through to her actual body.

"Is something funny, Naoko?"

"No sir, I…" Naoko straightened, then beamed nervously at her father, "…just, uh, thought of something funny."

He arched an eyebrow, not taking his eyes off the road. "And what would that be?"

Naoko pulled back into her mind, her eyes begging Kokoro for help, for her to front. Kokoro returned her plea with a smirk.

"Go on, Naoko," she teased. "Tell him!"

Naoko blew raspberries and fronted again, facing her father. She blinked, obviously struggling to come up with something until she finally spat it out. "Uh…you know that cake fight we had last night?"

Most of her father's face remained passive, minus his mouth, the tips slightly curling into a small grin. "Of course. What about it?"

Kokoro watched as Naoko struggled to come up with another response. Then she had an evil idea and pulled herself into control.

"Did you clean up Mom by licking the cake off her?"

Mr. Haneda slammed on the brakes, the seat belt tightened against her chest, knocking some of the breath out of her. Luckily, the street was mostly empty, save for a few cyclists and pedestrians. As Kokoro recovered, she saw him stiffen, gripping the steering wheel.

Kokoro felt Naoko panic, trying to shrink deeper into her mind. She herself was also nervous. It felt like one more wrong word, and they would be grounded again.

Mr. Haneda sighed, regained control of himself, and sat up straight in his seat. With his face hardened, he opened his mouth to speak. "...No. She did."

Another moment of awkward silence. Then came the laughter from both Kokoro and her father. She felt a rising heat behind her as Naoko's rage grew.

"Alright, jerk," Naoko said. "That's enough of you."

Unexpectedly, Naoko made a sudden move to seize the body, sparking a fierce internal struggle for dominance. Kokoro chuckled, resisting her advances while the body trembled. By the time Naoko broke through, their coffee had splattered across the dashboard and carpet of her father's car. Naoko turned towards him, her expression clouded with a frown.

Within the next few minutes, her father had found a convenience store and walked back out with a few rolls of paper towels as Naoko stood to the side, her face covered in her hands as her father cleaned up her mess.

"Father..." Naoko began. "I'm so sorry. I didn't mean to—"

"Never mind that," Mr. Haneda said. "Are you sure you're feeling okay, Naoko?" He stood up from his cleaning, a plastic bag full of used paper towels gripped in his free hand. "When we were driving, you went rigid before you spilled the drink. You seem like you're—"

"I'm fine!" Kokoro said with a smile after regaining control of the body. Naoko pulled back, arms crossed, feeling ashamed.

Eyes narrowed, he nodded, throwing the bag away in a nearby trash can. "Well, I had better take this to a cleaner before it stains."

"Oh." Kokoro frowned. "Does that mean we're leaving already?"

"I…" Mr. Haneda paused, scratching the back of his neck. "I am. You don't have to if that is what you wish."

Naoko stood up in their mind, moving closer to the front. Kokoro met her gaze before fronting again. "You mean…?"

"You are free to go," he said. "Let's just meet back here around six. After that, I'll take you out somewhere nice for dinner. How does that sound?"

Both Kokoro and Naoko leapt for joy upon hearing the words, though they were careful not to let it show in the body. Slowly, Naoko shifted into control, a smile adorning her face as she nodded slowly.

"Of course. Thank you, Father." Naoko bowed but didn't receive one in return. Instead, her father embraced her. Her cheeks warmed up, her heart fluttered inside her chest. He released her, then regarded her with a nod, beckoning for her to be on her way.

Kokoro could feel her excitement pulse within Naoko as she walked away, giving her father one last look before turning a street corner. She smiled.

Her precious Naoko was a butterfly, indeed.

Naoko couldn't stop thinking about her father's hug. It was the first one he had given her in forever, perhaps even since she was a small child.

Child. As she walked, Naoko heard the cries again, distant and faded. She mentally nudged Kokoro, who was back in their internal world, searching for the very same voice.

"Still nothing?" Naoko asked.

Kokoro slipped in with her, though gently, trying not to knock her from control. She shook her head. "I don't know why, but…I don't know. Every time I hear it, I feel a little more worried."

Naoko nodded, frowning. It wasn't the cries that scared her, not exactly. There was something more to them, something familiar. Dangerous, and yet tragic.

She inched forward. The cries echoed louder as her surroundings darkened. Something was in the distance that she recognized, a strange shape…no, a building obscured in shadow. Distorted groans and cries rang out and filled her with dread.

Kokoro grasped her hand and pulled her back. Naoko blinked and found that she had gone deeper, toward the 'unknown,' as they called it. The darkness.

"You were…wandering…" Kokoro said, as she struggled to catch her breath. "I caught you just in…time. I was afraid I would have lost you."

Naoko inhaled sharply and shook herself out of the strange trance, back into control of the body. They had walked further without realizing it. *Much* further. The streets had widened, and yet traffic was packed tight. The outside of the buildings were filled to the brim with advertisements for anime and soap operas. People in cosplay lined the streets, some of them in maid outfits, handing out flyers. Naoko arched an eyebrow.

"We're in Akihabara?"

Kokoro shrugged behind her as Naoko spun, taking in her surroundings. "But…we were just at the Meguro. That's like a two-hour walk!"

"Closer to three, actually," Kokoro pointed out. "The thing is, I don't remember it, either. I was too busy chasing you."

"Who was controlling, then?" Naoko asked, her brows furrowed, eyes widening. She recalled their conversation the night prior when she had asked Kokoro about the possibility of another.

Maybe she and I aren't alone, after all.

"I'm considering that too," Kokoro said, reading the thoughts that bled from her. "But for now, we just have to be careful."

Naoko acknowledged with a nod, then moved from the sidewalk to the brick inlaid street. The sun beat down from overhead. The constant flux of people around her made her world spin. She blinked and found herself inside a small café. A girl dressed in a maid outfit was standing in front of her, notepad in hand, fake cat ears poking from the top of her hair.

"Are you okay, Miss?" the maid asked, the higher-than-normal pitch of her voice shaking the fog from Naoko's brain. The girl tilted her head, though Naoko couldn't tell if it was her just being in-character or if she was genuinely concerned.

"I'm, uh…fine," Naoko answered, sitting up and smiling, though she was sure her nervousness was all but evident. She had blacked out twice, after all. Had some unknown taken control again?

"That was me that time, sorry," Kokoro said, her soft voice echoed. "At least…I think so? It was a bit blurry for me too."

"You think so?" Naoko asked, careful to keep her words from reaching her mouth. She was already on the verge of public embarrassment, something she wanted to avoid at all costs.

The maid blinked. "Perhaps a water, miss?"

"Er, yeah! Let me just…" Naoko pulled her wallet from her back pocket, to find it empty, when she had at least a thousand yen in it before. Her eyes widened as she turned back to the maid. "Um…never mind."

The maid smiled, then rollerbladed over to the counter, pulling bottled water from a hidden mini refrigerator. She returned, placing it on the table.

"It's on the house," she said with a wink, before shifting back to her mockingly cute demeanor. "But just this once. Okay?"

Naoko nodded slowly. The maid rolled off to another table filled with young men, who cheered her arrival like she was a celebrity. She beamed, nodding as they all afforded her compliments, occasionally eyeing her but never touching. Still, it bothered Naoko.

"I think it's kinda cute," Kokoro said, water bottle in hand, as she finished sipping it. Naoko hadn't even realized it, but Kokoro had slowly shifted their places. Back when they were first learning to coordinate, it was a protective habit of hers, something that she hadn't let go of yet. Despite how close they were and all the progress they had made, boundaries were still an issue sometimes. "I mean, she wouldn't be there if she didn't want to be?"

"I guess so." Naoko took another look at the girl as she turned away from the table. Her smile never dropped, and yet, she could almost feel the emotion radiating from her. No, not emotion. Resilience. A guard against doubtful thought. Even if it came down on her later, Naoko realized, it wouldn't matter as long as it held together when facing the world. She frowned.

"Anyway," Kokoro began. "We should get going. We still have one more thing to do, remember?"

Naoko arched an eyebrow. "And what would that be?"

A sly smile crossed Kokoro's gentle lips. She leaned against the window, her eyes fixed on something not too terribly far in the distance. Naoko followed her gaze and saw it: a sturdy white needle that pierced the blue sky, two observation decks fastened near the top, the same one they had seen earlier.

They were going to the Tokyo Skytree.

Within the hour, they had finished their walk from Akihabara, and Naoko found herself standing at the entrance of a small village-like wonder called Solamachi. The vibrant ambiance engulfed her as she stepped inside, the bustling atmosphere alive with an assortment of shops that catered to every imaginable interest, each intricately linked to the main attraction: the Skytree itself. Up closer, it looked much sturdier; columns of white, curving steel churned the bright blue above, defying the terrifying reality known as gravity with daring engineering.

Naoko had looked up at the towering marvel and stopped, her heart beginning to churn inside her chest. "We're going up there?"

"Yup!" Kokoro said. "I've been looking into this ever since our conversation the other day. I figured… Well, you know. That it'd be cool!"

Naoko pursed her lips. "Exactly how tall is this thing?"

"Six-hundred and thirty-four meters from ground to tip, I believe," Kokoro said. "To the first observation deck, it's about three-hundred and fifty."

"That's really high," Naoko pointed out. "Are you sure we can't do something…you know, safer?"

"It's perfectly safe, so don't worry," Kokoro said. Naoko couldn't exactly see it at that moment, but she could feel the excitement brimming within her, the desire to ride to the top and see the world from above. She wasn't exactly keen on it, but then again, Kokoro had gone through the trouble of fixing her life for her.

It's the least I can do.

Naoko swallowed, then tried to push herself forward. Her body froze, then sped-walk away from the tower and back into the inside of the Solamachi, tucking herself inside one of the hundreds of shops that lined the long hallway. She inhaled sharply and focused on a shelf filled with figures, trying to slow her ragged, panicked breathing.

Kokoro shifted next to her, her brows furrowed. "Everything okay, Nao?"

"I just need a minute," she whispered, closing her eyes, the world outside fading from view.

"If you don't want to, then we don't have to, Nao. I…just thought it would be fun."

Naoko turned to her, seeing her lips curl into a frown. Even though she knew Kokoro would never even consider forcing her to go, guilt still crept into her. Besides, it was time to repay her for everything she had done.

"No. We're doing this. I can do it."

"It's okay, really. We don't—"

Naoko stopped listening and briskly walked out of the shop, back out to the base of the Skytree. Within the next few minutes, they had visited an ATM, received their ticket, and were inside the elevator. The walls were coated in a shining onyx aluminum, a piece of brass artwork on one end, and the digital height indicator on the other.

She shrunk back into the corner as more tourists filed in. The lady manning the doors bid them farewell with a bow as the doors closed and the elevator began moving. Much to Naoko's relief, it was surprisingly smooth…and fast. It hadn't even been a minute, and they were already there.

The doors slid open, and they were greeted by another tour guide wearing a multicolored uniform. She bowed, then beckoned them out onto the ramp and finally the deck itself.

Naoko's eyes widened. The first observation deck was much, much bigger on the inside. Off to the sides were two staunch pillars imbued with artistic renditions of the Skytree, near a couple of historical and engineering exhibits. At the far end were the forward-slanted observation windows and black guardrails, brimming with an entrancing white light.

The panic melted away as Naoko made her way up and across, following the curvature of the deck around the inner structure. She smiled.

"This isn't so bad," Naoko admitted as she stopped to look at one of the observation windows. She approached it cautiously, as if it would shatter and the wind whisk them both to their doom. She froze, her heart beginning to twist in her chest.

"Breathe. It's okay." Naoko felt Kokoro's comforting warmth hold her fear at bay. "Just one step at a time."

Naoko inhaled and moved. The white light in the windows blended with blue as she inched closer, and finally, the distant, faded horizon came into view. Wedged in-between the ocean and the mountains was Tokyo itself. Decades upon decades of economic growth had filled it to the brim, the buildings growing higher, more tightly packed, and yet organized. Strangely beautiful. Why had she lived here so long and taken it for granted the way she did?

The mirror shimmered, her reflection. No, not hers. Kokoro's reflection that projected from her mind's eye came into view as she beamed with pride.

"See. I told you it wouldn't be that bad."

Naoko's eyes shifted beyond the city, back to the gleaming water of Tokyo bay. It had just hit her she had never been to a beach, not even once.

"Hey, Ko?"

Kokoro blinked. "What is it?"

"I think I know where I want to go next time," she said.

"Yeah?" Kokoro turned, trying to see where Naoko's gaze was focused. "And where is that?"

As Naoko stared at the glimmering water in the distance, she let her imagination pull her in like a tide. She could almost feel it, the waves pushing past her ankles, feet sinking into the sand, the salty breeze blowing through her hair as she gazed at the sea. But it was much more than that. All her life, Tokyo, despite its size and wonder, had been a cage of sorts. To her, that endless churning water was so much more. To her, that ocean meant that there was an entire world that lay beyond the horizon.

To her, it meant freedom.

"One day," Naoko declared. "I want us to see the ocean."

Kokoro met her gaze, then gently smiled. "There's nothing I would want more."

Naoko returned it and started to reply before something caught her eye. Not far off to the side, conversing with some other women was a familiar-looking foreigner woman dressed in skin-tight jeans, a loose hanging blouse, and sunglasses on top of her head. Her brown hair with gentle curls was brushed back behind her ears. Naoko blinked, brows furrowing.

"Claire?"

Claire froze, then faced Naoko slowly. She beamed, though she seemed nervous. "Naoko! Is that you, darling?"

Naoko didn't respond at first. She simply stared as Claire continued to inspect her before smiling.

"Ah, it is you!" Claire squealed, drawing attention from some of the other tourists. "It's really been a hot minute, hasn't it?" She placed a hand on her hip, shaking her head ever so slightly. "So, how have you been? Still doing school, or…?"

"The party," Naoko said simply. It may have been rude at that moment, but she didn't care. After so long not knowing the truth, it was time for answers.

"Oh. That." Claire's frown melted, her eyes widened slightly. She took the smallest step back. "I…uh…"

Naoko moved closer, her gaze demanding, though her voice had come out softer than she intended it to. "I…want to know what happened that night."

"Oh." Claire blinked, her voice trailing off. Then her eyes widened. "You mean…you don't remember?"

"No," Naoko said, shaking her head. "Only before. In the dressing room. After that, it's…" she trailed off.

Claire paused, looking off to the side thoughtfully. Then she turned to Naoko. "Well, if I'm being honest, things got out of control and…" She frowned. "We didn't take care of you like we should have. That's on us, me especially."

"I see." Naoko stopped for a moment, remembering her father's question from that night. "Hey, Claire?"

"Yeah, hun?"

"They said I took drugs, but I don't remember." Naoko looked up at Claire. "Did I really do that?"

Claire returned her gaze, then bit her lip. "Yeah, that was on me also. I should've known what your first time with that stuff would be like, and I shouldn't have pushed you so hard." Claire took her hands. Naoko's chest fluttered, her vision tunneled as she focused in on Claire's electric gaze. "I'm sorry, babe."

Naoko blinked, the feelings from before bleeding into her. For a moment, she was back in that courtyard, the day Claire had introduced herself and been so sweet to her, offering her arm and escorting her around the school like she was her prized possession. Despite what she had admitted to doing, Naoko wanted to forgive her. She just couldn't help it.

"It's…okay," Naoko said, nodding.

"Good!" Claire said, moving her hands to caress the side of Naoko's arm. "I'm glad."

Naoko smiled. Then, surprising her, her arm jerked away. She felt Kokoro stiffen within her and try to push herself into control, though Naoko held her off. She turned inward, brows furrowing.

"What is your problem, Ko?"

Kokoro didn't respond. Instead, Naoko kept feeling her try to tug her away from the front, her pulls becoming more intense.

"Relax," Naoko reassured her internally. "She's a friend. The same one from school, remember?"

The tugging lessened, though Naoko could still feel her tense, still not responding. Naoko arched an eyebrow. Why was Kokoro being so silent and yet so defensive?

"You okay, darling?" Claire asked.

"Um, yeah!" Naoko said nervously. "Sorry, just had a long day, is all."

"Hey, trust me. I get it, girly." Claire continued to assess her, eyebrows raised as she bit her thumb. "Wow. I'm sorry, I can't help it. You look amazing."

Naoko blushed and bowed slightly. Kokoro was still behind her in their internal world, but she wasn't trying to pull Naoko back, like before. She was simply watching.

"So…" Claire pursed her lips cutely. "How have you been?"

With a subtle tilt of her head, Naoko nonchalantly shrugged and let a radiant smile grace her blushing cheeks, but she didn't bother to hide it. It wasn't like her to flirt, but Naoko found she couldn't resist.

"Oh, you know. Good," she replied coyly.

"Yeah?" Claire nodded, her soft lips parting slightly. "So, what are you doing out here?"

"Not much," Naoko answered, quickly turning and briefly gesturing to the observation windows. "Just enjoying the view, you know?"

"So, you're by yourself?" Claire beamed. "And you're not busy?"

Naoko felt a strange urge to say 'yes' and walk away, but she knew it was just Kokoro trying to slip her thoughts into hers. She shook her head and smiled.

"How would you feel about hanging out with me for a while?" Claire asked, hands on her hips. "You know, now that I think about it, I'm not staying too far from here. Maybe we can go to my place and chill?"

Naoko paused and checked the time on her phone. It was almost three in the afternoon, a few hours before she was supposed to meet her father, so more than enough time. Kokoro was silent now, but Naoko knew she was watching this encounter like a hawk.

Her body stiffened. Instead of what she wanted to say, the words that came out were, "No, I'm meeting my father soon. Perhaps another time."

Naoko blinked. It was Kokoro, who had taken advantage of her hesitation and finally switched. She felt irritation burn within her as she snatched control of the body back.

"Oh. Well, okay! It's all good!" Claire flailed about for a moment, then offered her arm. "You don't mind if I walk you down, do you?"

Naoko, still holding Kokoro at bay, took it, and together they walked down to the exit elevator. The moment the doors shut behind them, Naoko's back was suddenly against the wall, a pair of lips pressed against hers. Her eyes widened as Claire pulled back with a smirk and whispered into her ear, "Just let me know if you change your mind, baby. I'm not far."

Naoko blushed as Claire pushed off from her chest and strutted out of the elevator. She blinked, taking a moment to process what had just happened.

Did she just kiss me?

Brimming with excitement, Naoko left the elevator and base of the tower, though her own body resisted her, like walking through molasses.

"Seriously, Ko?" Naoko growled. "I thought you were supposed to help me with this kind of stuff?"

Kokoro finally materialized, half of her vision now filled with the gray swirling mists. The surrounding air was heavy, her brows furrowed.

"Nao, I'm sorry, but please just listen," Kokoro said, her eyes intense. "I don't know how to explain it, but something is off about that girl. She's just…"

"Just what?" Naoko asked, hands on her hips. "What's off?"

"…I don't know," she admitted. "I can just feel it, okay?"

Clenching her teeth, Naoko inhaled sharply. The intense longing she felt earlier faded. Irritation and anger poured into her, its tendrils digging until the venom escaped her lips as words.

"What are you, jealous or something?"

The intensity in Kokoro's face slowly melted, her lips curled down. Her focused glare softened, eyes glistening.

"Don't you trust me?"

"I…" Naoko huffed and looked away, not wanting to meet Kokoro's gaze. "The question is, do you?"

"What? Of course, I do, Nao." Kokoro shook her head. "I just…"

"You say that, but then you take control every chance you get. I almost say the wrong thing, then suddenly you front and say the right one. I almost trip, and you're there, keeping me upright. I put the wrong answer on a math test, and you switch in and put the right one!" Naoko glared at her, wrath brimming below the surface like a volcano preparing to erupt. These were cruel words, but she had held them in for far too long. "What are you, my mother? My father? Or better yet, maybe you're more patronizing than both combined!"

The piercing silence hung between them as Kokoro reeled from Naoko's words, tears freely streaming down her cheeks. She frowned as the surrounding area shifted, darkening, blurring as she faded from view. Naoko could feel her further back in their internal world, sulking as she watched.

Finally, there was nothing between them but the darkness.

The anger that had felt so right before faded almost instantly. Naoko leaned against the misty wall, taking a moment to truly process the hurtful words she had told Kokoro.

What is wrong with me? For a moment, Naoko wanted to stop her pursuit of Claire, to run back into their world and beg on hands and knees for Kokoro to forgive her, even though she didn't deserve it. *Even so, what does it matter? She wouldn't forgive me, anyway. Not after what I said.*

Pushing the thought from her mind, Naoko looked to the entrance of the Solamachi, where Claire was slowly pacing and looking around, as if waiting for her. With a deep breath, she followed Claire back out into the streets.

第八章

CHAPTER 8

TRAGEDY

THE MOMENT NAOKO HAD FOLLOWED CLAIRE back to her place, Kokoro's heart had shattered. She had spent the entire walk there replaying Naoko's rejection in her mind, letting the words burrow into her soul. It felt like a complete betrayal, and yet, she was also guilty. She was a control freak, after all.

Kokoro curled her knees to her chest as the muffled words of Naoko and Claire's conversation rang across their inner world. No, *Naoko's* inner world. Kokoro wasn't even needed anymore.

The next thing she heard was the slamming of a heavy metal door, followed by the clacking of footsteps on concrete. Then it stopped.

"Hello again, love," another voice said.

Kokoro's eyes widened. Who was that?

"Shane?" she heard Naoko say. "I didn't expect to see you here."

Shane? Kokoro briskly stood up. *Her other friend from the party?*

"Oh. I forgot he was here. Whoopsie," she heard Claire say. "But since the band is back together again, why don't we all sit and talk?"

The air in the internal world grew dark. Kokoro immediately dug through it, fighting her way back to the front of their mind. Once she had reached it, she could see everything: They were in an old spacious loft, exposed beams held back the cracked concrete wall and aged ceiling. Across the loft were several pressed leather couches, a select few occupied by a few foreigners accompanied by scantily clad women in flashy clothing. Shane was sitting on a couch opposite Claire, flanked by two burly men in suits.

"What's the matter, Naoko?" Shane asked, never taking his eyes off her. "It's okay to get comfortable, love. So please, if you would take a seat."

Naoko stood between them before she slowly complied and sat on the couch with Claire. The three of them exchanged glances before she broke the ice.

"Where have you been?" Naoko asked. "I haven't seen you guys at school."

"Oh. That." Claire rolled her eyes. "Well, to tell you the truth, my parents pulled me out once they found out about our party and grounded me for a while."

"Oh. I see." Naoko nodded and turned to Shane. "What about you?"

"Me?" Shane lit a cigar and took a casual puff. "Same shit. Got grounded after John ratted us out."

"John?" Naoko blinked. "Where is he?"

"Don't know, don't care to be honest," Shane said. "Probably out snorting coke or whatever else. Who knows?"

"You're not friends anymore?"

"Nope, thank God," Claire said, her pursed lips slowly curling into a smirk. "That's okay. We don't need him. We have you."

Naoko's eyes narrowed ever so slightly. "Me?"

"Of course, love," Shane said. "Good to have a real friend to confide in, you know? Especially after my dad…eh, died. Company stock took a dive and so did he, right out of the penthouse window.

"Your dad?" Naoko frowned. "That must be hard on you."

"Yeah," Claire added with a false-sounding sincerity of her own. "But it really is the darndest thing, you know? I lost my mom, too."

"You did?" Naoko asked as her heart beat harder, loud enough to echo across the internal world. Kokoro carefully studied Claire's face, seeing not even the slightest grief or remorse.

Claire nodded, biting her thumb. "I guess she just couldn't cut it anymore." She flailed her arms before crossing them. "But, oh well. You know what they say. Gotta move on."

"I'm…sorry," was all Naoko could say. She briefly turned back to look at Kokoro. She frowned before fronting again. "Both of you. I'm sorry for your losses."

"It is what it is, love." Shane stood up and paced across the room, rolling his cigar between his fingers. "But like dear Claire said, just gotta keep the business going."

Naoko looked up at him, her eyes narrowing. "Business?"

Shane nodded and took another pull from the cigar. "Taking over from Dad was an adjustment, but I think we've got it handled. In fact…" He leaned against the window. "…I was looking to give you a little…er, job, so to speak."

"A job?" Naoko asked, pausing thoughtfully.

"Yeah," Shane said, smiling. "You said you wanted to get out of Tokyo, right?"

Naoko nodded, returning it.

"Got a buddy of mine in Australia," Shane continued. "He and I are real tight, so he'd take good care of you. You'd even get to see the world, like you want."

"See the world…?" Naoko paused, blinking. Kokoro's lips curled; she could feel a tinge of excitement, of possibility brim within her friend. Not even an hour ago, it had been their shared dream, to see the ocean, to stare off into the unknown, perhaps venture it one day.

Now, Naoko would make that decision on her own.

"I appreciate the offer," Noako began. "But I have school. My family." She turned inward again, weakly smiling at Kokoro. "I would like to visit one day, but for now, my life is here."

Shane, upon hearing the words, moved from the window and sat back in his chair, taking a puff of the cigar. He chuckled in what appeared to be disbelief.

"That's the thing, love. I didn't say you had a choice in the first place."

Naoko froze, her heart twisting in her chest. Kokoro could sense her heightened awareness, just one step away from complete panic. In that moment, she felt the exact same way.

"What did you say your father's business was again?" Naoko asked, her voice weakening with each syllable.

"Come on, love," Shane said, chuckling. "It ain't that hard to figure out."

At first, Naoko didn't reply, her eyes darting all over. Then she hesitated before opening her mouth to speak. "What you said that day after school and drugging me at the party?" She looked at Shane with horror. "You're traffickers."

Kokoro's eyes widened, a primal fear rising within her. For Naoko's safety, and even her own.

"I hate that word." Shane paused, his eyes focusing on her. "I'm a *businessman*. All I do is follow the money. Right now, that happens to be here in Tokyo…with girls like you."

"That's right. Usually, people come *here* for that kind of stuff. But when we met our friends here…" Claire gestured to the other men in the room, "…we figured, why not *export* instead?"

There was dead silence as Shane and Claire's hungry, twisted gaze dug into her. Naoko shifted uncomfortably, the hairs on the back of her neck standing up. Kokoro kept trying to front with her from their inner world, only to be rebuffed over and over, like tugging at a locked door.

"Naoko…" she warned. "We need to leave. *Now.*"

"Planning on going somewhere, love?"

They both froze. Without realizing it, Kokoro's words had slipped out of the body's mouth in a rushed whisper.

Naoko said nothing. Kokoro met her quivering eyes, asking…no, *begging* her to let her front. Her friend wouldn't budge.

"Come on, babe," Claire said, twirling a strand of Naoko's hair around her finger. "We're all friends here, right?"

Naoko froze as Claire walked in a slow circle around her, tracing her hand along her rear. It made Kokoro wish she was in control, so at the very least she could savagely punch the bitch for daring to touch her friend like that.

"I think you'll be his favorite. Shane's business partner," Claire said as she leaned in. "Such fine…*product.*"

Panic welled up in Naoko's chest. Kokoro was there with her, fighting to keep both herself and her friend from losing control.

"Claire's right," Shane said, taking a puff. "Promise we'll take care of you as long as you behave. If you don't…" His eyes narrowed. "…well, let's just say I'm not above selling damaged goods. Bruises heal, after all."

Naoko's eyes widened. Her flight instinct finally kicked in as she ran back to the door, but it was covered by two more men in suits. They pressed forward; her shaking legs threatened to give out beneath her.

"Ah, ah, ah," Claire warned. "Come on, now. Don't let it be like this."

Kokoro finally snatched control and sprinted, this time at another door across the loft, only to find it barricaded shut.

Oh no. No, no, no, please, no. Kokoro turned to face her friend, whose eyes trembled with not just fear, but regret.

"Ko, I just wanted to—"

"Don't worry about that right now. We've got to—"

"—I didn't mean it. What I said earlier."

Kokoro ignored Naoko and used her body to take another look around. There wasn't a need for an apology, because one way or the other, they were going to get out of there.

She spun, searching desperately for any and every chance to escape the impending horror, only to find them all blocked. Guards covered every single possible chance of escape, be it a window, a door, or anything. Those who didn't cover an exit advanced on her and Naoko, with Shane and Claire watching.

Kokoro paled. She now knew there would be no escape, so what could she do? Escape wasn't an option. She could fight, but it would only make it worse on Naoko's body. The mist wouldn't let them both retreat into the inner world, but maybe…?

Turning to the mist, Kokoro partially passed through, then screamed. "Help! Whoever else is there, please!"

At first, nothing happened. Then a strange silhouette appeared, walking toward them.

"Hey!" Kokoro waved. "Whoever you are! Please!"

Thankfully, the figure stepped forward. It reached, as if it were going to heed Kokoro's request, then paused, withdrawing it. It shook its head, stepping back.

"No. No, come back!" Kokoro begged.

Her cries went ignored. In the end, the figure turned, ran, and vanished into nothing.

Damn it! Kokoro panicked as she moved back through the mist and glanced at Naoko. *What are we going to do? How am I supposed to save us?*

Save her. The answer seemed so obvious now. The strange mist wouldn't let both of them pass, but that didn't matter, as long as Naoko was spared. As long as she was safe.

Yes. Kokoro nodded. *It doesn't matter what they do to me. It's not like I'm real, anyway.*

Kokoro eyed the approaching men one last time before she turned back to Naoko, gripping her hands tight. "Hey. Naoko. I—"

"I'm scared," Naoko said between ragged breaths.

"I know, it's gonna be okay."

"I don't want that to happen. I...I don't..."

"Naoko! It's okay!" Kokoro gripped her shoulders and shook her. "You're gonna be fine because it's not going to happen to you. It's going to happen to me!"

"No!" Naoko's eyes widened, brows furrowed as she shook her head in disbelief. "Ko, please don't."

"Here's what you're going to do, okay?" Kokoro began. "Just run. Run back as far as you can. Run so far that you can't even hear the voices or feel the pain. Find somewhere good, and safe. So, one day…after it's all over…"

"…I can come back," Naoko deduced, her voice cracking. "But you'll come back too, right?"

Kokoro smiled sadly. "I don't know. Probably not, so just in case, I wanted to tell you something. How proud I was to live this life. Not just that but living it with you. Just…thank you so much, Nao. For everything."

As the words left her mouth, Kokoro broke down, tears falling like rain. Why did it have to be this way? Why was the world so cruel and cold that it would separate her from her precious Naoko?

She looked up. The men had completely encircled them. Time was running out.

"Naoko!" she commanded. "You need to go, now! You—"

Kokoro froze. Something was off. Naoko stared at her with a sad, accepting smile.

"I'm sorry, Ko."

Before Kokoro could even process it, Naoko had pushed her through the mist. She attempted to move back through, but now it was as solid as rock, an impenetrable barrier.

Saving her precious friend, she knew, was now impossible.

"Naoko…Naoko, no! Stop!" Kokoro pounded on the translucent wall as a legion of shadowy hands grabbed Naoko, their iron-clad grips tightening on her fragile body. The world around them darkened as a twisted voice echoed across.

Kokoro's last glimpse of Naoko was of her face, a bittersweet combination of sadness and a faint smile. She fell back as the shadows consumed her friend and the world outside faded to black.

An eternity passed as Kokoro cried her heart out. It twisted in her chest, her thoughts pulsing, erratic, unstable. *Naoko, Naoko, Naoko* were the only words going through her head, endlessly repeating, tormenting her. And yet, it also provided a small mercy. Her mind eventually slowed to a crawl, to where the word her precious friend's name was like the dripping of a faucet.

Kokoro stared ahead blankly, either because she was too exhausted or because she just couldn't process it. Why had Naoko done that? Why would she save her, instead of letting Kokoro protect her like she always had?

She laid there for what felt like forever, the Sakura trees that used to adorn their inner world had now shed their precious pink flowers, leaving them barren, dark, and hopeless.

It should have been me. It should have been me.

A shrill sound filled the air around her, making the hairs on Kokoro's neck stand and chilling her to the bone. She sat up and listened harder; she recognized that sound. But what was it?

The haunting wails hit again. Her eyes widened.

It's that crying from before. Kokoro stood, listening. She and Naoko had tried a few times to find it, but the eerie weeping had either disappeared or frightened them so much that they didn't dare seek further.

It grew louder. Kokoro spun, trying to locate it, the sound of a young girl's tears howling across their inner world. The sobs were a story: pain, sorrow, and yet, they were also something else. A cry for help, yet a warning to stay away.

Kokoro stood shakily, only balancing herself after she had taken her first quivering step toward the sound. The darkness in front of her moved, clearing a path forward, the shadows twisting into barren tree branches that vaguely resembled spindly hands.

At the end of the path, she finally saw it: the outline of a strange building. Shadows danced against the light bleeding from the crooked windows.

The cries echoed again, this time from inside the building. Kokoro's eyes widened, then her brows furrowed.

Can't I at least save someone today?

Taking a deep breath, Kokoro pushed forward into the main hall of the building. The wallpaper was shedding, the buzzing lights flickered, the ceiling was so low that she was afraid that it would collapse any minute.

Then she stopped. Something was familiar about this place, but what?

The child's wailing continued, echoing off the rotted wooden walls. Kokoro closed her eyes and focused. She was rewarded with another cry, which she followed down a hallway to the right.

A sinister laugh stopped her in her tracks. She spun, behind her was a burly, shadowy figure. Luminescent tattoos infected the entirety of its body from its horned head to it's protruding toes. The Oni grinned.

"Where are you going, little girl?"

Kokoro immediately ran. Her heart thumped inside her chest, filling her with raw adrenaline. A door appeared at the end of the hallway, orange lights and dancing shadows flickered at the seams. The voice of the girl sounded again, louder this time.

Her eyes widened. Whoever the voice was, they were hurting. She had to—

Without warning, the floor gave way, sending Kokoro plummeting into darkness. She landed, but not straight down like she had thought. Her body rolled along cold concrete, as if it were thrown by something far larger than her.

Kokoro cried out as something stiff broke her tumbling. She spun, seeing that she was now in a different hallway, one lined with rooms, the sliding doors of which were demolished.

Pressing forward, Kokoro hesitated before looking in one of the rooms. In it was a statue of a naked woman, arm outstretched defensively, though half her body had been shattered.

Kokoro briskly stood, then exited the room, moving down the hall to look at the others. They differed in position, some were defensive like the first, and others simply looked away, as if to spare their eyes the horror that their bodies endured.

It's too late for them. Kokoro frowned. *The damage is already done.*

She quickly shook the thoughts and began looking for an exit. The rooms stretched on; the rest obscured in shadow. Kokoro heard footsteps, then immediately ducked into one of the rooms, behind the statue that was in it.

Kokoro froze, trying to keep as still, as quiet as possible. The shadows soon passed by in the hallway and faded as she breathed a sigh of relief.

"Thank you," she said to the statue that had hidden her, then paused. This one differed from the others. Instead of being broken, there seemed to be a tinge of hope in the stone eyes and a gentle, reassuring smile. Above all, it seemed…familiar?

"There you are, you little brat."

Kokoro's eyes widened. The far darkness gave birth to more Oni like the one earlier, all led by a lanky one with slicked back hair and a pair of shades. They marched in on her, white wicked grins flashing at her, their hungry gazes coveting her. Their ugly, stiff hands reached for her, some bearing knives.

No, no. Please no.

Kokoro could do nothing but sit down and curl up into a ball on the floor as the cries echoed again in the unknown. It was over. Soon they would have her, and everything she had done for Naoko would be left to waste. She could only hope that there was an afterlife, that she and her precious friend would reunite one day.

Clenching her fists and closing her eyes, Kokoro curled up tighter and prepared for the end.

Suddenly, one of the figures shrieked and fell to the ground. Another slammed against a wall and lost its head in a flash of dazzling silver. A third was impaled and torn to ribbons.

Kokoro rose, her eyes narrowed as she tried to identify the strange thing that was killing the monstrosities. As she focused, she realized that it was a blade, wielded by yet another humanoid figure made of a different kind of shadow, less sinister, more subtle, yet even more brutal. It flashed across the Oni as her surroundings burst into flame, the heat beginning to consume everything in sight.

She tried to move but found that she was too weak. No, not only that, but her entire body had shrunk, her voice pitched higher than before as she cried out in pain.

For some reason, Kokoro was now a child.

She struggled, but managed to get to her feet, following the figure. It had finished dispatching its foes and was shouting something indiscernible into the hallway where she had seen the statues of the women. The flames rejected her savior and consumed the rooms, haunting wails of horror and pain emanating from them.

The figure turned, looking at her. Shaking its head, it scooped her up and ran toward the exit. Kokoro coughed as she looked back at the hallway, watching the growing flames as they continued to roar. In them, she could see something—a small silhouette in the shape of a little girl, her arm outstretched. Kokoro's eyes widened as a strong pain erupted in her chest, like her soul itself had just been torn in two.

"Go back!" Kokoro wailed, reaching out. "Please!"

The shadow that had saved her muttered something indiscernible as it ran with Kokoro in its arms, before turning a corner to a bright light at the end of the hallway. A way out. An escape from the hell that pursued them.

Without warning, the figure collapsed to the ground, sending Kokoro tumbling away. She recovered and dared to glance back. The hellfire from the brothel snapped at her savior's heels, almost like the souls who died were trying to drag it to damnation. Kokoro, now unable to control her own body, limped over to it.

"Get up!" she said. "Get up!"

The shadow looked up at her, its vague face somehow downcast, filled with regret. It tried to wave her away, yet Kokoro insisted, placing her hands on its rough face.

Kokoro's brows furrowed. No way she was going to let it die. She shook the figure, screaming, begging it to escape with her.

Her efforts paid off. The figure rose, pulled Kokoro into its arms once more and limped from the dark building, shielding her from the flames.

Finally, they were out. The remains of the building was now a blazing inferno, the roaring fire wickedly whipping against the dark sky. The figure trudged forward to two others—the first being the shape of a man, and the second a woman—and passed her into the arms of the taller one. Kokoro watched as her savior nodded, then limped away into the far darkness, it's now-sheathed weapon in hand. A symphony of voices flooded Kokoro's mind as the man and woman wrapped her tight in what felt like an oversized jacket.

Exhausted, confused, and above all, heartbroken, Kokoro finally gave into the dark and let herself pass into the safety of sleep.

The first thing Kokoro heard upon regaining consciousness was a set of shrill, steady beeps. Her eyes fluttered open, her blurry vision focused. She heard hushed voices at the far end of the white room, their muttering slowly became recognizable words.

"...the exam we did shows no signs of penetration, though the significant bruising on her body shows she fought her captors. I didn't find anything broken, thankfully, but she will need time to recover."

"How long do you think she will be out?" another voice asked.

"Hard to say," replied the first voice as it hesitated. "It's even possible that she won't wake up."

"No!" a third voice said. "She has to! I couldn't live with myself, otherwise!"

Kokoro groggily turned her head, seeing Mr. and Mrs. Haneda in the corner, conversing with a doctor. On the other side was a small pull-out couch, sheets and blankets spread across it. To the left of it were two small suitcases, opened and stacked atop the other.

I'm in the hospital? Kokoro turned to look down at the bed she was resting on. *I thought Shane and Claire had taken us. What happened?*

"It's alright, Hana," Mr. Haneda said, comforting his wife. "She'll be alright. Our little Naoko will be okay."

Kokoro froze, her breath cut short as she realized something. Not only was she in control of the body, but she couldn't feel Naoko's presence. Not in the front, nor behind the misty veil. It was simply gone.

"No, no," she rasped. Naoko couldn't just be *gone*. She was a part of her! She had to be somewhere, right? Maybe she was just hiding somewhere so deep in their inner world that even Kokoro couldn't find her. It was possible, wasn't it?

She's alive. She has to be. Kokoro grit her teeth. *I need her to be.*

"Naoko?" a voice asked. Mrs. Haneda's eyes widened as her gaze locked on her. "Oh, Naoko! You're awake!"

Kokoro didn't even get the chance to respond before she was swarmed. Mrs. Haneda latched onto her, then pulled back, tears in her eyes. Naoko's dad knelt next to the bed as he gripped her arm.

"Naoko, I'm so, so sorry," he said with labored breaths, on the verge of crying himself. "I failed you. I couldn't find you, and…"

"It's okay!" Naoko's mother said, reassuring her husband by wrapping her arms around his neck from behind. "They did it. After so long, they found our baby girl. She's safe, Itsuki. Our Naoko is finally home."

Kokoro opened her mouth to respond. She had so many things she wanted to say, but all that came out was, "Naoko?"

Naoko's parents pulled back as the doctor observed from behind. They turned to look at him. "She knows her name! That's good, right?"

Head swimming, Kokoro strained her voice to speak again. They turned back, leaning in to hear.

"Where is…Naoko?"

The joy on their faces soon melted away. Mrs. Haneda blinked and pressed the back of her hand against Kokoro's forehead.

"I think she's a little confused, Doctor," she said. "Maybe it's like you said. She just needs rest, right?"

"I agree," Mr. Haneda said. "She needs to come home with us. She'll be more comfortable there, and—"

"I understand your concern. Unfortunately, I think it's better to keep her here just a while longer for observation. She was in that place for a good week and a half, so we—"

Their voices muffled as something caught Kokoro's eye. In the doorway stood a girl dressed in a school uniform, black hair pulled back with a pink hair clip.

Naoko!

Kokoro sat up briskly and slid off the bed to everyone's horror. She collapsed on the floor, then shakily rose to her feet. The doctor gripped her shoulder.

"Naoko, you're safe, but you need to lie down, okay?"

She ignored him and broke free of his grip, pushing past him. Her first steps were wobbly, but partially stabilized as crumbs of her former strength trickled back into her.

Kokoro reached the door and poked her head out into the hallway. Naoko had moved, standing at the end. Kokoro followed her, past a group of concerned nurses and doctors, out into the rain-drenched streets of Tokyo, the neon signs blinding her. She continued to run until she found herself in the middle of Shibuya crossing.

"Hello? I need help!" she asked, grabbed arms, shoulders, whatever was within her reach. "I can't find her. I can't find—"

"Get off, girl!"

A calloused hand shoved her away, into the center of the shifting traffic as Kokoro's legs finally collapsed beneath her. Her hands broke her fall as she splashed into a shallow puddle. She caught her breath; the shimmering water below finally settled, revealing the girl beneath the surface: ashen white hair with fading strips of black, a gaunt face and sunken eyes that had seen way too much tragedy for her short life on earth.

"There you are!" Kokoro's eyes widened; a smile finally touched her lips. "I—"

She paused. The face in the water mimicked her perfectly as her smile faded. The gleaming hope in her eyes slowly gave way to absolute horror.

Her fists clenched, the cold, unforgiving rain beat down on her broken body. She rose and turned her gaze skyward into the dark, hopeless clouds; the only light left for her was the soulless flashes of the neon street signs. Her chest heaved, her stomach twisting in knots as the mobs finally cleared the cold streets.

Since she had pulled herself from Naoko's darkness, Kokoro had never been alone. Now, in the decrepit remains of her beautiful world, she was all that remained.

CHAPTER 9

THE WHITE SILENCE

"SO THAT'S HOW IT HAPPENED?" Dr. Maeda asked.

Kokoro nodded slowly, pushing some of her ashen hair behind her ear. "Yeah. That's how I lost Naoko."

Silence hung in the cold air. Both Kokoro's throat and chest tightened. Dr. Maeda frowned.

"I understand. Loss is difficult."

Kokoro drew in a deep breath, closing her eyes, desperate to keep control of herself. "It's just the world we live in, isn't it?"

"It isn't all bad," Dr. Maeda countered. "There are good things. Beautiful, even."

"And this world, for some damned reason, just loves trampling them," Kokoro growled, her voice cracking, her face hidden in her hair.

Dr. Maeda frowned. Kokoro clenched her fists in a desperate bid to stay in control, though her emotions worked against her. Every breath threatened tears, every thought threatened pain.

"I'm sorry, I—" Breaths becoming shallower, Kokoro gave up her struggle for composure and let her tears flow, the already-weak dam of grief inside her shattering and soaking her cheeks, dripping down to her clenched hands. "I just miss her so much. She was the reason I exist, and now? I don't know what to do. I can't do this without her."

"I understand," Dr. Maeda said. "That's why we're here. I know it hurts, but talking about this is the first step."

Wiping her tears with her sleeve, Kokoro managed to look at him. For several months now, she had been at these appointments with him relaying her story, piece by aggravating piece. Dr. Maeda wanted every little precious detail he could manage from her, any piece that would help him solve the puzzle. On the one hand, it made her feel just a little better, being able to empty the grief from her soul, even if for only an hour. On the other, it was excruciating, like ripping out her own heart for Dr. Maeda's calculating, almost robotic gaze to analyze.

Not that she could blame him. It was his job, after all.

A scoff slipped from Kokoro's lips that became a short laugh. The doctor watched intently, his gaze piercing her from behind his glasses as he held his notes in his hand.

"What's got you laughing?"

"Nothing, I just…" Kokoro shook her head, blinking tears from her eyes. "Am I just insane?"

Dr. Maeda opened his mouth to reply but stopped. He paused to draw in a deep breath, as if he were being careful with his next words.

"If I'm being honest, I think everyone is a little insane. Sometimes it's just about survival. Often when people survive such things they come out with scars."

"Makes sense," Kokoro replied. The hint of a smile crossed her lips, then faded. "I guess I'm just a little crazier than anyone else. Otherwise, why would I be here?"

"That doesn't mean anything," he said. "We're just—"

"—here to help me. Right." Kokoro frowned. "Crazy or not, I'd give anything to have her back. To see her, to hear her voice, to…I don't know. I should have been the one to die. Not her."

"Please understand that I'm not trying to be insensitive. When you say that she 'died,' what exactly do you mean? What is that like for you?"

"I've already told you," Kokoro said.

"Humor me," the doctor replied. "Please."

Kokoro sighed. "It's hard to explain, but I can't feel her anymore. Even when I was in control, I knew that she was still *there*, even if I couldn't see her."

"See her?" Dr. Maeda asked. "When you say she's 'there' is it like how I'm 'here' now? Or is she internal?"

Kokoro paused, eyes narrowing in deep thought. "We had our own little world where we could talk and spend time together. When I was there, it was like you are now. Just…right in front of me. I could hear her. Touch her. When she was scared or unsure, I would take control while she would stay back. When she was up front, it was the other way around, like being in a passenger seat."

"Ah, yes. I remember," he said, flipping to a page in his notebook. "This 'inner world' you mentioned. It was a safe place for you and Naoko, correct?"

"It was. Now…?" She avoided his gaze. "I don't know. I haven't gone in since. It doesn't feel safe anymore."

Dr. Maeda scribbled a few more notes. "Tell me, have you ever explored beyond that part of it? To the dark areas?"

The body seized up as Kokoro remembered her brief venture into the building with the Oni, the cries, and the silhouette of the young girl. She shook her head.

"I see." The doctor's eyes narrowed, almost like he could see right through her. "Besides Naoko, have you seen anyone else there?"

"Not exactly. There was this one time, but…" she paused, the memory of that strange silhouette came to mind, how it abandoned her and Naoko to Shane and Claire, "…but it turned out to be nothing."

"So, this inner world of yours sits unexplored, with possibly others roaming about." Dr. Maeda took off his glasses. His eyes seemed to glow in the moonlight. "Then how do you know she's dead?"

Kokoro shuddered, her grip on her pants tightening. The answer felt so obvious, and yet…

"I don't know. More than anything, I want her to be here, with me." Her thoughts drifted to Naoko's parents as her body stiffened. "With everyone."

The doctor's eyes narrowed slightly as he clicked his pen a few times. "Have you considered this a possibility? Or looked for her?"

"Why?" Kokoro's eyes narrowed. "You mean she might not be dead after all?"

He hesitated. "Not in the same way you're thinking. Alters can't really 'die,' but they can go dormant."

"Alters?" Kokoro froze. Suddenly it all clicked, the endless probing, the repeating questions. "You know what's wrong with me, don't you? The reason I'm here and not Naoko?"

Dr. Maeda nodded with a gentle, encouraging smile. "I do. Are you ready to hear it?"

Silence filled the air. Kokoro pulled her arms in, clutching her abdomen, fingers wracking her throbbing head. The hair on the back of her neck stood up as she felt someone watching through her eyes, like she had when Naoko was still around. But this was different. Whatever this presence was, it was calm, focused, yet…intense. When Kokoro tried to pull away, the presence pushed her back, forcing her to face the truth. Her vision tunneled, focusing in on the doctor as he awaited her answer. Finally, she gave in, sighing.

"I already know." Kokoro dipped her head. "I'm not real."

The doctor blinked, then folded his hands together, elbows resting on the desk.

"On the contrary, you are very real. Equally as real as Naoko, in fact. Both of you are your own person, yet parts of a greater whole. A system."

"I…" Kokoro's eyes narrowed. "I don't understand."

"It's called Dissociative Identity Disorder," he explained. "You are what's called an 'alter.' You, and likely others, formed in Naoko's mind to protect her and help her function."

"So…I was meant to help Naoko." She nodded. "That makes sense, but why? If you say I'm part of Naoko, and yet…"

"You are your own person, yes," Dr. Maeda continued. "The initial fracture is caused by repeated childhood trauma. The young mind can't process it, and so it splits, and the 'alters' develop from there."

Kokoro sat up straight, her skin crawling. As the cries of the child began to manifest once more, the visions of that dark place nestled in the depths of shadow. Could that really have been it, the thing that started it all?

"I've had hints. Heard the cries, saw that vision," Kokoro admitted. "But I don't know what it is, nor do I remember anything like that happening to me or Naoko. Not even from her memories."

"That's the whole point," the doctor replied. "Amnesiac barriers, separating you and Naoko from the trauma, sometimes from each other. Think about it: you *know* what happened to Naoko, but you don't remember it yourself. That entire time you were trapped inside?"

Kokoro barely let the words slip from her mouth. "She protected me."

Dr. Maeda paused, his eyes focused on her. He scribbled a few more notes into his pad and looked back at her. "Yes, she did. Despite your intent, she made the choice to shut you out and keep you away from it all."

"I know, but…" Kokoro frowned. "…why? I don't get it. I was supposed to protect *her*."

"I'd be lying if I said I knew." The doctor returned the frown. "The truth is, only you can answer that question."

She avoided his gaze. "I don't know how."

"Things like this take time." He smiled encouragingly. "So don't be hard on yourself. You're doing great."

"Right." Chest heaving, she gripped her arms, nails digging in. She brought herself to look at Dr. Maeda. "I'm sorry. Can we be done for today?"

Dr. Maeda sat back in his chair, slowly nodding. "Of course. I apologize if I've overstepped."

"It's not that, I just need time," Kokoro said. "To process."

"I understand." The doctor nodded, then the door to the room opened behind her, out came a familiar blonde nurse with sharp, alluring eyes. She stood by with a gentle smile, one hand over the other resting down. "As usual, Sakura will escort you back to your room. We will speak again soon."

"Thank you." Kokoro stood and bowed, then followed the assistant out the door, into the long, drab hallway. Several more doctors and nurses passed by with their own patients, some of whom wore straightjackets or were tied down to their beds. As they walked by, Kokoro briefly looked into one of their eyes and saw nothing but the empty black staring back.

Kokoro frowned, rubbing the bruises on her wrists. During her first days in the facility, she was much like them: hopeless, forgotten, bound to the hospital bed with nothing to look at but the maddeningly plain ceiling and nothing to do but drown in her own tears. It wasn't until Dr. Maeda took her on as a patient that she was finally released from it, but even then, things weren't much easier.

They arrived at her room. It was a tiny space with a soft wooden floor and a small metal stool. A shallow sink was built into the wall, and a large, thick window that allowed her to gaze out into the cold world beyond it. Kokoro's shoulders sank as she moved to her small bed in the corner and sat down, pressing her back against the wall with her knees tucked in.

The assistant finished tidying up a few things, then stood straight, gesturing as she smiled gently. "Okay, here we are."

Kokoro managed a weak smile. "Home sweet home, huh?"

"It doesn't have to be," Sakura said, frowning. "This place is just temporary. Your real home is beyond these walls."

Out there. Lips curling down, Kokoro turned to the window and stared at the cold world beyond. The snow fell just outside, contrasting the darkness and flashing of the soulless city lights as the night swallowed the sun. There was a strange, cold beauty to it, the way it covered the ugly concrete below, as if it were trying to conceal the blemishes that humanity had inflicted upon nature for so long. *The white silence.*

"I know, but…" Kokoro continued to stare out the window. "It's safer here. I have to protect what's left of Naoko."

Sakura frowned. With a sigh, she made her way to the door. "I'll be back shortly. In the meantime, let me know if you need anything." She bowed, before passing through to the hallway.

Kokoro returned it, and soon the thick door was shut behind her. She faced the outside world again, but only saw Naoko's face with her precious, sweet eyes, though her once-beautiful dark hair had completely whitened from root to tip. The different doctors she had seen had tried to explain it away. 'Marie Antoinette Syndrome' they had called it. Too much stress, more than a normal person was meant for. Some even offered the possibility that the color would return with time, but Kokoro knew the truth. As far as she was concerned, she would always be the ghost of Naoko Haneda, nothing more.

After an eternity of staring out into the cold dark, a knock came at the door along with a muffled voice. "Kokoro? It's Sakura with Dr. Maeda. We have some news for you."

Sighing, she turned from the window and rose from her bed, preparing to welcome them with a bow. Then, a flash from the window caught her eye.

Kokoro spun to face it. Her eyes narrowed as the reflection flickered, and she struggled to differentiate reality from the image in her mind's eye. The figure solidified until it became a tall young man wearing khaki dress pants and a blue polo shirt, face cast in shadow.

The darkness faded, revealing his face. He looked like a strange cross between Naoko's Dad, Dr. Maeda, and even Mr. Takeda from school, the only difference being his age and unkempt red hair. The young man pushed his glasses to his nose and regarded her with a nod.

"Kokoro?" The knock came again. "Are you alright?"

Kokoro jumped, accidentally tipping over the small stool. She recovered it before answering. "I'm here, sorry!" She looked back at the window to find the image of the young man had disappeared. She shook her head and faced the door again. "I'm okay!"

The door handle clicked, then opened. Dr. Maeda walked in, flanked by Sakura. They both smiled.

"We wanted to talk to you, if that's okay," he said, gesturing to the chair that she had knocked over previously. "Do you mind if I sit?"

Kokoro eyed them both and nodded. Dr. Maeda took the chair and put some distance between them. Sakura placed a set of clothes at the foot of the bed, then planted herself next to Kokoro, gripping her hand reassuringly. It wasn't necessary, but Kokoro appreciated it, nonetheless.

"So, we actually have some good news for you," Dr. Maeda began. "The discharge process was a little complicated, but it's done. I've approved your release. You're going home today."

"Oh. Thank you." Kokoro blinked and tried to manage a smile.

Sakura frowned. "Do you not want to go home?"

"It's not that. I do want to go home, it's just…" Kokoro sighed.

Dr. Maeda's brows furrowed. "It's just what?"

Kokoro paused. She thought back to their earlier session and the diagnosis he had given her. It made sense, that she would be part of Naoko, that she was meant to help protect her. At the same time, something had bothered her, even from her earliest days. She had always assumed that she was a figment of Naoko's imagination, and that she would be the one to disappear in the end. If she was real, then…?

"Doctor Maeda?" she asked, breaking the silence.

He blinked and motioned for her to continue.

"If I really am my own person, then…" Kokoro dipped her head, swallowing. "Do you think I have a soul?"

The initial look of encouragement on his face faded, replaced with a frown. "There are some who would disagree, but I choose to believe that you do."

Kokoro met his concerned eyes and managed a weak smile. "So, Mr. Haneda is on his way, huh?"

"Yes," Sakura said. "He'll be here soon."

"And that brings me to discharge conditions," Dr. Maeda said, opening the folders in his hand. "Your release is contingent on your attending further appointments for treatment. Some will be with me, some with other doctors for therapy." He looked at her. "And for the therapy, we would like to involve your parents."

Kokoro paused and blinked, though it took approximately one second to come up with an answer.

"No. Under no circumstances do I want them to know that Naoko is gone."

"I know you are of age and can continue to deny the release of your records, but I don't recommend it." Dr. Maeda sighed. "I think the therapy will go better if they know. I have other avenues I can pursue to ensure they are involved…if I have to."

"*No*," Kokoro reiterated stiffly, then stopped. "At least…not until I can figure out how to tell them myself. At least give me the chance to do that." Her eyes met his. "Please."

Dr. Maeda paused thoughtfully, then sighed. "Alright." He sifted through a few more of his papers, then looked at Kokoro. "So, how do you feel about it? Going home?"

Kokoro considered his words, then glanced around in her padded room. Despite the crying, yelling, and loud slamming that occasionally filled her nights, it was familiar to her. Small, constrictive, and yet it was also simple. Impenetrable to all but a few. *Safe.*

"Do you really think it's okay for someone like me to be back out into the world?" she asked.

"Why wouldn't it be?" Dr. Maeda asked. "You're not dangerous, if that's what you're worried about."

"More like the other way around." Kokoro shook her head. "The outside is horrible. I don't know if I can face it, especially not without her."

The room fell dead silent. The snowfall outside stopped, the gray skies erupted, allowing light to bleed through the clouds and window. Sakura placed her hand on Kokoro's.

"I don't want to speak for your friend, but I don't think she would want you to stay like this, all cooped up," she said. "She wouldn't want you living in fear."

"How would you know that?" Kokoro asked, eyeing her.

"Because I know what that's like," Sakura replied. "I let it keep me trapped and make my decisions for me, until finally…" She looked at Dr. Maeda and smiled. "…I learned how to be brave. Now, I try to help others do the same."

The tension in the body slowly subsided, the muscles relaxed. Kokoro frowned. "I didn't know."

"Everyone has a story. How will you know how yours turns out otherwise?" Sakura gripped her hand tight. Kokoro squeezed back, if only slightly. The breath within fought to escape her lips.

"It's going to be difficult, isn't it?"

"It seldom isn't, if at all," Dr. Maeda said. "I know you said you feared that darkness because it had taken Naoko, but the truth is that one day you will have to confront it. It may take years, decades even. It will be terrifying. It will probably tear you apart in ways you couldn't imagine, and yet, it must be done if you want to heal." He glanced at his assistant. "Like Sakura said. Facing the dark despite the fear trying to hold you back. That is what it means to be brave."

Kokoro met the doctor's eyes, taking in the words. She nodded slowly.

Dr. Maeda regarded her before standing and making his way to the door. "If you want to stay here, we understand. We'll walk out of here and let you shut the door behind us. You'll be safe." He eyed her. "But would that honor Naoko? Or her dream?"

Kokoro paused, considering his words. She opened her mouth to speak, but stopped, avoiding his gaze.

Dr. Maeda sighed as he and his assistant walked to the doorway. "I'll leave you to think about it for a few minutes. Sakura and I will be just outside."

Kokoro nodded, and soon she was alone. She inhaled sharply, running her fingers through her hair, standing up to stare out of the cold window. The images of her friend's last moments were burned into her psyche, her smiling face consumed by shadows. She didn't want to imagine the horrors Naoko had to endure just to protect her, and yet it kept her up every night. Without her, what did she have to live for?

For a moment, her surroundings changed. She was back in the Tokyo Skytree, staring out…no, staring *in*, back at her sweet friend, a precious smile on her face.

I want us to see the ocean.

The images faded, the observation window of the Skytree replaced with the one in her padded room. Kokoro took several deep breaths to try to keep the tears back. Deep down, she wanted to collapse and give into her grief, but found that she couldn't. How could she just sit here, all pathetic, while Naoko's dream remained unfulfilled?

They're right. Kokoro changed into the jeans, t-shirt and a gray, slightly oversized turtleneck sweater that Sakura had left on her bed. She hurried out of the room, where they waited. *One way or another, I'll reach that ocean.*

Kokoro nodded and pulled ahead as they walked. Soon enough, they had arrived at the long hallway that led to the entrance. The doors were wide open, the space between filled with a burning bright light. She bid them goodbye and ventured forth, to the dangers and beauty of the cruel world beyond.

第十章
CHAPTER 10
THE OTHERS

THE FIRST TWENTY OR SO MINUTES OF THE RIDE back home was filled with silence, minus the quiet drum of the radio. Mr. Haneda would occasionally eye Kokoro, as if she would suddenly jump out of the car into oncoming traffic.

"So, I bet you're happy to be out of there, right?" he asked.

Kokoro cringed slightly. If he had to break the ice, why did it have to be with such a stupid question?

"Not really," she answered. "But I needed to leave. Otherwise, I probably would have let myself stay." Kokoro briefly looked out of the window to the towering buildings and the starless black above.

Either the world was much, much bigger or she was that much smaller. She shrunk from the window, dipping her head. "It was safe."

"I understand. I know you've been through a lot." Mr. Haneda paused, clenching the steering wheel. "Even so, I'm glad you decided to come home. After you were gone, I…" He shook his head, his brows furrowing. "No. This time, I *will* keep you safe. Nobody will ever touch you again. I swear it, Naoko."

Kokoro tensed upon hearing her friend's name. She was supposed to keep Naoko safe too. Turns out, they had both failed in that regard.

"Thank you…Father," she said, careful to maintain the charade, though it felt so wrong saying the word. She inhaled and turned to him. "So, what did Dr. Maeda tell you?"

"Not much." Naoko's Dad shook his head, then arched his eyebrow. "He did say that you opted to keep your medical information from your time there confidential."

Kokoro paused for a moment, considering how to reply to that. In the end, she just frowned.

"Nothing serious," she lied. "Just a lot of stress. I've been learning to deal with it."

"I…understand." He appeared to accept her explanation, nodding. "And I agree. There's nothing wrong with you, I think you just need time."

Kokoro hesitated as she thought back to her conversation with Dr. Maeda and Sakura. All along, she had just assumed she was a short-lived spark that would extinguish when she wasn't needed. To hear that somehow she was a part of Naoko, yet her own person? That she was *real?*

She glanced at Mr. Haneda. How would he react to the news that the girl sitting next to him wasn't even his daughter? After all, she could barely make sense of it. How would he?

"Naoko?"

Kokoro blinked. They were at a stoplight. Mr. Haneda stared at her, frowning.

"Oh. Yeah, sorry. You're right." She sighed. "I just need time at home. I'm looking forward to it."

He gave Kokoro a gentle, reassuring smile. She returned it, though truthfully, she felt like breaking down. Mr. Haneda had changed so much, becoming so much kinder and caring. Kokoro couldn't help but think how happy Naoko would have been.

The light turned green; the car gently trudged through the light snow. Kokoro shivered and pulled her oversized sweater down further, crossing her arms. Naoko's Dad responded by reaching to crank up the heat but turning the radio knob instead.

"...the winter storm shows no signs of letting up, so prepare yourselves for even more snow. In other news, the number of missing girls has continued to skyrocket. The police continue to..."

Kokoro's eyes widened as he quickly turned it back down. She faced him and frowned.

"There are more like me, aren't there?" she asked. "Girls that have gone missing?"

"Unfortunately." Mr. Haneda sighed. "We've been working on this case even before they got you. Hell, we're lucky that *we* got to you before they could ship you off somewhere."

"Any leads?" Kokoro asked without really thinking about it. The words had simply slipped out of her mouth, her own voice seemed rigid, yet distant.

Mr. Haneda shook his head. "At first, we thought maybe some of the Yakuza were involved, but no. They're in the middle of a conflict with some of the other gangs, who we believe to be the actual culprits behind the disappearances. The two events are undoubtedly related."

"It's not just them," she said. "I already know the names of the people who—"

"Claire Hanson and Shane Dreybuck," he said. "Foreign nationals. We already have extradition agreements with their home countries once we catch them, assuming the Yakuza don't get to them first."

Kokoro blinked. "How do you know their names?"

"A former associate of theirs. An insider," he said. "The same one that rescued you, in fact. Thanks to him, we liberated about a dozen other girls from that same facility. He was supposed to be sent back to his home country, but…"

Kokoro arched an eyebrow. "Do I know him?"

Her father met her eyes and hesitated. "I can't reveal his name, but he seemed to be familiar with you. Either way, I'm grateful. Without him, we could have lost you forever."

But you did lose Naoko. Kokoro frowned. *We both did.*

"Right," Kokoro said, resting her head against the seatbelt and biting her lip. The dark sky slowly grew as they drove on, blurring into the shops and restaurants of small business districts and, finally, the residential areas.

The next minute, they pulled into the driveway. Naoko's mother was there, waiting. The second Kokoro had stepped out of the car, she latched onto her and began crying.

"Naoko," she said. "My dear, sweet, baby girl."

Kokoro tightened her grip on Naoko's mother, then finally released as she smiled sadly. Her father walked up to them and wrapped an arm around each of them.

"Why don't we head inside?"

Kokoro nodded and escorted Naoko's mother into the house, flanked by her father. Ahead was the kitchen table, where they had the cake war the night before she and Naoko were taken. Kokoro clenched her jaw and swallowed to keep herself in check.

She turned to look at Mr. Haneda, who took a quick look around outside, then closed the door, slipping his shoes off. After that, she not only heard the familiar squeak of the hinges, but also the clicking of about four locks, when she distinctly remembered it only having one.

As Mr. Haneda joined them at the kitchen table, Naoko's mother beamed at her, the tears on her cheeks beginning to dry up. "So, how does it feel to be back?"

"It feels…good," she lied, smiling reassuringly for their sake. She paused for a moment, trying to think what Naoko would say before continuing. "Although, I'm pretty sure I've flunked out of school by now."

"Don't worry about that," Mr. Haneda said with a reassuring smile. "That can wait."

"He's right," his wife added. "For now, you just relax. If you need anything, we'll both be here."

Kokoro smiled, then twisted a few locks of her ashen hair. Mrs. Haneda giggled.

"Oh my. You're not supposed to go white and gray yet! You're so young! When did you dye your hair?"

"I…didn't," Kokoro answered. Naoko's mother frowned.

"I had no idea, Nao. If you want it changed back to the way it was, we can—"

"No!" Kokoro said quickly, before lowering her voice. "I mean…no thank you. I appreciate it though."

Kokoro nodded, the pleasant numbness she had managed to feel earlier now threatened to fade. Mr. Haneda cleared his throat.

"Well, enough of this downer talk. Because right now, this is a cause worth celebrating. Our sweet Naoko is finally home."

Her eyes stung. Kokoro gripped one of her bruised wrists so tight she might have broken it. Despite her best efforts, the tears fell, and they fell hard.

It should have been me. It should have been me.

Naoko's parents quickly took her side, embracing her. "It's okay, it's okay. You're safe now. We've got you, Nao."

Kokoro shifted her grip to Mrs. Haneda's arm as she sobbed. Why? Why was she here, and not Naoko? These were her parents, this was her life! How could she be so stupid as to give it all up for her?

The tears finally stopped as Kokoro regained control of herself. Naoko's parents loosened their grip and allowed her to stand up. She briskly moved from the kitchen to the stairs but stopped.

"I'm sorry," she said, her throat swollen. "May I be excused?"

"Of course," Mr. Haneda said, standing up straight as he exchanged glances with his wife. "Take all the time you need."

Kokoro regarded them with a gentle smile before climbing the steps to Naoko's room, flicking the light on. The dresser across from the bed was lined with cards, some of them saying 'Get well!' Others offered prayers for Naoko's safe return.

She clenched her jaw. Did they not know their prayers would be in vain?

Kokoro huffed and turned the light back off. She removed her turtleneck sweater and pants and crawled into bed beneath the covers, curling into herself. She stared aimlessly as she interlocked her hands, desperate to feel something from Naoko. *Anything.*

Instead, there was nothing but the feeling of cold, clammy skin.

Slowly releasing them, Kokoro pulled one of the pillows close to her. She didn't have the energy to cry anymore, so she just laid there until the merciful darkness finally took her into the night.

Kokoro awoke and felt like she had been hit by a bus. All night as her head throbbed, sleep had eluded her and hid among the noises in her mind that were like the chattering of a crowd. Along with that, her mind danced under her closed eyelids, twisting shapes and brief glimpses of faces passed by.

A flashing light caught her eye. She looked to the side and saw Naoko's phone on the nightstand. Her eyes widened as she picked it up.

Wait, when did they get this? Kokoro paused, then unlocked it with her finger. *Did Claire and Shane have it?*

A knock came at her door, causing Kokoro to jump. She frantically checked herself, but then arched an eyebrow upon finding that she was dressed in a pair of clean pajamas.

"Naoko? Are you awake?"

"Um, yeah!" Kokoro answered. "Come in!"

Mr. Haneda slid open the door. "Oh. I see you found your phone."

Kokoro blinked as she looked down at it. "Where was it? Was it at the place…"

"...where they kept you?"

She nodded.

"It was," he said. "We took it in for evidence, grabbed all the necessary data, then double checked it for any spyware programs and whatnot. It looked like they were about to wipe and destroy it to keep anything from leading back to them. We're lucky they got lazy."

Kokoro inspected the phone. It largely remained the same, minus the thirty missed calls and texts from Naoko's parents and friends.

"I can have it back, right?"

Naoko's dad smiled. "Of course. We were only borrowing it to try to find those other girls."

She frowned. "Any luck?"

"Unfortunately, no." He shook his head. "We *will* find them, though. No matter what it takes."

Kokoro managed to smile. Mr. Haneda straightened his posture.

"Anyway, your mother and I are making breakfast downstairs. We would love it if you could join us."

"Oh. Of course," she said, looking down at the phone one more time. "Do you mind if I take a few minutes to myself first?"

Mr. Haneda regarded her with a nod. "Take your time, Naoko. I'm sure it would help to send your friend a message to let her know how you are doing."

"Right." Kokoro nodded. "I'll be down soon, I promise."

He beamed and slid the door shut for her. She turned back to the phone, opening the app drawer to see the messages, but noticed something. On the internet app, there were no less than fifteen tabs open.

Kokoro's eyebrow arched as she clicked into the app, flipping through the different pages. Some were articles, others were videos, all dedicated to the thing Dr. Maeda had diagnosed her with.

What the…?

Her eyes widened as she continued to flip through to the end. The second to last tab differed from the rest: a forum. Kokoro skimmed the different posts, one of which read:

Tips for interacting with an unaware host for the first time?

Kokoro continued to read the replies. Most offered different suggestions and encouragement. One comment in particular caught her eye, posted three hours ago by a user called 'Fractured_5oul(s)', the same account that had posted the question…and the same one the phone was logged into.

We appreciate the advice, everyone! Wish us luck with—

"Kokoro?"

She jumped up from the bed and dropped the phone, looking around for the source of the voice. It had seemed like it had come from everywhere and nowhere all at once, like her own thoughts, yet also as if someone were right there with her. The one multiplied into an indiscernible chatter at first, then finally separated again. This time, each voice was its own.

"Think she'll see us?"

"Who gives a shit?"

"Come on, Ikiryo! Don't be so mean!"

"Go to hell."

"Everyone, calm down! She's seen me before. Just hang back. Let me introduce myself first."

Kokoro blinked as her heart thumped faster in her chest. What were these voices? *Who* were they?

"Kokoro! The mirror!"

She turned to face it, though she hadn't meant to; Naoko's body had moved on its own. Kokoro approached it slowly, the reflection mirroring her perfectly. At the same time, she felt a strange, comforting, yet firm presence creep into her.

"What am I supposed to see?" Kokoro asked out loud, though something from within beckoned her to lower her voice.

"Trust me. Just…focus. Look harder."

Kokoro hesitantly obeyed. Slowly, her reflection shifted and blurred, until it finally sharpened again. Now, it was a young man in a polo and khakis, around her age. Behind his glasses were a pair of sharp, discerning, yet kind eyes. His face was rigid, yet fair. His red, unkempt hair was swept to the side.

Her eyes widened. It was the same boy from the window in the psych ward, right before she had been released.

"My name is Hideaki," the young man in the mirror explained. "I'm—"

"—like me," Kokoro said, the realization dawning on her.

Hideaki gave a small bow. Kokoro hesitated.

"You…want me to go back inside, don't you?" she asked. Hideaki nodded again, and Kokoro took a step back. "I…I can't," she said, thinking of the shadowy figures, the building, and the cries of the little girl. "It's not safe. Not anymore."

"This part is," Hideaki said in a disarmingly calm tone. "We made it that way for you. Please, Kokoro…just trust me. Trust *us*."

The next thing she knew, her hand was on the mirror even though she didn't remember placing it there. Withdrawing it, Kokoro spun, her eyes scanning around her. Of course, nothing really changed; she was still in Naoko's room. The lights hung from the ceiling, the Sakura tree was…

Kokoro froze. The Sakura tree wasn't a painting on the wall anymore. It was as solid as the ones that lined the Meguro. She caught her breath and approached it, placing her hand on one of its beautiful pinkish-white flowers.

"It really is gorgeous, isn't it?"

Kokoro turned toward the voice. Hideaki was now next to her, admiring the Sakura as much as she was.

"Right," she replied, assessing him. "It kinda reminds me of…"

"When you first told Naoko about you?" he asked. Immediately after, his face flushed. "Sorry. We didn't mean to pry in your memories. They just sort of came to us, like a dream, or a leaf in a gust of wind." He frowned. "We even felt it. The pain."

"I didn't even know you were here, but I'm sorry. I didn't mean for it to." Kokoro's lip curled down, then her face contorted in confusion. "Wait a minute…'*we?*'"

"Oh, come on, Hideaki! Just get on with it!" a voice said from the swirling void. "I'm tired of waiting!"

"I'm getting to it, Ikiryo," Hideaki growled. "Calm down!"

Vertigo overtook Kokoro as they argued back and forth, their voices blending into pointless banter. Without warning, Hideaki reached into the fog and pulled someone from it: a young woman about her and Naoko's age, dressed in rebellious black leather laced with crimson strings, torn shorts over striped leggings with knee length, high-heeled boots. Her dark hair ran down her back in a loose ponytail, her misshapen bangs fell down either side of her face, which was practically coated in makeup. On her ears were several small spikes, with a large, plastic loop embedded into the bottom ear lobe.

"We want to make a good impression," Hideaki emphasized through gritted teeth. "She is the host. Remember?"

"Yeah, don't remind me." Ikiryo gave him the finger, before fixing her hostile gaze on Kokoro, her eyeliner-dashed eyes narrowing.

Hideaki rolled his eyes as more figures emerged from the swirling fog. The first was another young girl about ten years of age, her strikingly golden hair tied into two cute little pigtails with hair ties on each one. She wore a yellow t-shirt adorned with stitched sunflowers and faded jeans interspersed with several beaded designs.

The girl stumbled forward as she broke free of the mist. Kokoro lunged and caught her just before she fell.

"Are you okay?" Kokoro asked.

The girl nodded and latched onto Kokoro, who froze as she felt something strange bleed into her. As the anxiety she had felt earlier vanished, it was replaced by a sense of happy calm, like the warm, gentle breeze that follows rainfall.

"Sorry." The girl blushed and pulled away, the pleasant feeling going with her. "I could sense that you needed a hug."

"Oh." Kokoro paused as she tried to process what had happened. "Well, thank you, err…"

"Sunshine," the young girl answered as she beamed.

"Right. Thank you, Sunshine." Kokoro returned her smile, albeit with a slightly sad one. "I really did need that."

Sunshine nodded sheepishly as the mysterious wall of fog shifted again. The second figure came through: a tall, dark, masculine body that seemed like a window into space itself. Stars, distant planets, even entire galaxies somehow drifted around in its seemingly impossible form. In what Kokoro assumed to be the head were two evenly spaced lights shined brighter than the others on its body, a pair of eyes.

Kokoro turned from Sunshine and approached it slowly. With this one, she felt a strange sense of…nothing. She wasn't happy, and yet the grief that had hung on her had melted away as well. There was only a sense of calm and silence, with the feeling of drifting endlessly in the dark.

"Ah," Hideaki said, pulling her back a little. "That is Void. He's friendly, but you have to be careful, otherwise…"

"I'll get lost," Kokoro deduced.

Hideaki nodded. "He doesn't mean it. It's just what he is. Whenever you're around him, you won't be able to feel emotion, good or bad. He absorbs it."

Kokoro continued to assess Void as he stood next to Ikiryo, who seemed slightly less irritated than she was before. She wondered if perhaps that was Void's role, to be some kind of dampener.

A slapping noise shook Kokoro from her thoughts. She looked around at the swirling mist for another figure, but none had arrived. The noise echoed again, allowing her to pinpoint its source: an Ogon Koi, flopping around on the ground below.

"Fishy!" Sunshine ran over worriedly and scooped it up in her arms. Kokoro's eyes widened.

"Uh, shouldn't we find some water? Or maybe we can make some, so we can…"

"Don't worry. He doesn't really need water." The worried look melted from Sunshine's puffy face as she continued to hold it. She beamed. "Besides, he's not that kind of fish. He likes to be held instead."

Kokoro turned back to Hideaki, hoping for an answer. He shrugged, obviously just as confused as she was.

Sunshine beamed and held Fishy out for Kokoro to pet. She hesitantly reached and did so, but found that despite his appearance, he didn't feel slippery and scaled. In fact, he felt soft, like the stained cotton of an old stuffed animal.

Kokoro blinked as Sunshine handed Fishy to her. She clung it tight to her chest, almost instinctively. It felt…comforting. Familiar.

Fishy wriggled in her arms. Kokoro briskly gave him back to Sunshine, who calmed him by bouncing him on her shoulder like a baby.

"Okay, we're all here. Good," Hideaki said, nodding to each of them before turning to Kokoro with a small bow. "Anyway, apologies for the sloppy introduction. I've only just found them not too long ago."

"Found them?" Kokoro asked, glancing around at the new arrivals. "I mean, I'm honored to meet you and all, but why? What's so important about me that you would bring them all here?"

"Ditto," Ikiryo eyed Kokoro with disgust.

The entire space around them fell silent as Kokoro tensed, her jaw tightening as she felt a strange wrath within her. Why was she even here? Why would a bitch like her even exist in Naoko's mind?

"Sorry about Ikiryo," Hideaki said with an exasperated sigh. "We've been trying to get her under control, but it has proven…difficult. That may just be her nature."

Ikiryo glowered at her, eyes digging in like a parasite beneath the skin. Kokoro turned back to Hideaki. "So, I assume you know about what Dr. Maeda said? About the—"

"—the DID, yes. I've been doing research, most of it last night," Hideaki said as he rubbed his chin in deep thought. "I apologize for the confusion. Also, the lack of sleep."

Kokoro arched an eyebrow. "That was you?"

"I was curious." Hideaki nodded. "I wanted to know more about what I was, what *we* were."

What we were. Kokoro pondered the words as Hideaki fell silent, waiting for her answer. All this time, Naoko had been right. There *were* others.

Kokoro's brows furrowed as she thought back to the day everything went wrong: the three-hour walk to Akihabara, the mysterious presence she felt around her and Naoko in the tower, and finally that silhouette that had abandoned them.

"Hey, Hideaki?" she asked, looking up from her thoughts. "I have a question, if that's okay."

With a respectful nod, Hideaki beckoned her to continue.

"Before…the day that Naoko…" she clenched her jaw, both unable and unwilling to finish that particular sentence. "We thought that someone else might have been there with us." She glanced around at all of them. "Was that one of you?"

Hideaki blinked. "I'm…not sure." He turned, looking at his companions. "Not that I know of. I can't speak for them, but I can tell you for certain it wasn't me."

"Me neither," Sunshine said with a frown. Fishy flopped in her arms, likely echoing her sentiment. Kokoro looked at Void, who shook his head.

"Ah." Kokoro sighed, then turned to Ikiryo. Her rebellious expression had faded slightly as she eyed Kokoro. Her brows furrowed for a moment as she reached to scratch her forearm.

"Same here," Ikiryo said. "No clue."

Kokoro's eyes narrowed. Hideaki touched his chin thoughtfully.

"Hmm. Assuming none of us is lying, there could technically be more of us, I suppose. Though…" He briefly eyed Ikiryo. "…some are more elusive than others."

Ikiryo's jaw tightened as she glared at him. A loud knock rang throughout, causing everyone minus Void to jump.

"Naoko?" Mr. Haneda's voice reverberated throughout the inner world. "Everything okay?"

"Wait a minute," Kokoro's eyes widened as she turned to Hideaki. "I'm sorry. I have to go."

"Of course." Hideaki bowed slightly. "We can get you caught up later."

Kokoro opened her mouth to speak further, then opted not to. Instead, she turned to the four of them with a sad half-smile. "I'm sorry. It was really nice to meet you all."

"Sure," Ikiryo quickly eyed her, scoffed, then vanished into the mist.

"Right," Sunshine added, beaming as Fishy momentarily wriggled in her arms. "We're here if you need us."

Void said nothing and nodded.

Kokoro nodded and moved back to the mirror by the Sakura, pushing through the shimmering glass and back into the real world.

CHAPTER 11
SHATTERED INDIFFERENCE

KOKORO NEARLY TRIPPED DOWN THE STAIRS on her way to the kitchen. The smell of miso soup, steamed rice, and fermented soybeans filled her nostrils. Once she had made it down the steps, she found her place at the table next to Naoko's mother and father.

"Ah, Naoko." Mr. Haneda smiled as he and his wife removed their aprons. "You made it. You were up there for a while."

"Sorry," she said sheepishly. "I just had a lot of catching up to do."

"I imagine so. That Sayuki girl was practically blowing up your phone when you were in the ward," Naoko's mother said. "She must be a good friend of yours."

Kokoro nodded and smiled. Beneath her haughty and rough exterior, Sayuki was a sweet girl. She only wished that Naoko had the chance to truly see it.

"Well, speaking of Sayuki…" Naoko's dad began as he cleared his throat. "…we invited her to join us for breakfast. We hope you don't mind."

Before Kokoro could even process it, the doorbell had rung. Mr. Haneda stood and made his way to the door, opening it.

"Ms. Sato," he regarded her with a quick bow before he moved aside. Sayuki stepped in, her eyes searching frantically, settling on her and widening. She ran over, not bothering to take her shoes off at the door. The next thing Kokoro felt was her tight embrace.

"Naoko… Oh, Naoko!" She pulled back and placed her hands on Kokoro's cheeks. "You're alive. I was so worried, I…"

Kokoro smiled back and hugged her tightly. She released Sayuki and gave her a small half-grin.

"Ms. Sato," she teased in a voice mimicking Mr. Haneda, "aren't you forgetting something?"

"What? Oh." Sayuki's cheeks flushed as she moved back to the front door, removing her shoes and apologizing to Naoko's dad with a deep bow. He laughed it off and beckoned her to join them at the table. She settled in close to Kokoro, practically attaching herself to her hip.

Kokoro chuckled as they gave thanks for the meal and began to dig in, first with the miso soup, followed by rice. The mysterious main dish was dead center in the middle of the table, and there was a strange, awful smell emanating from it.

"Ah." Mr. Haneda noticed her staring at it. "I assume you're ready for this?"

Before she could protest, he lifted the cover to reveal grilled fish. Her chest tightened, her stomach immediately twisted in knots, threatening to spill bile across the dinner table.

Kokoro pushed back off her pillow as she averted her gaze, trying to shake the sudden disgust. It was like looking at the corpse of another human.

What's happening? I've had fish before. Why am I…?

"Are you okay, Naoko?"

She blinked to find Sayuki and Naoko's parents staring at her worriedly.

"Oh." Kokoro blinked. "Sorry. I don't know what came over me."

Sayuki and Mrs. Haneda frowned. Mr. Haneda was inspecting the fish, perhaps wondering if he had cooked it wrong. He met his wife's gaze and shrugged.

"It is a little strange," he said. "You used to love fish."

"I do, I…" Kokoro sighed. "Or I did. Sorry. It's not that it was cooked wrong or smelled bad. I promise."

Mr. Haneda briefly assessed her, nodding as he covered it back up. "Preferences change all the time."

"May I be excused?" Kokoro blurted out, then blinked. She hadn't meant for those words to come out. Why had they?

"Of course." Mrs. Haneda gave a sad smile and gestured to Sayuki. "Besides, I'm sure the two of you have much catching up to do. Your father and I will be outside for a moment, anyway."

Sayuki smiled and took Kokoro's hand, leading her from the table up the stairs. Kokoro's vision blurred her, her brain fogged. When she had regained focus, she was planted on the floor, knees tucked under, with Sayuki sitting on the floor across from her, her hands comfortingly on her knee.

"Are you sure you're alright, Nao?" Sayuki asked. "I know you've been through a lot, but I didn't think a fish would scare you like that."

Kokoro paused. Was it one of the others, or…?

"Sorry about that," a voice from the inner world said. It was Hideaki. "We had a brief incident. It's under control now."

"What happened?" Kokoro asked inwardly, careful not to say the words out loud.

"Fishy freaked out," Sunshine said. "But I calmed him down. He's okay now, just a little shaken."

Of course. He must have reflexively taken control.

"I don't know. Still just getting used to things, I guess." Kokoro smiled sadly, pulling herself back into focus to continue her conversation with Sayuki. "It's…been rough. Especially since I lost Naoko."

"What do you mean? You're 'Naoko.'"

Kokoro froze. Sayuki's eyes narrowed. The two of them stared at each other as the room fell silent. Even the others didn't utter a peep.

"You're right." Kokoro tried to laugh it off. "I'm sorry. I'm just tired and my brain is scrambled, that's all."

"Are you sure?"

Kokoro nodded nervously, but Sayuki wasn't buying it.

"Nao, come on. You know you can talk to me if you need to. After all, you've been there for me." Sayuki frowned, then gripped her arm. "I never thanked you."

"It's okay." Kokoro smiled, hoping to cut off the conversation. "You're a good friend. Trust me."

"It's not that, I...I can't even imagine what you've gone through." Sayuki scooted closer, just within reach of Kokoro's hands. "Just...why? Why did that have to happen to such a sweet girl like you? Especially when you think about how I treated you before you became my friend. You didn't deserve any of it, Naoko. I'm just glad that you came back. Because without you, I..."

Kokoro drew Sayuki in for a hug, taking in her warmth while also trying to comfort her. Her hands rested on the top of Sayuki's back by her hair, then drifted down to her hips. She pulled away, seeing her friend's cheeks flush. Their eyes locked, their gazes deepening. The two held the stare until Sayuki closed her eyes and leaned in.

Her head suddenly throbbed. Kokoro swallowed as her throat constricted, her heart beginning to thump in her chest. Without warning, or meaning to, she shoved Sayuki away and backed herself against the window.

"Are you kidding me?" Kokoro hissed. "You would dare try to kiss her, despite everything you put her through all those years?"

"I'm sorry!" Sayuki frowned as she desperately tried to explain. "I misunderstood. I—"

"Sorry doesn't cut it. Who do you think you are? Honestly, it's people like you that made her the way she was, whether it was you, her father, or—"

Kokoro paused, but the body continued to disparage Sayuki with venomous words as the poor girl's eyes widened.

What's going on? Kokoro watched in horror. *Why am I acting like this?*

Realizing she was back in the inner world, she spun and looked around. Who was saying those horrible things to Sayuki?

Kokoro heard the muffled words behind a wall of mist and then pushed through. Ikiryo was in control, the others trying and failing to pull her back.

"Ikiryo!" she called. Ikiryo stopped and turned to face Kokoro, chest heaving, brows furrowed, eyes filled with a pent-up rage. Void finally appeared and placed a hand on her shoulder. Slowly, she calmed down. She growled, pulled away, and shoved her hands in the pocket of her leather jacket.

"Why?" Kokoro asked, horrified. "Why would you ever hurt my friend like that?"

"The question is, why would you let someone touch Naoko like that again?" Ikiryo stopped at her side, eyeing her. "Besides, I may have said the words, but I wasn't the one thinking them, was I?"

Again? Kokoro blinked, pondering it, then shook her head. "No. I would never..."

"But you did," Ikiryo pointed out, her glare reforming and burning into her. "You won't admit it. Yet, you still became friends with Sayuki, knowing how she had treated Naoko."

Kokoro returned the glare. "That was before. She's different now. Better."

"Sure." Ikiryo shrugged, scoffing. "But did Naoko feel that way, or were you just trying to force it on her?"

Kokoro screamed and lunged, but Hideaki stepped between them, arms spread. He turned to her, brows furrowed.

"Calm down," Hideaki urged, then turning to Ikiryo accusingly. "This is what she does. Don't fall for it."

Baring her teeth, Kokoro shoved his arm aside to move past Hideaki, but felt another hand on her shoulder. The anger within her cooled, her mind cleared as reason filled the gaps. Ikiryo spun, walking into the swirling mist before Void could get the chance to calm her too. Kokoro moved to go after her but was stopped by Hideaki.

"Leave her for now." He stared where Ikiryo had gone, then turned to face the front, the window to the outside world. "Right now, we have more pressing matters."

Kokoro turned and froze. Sayuki was still sitting in front of her, tears streaming, a look of absolute betrayal affixed to her face.

Oh no. She stepped forward as the others avoided her gaze. The light engulfed her, then finally solidified into the familiar shapes of Naoko's room.

Kokoro knelt down with her crying friend and took her hands. "Sayuki, I am so, so sorry. I didn't mean—"

"—is that how you feel about me?" she asked. "Is it really my fault? What happened?"

"No! No, of course not." Kokoro's eyes stung, her desperation so raw that she felt Void struggling to keep them in check. "I'm sorry. Everything I said was wrong. You *are* a good friend. What happened to Naoko wasn't your fault."

"Why do you keep talking about yourself in third person like that?" Sayuki asked, her soaked eyes narrowing.

Kokoro froze; she had slipped up again. How should she explain it?

"Naoko," Sayuki said, backing up slightly. "You're scaring me."

"No, no, I..." Kokoro clenched her fists. "Sorry. It's just complicated."

"How so?"

Kokoro paused, unsure of how to answer. She briefly turned to the others in the inner world, though they met her with the same hesitant look. Regret in his eyes, Hideaki shook his head. She bit her lip and allowed herself to regain full control again, meeting her friend's frightened, confused gaze.

Her heart thumped in her chest. This moment was important...no, *critical.* Whatever she was going to say to her, she had to be careful and concise. One wrong word could send the only other true friend she ever had running.

Kokoro paused, an idea coming to her. She lifted her chin and smiled at Sayuki.

"Actually...my name is Kokoro. Even though we've technically known each other for a while now, it's nice to meet you."

"Like the PULSE star?" Sayuki blinked.

Kokoro swallowed. It stung a little, being reminded of what she really was: a copy meant to help Naoko. Between that and the fact that she had failed in her purpose, she couldn't decide which hurt more.

"Yeah," Kokoro said. "But not exactly. I started existing when Naoko needed me. I was in her mind with her. When she needed help, or felt horrible, or needed to be protected, I would take control. That was my job. I was her protector."

Sayuki tilted her head. "Are you like…a spirit? Or a ghost?"

Kokoro paused. Sayuki hadn't run away or called her crazy yet. That meant that she was at least listening, even if she couldn't quite understand.

Progress. Kokoro nodded. *But how should I break it down, so she'll understand?*

Without warning, her back straightened. She went from sitting cross-legged to the Seiza pose, her legs tucked under her, her hands resting on her knees. The body inhaled sharply.

"It's called Dissociative Identity Disorder," she said, her voice rigid. "It's when an individual has two or more separate personality states, or 'alters,' that can alternate and take control of the body. This happens for many reasons. The first of which…"

Kokoro blinked, then looked to the side. Hideaki had taken control with her and was rattling off everything he had learned. Her friend blinked, staring in amazement as she took in the new information.

He's great at explaining things. Kokoro blinked as Hideaki continued on.

"So, it's like multiple people in one body," Sayuki said, her eyes attentive, intrigued. She arched an eyebrow. "And Naoko is the original, right?"

Kokoro watched as Hideaki paused. Then, he pulled a blank sheet of paper from one of Naoko's old journals, and promptly tore it into exactly six pieces. He laid them out in front of Sakura.

"Which one is the 'original?'"

"None of them, and yet…" Sakura blinked. "All of them?"

"Correct." Hideaki gestured to them once more. "Which one do you think is in control most of the time?"

"The biggest one," Sayuki answered.

"Excellent." Hideaki smiled, then grabbed a pen and drew his name on one of the side pieces, the second largest. "This one is me. Hideaki."

"Oh. Hideaki, huh?" Sayuki smiled at him. "That's a lovely name." She paused, staring back down at the papers. "And the biggest one is…?"

"Kokoro," he said, nodding. "She was having difficulty explaining, so I…well, stepped in."

"Like she did, as a protector for Naoko," Sayuki theorized.

"Yes," Hideaki confirmed. "Very much like that."

"What about Naoko? Which piece is she?" Sayuki's eyes softened as she scooted forward slightly. "Can I talk to her again? If it's okay, I just wanted to apologize. For everything."

At that moment, the entire body chilled, as if blanketed in a sudden snowstorm. Hideaki froze, as if unsure of how to respond. Kokoro placed a reassuring hand on his shoulder and let him know it was okay. He nodded in relief, then faded back into the depths of their mind as she bled into the front.

The chill of the room filled Kokoro as she struggled with her words while Sayuki watched her curiously. Her gaze fell to the pieces of torn paper set up neatly at their feet. While biting her lip, she grabbed one of the pieces and pulled it away, cupping it in her hand. She looked up just in time to see Sayuki's heart shatter in her eyes.

"Kokoro, if that's you, I…I'm sorry." Sayuki scooted closer and latched onto her. "I'm so, so, sorry."

She melted into Sayuki, accepting the embrace. Void was there, but she warded him off as he tried to calm her. This pain was like a raging river; damming it up too long did her no good.

The door slid open as Kokoro and Sayuki turned their heads. Naoko's dad was there, his eyes alert. When he realized what was going on, his focused expression softened.

"Oh. I'm sorry. I didn't mean to interrupt, I…"

"It's okay," Sayuki said, though her quivering betrayed her words. "She's okay. I've got her."

He nodded solemnly, then slid the door shut as he took one last look at Kokoro.

Sayuki sighed and held her close. She pulled back, brows creased. "Does he know?"

"No," Kokoro said. "And he can't know. Promise me."

Sayuki nodded quickly. Kokoro sighed with relief.

"Good, good. I…" Kokoro leaned against Naoko's dresser, clutching her head as it throbbed. She could feel them all trying to cram their way into control of the body to help her.

"Back off, guys," Kokoro said internally. "I'm fine."

Slowly, the pulsing sensation in her head stopped. Sayuki sat nearby and held her hand comfortingly.

"So, what now?"

Kokoro stopped for a moment to consider it. Sayuki was right. Where should she go from here? Should she just keep living Naoko's life, even though it would all be just a lie?

"I don't know," she answered with a brutal honesty. "Without her, I'm lost."

"But you're not alone," Sayuki said. Though she was undoubtedly hurting too, she managed a brave, reassuring smile for her. "Whatever happens now, just know that I'm with you, okay? No matter what the future holds."

Kokoro paused, staring at her and delving into her thoughts. What did the future hold? Even if she wasn't alone, what *could* she do?

Naoko's phone buzzed nearby. Kokoro turned and quickly grabbed it. It was a pop-up headline from a news app. More missing girls reported, breaking even last month's record. No doubt the work of Claire, Shane, and whoever else was helping them, kidnapping innocent girls and forcing them into a life filled with horror.

More girls that could suffer the same fate as Naoko.

Kokoro clenched her teeth. What the hell was wrong with her, wallowing in her own emotions while others continued to suffer? Unlike them, she had the privilege of a robust support system—Dr. Maeda, Sayuki, and, notably, Naoko's parents, with her father having the entire police force at his back. What did they have?

"There's something I have to do," she said. "The ones that took Naoko from me are still out there. Somehow, I've got to find them and put a stop to this all."

"You mean…you want to go after them?" Sayuki asked.

"I don't want to. I *have* to." Kokoro pursed her lips. "For those still trapped. Above all, for Naoko."

The silence and disbelief that filled the air was just as cold as the world outside. She turned and waited for the words of disapproval from her friend, for her to talk her down.

"Okay," her friend said. "I'm in."

"What?" Kokoro blinked, then shook her head. "No, no. I mean…thank you, but no. This is dangerous."

"You don't think I know that?" Sayuki protested. "I know what can happen, and truthfully, it scares me. But I'm more afraid of losing you."

Kokoro met her concerned gaze, silent, the need to keep her friend safe and the fear of being alone tearing at one another in her soul. What should she say?

"I…thank you." Kokoro's lips curled as she knelt. "I'm glad for you, but I wouldn't forgive myself if they took you too."

Sayuki paused, then fell to her knees, embracing her. Her hands slipped from her upper arms down to Kokoro's wrists, then finally her hands. "Look...I'm not giving you an option here. I'm gonna help you with this, one way or the other."

Kokoro opened her mouth to protest but was met with a finger to the lips. Her cheeks flushed as she gazed into Sayuki's enchanting brown eyes, her sweet smile filling Kokoro with warmth like a fireplace.

"So just...accept it, okay? I wasn't there for Naoko. But I *will* be there for you." Sayuki turned her gaze to Kokoro and smiled gently. "For all of you."

Kokoro stared at her friend. In her own way, she was a butterfly, too. She had watched as she slowly emerged from the cocoon of cruelty, indifference, and pain, spread her wings, and embraced the kind girl that Kokoro could see was there all along.

Sayuki beamed and stood to her feet, offering her hand to pull Kokoro up. "Like it or not, you're not alone anymore."

"She's right," a voice suddenly said. The part of Naoko's room that held the painted Sakura tree had blurred with the internal world as Hideaki, Sunshine, Fishy, Void, and even a reluctant-looking Ikiryo stood, albeit far off in the distance. Hideaki stepped forward and knelt next to Kokoro and Sayuki, as if he were physically there with them.

Hideaki nodded, extending his hand in a manner identical to Sayuki. "Just know that whatever you need, you have us as well."

Kokoro blinked, her chest fluttered, raw emotion overwhelming her. She gritted her teeth, pocketed the phone and clasped Hideaki's hand in the inner world, and Sayuki's in the real one as she stood, her body tense, a new fire burning within her.

"You're right," she said to both. "I can't do this alone. Not without you."

They both stared at her, on separated planes of existence, yet their facial expressions were mirrored. They simultaneously nodded.

Kokoro returned it, then stared out of the window into the snow-capped city. For once, just once, she wanted to make the world a little less cold.

Leaving the house, even for an appointment with Dr. Maeda, had proven far more difficult than Kokoro had thought it would be. Only with the explicit promise of checking in every thirty minutes to an hour, along with being escorted by Sayuki, was she able to go.

Kokoro closed the door to Mr. Haneda's car and bid him goodbye. She watched him carefully as he turned the corner, then moved toward the opposite corner, away from the psychiatric hospital. Sayuki, having made her way from the other side, held her fast.

"Come on," she said. "I know what we agreed, but…just do the appointment first. Please?"

Kokoro met her eyes then sighed in defeat. For the past couple of days, she and Sayuki had been digging into the disappearances, visiting forums, social media, anything that gave them a hint as to Claire and Shane's whereabouts. They had found a lead: an anonymous PULSE user on a private forum who was investigating Naoko's former friends as well. He had messaged them and asked to meet in person, claiming to have more information. Sayuki thought it was a trap, a means of luring girls and curious people to their doom.

Even if they're not who they say they are, it's still something. We just need to be smart about it.

Sayuki nudged her, taking her out of her train of thought. They had already checked in, and Sakura stood nearby with a smile, ready to escort her to Dr. Maeda's office.

Kokoro blinked and followed her, wondering how time had passed so quickly. It took her a moment to remember that she and the others had agreed to switch more often. When she focused, she felt Hideaki next to her, guiding the body, observing every detail of their surroundings, taking mental notes.

She turned to him. "How does it feel?"

"Fine," he answered, still focused on the outside. "I remember this place. This is where…"

"…they kept me?" Kokoro asked.

"That," Hideaki said, "and it was here that I became who I am now."

Kokoro blinked as she felt something bleeding from him, only to stop. He briefly glanced at her, cheeks flushing in embarrassment.

"Sorry," Hideaki said. "I try not to let it all out."

"Let what out?" she asked.

"Emotion," he told her, eyes lowering. "For me, it's…powerful. Not something I want to burden you or the others with. Besides, I feel like it's my job to stabilize us."

"It's not all bad," Kokoro said, smiling. "Maybe we can help you embrace and control them?"

"I…appreciate the offer." Hideaki returned it. "I've always preferred the clarity that comes without it. And yet, with this place, it's hard." He looked forward, brows creasing. "This is where I was 'born,' after all."

"I know that feeling," she replied, thinking of her own 'birth.' She was formless at first too, like him, but had found her identity in the idol that Naoko had relied upon for her sanity. Even now, she wasn't sure if Naoko had subconsciously made her that way or if it was born out of her own desire to help her addled friend. She frowned.

"Hey, Hideaki?"

"What is it, Kokoro?"

"Do you remember before you were…well, you?"

"Vaguely," he said. "If I existed at all, it was only for things like schoolwork, tests, or studying. Other than that, it was mostly just…darkness, like an ocean of shadow. I was there, struggling to keep my head above the waves. When I couldn't…"

"…you were drowning."

"Yes." Hideaki nodded. "Exactly that."

"I'm sorry." Kokoro's lip curled down, thinking of how she had saved Naoko from the same thing he had described. "If you don't mind my asking, how did you escape it?"

Hideaki straightened. The body stopped. The view of the outside faded as he turned to her.

"Honestly, I don't know. One minute, it's just…nothing. Next, I'm suddenly 'here.' Alive."

Kokoro blinked. "How did you find the others? Or me?"

Hideaki rubbed his chin. "At first, I wandered aimlessly, finding nothing but the shadows. Then, I saw this strange, fading light. It helped me navigate and pass those barriers between us. Eventually, one by one, I found them. The last one the light led me to before it disappeared was…"

"Me," Kokoro surmised.

Hideaki confirmed it with a nod.

"I see," Kokoro said, nodding as she turned her attention back to the real world. Sakura had led them to Dr. Maeda's office and beckoned at them to take a seat. She smiled, bowed, and left them alone with the doctor, who smiled from behind his desk.

"How are you today?"

"Doing slightly better," she answered, feeling Hideaki nearby. His presence usually calmed her and cleared her thoughts, but instead, she felt the slightest hint of something else. Was it anticipation?

"That's good," Dr. Maeda said with an encouraging smile. "These next few sessions are follow-ups. We're going to be focusing on—"

"I have a few questions if you don't mind, sir!" Kokoro unexpectedly said.

"Oh. Of course," Dr. Maeda replied, eyebrow raised. "What questions were you hoping to ask?"

Kokoro paused, drawing a blank, unable to respond. Then Hideaki's voice echoed as he materialized ahead of her, her peripherals blurring. "Sorry. I didn't mean to push you back like that. I just got—"

"—excited?" Kokoro asked.

"Yes. I apologize for letting it out." Hideaki's brows creased as he bowed. "I just…I wanted to learn more."

"Just do what you need to do," she said.

"Are you sure?"

Kokoro nodded, a smile reaching her lips. She didn't mind. This kind of thing was Hideaki's specialty, anyway.

"Right." Hideaki nodded sheepishly, vanishing as he gently assumed full control of the body, with her just behind him, watching through the body's eyes. He stood up, hands rigid at his sides as he bowed.

"Pardon my earlier outburst, Dr. Maeda. It is a pleasure to speak to you again."

Dr. Maeda blinked, then nodded his head with a chuckle. "Ah, Hideaki! It's been a while."

"Wait." Kokoro blinked. "You've spoken to him before?"

"On four occasions during our time in the ward," Hideaki confirmed. He turned to her, eyes downcast. "Sorry for keeping it from you. We figured it would be best to, ah…take it slow."

"Oh." Kokoro paused, then smiled. "So, are you gonna ask him questions or what?"

Hideaki nodded, then pressed forward through the mist and into control of the body. "Apologies once again. I was explaining the situation to Kokoro."

"Of course, Hideaki." Dr. Maeda smiled. "Anyway, what questions did you have? I'd be happy to answer to the best of my ability."

Hideaki nodded, hands on knees, body stiff. Despite his best efforts, his excitement at learning something new bubbled over, bleeding out to her. She continued to watch as he took copious notes with a pad he had borrowed from the doctor. Every so often, he would look up to ask another question, only to write another down not even a second later.

Better him than me. Kokoro let herself sink back into the inner world, walking over to sit under the Sakura tree, which had grown slightly since she had first seen it. She took a deep breath, closed her eyes, relaxing her back against the safe trunk, letting the sway of the branches lull her into a restful sleep.

CHAPTER 12
AN UNEXPECTED ALLY

BY THE TIME KOKORO HAD WOKEN UP, the session had finally ended. Hideaki was still in control, sifting through his newly taken notes and a pamphlet like a student cramming for exams at the last minute. Kokoro briefly fronted with him, viewing them through the body's eyes. The scratches on the paper barely resembled words.

"Learn anything interesting?" she asked.

"Not as much as I'd like, but…" He smiled with satisfaction as he partially pulled back to face her. "…but enough for now. Thank you, Kokoro."

Kokoro beamed as Sayuki escorted them from the building out onto the snow-filled streets, and finally to a bench that was fairly exposed, but to her, that was a good thing. To her, it meant the possibility of being snatched by Shane and Claire's goons was much, much lower.

"So, how did it go?" Sayuki asked as she planted herself next to them.

"Very well, as far as I'm concerned," he said, his rigid tone bleeding through Kokoro's voice as he held up his notes. "I learned quite a lot, specifically about system roles and their functions. I didn't realize how much of an iceberg our condition was."

"That sounds…um, interesting." Sayuki stared blankly. "It's Hideaki, right?"

"Right," Hideaki said, nodding as he flipped through his notepad. He blinked, looking at her. "Oh. Sorry. Would you prefer to speak to Kokoro?"

Sayuki smiled. "If it's okay."

Hideaki nodded, stuffed his notepad and pamphlet into the bag slung across the body's shoulder, then pulled back into the inner world. Kokoro blinked, and found herself in control, her body engulfed in a sudden chill as the snow fell around them. She shivered and faced Sayuki.

"Is that you?" her friend asked, eyebrow raised.

Kokoro inhaled sharply and nodded with a smile.

"Good!" Sayuki returned the smile. "Sorry if I get it mixed up sometimes. This whole thing is still so new to me."

"It's okay. Same here, honestly." Kokoro leaned closer to her, looping their arms for further warmth…and for comfort. Even if she had braved it, the outside world still towered over her. "By the way, did our mystery man say anything else since I was in there?"

"He said he would be nearby soon," Sayuki said, flicking through the messages. "The thing is, I'm not sure what to look for. He didn't give us any description of him, only the location. Seems sketchy to me."

Kokoro looked up from Sayuki's phone and glanced around. The street next to the psych ward wasn't too packed, thankfully, giving her a good look at everyone around her. Most of the people nearby were doing the same thing: scrolling their phones, walking, or minding their own business.

A familiar, sadistic laugh rang out. Kokoro froze, then nervously glanced around. What was it?

Could it really be…?

Finally, she located the source. It was nothing more than another set of girls on a bench close to them, giggling at something they saw on their phones.

Kokoro's eyes slid shut, forcing that tense breath she held from her lungs. She had to focus. No time for panic now. How were they supposed to find the informant? Would he find them? Was he even there?

As she turned in her seat, something caught her eye. Leaning against the base of a tree about twenty meters away was a tall, masculine figure in a hooded leather jacket. Most of the stranger's face was obscured in shadow, with only part of it being illuminated by the burning end of a cigarette. She couldn't see the person's eyes, yet somehow, she could feel his stare burn into her from afar.

The panic returned. Kokoro turned back around quickly, moving her gaze elsewhere, yet keeping her peripherals locked on the stranger. She nudged Sayuki.

"Behind us."

"What is it?" She immediately caught sight, then did the same as Kokoro, averting her gaze. "I see. Think that's him?"

"It could be." Kokoro fidgeted. She felt a firm, familiar presence behind her in the inner world, analyzing. "Might also be one of Shane's goons."

"I hope not." Sayuki quickly turned. Her eyes widened as she lowered her voice to a hushed whisper. "Ko! He's moving closer."

Kokoro paled, her chest tightened. She was tempted to look back, and yet, she didn't dare. If it was one of Shane and Claire's men, then it would do nothing but tip them off.

"We need to go," Sayuki insisted, tugging on Kokoro's arm. "This doesn't feel right."

Kokoro's body locked with indecision. On one hand, what if it was one of their men? On the other, what if it was the informant? What if they were one and the same?

Despite fighting both her friend's tugs and her own flight instinct, Kokoro stayed put. "We're out in public. He can't—"

Her vision twisted and blurred, the dark churning around her. When the world finally came back into focus, she and Sayuki were moving through a thick crowd, keeping their arms locked tight onto each other. Her head throbbed, her body seemed to move on its own.

"What?" Kokoro looked around, then at her friend. "What are you doing?"

Sayuki shook her head. "I'm sorry, Ko. This just scares me too much. We needed to leave."

"Agreed," Hideaki echoed from the inside. "He's still tailing us."

Kokoro briefly turned, seeing the mysterious hooded man follow them through the crowd from about ten meters behind them. Nine. Eight, now five. Her eyes widened, her chest tightened, the thumping in her ear drowning out the surrounding crowd.

The stranger, whoever he was, got closer by the second.

She blinked and found herself in an alleyway, crouched behind a small concrete outcrop with Sayuki tucked close. Kokoro tried to stand and look around but was pulled back down and met with a pleading stare from her friend.

"Don't. He's too close."

Kokoro wanted to protest, to face the mysterious goon, but found that she couldn't. Her body froze, her jaw clenched shut. Fear reigned supreme as she stayed hidden, hoping that the looming shadow approaching them would give up and go away.

The stranger got closer, moving across the light that bled into the alleyway. It grew, the footsteps sounding closer and closer. Kokoro and Sayuki froze, keeping perfectly still, the silence on the outside mirroring that of the inner world. Slowly, she felt a strange rage fill her, stiffening her body and resolve. Her fist clenched.

"Oh, forget this," a snappy voice echoed from the inside as Kokoro found herself ejected from cover.

"Hello? I'm looking for…"

Before she could even register it, Kokoro had struck the stranger square on the cheek, causing him to stumble back and fall.

"Whoa, whoa! Easy now! I ain't a threat!" The hood fell back, revealing a young man with dark skin, medium length hair and a short beard. He rubbed his cheek. "Bloody hell, you punch hard for a girl."

Kokoro's eyes widened. It was John, one of Naoko's three foreigner friends from school.

"Sorry if I spooked you. I just…" John's eyes locked with hers. "Wait, Naoko? That you?"

Kokoro didn't know how to answer. She pulled back and allowed John to stand, Sayuki following suit. He assessed her, laughing with relief.

"Oh, you made it! Thank God! I was worried that—"

Kokoro's body moved against her will, pinning him against the wall with such strength that it surprised even her. While she couldn't see him, she could feel Ikiryo nearby, her rage bleeding out and filling Kokoro with burning adrenaline.

"Why the hell are you here?" she hissed. "You were their friend too! How do I know you didn't help sell her out?"

John blinked, eyes narrowing. "Hold on a minute. First things first, I ain't their friend anymore. Shane and Claire can shove a cactus up their arses. Second, I'm the one that saved you!"

Kokoro's grip softened as she let go of his jacket. Ikiryo backed away slightly, allowing control to sip away and back to Kokoro. "Saved…me?"

"Yeah, from that place they kept you in." John's brows raised. "Do you not remember?"

"I…" She stopped, her mouth gaping open. The truth was, she didn't. Naoko had locked her out for so long. "I don't. I'm sorry."

"Hey, hey, I get it. Trust me. It was hectic." John sighed, crossing his arms and leaning against the concrete wall. "Anyway, you wanted information, right? So let's talk."

Kokoro looked around the dark alleyway, then back at John. "No, not here. Somewhere public."

Somewhere safe.

"Oh. Of course." John blinked, scratched his beard thoughtfully. "There's a ramen joint nearby, nice and open, lots of people. I'll buy."

Kokoro exchanged a glance with Sayuki, then nodded. Soon they were following him, out of the alley and back into the snow-filled sidewalk.

The ramen shop they had entered was called Danger Noodle. It was small, only fitting two small tables and a booth by the window. On that window was a large, neon sign of a happy-looking green snake wrapped around a ramen bowl, a cup of sake coiled by the end of its tail. Despite the crowds outside, the place was mostly empty aside from the chef who meandered behind the counter. John nodded to him, and soon they seated themselves in the booth as the snow glided from the heavens to the cold ground just outside the window.

The phone buzzed in her pocket. Naoko's dad had messaged her, asking for her whereabouts. She quickly replied.

Getting a quick bite to eat. We're safe. We'll be back soon.

Kokoro tucked Naoko's phone into her jacket and rested her arms on the table, staring across at John. He was sticking his nose in the menu, though it seemed less for food choice and more to obscure his face.

Almost like he's hiding. Kokoro tilted her head. *But from who?*

John looked up and placed the menu slightly off to the side. The server came by, orders were soon placed, though he requested to keep the menu with him. He met Kokoro's eyes.

"I'm guessin' you want some answers?"

Kokoro and Sayuki nodded simultaneously, their eyes fixed on him. He sighed.

"Alright, suppose I owe you that after scarin' ya." He rested his elbows on the table and leaned in. "So, what do you wanna know first?"

"Shane and Claire," Kokoro said immediately, her tone unexpectedly harsh, though it wasn't from Ikiryo this time, but rather, it was all her. Hideaki wasn't fronting with her, but she could feel him not far behind, his intense focus bleeding into her. She was glad for it; for this, she needed it to dull her anger's edge. "You said you're not friends with them anymore? Why should I believe you?"

John opened his mouth to answer, but then the food arrived: three bowls filled to the brim with Miso ramen. He immediately dug in, like he hadn't had a meal in forever. After a few minutes of his slurping, he finally met her eyes to give her the answer.

"You know that party we had a while back? The one in their club?"

Kokoro nodded quickly. The faint whirr of the police siren stirred in the back of her mind, a fragment of Naoko's distant memory. There wasn't much there about that day, but the one thing she could see clearly was the face of Mr. Haneda, horrified at what his daughter had done. She couldn't recall much, but she needed to know, regardless.

"What do you remember?" John asked.

"Not much," she admitted. "Just what happened after. When you turned Naoko in and got her arrested."

John blinked, then arched an eyebrow. Kokoro silently cursed to herself for slipping up like she had done with Sayuki those days before. She couldn't out her and the others to John, not until she was sure she could fully trust him.

"Uh…you know I saved your ass, right? *Twice.*"

"You mentioned that earlier." Kokoro's eyes narrowed, if only slightly. "How?"

"Don't know if you know this, but they gave you something that messed you up." John took a careful pause between his words. "You were trippin' bad, and nobody even bothered to check on you. Everyone was grabbing on you and trying to have their way."

"Yeah," Kokoro said, remembering the conversation with Claire in the Skytree, her false sincerity that had lured Naoko back in like a moth to the flame. She took a moment to carefully parse the words together. "Claire pressured me."

"That tracks," John continued. "I didn't realize it at the time, but Shane and Claire were trying to sell you off. I tried to help, and Shane had me kicked out. I couldn't get back in, so I called the cops."

"And that's the truth?" she asked.

John met her eyes. "I swear it."

Kokoro listened intently to his tone, his voice threatening to break, probably from guilt. Hideaki wasn't saying anything, but she could feel him analyzing John. She paused for a moment, reluctantly thinking back to the day in that cursed loft where Naoko was taken from her. Shane and Claire made it plain as day that John was out of their trusted circle.

"Alright. I think I'll believe you," Kokoro finally said after the silence had hung between the three. She briefly sunk back into the inner world to Hideaki, hand on his chin thoughtfully. He met her eyes and nodded in concurrence.

"That's not all." John's sudden declaration had snapped Kokoro out of her mind and back to reality. "After that, I told my dad and we started working with the police on them. We managed to get their businesses cut off, some of their partners, but we never could get them directly. Next thing I know, it's a damn corporate war. Board of Directors voted us out, and we were on the street. Didn't stop us, though. We kept informing the police, and doing what we could. Eventually, we found their new place. The police were too slow respondin', so we snuck in and got out as many girls as we could. You included."

Kokoro's eyes shot open. Mr. Haneda had mentioned an informant, one that had helped free them. Could it have really been John?

"That's noble of you," Sayuki said, filling in the silence. "I'm sure…"

"I don't remember that either," Kokoro said, interrupting her friend. She took an apprehensive glance at her friend, then back to John.

"You don't?" he asked warily.

"That day, or any of it," Kokoro replied. "What exactly happened?"

John leaned back in his seat, rubbing his hands together, his curious eyes narrowed. "You don't even remember what you told me?"

Kokoro blinked and shook her head, leaning in to listen.

"You said that you weren't going to make it and you asked me to 'protect your friend.' But that's the thing I don't get. I mean…" he gestured to her. "…you *did* make it. You're sitting right here, for Christ's sake."

Kokoro's body stiffened. She felt Void's, Hideaki, and Sunshine's warm embrace from inside, and Sayuki's reassuring hand on the outside, rubbing her back.

John noticed and held his hands up in a futile attempt to avert the effect of his words. "No, no, I didn't mean-ah, sorry." He sighed, hand on the back of his neck. "Didn't mean it like that. I know you've been through a lot. I just—"

"It's okay, John." Kokoro took a deep, cold breath and met his eyes. "I promise."

"You sure?"

Kokoro nodded.

"If you don't mind me asking, what friend were you talking about? The one I had to protect?" John looked at Sayuki. "It wasn't you, was it?"

"No," Kokoro hesitated, exchanging a quick glance with Sayuki. "I mean, she *is* my friend, but it's complicated. Something I really don't want to talk about, if that's okay."

"'Course," John said, eyeing her with a slight wariness. "Anyway, down to business. The message said you were looking for info on Shane and Claire, right?"

Kokoro nodded quickly. "I want to make sure this doesn't happen to anyone else ever again."

"And how exactly are you planning to do that?" he asked. "Gathering info for the police is one thing, but trying to take them down? I mean, me and Dad had resources and even we barely pulled off saving you. What makes you think you can?"

Kokoro's eyes burned into him, though it wasn't meant to intimidate. The grief that had slowly strangled her for the last few months had finally transformed into something useful: motivation. Fuel for the ever-growing fire burning within her.

"You really want back in?" John stopped, eyeing her. "After what they did to you?"

Hesitation grappled with determination. She had promised herself that she would do anything to protect what was left of Naoko.

And yet…

"Yes," Kokoro finally replied. "More than anything, yes."

The air thinned. John leaned back in his seat, assessing them both. Sayuki slipped her hand into Kokoro's and squeezed as they waited for his answer.

"Alright, then." John closed his eyes and nodded. "Only if you're absolutely sure. Shit's dangerous out there."

Kokoro's brows furrowed. She nodded.

John returned it. "I guess I'll begin with the latest. The good news is that thanks to our snoopin', the police know their names and seized all their assets and properties. They know the last one was an old apartment building, the same one they had you in, which we managed to bust just a few months ago. Saved you and about fifteen other girls, though me and Dad had to jump in before they packed up and left."

"Okay," Sayuki said. "And the bad news?"

John sighed. "Bad news is that they're still up in running in Tokyo somehow. Girls disappear faster than we saved them. Even without their companies, somehow Shane and Claire are makin' enough to keep their hustles going. Dad first suspected that maybe some Yakuza were helping, but—"

"—The Yakuza are hunting them instead," Kokoro said, remembering her conversation with Mr. Haneda in the car a few days prior.

"Yep. From what I hear, they're out for blood. Not too privy to having their territory violated."

"So, who is helping Shane and Claire?" Sayuki asked. "There's no way anyone can fly under the radar for long, especially if the Yakuza are after them."

"Mostly the other gangs, working to keep the police and Yakuza off their ass while they work, and it's mostly been succeeding since the Yakuza don't have the numbers they used to have. Me and Dad informing was giving the police an edge at first, though…" John hesitated, looking out the window, then behind. He turned back and leaned in, "…we found when info was passed to the police, it often took a long time for it to reach the chief. Half the time when they got there, Shane and Claire had already cleared the girls out, like someone warned 'em."

"A traitor?" Sayuki asked.

"Dad thought so," John said. "The police here are pretty good, but they ain't perfect. Corruption's everywhere, unfortunately. Almost makes working with them kinda pointless."

"So, that's where we come in," Kokoro said. "We have to stop Shane and Claire ourselves."

"Gonna be impossible, but yeah. Got some unfinished business with that bastard, anyway," John said, sinking back into his seat. He met her eyes. "That aside, this time, it's going to be different. I won't let them hurt you again, Naoko. That's a promise."

Kokoro briefly shuddered, thinking of her Naoko, of her final smile before being taken by the dark. She shook the memory from her head and managed a weak smile for him.

John returned it. "Anyway, I'm sure you two have to get back." He slid from the booth, hobbled over to the counter, and emptied the remaining contents of his wallet to pay for it. John then poked his head out of the door, eyeing the surroundings. He beckoned them forward and walked them to the edge of the sidewalk, where he waved down a cab to take them home. "You two stay safe and keep in touch, alright? We'll get some plans together and try what we can to find them."

Sayuki opened the door and slid in. Kokoro stopped just before and looked at John.

"What about you?" she asked. "Going back to your dad?"

The gentle smile on John's face faded. He avoided her gaze, shoving his hands in his pockets.

"Dad's dead. They got him the same night we saved you."

Upon hearing the words, something in Kokoro broke, her heart pouring out with it. Assuming what he had told them was true, John had sacrificed everything to save her and the other girls. And now, that sacrifice had cost him his father.

"I didn't know that. I'm sorry, John." Kokoro frowned. "Where are you staying?"

"I'll find somewhere." He smiled, though his eyes quivered. "Don't you worry."

Kokoro bit her lip as he turned away. After all, this was the man who had saved her not once, but twice. Despite losing everything, even his father, he continued on, determined to stop his former friends. She wanted more than anything to pay him back for all the good he had done.

That, and she knew what it was like to be alone. She didn't want him to have to endure that anymore.

Her heart twisted in her chest, a strange sense of warmth filling her. Without warning, she pushed forward and latched onto him.

Kokoro blinked in surprise. She turned back into the inner world, seeing Sunshine next to her. The young girl's cheeks flushed.

"Sorry," Sunshine said, slowly letting Kokoro front again. "I didn't mean to snatch. He looks lonely, and I just wanted him to feel better."

Kokoro met the young girl's wide, innocent eyes that, along with her hair, emanated a light of their own. This was the thing she admired so much about Sunshine: her being a light to everyone around her.

"I know," she finally said, smiling. "I was thinking the same thing."

Sunshine beamed and disappeared into the mist, leaving Kokoro in control. She blinked, and she was back in the real world, embracing John.

At first, he stiffened, as if unsure of how to react. Slowly, he returned the hug, his brows creased.

"Thanks, Naoko. I needed that."

"Come with us," she said. "I can talk to my father. He can…"

He pulled back. "Thanks, but I can't. Only a matter of time 'fore I end up like Dad."

"A matter of time?" Sayuki asked, looking at Kokoro as she frowned.

"Yeah," John said, eyes downcast. "Shane and Claire know what me and Dad were doing. They've got their goons out and about, tryin' to find me."

Suddenly, everything made sense. The reason he wore the hood, why he hid his face behind the menu and stuck to the shadows. Shane and Claire knew what he was doing and wanted him dead. By heeding their request to meet somewhere public, he was willingly putting himself in danger, just so they could feel comfortable and safe. Kokoro bit her lip.

How could I have misjudged him?

"Please." She immediately gripped his wrists, her pleading eyes gazing into his. "I don't want to lose you, too."

Kokoro held the stare with Naoko's friend for what felt like forever. He then sighed, finally giving in. They slid into the cab along with Sayuki, and soon the car took off into the silence of the cold Tokyo night.

CHAPTER 13

TAINT OF COWARDICE

"ARE YOU SURE ABOUT THIS?" SAYUKI WHISPERED to Kokoro as the cab took off from the curb.

"Positive," she replied, glancing over at John as he stared out the window. In his ears were a pair of cheap headphones, music turned so loud that everyone in the car could hear it.

Sayuki sighed. "If you're sure. Besides, what is your father going to say?"

Kokoro paused. It wasn't something she had considered when she asked him to come along. She was more concerned that the man who saved her life not once, but twice, had lost everything because of what he had done for her. It didn't matter if her father agreed or not. Somehow, she *would* repay the favor.

"He'll understand. If not…" Kokoro glanced at her friend. "…then I'll figure something out. We owe him."

Sayuki nodded, lowering her eyes, her lip curled. From inside, Kokoro felt a strange sensation, possibly a bleed-through emotion from one of the others. Her eyes locked on her friend, and suddenly she wanted nothing more than to smother her in as many hugs as she could provide. She shook her head, letting herself drift back inward to make sure she didn't address her counterparts out loud. "Sunshine, is that you again?"

"Sorry!" the real world vanished, replaced with their inner one as Sunshine materialized next to Kokoro. Fishy was clutched to her chest, occasionally shifting in her arms. "I figured she needed a hug, too."

"No, she's just jealous, you idiot," a voice said. Ikiryo walked out from the mists. She regarded the young girl with a careless stare. "You're probably the only stupid enough not to know it at this point."

"That's not nice!" The glow in Sunshine's hair and eyes faded slightly. Ikiryo scoffed.

"So?"

"You. Back off," Kokoro stepped up to her, meeting her challenge. She shook her head. "Why are you so damn critical all the time? Why can't you just get along with everyone?"

Ikiryo's stare solidified, brows furrowing. "How would you feel if I told you to just stop being you? I am what I am."

Kokoro clenched her jaw. It was hard for her to imagine why someone like that would manifest in Naoko's mind. What was she, anyway? What purpose did someone like her serve?

"Fine," Kokoro finally said. "Do what you want, just not here. We don't need someone like you around. All you do is make your stupid comments and put people down. It's fine if you're miserable. Just don't drag down any of us with you!"

Ikiryo's glare wavered, if only briefly. She stepped forward, only to be stopped by Sunshine.

"Both of you, stop!" Sunshine begged, trying to push them apart, desperately flaring her light. At her touch, Kokoro felt torn, like the light and dark were trying to pull her apart at the seams. Something rushed into her from Ikiryo, faded images interspersed with vivid emotion that blurred and twisted together. Finally, it solidified into memory, streets stretching out, tall buildings with endless light stretching as far as the eye could see until it had formed the Tokyo that she had known her entire existence.

Kokoro blinked and looked forward. Ikiryo was walking ahead, hands tucked into pockets as she walked forward, eyes downcast, avoiding the world around her.

What is this? Kokoro's eyes widened as she watched Ikiryo. *A memory?*

Another blur of light and shadow and she was in a classroom, seated in front of Naoko's old teacher, Mr. Takeda. The rest of the class's faces were unreadable, plain. Soulless.

"No problem, Mr. Takeda," a girl seated next to Ikiryo quipped. "Naoko's all over it. She seems more the type for girls, anyway."

Next to him was her friend Sayuki, though she was like she was before Kokoro ever met her: insecurity buried beneath the facade of arrogance.

Ikiryo's brows furrowed, teeth grit. Kokoro could feel rage, hurt emanating from her like steam from a smoldering rock. Above all, she felt something else, something worse: the need to bite back.

"At least I didn't *kiss* a girl," Ikiryo hissed.

Memory-Sayuki's cheeks flushed red as laughter echoed. Kokoro's eyes widened in realization.

This isn't just Ikiryo's memory. This is Naoko's too!

Their surroundings shifted again in the blink of an eye. Ikiryo was sitting and chatting away with Claire as she brushed and sprayed her hair. The images blurred, then refocused as she saw Ikiryo smirking and strutting down the stairs to the synthetic beat. It wasn't long until she was on the dancefloor, her eyes glossed over, the image shifting between a worried Naoko in a yellow sunflower shirt and Ikiryo in the viridescent green dress as she lost herself in the euphoria.

Kokoro blinked. She was back at the Solamachi Village, at the base of the Skytree, though this time it seemed different. Unstable. The area around her was warped as well, fading from solid to black as if in peripherals. She clutched her throbbing head, trying to find something, anything, to latch onto.

Just then, she saw something. A girl dressed in a tank top and jean shorts up ahead, black hair a waterfall past her shoulders. Her eyes widened.

Naoko?

"You…you're okay!" Heart fluttering, Kokoro stepped forward. "I can't believe—"

"What are you, my mother? Or better yet, my father? Or maybe you're more patronizing than both combined?"

She froze at the familiarity of those words; one of the last Naoko had ever spoken to her. Her brows furrowed, her eyes burning into Kokoro. Behind her was the silhouette of a woman, one that solidified, shadow morphing into black leather clothing with interspersed blood laces. The now-recognizable face held a jealousy that was unmistakably focused on Kokoro.

"Ikiryo?"

Ikiryo blinked. Her glare faded, replaced with something resembling shame.

"The things she said. That was you?" Another thought hit Kokoro, remembering when Hideaki had called her 'elusive.' Her eyes flicked to Ikiryo. "You were there the whole time…*hiding*."

Ikiryo avoided her gaze, bangs shielding her eyes from view. She slowly nodded. Kokoro's chest tightened. Her lip quivered.

"You *bitch*."

Ikiryo faced her again but stopped. She slowly turned around, eyes widening in horror as a familiar thick metal door appeared behind her.

"Ikiryo?" Kokoro asked warily. "Is that what I think it is?"

Panic immediately set in Ikiryo's eyes. "No…no, no, please don't."

Kokoro eyed her for a moment, then huffed. "You have a memory there too, don't you? The day I lost her?"

Ikiryo stood silent. Kokoro pushed past her.

"No! Please!" The girl's breaths became shallow as she tried to grab Kokoro. "I'll do anything! Just don't—"

The streets faded, the blurred area around them darkened. Behind Ikiryo were a set of shadowy figures, greedy hands reaching out to grab her. Her eyes widened, her entire body so still it was like a tree.

"—I didn't mean it. What I said earlier," a familiar voice said.

Kokoro tensed as her gaze followed it. The figure of Naoko was there once more, but she was frozen, tears streaming down her face. It was the moment that had changed everything. She continued to watch, seeing her memory doppelgänger pierce the mist, calling desperately for help.

Kokoro looked over at Ikiryo. Her earlier stillness vanished as she shook. Her eyes darted between Naoko and the hands that reached to grab her.

"Come on, come on, Ikiryo!" she told herself, shaking her head. "Protect Naoko. You…"

Ikiryo froze. The shadowy hands moved past Naoko and Kokoro, then reached for her, twisting like vipers following their prey.

"No…no!"

Ikiryo screamed, turned, and ran. The memory faded as she continued to sprint away from the blackened tendrils. She broke through the barrier between the darkness and the rows of Sakura that made up the world Kokoro had made for Naoko. Catching her breath, she leaned against the trunk. She then slid down, tucking knees to chest, face rigid as she processed her own cowardice. The tears began as the petals fell to the ground and died around her.

"Naoko," Ikiryo rasped. "I'm so, *so* sorry."

The vision shattered as Ikiryo pulled away from her and Sunshine, chest heaving. Her eyes locked with Kokoro's, though the anger from earlier had faded. Instead, her usually arrogant eyes held only pain.

"You…you were there with Naoko. Even when they took her," Kokoro said, her voice threatening to break. "You abandoned her."

Ikiryo grit her teeth, eyes glistening, as if trying so desperately to keep herself under control. The silence between them at that moment was louder than even the morning train. With one last shameful look, Ikiryo turned and sprinted into the mists.

"Wait!" Kokoro called out.

Something stopped her. Void and Hideaki had materialized in front of her, blocking her path.

"What are you doing?" Kokoro asked. "Let me go. She…"

"Leave her," Hideaki said, his eyes lowered. "Please. It's a lot for both of you to process, her included."

"But…"

"He's right." Sunshine frowned. "She's just dealing with too much bad stuff right now."

Kokoro frowned, gazing ahead worriedly. Despite her having abandoned Naoko when she was needed the most, she couldn't help but feel pity for her.

"Isn't there anything we can do?"

"She'll be fine," Hideaki reassured her. "For now, we've got to get back."

Kokoro looked at the swirling mists that had taken Ikiryo. Reluctantly, she turned away, letting the painful truth sink in.

"Kokoro?" Sayuki whispered, nudging her. "We're almost there."

She blinked until her surroundings came back into focus. John had woken up from his nap and was pulling his headphones from his ears while Sayuki was wrapping up her coat. Naoko's house wasn't much further.

She sighed and stretched, her mind still on Ikiryo's memories. All this time, she was there, even before Kokoro had existed. And yet, she ran away, just when Naoko needed her the most.

It should have happened to her, the cowardly bitch. Kokoro shook her head, immediately feeling shame. How could she ever wish evil like that upon someone, even Ikiryo?

The taxi pulled along the side of the driveway, the final jolt shaking her from her thoughts. The three of them quickly opened the door and slid out. Kokoro quickly bowed and paid the driver.

"Nice little place you have ere'," John said, eyeing her house. "Are you sure about this? You really think your dad will let me chill for the night?"

Kokoro pursed her lips. She didn't know for sure, but she was determined not to let him freeze out in the snow. She nodded, pushed forward, and knocked.

For a moment, there was no reply. Next came the click of the four locks, then finally the door creaked open to reveal Mr. Haneda.

"Naoko?" he asked. "You're late. What were you…" He froze, then stepped forward, eyes narrowing in disbelief. "*John*? Is that you?"

Throwing his hood back, John nodded with a weak smile. After staring for a solid minute, Mr. Haneda stepped forward with a quick bow. After that, he latched onto him with a smile.

"It is you!" He pulled back from the hug, beaming. "Ah! You're alive! We were worried after you disappeared from the station!"

"Yes sir," John replied, laughing. "Don't worry. They didn't get me yet."

Mr. Haneda turned to Kokoro and nodded. Then he placed a hand on Sayuki and Kokoro's back, glancing around and pushing them toward the door. "Well, we should get inside. Quickly."

Kokoro nodded and obeyed. Soon enough, all three of them were in the dining room, shoes removed, as Mr. Haneda quickly secured the door. Naoko's mother walked in from the living room, eyes narrowed.

"Oh. Do we have another guest?" she asked, eyeing John's unkempt appearance.

"Hana." Mr. Haneda walked over to her, leaned in and whispered. Her eyes widened.

"Wait. John?" she asked, tears forming in her eyes. She quickly moved and gave him a quick hug. "You brought our sweet girl back. I'm glad I finally get to thank you in person."

The skin on John's cheekbones suddenly lightened as he returned it. To them, he was the man who had brought Naoko back to them. To Kokoro, he was the one who tried. How would they react if they knew the truth?

Even more reason to keep it secret.

"Well…" Naoko's parents smiled warmly at John, then Sayuki. "Can we get you two something to eat?"

"I'm alright," John said with a quick, awkward bow. "I…uh, appreciate it, though."

"Are you sure?" Mrs. Haneda asked. "I mean, we must do something to repay you. I'm sure—"

"John has nowhere to go," Kokoro suddenly blurted out in a slightly higher pitch, blinking in confusion. "Can he stay with us tonight?"

The entire room first turned to her, then back to John, whose eyes were downcast. All it took was a quick glance and they were in agreement.

"Of course," Naoko's parents said in unison. John's eyes widened, his lip quivered as he smiled weakly. Kokoro could tell this was the first bit of kindness that anyone had shown him in forever, if any. She didn't know exactly what he was feeling, but if she had to guess, he must have felt a heavy weight lifted from his shoulders, if only for the moment.

"Thank you." John turned to Kokoro and Sayuki. "Thank you all."

Kokoro returned it. She felt another presence nearby: bright, warm, and brimming with love. She turned to find Sunshine next to her. A youthful smile that could outshine any star adorned her puffy little face.

"You again, huh?" Kokoro asked.

Sunshine beamed with pride. "Yup. You were taking too long."

Kokoro shook her head and smiled. Mrs. Haneda took a whiff of John, her nose crinkling.

"Uh, sorry about that." John chuckled nervously. "Don't mean to be pushy, but do you guys mind if I shower too, or…?"

"Yes, absolutely!" Naoko's mother quickly said, nodding. "In fact, you can take one now!"

"I don't have a change of clothes." His cheeks flushed. "Maybe I can run to the store, and…"

"I have something you can borrow," Naoko's dad said, pushing past them to guide John up the stairs and out of sight.

Kokoro and Sayuki exchanged glances, then burst into laughter. Polite as they tried to be, the one thing Naoko's parents never tolerated was a bad smell.

Time had passed quicker than she realized. Next came the slow, irregular thumping of feet down the carpet stairs. John emerged, clad in a pair of Mr. Haneda's pajamas. Kokoro and Sayuki pursed their lips to resist giggling.

"Cozy?" she asked teasingly.

John rolled his eyes. "Haha yeah, funny. It's just for a bit while my clothes wash." He sighed and made his way back into the living room with her and Sayuki, laying against the couch, elbows on knees. Kokoro watched as he dipped his head, letting out all the tension in his body with a deep sigh. He looked up and met Kokoro's eyes. "You know, you didn't have to do this, but…I did need it. Appreciate you lookin' out for me."

Kokoro beamed. "It's what friends are for, right?"

"Funny you say that." John shifted, let his legs stretch out as he laid against the chair. "After the company went under, I didn't think I had any left. It felt like it was just me and Dad against all that bullshit."

"You don't want to go home?" Sayuki asked.

"I do. All the damn time, actually," John said, chuckling. "But right now…I just can't."

"Why not?" Kokoro asked, arching an eyebrow. "Did they not offer to take you back?"

"As a matter o' fact, the Government was about to ship my ass home on a plane. I mean, I thought about it. But knowing what Shane and Claire were doing? I just couldn't. But now that Dad's gone, I don't know anymore." John's eyes lowered in defeat. "Honestly, maybe I should. It's starting to wear on me a bit."

"I don't want to see you go, but…" Kokoro smiled sadly. "I understand. You've done enough for us."

John met her gaze, the apprehension in his eyes evident. Kokoro could almost see his wounded soul behind them, fighting, tearing itself to pieces in agony over his next answer. They held the stare for about a solid minute until he finally opened his mouth to speak.

"I made a promise, didn't I?"

Kokoro blinked. "Are you sure?"

"More than anything." The conflict in John's eyes faded completely. His brows furrowed. "I've gotta put a stop to this. The bastard and bitch are going down."

"Same here," Sayuki added. "Whatever we have to do. Whatever comes next."

Kokoro smiled at her friends, nodding. She turned to John. "So, any new info from that PULSE forum?"

"Damn right." John grinned, pulling out his cracked phone. "A couple of users were keepin an eye out found where Claire's been snoopin' for new girls. I was looking to scope it out in the morning."

"You're not going without us, are you?" Sayuki asked.

"'Course not. This is your fight too, ain't it?" John balled his hand and held it in front of him. Kokoro smiled and bumped fists with him, looking at Sayuki until she finally joined.

John eyed them both as if looking for any sign of hesitancy in their eyes. "Alright, it's settled then." He nodded as the three of them withdrew. "First thing in the morning. We'll find Claire and figure out what the hell is going on."

"Hope so," Kokoro said with a weak smile. Truthfully, she wasn't even sure if they could. Even so, it made Kokoro feel better knowing that she was finally doing something instead of wallowing in grief.

"We will," John reiterated, returning it. He yawned and stretched out on the couch, one hand behind his head as he scrolled his phone. "You two sleep well now."

Kokoro and Sayuki nodded and stood to their feet in unison. The two girls headed upstairs into her room, closing the door. Sayuki yawned and plugged in her phone. Kokoro did the same and opened her drawer, pulling out a set of pajamas.

"Think we'll find anything?" her friend asked.

"Who knows?" Kokoro began to pull her shirt over her head, but stopped upon noticing Sayuki, whose wide eyes were fixated on her, her cheeks red. Kokoro felt her own face warm as she slowly pulled her sweater back down. "Err…sorry."

"Um…it's fine!" Sayuki beamed nervously, collected her night clothes from her bag and shuffled out of the door. "I'll, uh, just change somewhere else."

The door slammed shut, footsteps thumped against the carpet floor as her friend made her way to the restroom. Kokoro resumed changing and soon donned her pajamas. For reasons she understood but didn't want to acknowledge, she shifted over to her mirror and messed with her pale hair, brushing half of it behind her ear.

"You know, I'm not one to agree with Ikiryo," a voice said, "but her body language shows that she seems to like you."

Kokoro blinked, then resumed messing with her hair. "She tried to kiss us, so believe me. I know."

Hideaki materialized in her reflection behind her, eyes halfway hidden in his shimmering glasses. "You know, this is not really my thing, but it's painfully obvious. I think you like her, too."

"It's always nice to hear from you, Hideaki," Kokoro said, brushing one side, "but you assume too much."

Hideaki crossed his arms. Kokoro sighed.

"Okay, maybe a little." She sped up her brushing, her comb now gliding through her hair. "But that wouldn't be fair to you guys, would it? We're all in this together. I can't just…"

"It's fine with me!" another, higher-pitched voice said. Sunshine, with Fishy in her arms, came into view in her mind's eye next to Hideaki. "I like her. She's really sweet."

Kokoro continued to brush, glancing at Sunshine before turning her gaze back to her hair. "Okay. What about Ikiryo? She didn't seem to like Sayuki very much." She paused, thinking back to the time she had taken control specifically to rebuke Sayuki in what she claimed to be defense of Naoko's memory.

Even so, Ikiryo abandoned Naoko. Makes her a bit of a hypocrite, doesn't it?

Kokoro sighed, brushing the other side of her hair, gazing at her reflection. She stopped, slowly putting down the brush as a realization hit her. When Ikiryo insisted she felt the same, she wasn't talking about her, 'Kokoro.'

She was talking about Naoko. Her feelings, not mine.

Kokoro frowned and looked in the mirror. Despite the differences, sometimes she couldn't help but see it as *Naoko's* body. Even though she was gone, she couldn't disrespect her memory by becoming *that* close to the girl that tormented her all those years, whether she liked her or not.

"I'm sorry, guys," Kokoro finally said. "I do like her, but I just can't."

Sunshine's light dimmed as her lip curled. Hideaki closed his eyes and dipped his head. "We understand. Just know that whatever you decide, we support you."

Kokoro smiled weakly. "Thanks, guys."

They nodded and vanished just as a knock came at the door. Kokoro slid it open to find Sayuki, dressed in her nightclothes, though something was different. Her hair was brushed as well, albeit with a bow that tied it into a pretty ponytail.

Kokoro blushed. She moved aside and beckoned her friend into the room. Sayuki gently sat on her mat next to Kokoro's bed that she had set up from the previous days, her legs tucked to the side as she leaned on her arm. She met Kokoro's eyes, her gaze soft.

Kokoro gazed back at her. The room fell silent. She carefully sat down on her bed, gripping her pajama legs as she fought the urge to jump into Sayuki's arms.

"You look nice," Kokoro finally said, chuckling nervously. "Especially for bedtime."

Sayuki smiled, twirling some of her hair in her finger. "Thanks. So do you. You always look nice."

Kokoro blushed and quickly looked away. She settled under her sheets, turning the other way so Sayuki couldn't see how red her face had become. She heard her do the same, her movements slow as she too laid on her mat.

"Well…" Sayuki began, disappointment evident in her voice. "…goodnight, Kokoro. See you in the morning."

Silence filled the air for about five seconds before Kokoro shattered it with her impatience.

"Okay, okay, I'm sorry!" Kokoro spun to face her, digging her hands through her hair in frustration. "I know you like me. I like you too, but…I just can't."

Sayuki turned around, frowning. "Why not?"

"Because it's…" Her lips quivered as she struggled with the words. She gestured to the body as she spoke, "…it's me, yet it's still *her*. I do feel that way about you, but Naoko—"

"—hated me," Sayuki finished for her.

Kokoro bit her lip and nodded.

Sayuki laid on her back, her hands resting on her belly. "I know. I deserved it for the way I treated her. If I could go back, knowing then what I do now, I'd do it all differently."

"How so?" Kokoro asked.

"For one, I wouldn't have treated her like that. If I had just been honest with myself, maybe things would have been different. Maybe I would have had a chance with her."

Kokoro's eyes widened. "You mean…?"

"Yeah." Sayuki faced her, eyes downcast. "I liked her. Even back then."

"Oh." Kokoro blinked. "Not to be mean, but you sure had a funny way of showing it."

Sayuki's cheeks flushed. "People grow, don't they?"

"They do, yes." Kokoro chuckled, then relaxed, her eyes on the ceiling.

"Hey, Kokoro?"

"Yeah?"

"I gotta ask. The entire time we were friends, was any of it her? Or was it all you?"

Kokoro frowned. "Pretty much just me. I was trying to get her to come around on you, and she almost did, but…"

"…you ran out of time. I figured." Sayuki frowned. "I'm sorry."

"Yeah. She was my butterfly," Kokoro said, her voice cracking. "I miss her, Sayuki. I miss her so much."

Despite keeping her eyes up, Kokoro felt Sayuki's pitying gaze focused on her. Sayuki eventually did the same as Kokoro, her eyes staring up at the stars.

Kokoro blinked as she felt Sayuki's hand rest on hers. She hesitated for a moment, then gripped it tight. They stayed that way, never moving until the numbing darkness took her.

CHAPTER 14
PART OF THAT WORLD

"HEY," A GENTLE, FEMININE VOICE SAID. "Wake up, sleepyhead."

Hideaki startled awake. The darkness vanished in a flash, replaced with Kokoro's room. In front of him was Sayuki, leaning forward, her face inches from his. He instinctively recoiled.

"Wait, did I scare you?" Sayuki pulled back. "I'm sorry. I wasn't trying anything, I just—"

"I know," he said quickly, standing to his feet and greeting her with a quick bow. Sayuki arched an eyebrow.

"Hey, wait. You're one of the others, aren't you?"

"Hideaki," he said, reaching to push up the glasses he normally wore, but finding there were none. He felt naked without them. His own voice also felt so foreign to him, every utterance done in a feminine tone that didn't suit his words.

"Oh. Hi, Hideaki. It's good to see you again." Sayuki's cheeks flushed. "Sorry, I'm still just not used to this."

"It's quite alright," Hideaki reassured her, glancing down at Kokoro's body. "I'd be lying if I said I was too. I'm trying my best to understand it all and try to organize us, if that makes any sense."

"I think so." Sayuki's nose crinkled. "I don't mean to be rude, but is Kokoro in there?"

Hideaki paused. He slowed his breathing, closing his eyes and trying to sink back into the inner world. He looked around the swirling mists, then tried to walk through them, but found he couldn't. The vague world behind it seemed to stretch back farther from him, denying him.

What's going on? Where is everyone?

He turned, still seeing the real world close to him, the light from it pulsing, beckoning him to stay in control. The mists seemed to breathe slow and steady, as if they were asleep. Perhaps Kokoro was, too.

Hideaki sighed. A blur of light and shadow later and he was back in front. "She's probably just resting."

Sayuki frowned. "But she's okay, right?"

Hideaki met her concerned gaze and gave her a reassuring smile. "I promise."

"If you're sure..."

"I am, I assure you. Whatever needs to be done today, I'm more than capable of handling it."

"Okay. Good." Sayuki beamed nervously. "So, I guess you're gonna help us find Claire, then?"

Hideaki's brows furrowed upon the mention of the name. He didn't have the same hatred for her Kokoro held, and yet, it still unnerved him. After all, wasn't Claire the reason for their previous host disappearing? He didn't know Naoko much at all, and he wasn't around to experience what had happened to her and Kokoro. Despite that, he still wanted to help achieve justice in any way he could.

"Right," he finally told Sayuki. "I'll do what I can."

Also, it's probably better that I investigate this than Kokoro. I can look at things more objectively.

"Good." Sayuki blinked. "So, I guess that means we should get ready then, huh?"

Hideaki glanced around the room, then his eyes fixed on the dresser. He pulled open the drawers and sifted through, looking for something warm to wear. If the last few days were any metric to judge the rather frigid weather, then he would need at least two layers to keep the body warm.

Also, something to make her less conspicuous. A strand of ghost-white hair fell across his eye. *She'll stick out like a sore thumb otherwise.*

He stopped, feeling Sayuki's gaze intensifying. He spun to face her. "Err...I don't mean to be rude, but..."

"What?" Sayuki snapped out of her trance, her face flushed. "Oh. Right. I'll just…um…"

A second later, the door slid shut behind her. Hideaki sighed, pulling off the pajamas and sliding on a soft pair of jeans, a plain blue hoodie, and a thick top overcoat with a ball cap. He inspected himself in the mirror, tucking in as much of the body's hair as he could, pulling the hood over when he was finished.

Hideaki nodded with satisfaction and stepped out of the room, descending the steps with precision. At the bottom stood a still-blushing Sayuki and a cleaned-up John stood with Mr. Haneda. He turned to Hideaki and smiled.

"Good morning," Mr. Haneda said with a smile, then cocked his head. "Are you going somewhere today?"

"We were going to…ah…" Hideaki eyed John and Sayuki, hoping one of them would intervene. In the time he woke up to now, he had thought of practically everything about their day except a good excuse to leave the house.

"Actually, they were gonna see me off, sir," John said. "I was heading out here in a bit."

Hideaki sighed gratefully, which earned an eyebrow raise from Mr. Haneda. He turned back to John and frowned. "You're not staying longer?"

"'Fraid I can't," John replied with a weak smile. "But I appreciate everything you and the missus have done for me."

"Of course." Mr. Haneda regarded him with a nod. "But where will you go?"

"I…" John briefly eyed Hideaki. "…an old friend is in town. Gonna try to catch her if I can."

"I see." Mr. Haneda turned to Hideaki and Sayuki. "And you wish to go with him?"

"With your permission, Father," Hideaki said with a sharp bow, drawing raised eyebrows from both John and Mr. Haneda. Sayuki watched nervously, being the only one who knew that Hideaki was the one in control. His cheeks flushed slightly as he realized his mannerisms were far too different from Kokoro's. At the very least, she could mimic their original host better than he could ever hope to.

"Hmm. Alright. But remember the rules," Mr. Haneda said. "Check in every hour and be back by seven tonight."

"Yes, sir," Hideaki said. As they prepared to step outside, Mr. Haneda stepped forward.

"Oh, John. One more thing." His brows furrowed slightly. "That…*thing* we discussed last night. I'll look into it." His gaze fell, and his face hardened. "Though I hope it isn't true. For their sake."

"For the record, I hope not either, sir," John replied. "But just to be sure."

"Just to be sure," Mr. Haneda repeated. John held out his hand, and he took it, eyeing him with resolute respect. "You stay safe. Okay, John?"

John nodded and soon the three were out the door, walking down the sidewalk as Mr. Haneda eyed them from the driveway. Then they rounded the corner, walked down the long street, and arrived at the train station. Hideaki quickly swiped the cards and waved them through the terminal.

"Ahh," John said, stretching. "Feels damn good to be in some clean clothes again. Thanks for letting me stay, by the way. I appreciate it."

Hideaki nodded quickly, his forward gaze never wavering. "You're welcome, John."

"You alright, mate?" John arched an eyebrow. "You actin' kinda stiff this morning."

"Just…" Hideaki paused, trying to think of a valid explanation that might temper John's newfound curiosity. "…not feeling myself. Didn't sleep that well."

"Ah." John nodded, apparently satisfied. "Understandable."

"So, Claire." Hideaki turned to John. "Where is she operating?"

"If the forums are right, by Shibuya Crossing," he answered, reading from the PULSE app on his phone. "Offering drugs, throwin' parties, anything to lure them in like they did you. Mostly, she sticks to the back alleys and deep clubs, but she's also been seen out in the open once or twice."

As John said the words, half-formed memories of the body running through the rain-drenched streets, the soaked hospital gown weighing it down filled his mind. A foreign sensation, yet intimately familiar.

Ironic that we're now going back to where it all began.

"I see," Hideaki replied to John, pushing Kokoro's drifting memory from his mind. "And you're sure it's her?"

"Pretty sure," he said. "Photos from the forum were blurry, but I'd recognize her anywhere. Doesn't matter if she changed her hair or not."

"Ah." Hideaki nodded. "What about Shane? Is he nearby too?"

"No, unfortunately. Haven't been able to get a beat on him, damn snake. Doesn't matter much though, because…"

"…Claire can lead us to him?" Hideaki finished for him.

"Now you got the idea, mate." John grinned. "For now, we just gotta hold back and observe. Would be reckless to go in and face her head-on. She's still got guards hangin' around somewhere, I'm sure."

"Agreed," Hideaki said, pulling his hood forward. "But assuming we manage to locate Claire, Shane, or both." He looked at John. "What then?"

"Well…" John hesitated. "This is the part you won't like. You remember when I saw when we formally informed the police? How it seemed like the info got slowed the minute it got to the station?"

Hideaki nodded.

"So, we jump the chain," John said. "We go straight to your dad and have him bring the whole damn force down on their asses. And if we can get our hands on Shane and Claire ourselves…" He cracked his knuckles. "Even better."

John looked over at him, eyes filled with anticipation, perhaps expecting a complaint or rejection.

"That…sounds good to me." Hideaki nodded in approval. "Logical."

John returned it, albeit with a confused look on his face. The train soon arrived and the three of them shuffled in. John and Hideaki grabbed a support ring as Sayuki took a seat. She shifted around a moment, then briefly eyed him.

She's wondering about Kokoro. Can't suppose I blame her.

With that thought, Hideaki paused and closed his eyes, and once more allowed himself to sink back into the beginning of the inner world. He was met with the same shifting mists that refused to let him pass.

Hideaki sighed and pulled himself back out. Time, like the low-crop buildings, trees, and eventually skyscrapers outside the window, seemed to blur, the train wheels rolling rhythmically along the tracks. With a chime, he, John, and Sayuki had reached their destination: Shibuya Crossing, often called the 'Heart of Tokyo.' It made sense to him that Claire would pick such a place as her new prowling grounds.

"Come on," John said, gesturing Hideaki forward with his hood up. Before he could move, Sayuki scooted close and locked arms with him. He briefly recoiled, then forced himself to relax. Just the day before, he had signaled his support for them, but being in the middle was far harder than he thought. Sex, love, intimacy—these were foreign concepts to him. Not bad by any means, but simply…unappealing.

The three of them moved forward, off the train, out of the station and into the churning crowds. His and Sayuki's locked arms drew the occasional arched eyebrow from passersby, though thankfully not many. Hideaki preferred it that way. The less attention, the better.

He looked up. They were now near the crossing, crowds of people walking down the lines to make their way across the street. It was haphazard yet organized. The perfect blend of manic chaos and orderly synchronization.

Just like us.

With Sayuki's arm still looped in his and John leading them, Hideaki inspected the faces of those who passed by. Despite being a prominent member in the system, when he tried to pull a mental image of Claire, his mind went…blank. Instead, he focused on looking for signs of blonde hair: not exactly perfect, but a good place to start, and John could easily decipher his former friend from the rest.

Strangely, a hint of excitement brimmed just beneath the surface. Remembering Kokoro's words from the psych ward, Hideaki paused, contemplating that feeling, trying to place it. To *understand* it.

Ah. Once Hideaki realized what it was, he nodded, satisfied. *Naoko's father is a detective. Maybe I'm taking after him more and more.*

Hideaki pulled himself from his thoughts, feeling Sayuki gripping his arm tighter. He turned, whispering, "Are you alright?"

"I…" Sayuki hesitated. "I've been here so many times. But this time, knowing what's out there? It feels so…" She trailed off.

"Dangerous?"

Sayuki nodded. Hideaki placed his hand on hers reassuringly.

"I may not be Kokoro," he said. "But don't think for a moment that I won't protect you like she would. If you're important to her, then you're important to me."

A spark of warmth spread across Sayuki's face, and her timidity melted away, replaced with the gentlest of smiles. Together, they walked out of the crossing and into one of the alcoves, endless hanging lights and stores lined up on either side. A group of young girls were performing nearby, dancing with near-perfect synchronicity.

Perfect targets for her, he thought, glancing around. *Are we getting closer?*

"There!" John said, tapping Hideaki on the shoulder, stopping him in his tracks. Further ahead, past the alcove, was a shopping center, filled to the brim with people. Near the entrance to the store was another group of young women, the sounds of laughter and giggling constantly erupted as they ignored the world outside. In the middle was a foreigner girl, who held their attention like nothing else mattered. Her now-blonde hair was cropped just above her shoulders, over her thick fur jacket and tight jeans. Her shrill, confident voice seemed to penetrate both the obscuring mental fog from earlier and the crowd, drawing even more poor girls in with an authenticity as faux as her soul.

It was Claire Hanson, the woman who had taken their first host from Kokoro. From them *all.*

Hideaki's eyes widened. His heart twisted in his chest as he felt something trying to erupt from within—a feeling. What was this?

Rage? It kept growing, his head throbbing as he fought to keep from being pulled back into the dark.

Damn it, Hideaki thought as he continued to pull himself into focus again and again. *Where's Void when you need him?*

Sayuki took notice as Hideaki pulled off to the side, clutching the body's forehead, sweat beading down. Whoever was trying to force their way into the front was vehemently determined…and beyond furious.

Hideaki gritted his teeth, focusing ahead on Claire. He felt tempted to give in, to lunge at her and beat her for what they had done. But he couldn't…no, he *wouldn't*. Someone had to keep a level head. Someone had to keep them organized, focused, and wise. And unless he wanted everything to fall apart, that someone *had* to be him.

For now, all he had to do was keep whoever was pulling at bay long enough to gather the intel they needed. Then perhaps, in time, they could find the missing girls and give Naoko the justice that she deserved.

When Kokoro awoke, it felt like she was in a dream. The inner world had changed, expanded. The lone Sakura that had been the center before had grown taller, its petals bright and vibrant, yet never leaving their branches.

She stared up at it, pondering it for a moment before she shook herself out of it. There was no time for this; they were supposed to track down Claire.

Kokoro tried to walk into the mist, back into control of the body but found that she couldn't. The mist seemed to both stretch infinitely and push her back, denying her.

"Damn it," she hissed, seeing no other option but to turn back around to the Sakura. She spun, then stopped in her tracks. Now, there was a small stream that flowed from the raised base of the tree, down to the infinite nothing of their world. Against the branch, leaned Ikiryo, legs tucked in and arms resting on them, head hidden in her pitch-black hair.

So, this is where she ran off to. Kokoro tensed. *I suppose it makes sense. She is a coward, after all.*

Ikiryo was whispering something to herself, over and over. They were her own, poison-filled words, aimed back at herself.

"Ikiryo?"

The girl stopped and turned to meet Kokoro's gaze, eyes drowning in pain. Kokoro could see memories in each drop, and with them, deep regret. Her nails dug into her arms, tiny drops of blood falling into the stream, along with her tears. Her form seemed to flicker as if it were a dim flame that threatened to extinguish forever.

Kokoro stayed put as she watched Ikiryo cry. She could feel her struggle to keep the pain from bleeding out, and yet, it still did. Her heart was like a shattered dam, its humiliating contents out for the world to see. Not really knowing how to break the ice, Kokoro said the first stupid thing that came to her mind.

"Fancy seeing you again."

Ikiryo stopped crying, if only to regard Kokoro with an annoyed look. She groaned and rested her chin back on her knees.

"What are you doing here?"

"The question is," Kokoro asked, "what are *you* doing here?"

"What do you think?"

Kokoro frowned. She slowly lowered her back against the trunk opposite Ikiryo. For a long moment, they sat in silence, hearing only the whisking of the branches.

"Feel like talking about it?"

A wry chuckle escaped Ikiryo's crimson lips. "Sounds like I don't have much of a choice."

"Not if you don't want to," Kokoro said. "I would never force you."

"That's…" Ikiryo perked up, surprise manifesting as an arched eyebrow. "…not what I expected. I would have thought that you'd beat me down until you were satisfied and then some."

"Not gonna lie, I thought about it," Kokoro admitted. The conversation drifted into silence once again. Ikiryo dipped her head to avoid Kokoro's piercing gaze.

"Go ahead," Ikiryo said, her voice almost hushed. "It's what I deserve."

"No, it isn't." Kokoro frowned. "You don't deserve to be in pain like this."

"Bullshit." Ikiryo shifted, tucking her legs and arms closer, nails digging into her skin. Shadow itself seemed to burrow and spread under her skin like venom in her veins, darkness eating her from the inside out like a parasite. "It should have been me."

It should have been me. The familiarity and damning nature of the words tugged at Kokoro. Shaking her head, she reached to place a reassuring hand on Ikiryo's shoulder. "No. I don't agree."

The girl froze and loosened her body. Her soaked eyes bled makeup down her cheeks. "How can you even say that?"

For a moment, Kokoro stiffened, unsure of how to answer. She slowly gazed up at the shifting mist ceiling as the Sakura tree grew larger, almost daring to pierce it. If it did, what would be beyond? Would it be the starry night sky that she and Naoko had been under so many times? Would it be the darkness that took her? Perhaps the mist wasn't a cage, but a shield, to protect them not just from the outside but from the horrors within their shared world.

Ikiryo is a part of that world too.

"Because even though you're a bitch sometimes," Kokoro continued, "you exist, and you deserve to."

At first, Ikiryo didn't reply. Instead, all that came was a scoff.

"I still don't agree, but…" She turned to glance at Kokoro. "Thanks, I guess."

Kokoro managed to smile for her. Just then, the mist wall that had separated her from the front lit up, solidifying images from the outside flashing across. She rose from her spot at the Sakura, walked over and tried to pass through, but found she still couldn't.

"Hello?" Kokoro called. "Whoever's up there, tell me what's going—"

She stopped, seeing a familiar woman dead ahead, mingling with other girls just like Naoko: blissfully unaware, fragile. *Vulnerable*. Her appearance had changed. She had dyed and cut her once brunette hair, but the twisted, shallow smirk on her face all but gave her away.

"Claire…?" Kokoro's voice was halfway between a hiss and a whisper, but it was enough for Ikiryo to rise from her sulking and join her. Their eyes briefly locked, before Ikiryo pounded on the veil that kept them from control of the body. "Hey! Let us in, now!"

The thumping reverberated through the inner world, the Sakura's branches shifting, as if from a giant's footsteps. A rigid voice echoed with it.

"Whoever that is, knock it off! I'm trying to focus!"

"Hideaki? Is that you?" Recongizing the voice, Kokoro pressed her face against the mist that—despite being as transparent as glass—was as solid as brick. "Is that really Claire?"

Silence. Finally, a reply came, "…yes."

Ikiryo slammed her fist into the wall, and Hideaki cried out in pain again. After a few breaths warped by the inner world, his voice sounded again, "Both of you! Calm down!"

Kokoro and Ikiryo exchanged a perturbed glance with one another, then faced the mist again. Together, they slammed into it, almost breaking through and eliciting another howl of pain from Hideaki.

"First off, don't tell us to calm down," Ikiryo pulled back, her brows furrowed. "Second, you need to let us through. *Now.*"

"You'll just endanger us all and ruin our plan," he warned through huffs. "No way I'm letting you run the body with Claire around."

"Hideaki," Kokoro said as grit her teeth, "give us control or so help me, we will *drag* you out."

Hideaki continued to resist, holding both her and Ikiryo back, the inner world shaking violently as they struggled. Suddenly, she felt her fire dim with the presence of a hand on her shoulder. The anger faded, as if being smothered by the vacuum of space itself.

Kokoro spun to see Void towering over her. She tried to fight but felt him sap both her strength and rage from her. She and Ikiryo collapsed, their once-combined strength spent.

"Let me handle this for now, okay?" Hideaki assured her. "We *will* take her down. For now, just stand back. Please."

"Fine," Kokoro scoffed and stood, swatting away Void's hand. Ikiryo also rose, calmer than before, and yet the fire in her eyes didn't dim completely. She met Kokoro's gaze, understanding passing between them.

"Thank you," Hideaki said, relief in his voice. Kokoro watching as they trailed between the middle and center of the crowd, following Claire. Kokoro briefly made out some of her guards that, despite their casual clothing, stuck out like a sore thumb.

Claire shifted away from the crowd, flanked by two of them. Kokoro felt her chest tighten.

"She's getting away."

"I know," Hideaki said. "Like John said, our job here today is to gather information, evidence, if we can. We've confirmed that she's operating in Shibuya ward, and that means Shane is likely not far. If we can locate wherever they're operating at, then we go straight to Naoko's father."

"So, he can bring the police force directly," Ikiryo surmised, arms crossed. "Without the risk of having the information leaked or slow walked."

"Exactly," Hideaki's voice echoed back. Kokoro and Ikiryo continued to watch as Claire walked down an alleyway, flanked by two of her guards. Unlike the rest of the shopping plaza, the narrow alleyway that held her escape van was fairly closed off.

"Damn," Hideaki said, though it wasn't directed toward her or Ikiryo. "We can't follow them any further unless we want to get spotted. It's safe to assume those guards are armed."

"Ah, shit. You're right," John replied. "I'm gonna call your dad and see if he can't get some of his boys to tail them."

"Understood," Hideaki replied. Kokoro watched as he tried to inconspicuously monitor Claire. The bitch soon made her way into the alleyway, though something was different about her. For one, she seemed nervous…especially around her own guards.

Kokoro's eyes narrowed as she watched a guard open the sliding door to the van, then tried to shove her in by the arm. She eyed him with a mix of fear and indignance as she shoved his hand away, loading herself into the van. The lights turned on as it slowly backed out of the alleyway.

"John!" Hideaki called through Kokoro's voice. "The plate!"

"Right, right… Ah, damn. Some of them are still looking out, and your dad's not picking up either," Kokoro heard John growl, then pause. "Wait, I got an idea. Sayuki, Naoko, come here."

"What? Why…" Hideaki trailed off, then his voice picked back up with excitement. "That's perfect! Alright, here it comes. On the count of three…"

Kokoro arched an eyebrow, then looked at Ikiryo, whose arms were still crossed with a confused look. Finally, she heard Hideaki's voice echo back to them.

"We got it! The license plate to Claire's van!"

"Oh." Kokoro blinked. "But didn't John say that some of the guards were still looking around?"

"We, ah…" Hideaki paused. "…took a selfie. Managed a clear shot of the plate in the frame. Not the best way, I admit, but it's less conspicuous, and it worked. It looked like they didn't suspect a thing. Now, Mr. Haneda can trace it once John gets ahold of him."

"Good," Kokoro said with a smile, turning to Ikiryo once more. Her earlier look of determination had faded, replaced instead by a shard of the shadowy guilt that had plagued her earlier. Kokoro stepped closer. "Hey. How do you feel?"

Ikiryo paused, searching within herself. She slowly smiled. "Better. Not good, but…better."

Kokoro returned it. Together they faced forward as Claire's van turned a corner, out of view. She clenched her fists, furious that they had lost their chance.

But like Hideaki said, Kokoro relaxed her hands, taking in a deep breath. *We need to play the long game if we wanna find those girls. I can't let my hatred cost them their freedom.*

"Claire," Ikiryo said, moving over to Kokoro. Her face stiffened as a hint of her earlier determination returned. "She has to pay."

"Agreed," Kokoro replied, nodding. After being at odds for so long, she and Ikiryo finally had a common cause.

A smirk briefly crossed Ikiryo's face, before it slowly faded. "Hey, Kokoro?"

"Yeah?"

"I just wanted to say thank you for earlier. Can't say I feel all the way better, but still." A gentle smile came to her lips. It looked good on her. Healthy, even.

Kokoro returned it. "Same to you, Ikiryo. Just don't go running off again, okay?"

"No promises." Ikiryo chuckled half-heartedly. "Anyway, see you around?"

"Of course." Kokoro beamed. "Just stay close, okay? I'll need you when we find Claire."

Ikiryo nodded, then slowly walked away, vanishing behind the Sakura. Kokoro turned around to face the mist and finally pushed forward into the outside world.

第十五章

CHAPTER 15

EXPOSURE

WHEN KOKORO FINALLY REASSERTED CONTROL over the body from Hideaki, he and Sayuki had already taken the train and were now on the long street back to Naoko's house. The sun was falling from its perch in the sky. She vaguely remembered something John had said to her before about him staying somewhere close to Shibuya Station to keep an eye on Claire, but the exact details seemed fuzzy.

"Are you okay, Hideaki?" Sayuki whispered, leaning in. Kokoro turned and smiled.

"Sayuki. It's me."

"Oh." Her friend blinked. "Sorry, I just…ever since we saw Claire, you…er, Hideaki was acting all quiet. He wouldn't answer me when I tried to talk to him."

"Like he was zoning out?"

"Right." Sayuki nodded. "I got worried."

Kokoro arched an eyebrow. "About him?"

"About you, and…" she smiled softly, "…him too. He's a bit like a robot sometimes, but he's also really sweet."

"Aww," Kokoro teased. "What? Developing a crush?"

"I like girls, you know that." Sayuki's cheeks reddened. "One person in particular."

Kokoro felt her face flush, then paused as a less pleasant idea came to mind. "Hey, Sayuki?"

Sayuki faced her attentively. She smiled warmly and nodded. "Yeah?"

"Since we're on the subject," Kokoro began, taking a deep breath. "This DID thing? The others? I'm not sure what you had in mind, but I don't think they're going away. And honestly, I don't want them to."

Sayuki's nose wrinkled. "Why would that be an issue?"

"It's just…you like me, and I like you, but…" She hesitated. "We're kind of a package deal. All of us. It'd be new territory, and I don't know if I'd be able to meet all of your needs because of it…"

Kokoro trailed off as she rubbed her hands nervously. The next thing she felt was a third hand, wrapped in a cotton glove, resting on hers reassuringly. Despite that, the warmth bled through as Sayuki smiled.

"I told you, I'm in no matter what happens, and I'm here," she said, "for *all* of you."

Kokoro's face grew so hot she thought it might pop off. She felt a calming presence, and thanks to that, could return Sayuki's smile, their hands interlocking.

"Okay," Kokoro said, beaming sheepishly, before continuing to walk. Eventually, they arrived. The clicking of the front door's four locks snapped her back to full awareness. With Sayuki beside her, Kokoro stepped inside and removed her shoes.

She stopped. In the living room, she heard a harsh, familiar voice conversing with a calmer, more analytical one. She peeked through to find Mr. Haneda in his detective uniform, phone in hand, as his wife sat on the couch, rubbing her forehead in frustration.

"…no, no, you're lying. Naoko is fine. You need to retract this diagnosis. I don't want this affecting my daughter's future!"

"It won't affect her future," Dr. Maeda's voice echoed from the phone's speaker. "With the right treatment, she and her alters can…"

"Alters? Come on, Dr. Maeda. They are *delusions*. I'd expect someone with your reputation would know that! Besides, she'll eventually drop it. Whatever is wrong with her, she *will* heal."

"It's not temporary, I'm afraid. Naoko has had this disorder since childhood. It's not something that just goes away."

"Itsuki…" Naoko's mother said. "Dr. Maeda is right. You know what happened to her, before we…"

Naoko's mother stopped once she had laid eyes on Kokoro. She nudged Mr. Haneda, who spun to face her. His brows furrowed as she spoke into the phone one last time.

"Enough of this for right now, Doctor. Retract it, or I will get legal involved." Naoko's dad pressed the end call button and pocketed the phone. He reached to the kitchen counter and pulled a stack of Hideaki's notes, along with the annotated pamphlet Dr. Maeda had given him at their previous session. Kokoro felt her heart pulse hard within her chest. The chatter in her mind grew louder.

"Damn it!" Hideaki cursed, a rare panic in his voice. "I forgot to hide the notes. I'm sorry."

"It's fine," Kokoro reassured him internally, though she herself tried to stay in control. After all, her worst fear had just come to pass. Naoko's dad had discovered the truth.

"Naoko." Mr. Haneda pressed forward, the papers in hand. He didn't appear angry, not with her, at least. "I don't know what sort of junk ideas Dr. Maeda has been trying to cram into your brain, but—"

"He's not trying to indoctrinate her!" Sayuki interjected. "He just—"

"Sayuki," Mr. Haneda's mouth drew into a hard line. "I appreciate what you've done for her. You should head home tonight. I'm sure your mother is worried sick."

Sayuki's lip curled as she glanced at Kokoro. She had been at her side in the weeks since her return from the psych ward, but now it was time for her to handle things on her own.

"I'll be fine," Kokoro reassured her with a gentle whisper.

Sayuki glanced warily at Mr. Haneda. "Are you sure?"

"Promise." Kokoro gave her a smile. "I'll call you later, okay?"

Her friend returned it, albeit with a weaker one. She nodded, then walked back out of the house and into the night. Mrs. Haneda's brows furrowed, her eyes dug into her husband like a rake into the ground.

"Itsuki. There was no need for that. She was…"

"Enough!" Mr. Haneda spun, jutting his finger at her. She glared back at him, then looked at Kokoro worriedly as he moved closer, placing his hands on her shoulders reassuringly.

"Naoko," he continued, his eyes softening from their earlier hardness. "You're okay. I know you've been through a lot, things that no girl should ever have to endure, but you're still my little girl. You're not this…*Kokoro*, or whoever else. You are Naoko. My daughter."

Kokoro froze, her muscles tightening as her stomach churned, tears streaming down her face.

"Naoko," he said once more, brows furrowed in loving concern. "Please listen. I know this is hard, I just…"

"I'm not her," Kokoro said, her voice low. Naoko's parents blinked in unison, taken aback as she caught enough breath to continue. "I wish I was. I really do, I just… I'm not."

Mr. Haneda's eyes bore into hers, as if reading her like a book. She knew what he was doing; digging for lies, searching for the truth, something his years as a police officer had burned into him.

"I…understand," he finally said, his gaze softening. He took a moment, resting his hand on the rail leading up the stairs as he pondered in silence. Finally, he moved past her to secure all four of the door locks before turning to face her again. "Either way, you're going to be staying here for a while."

Kokoro's heart dropped. "Until when?"

He didn't answer. Instead, he walked into the kitchen, where he pulled different ingredients from the cabinets. Kokoro moved toward the kitchen island and braced herself against it.

"How long do I have to be here?"

Mr. Haneda stopped, not bothering to meet her demanding gaze. "As long as it takes."

Kokoro's eyes widened. Mr. Haneda's wife moved up and grabbed him by the arm. "Itsuki! Why—"

"Hana," he growled. Turning back to the kitchen island, he briefly gestured to Kokoro before silently chopping the ingredients that were laid out from earlier. "Please go upstairs. Your mother and I need some time to talk."

Kokoro exhaled in disbelief, eyes darting between them. With an indignant huff, she ran up the stairs into Naoko's room, sliding the door shut behind her. She made her way to the bed and sat. Kokoro curled her knees to her chest as she fought to control her ragged breaths. With every thumping heartbeat, her room dissolved, and the mist of their shared inner world took its place, until the lone Sakura tree materialized.

Suddenly she felt herself relax, as if all the panic and fear within her were sucked out into a…

"Void," Kokoro realized. She turned and found the tall emptiness contained within a body inside, his star-eyes gazing at her in concern. She smiled at him.

Void nodded, retracted his hand and took a few steps back. The next set of hands she felt was Sunshine; her small arms wrapped around her neck. The nothing within her then filled with a warm light, like a star against the night sky.

"Everything alright, Kokoro?"

"Yeah," another voice said. "You okay?"

She turned. The first voice belonged to Hideaki, eyes halfway hidden behind his glasses. Next to him was Ikiryo, arms crossed, face rigid but eyes softer than before.

"I'm okay, thank you, though." Kokoro first smiled at Sunshine, then turned to the others. "All of you. I needed that."

"That's what we're here for!" Sunshine beamed, then frowned. "So…I guess he knows now, huh?"

"Guess so." Kokoro sighed, shaking her head. "Now I guess we're stuck at the house for a while."

"That's my fault," Hideaki said, face downcast. "I didn't take enough care to hide the notes."

"It's okay!" Sunshine turned to Hideaki and beamed. "Mistakes happen."

"The question is, what are we going to do now?" Ikiryo asked, eyeing them. "No way he lets us leave now, especially since he thinks we're batshit crazy."

Kokoro stopped to ponder her words. "What are you suggesting?"

"We get the hell out of here," Ikiryo said. "Stay with Sayuki or something. We can't afford to screw around, not while Shane and Claire are still free."

"I don't think that's advisable." Hideaki stepped closer to Ikiryo. Their eyes met, but the normal tension, sometimes hatred, seemed dormant. Hideaki's tone toward her was calmer, less condescending, and in return, Ikiryo's was firm, but respectful.

"Why not?" Ikiryo asked.

"We need to move forward, I agree, but not so recklessly. Besides, can we really do that to Naoko's parents again?"

"Naoko is gone, and now they know," Ikiryo scoffed. "What difference does it make, anyway? It's not like it would be—"

Kokoro stared at her, eyes pleading. Ikiryo's furrowed brows softened. Her gaze lowered.

"Sorry." Ikiryo sighed. "I'm trying."

"I know. It's fine." Kokoro exhaled. "But you bring up a good point. What's going to happen to us now that they know the truth about Nao?"

"If I may," Hideaki began, stepping forward, "I think this is true of Naoko's mother, but not her father."

Kokoro arched an eyebrow. "What do you mean?"

"Think about it, his expression, the way he said your name like speaking to a child. In other words, he thinks 'Naoko' is pretending to be 'Kokoro' as a form of escapism."

"So that's why he's keeping us here," Kokoro theorized. "He thinks 'Naoko' is delusional and wants to snap her out of it."

Hideaki nodded. "Precisely. Our best option is to play along and—"

"—and hope he believes it and lets us out?" Ikiryo asked. "Do we even have that kind of time?"

Hideaki pursed his lips. "Unless you have a better option."

The surrounding space fell silent. Kokoro sighed.

"Alright. For now, we stay here, lie low, play along, trying to be as convincing as possible," Kokoro declared, eyeing each of them. Hideaki nodded approvingly. Ikiryo reluctantly did the same. Sunshine beamed, Fishy flopped in her arms. Void simply stood. His lights-for-eyes seemed to shine brighter than usual. Kokoro nodded. "Tomorrow, we—"

The vibrations from her cell phone shook Kokoro back into reality. She picked it up to find Sayuki had called her over five times in the last ten minutes, leaving messages counting over twice that. Kokoro blinked and dialed her back, only to be immediately received.

"Kokoro? That's you, right?" Sayuki worriedly asked. "Are you okay? I'm sorry, I should have…"

"Sayuki." Kokoro smiled. "I'm fine. Promise."

"You're not in trouble or anything?"

"Not trouble, but…" Kokoro hesitated. "Naoko's dad is keeping us here for a while."

"What?" Sayuki's voice trailed off. "How long?"

"Who knows?" Kokoro said. "Hopefully, not long, though. Are you and John going to keep an eye on Claire?"

"As much as we can," Sayuki replied. "Don't worry, though. We'll keep you in the loop."

"Thank you." Kokoro smiled. "Just stay safe for me, okay?"

"Of course." There was a brief silence on the other end of the line before Sayuki's soft voice spoke again. "Sleep good, Ko."

The call ended with a click. Kokoro stared at the now-darkened screen, at the reflection. It was like the mirror she had seen earlier, in the middle of her conversation with Mr. Haneda, only this time it was showing Nao's face instead of hers.

A thought came to her. What if Mr. Haneda was right? What if she really was 'Naoko,' and 'Kokoro' was just a delusion? She was in a psych ward, after all. Maybe the key to everything was simply acknowledging it.

She pulled up the phone and gazed at the reflection once more. The same image of Naoko's face with pale hair was there, but there was also more. Afterimages, like the infinite mirrors in a barbershop, stretched behind. She angled it, and saw Hideaki's face, followed by Ikiryo's, Sunshine's, then Void's.

Kokoro frowned. No. This, like the mirror on Naoko's dresser, was also truth itself, as much as she didn't want to admit it. She could pretend all she wanted, and never in a million years would she truly be Naoko Haneda.

Plugging in the phone, Kokoro crawled into the low bed, curling in the sheets to protect herself against the cold. She closed her eyes and found herself under the Sakura again with the others. Hideaki and Ikiryo were adjacent, their backs resting against the trunk, with Sunshine huddled in the middle. She almost wished she could take a picture.

A noise caught her attention from the front. Void had poked the upper half of his body out of the misty wall. He regarded her with a small wave before disappearing back into control of the body.

Kokoro smiled. She took one more glance around, then stared upward, counting the falling petals in a trance-like state as the time passed by with the gentle wind.

"Hello? Naoko? Are you up?"

Without realizing it, Ikiryo instinctively grabbed the phone and prepared to throw it. Then she froze.

Wait a minute. Why am I in control?

Ikiryo lowered the phone and ran over to the mirror. Her own appearance was gone, replaced with Naoko's soft face. For the briefest moment, excitement brimmed, but it soon faded as the stinging reminder set in. Naoko was gone, and it was all because of her and her stupid obsession with the bitch known as Claire.

If I hadn't influenced Naoko to go after her…

Ikiryo frowned, pulling away. Without warning, the door slid open, and Mr. Haneda stepped in. "Oh. So, you are up."

Ikiryo froze. Naoko's dad hadn't ever spoken directly to her before. She had always hidden behind Naoko, a stalking cat in the tall grass, wanting to lash out and defend her. But she never did. She often told herself it was for Naoko's sake, but in reality, she was chasing her own selfish desires. Every step Ikiryo took, whether at school, Shane's nightclub, or anywhere else, seemed to push Naoko even closer to that ominous iron door.

"Naoko?"

"Oh." Ikiryo blinked, bringing herself back into focus. "Yeah, what's up?"

Naoko's dad arched an eyebrow. "I'm making breakfast. I was wondering if you'd like to help me.

Ikiryo stopped, briefly turning inward, praying that another would come to take her place. There was only the silence of the swirling mists and her frustrated sigh as she faced Naoko's dad once more. "I…guess so."

He nodded. "I'll be downstairs."

Ikiryo returned it, never taking her eyes off him as he vacated the room and descended the steps. She took one last look at the mirror, at Naoko's soft face, then briskly turned away, following Mr. Haneda.

She stopped. The bedroom door to Naoko's parent's room was open. Naoko's mom was lying on the bed, curled into herself. She glanced up, her eyes hollow and bloodshot. A tear streamed down her cheek as she returned her head to the pillow.

Ikiryo frowned, then forced herself past the room and down the steps. A familiar, delightful smell filled her nostrils and practically lifted her into the air. Her eyes hungrily darted over to the kitchen counter, where tiny chunks of cooked chicken marinated in soy sauce, sake, and mirin within a small saucepan. Close to it was the rice cooker which he had just dumped its contents into.

It smells so good. She blinked, surprised at her own lust for food. *But I've never even had it before. Why am I so…?*

"Hiya!"

Ikiryo nearly screamed out loud. A young girl had materialized next to her in the inner world, her glowing blonde hair tied into cute pigtails with flower bands.

"Oh." Ikiryo took a deep breath to regain control of herself. "Hi, Sunshine."

"Sorry. Didn't mean to scare ya." Sunshine beamed. "Just smelled the Yaki Oni giri. It's my favorite."

"Oh. I see." Ikiryo blinked, noting something absent from Sunshine's arms. "Where's Fishy?"

"He wanted to stay back with the others while they were sleeping," she explained, smiling. "So, I thought I'd come talk to you!"

"Oh. Great," Ikiryo huffed and turned back to the front. Mr. Haneda continued to prepare the food as he smiled at her.

"Want to come help?"

Ikiryo blinked. Next thing she knew, she was at the counter next to him, rolling the chicken and rice into rounded triangles on a bamboo cutting board, her long sleeves rolled back.

"It's been a while since you've had this, hasn't it?"

She looked over at him. He was so…different. Calmer, gentler. Caring. A far cry from how uptight he was with Naoko in the months before.

"Yeah," Ikiryo finally said, "a long time."

"You used to love this, *Naoko.*" The way he said her name was sharp, intentional, almost like a reminder. "Back when you were a little girl, remember?"

A little girl? Ikiryo froze. She didn't have any memories beyond her brief time with Naoko. Hell, she probably didn't even exist before the last few years. How was she supposed to remember anything, especially when said memories weren't even hers?

"Of course!" she found herself saying in Naoko's voice, albeit at a much higher pitch. "It was my favorite!"

What the hell? Ikiryo blinked. *Why did I…?*

"Sorry! Didn't mean to snatch," Sunshine's disembodied voice echoed. "You just looked a bit stressed. Hope you don't mind."

"Please do." Ikiryo briefly turned, but the strange mist now seemed solid. With that, any hope of an exit from the awkwardness of dealing with both Naoko's dad *and* Sunshine were dashed to pieces.

Ikiryo growled, then sighed. She would just have to be content with watching…for now, at least.

"Good." Sunshine fronted again and continued her work, looking at Mr. Haneda. "Sometimes, you'd let me add my own ingredients!"

"Ha!" He chuckled. "Candy, chocolate…ah, yes. I remember those days. You were quite creative back then." He smiled, though the edge of his lip curled down. "You were our little Nao. Our sunshine."

Ikiryo's eyes widened in realization. Sunshine beamed, her light growing brighter as she swelled with pride.

"You were there too?"

"Only a few years," Sunshine explained internally, careful not to let it slip out through the body's mouth. "Those years were her happiest. Naoko's. I just did what I could to help."

Ikiryo frowned, her gaze falling. "At least you *could* help."

"And you don't think you're helpful, too?" Sunshine asked.

"You already know the answer to that," Ikiryo said, her voice trailing off. "I'm the idiot that started this mess."

"Maybe." Sunshine happily continued to marinate the cooked chicken, placing a small piece of seaweed on each one. "Doesn't mean anything, though."

"Doesn't mean anything?" Ikiryo's eyes narrowed. "What am I supposed to do? Pretend like it didn't happen, that I didn't lead Naoko right to Claire in the first place?"

"Oh no, I'm not saying that. You absolutely fucked up," Sunshine replied, looking back inward with a bright smile. Ikiryo blinked, shocked to hear such damning words from her, of all people. "What I'm saying is that you shouldn't hold it against yourself forever. You still deserve to exist, ya know."

Deserve to exist. The same words Kokoro had told her before. Ikiryo sat down, drawing her knees up to her chest. "Do I really, though?"

"Only you can decide that, but I think you do!" Sunshine said, before turning her full focus back to the food she was preparing. Ikiryo clutched her ears as Sunshine hummed to herself. The irritating high-pitched tune echoed back a thousand times louder, as if she were in a tunnel.

Finally, the travesty that was Sunshine's so-called 'music' ended. Ikiryo sighed in relief, then blinked. They were now seated at the table opposite Naoko's dad, the delicious oni giri delicately placed on the plate in front of them. Sunshine, still in control, clasped her hands together and gave thanks for the food before greedily digging in.

Naoko's dad laughed. "I take it I did good?"

"Oh my gosh," Sunshine said, mouth full of food. "You did amazing!"

"Good. I'm glad." The smile on his face slowly faded. "By the way, I wanted to apologize."

Sunshine momentarily stopped chewing. Ikiryo's eyes widened and focused on him.

"For what?"

"I know I haven't been a good father these last few years. I've been strict, inconsiderate. Everything that's happened, I...I just can't help but feel a little responsible."

"You aren't. I am." Ikiryo blinked, the hairs on the body's neck standing up. She had switched back into control without realizing it. She felt Sunshine not far behind her, her usual warmth dimmed.

"Naoko." He reached across, grabbing her hand. Ikiryo almost recoiled, both at the mention of the name and the touch, but mustered every ounce of mental energy she had to resist the instinct. "None of this is your fault."

Ikiryo bit her lip, fighting back the pain that wanted to escape her eyes. Ultimately, she couldn't. There was no point in dodging the cold truth.

"Naoko…"

"Please." Ikiryo met his eyes. "Please stop saying her name."

Mr. Haneda blinked and withdrew his hands. Silence filled the kitchen, only the ever so quiet hum of the air conditioner could be heard.

"Her name," he said, closing his eyes. "So this delusion still holds you."

"No, Dad," Ikiryo quickly said, her quivering body betraying her attempt at deceit. "I-I'm fine. I promise."

Mr. Haneda was now directly in front of her, hands reassuringly on her shoulders. "Naoko. These voices in your head…they're temporary, okay?" His hands moved to her cheeks. "You are my daughter. One way or another, I will help you shed this fantasy and you will get better."

The world around Ikiryo spun, the body shaking uncontrollably as he brought her into his embrace. There was no stopping the tears now.

"I failed you before." Naoko's dad pulled back slightly, nodding. "I will *not* fail you again."

Ikiryo broke into a sob, pulling herself free from his grip, running up the stairs and into the room, sliding the door shut behind her. She collapsed on the bed, pulling the blankets close, desperate for warmth, comfort, anything as she gasped for air through her sobs. For what seemed like an eternity, she stayed there, neither eating nor drinking. Naoko's room slowly faded, first replaced with a strange, numbing feeling of nothing that slowly gave way to the familiar mists, then to the Sakura tree which she was now leaning against.

"Ikiryo…?" A concerned Sunshine was now in front of her, Fishy now snuggled in her arms. "Are you okay?"

She met the young girl's innocent, caring eyes. How could Sunshine be so kind to her? How could anyone?

"Go away." Ikiryo curled tighter and turned the other way. "I don't want to talk."

"It's gonna be okay." She smiled warmly. "I promise."

"You say that," Ikiryo scoffed, "but how do you know? You've never lost anyone."

At that moment, Ikiryo heard the cries of another little girl, far off in the distance. Sunshine pulled back, her eyes wide, her lips curled down. Fishy flopped around in her arms, and Sunshine immediately bounced him on her shoulder like she usually did.

"It's okay, it's okay." Sunshine's light dimmed as tears streamed down her cheeks. "We'll find her again."

Find who again? Then it hit her. Whatever those cries were, whoever they belonged to, Sunshine knew who it was, and it was abundantly clear that she missed whoever it was dearly.

"I-I'm sorry," Ikiryo began. "I didn't know."

"Like I said," Sunshine said, her voice soft, sad, yet with a hint of hope. "Everything will be okay in the end. It *has* to be."

Ikiryo frowned. As Sunshine noticed, she held out Fishy and managed a smile, albeit a weak one.

"Now you try. You'll feel better, I promise."

Though she hesitated at first, Ikiryo took Fishy and did like she had: placing him on her shoulder and bouncing him up and down like a baby. Immediately, some of that unbearable, unseen weight parted from her, enough that she could think straight.

"You're right," Ikiryo said, then paused. Her brows furrowed as she looked at the little girl. "Sunshine? Why do you think I deserve to exist?"

Sunshine didn't even hesitate. "Because you're one of us, Ikky." She beamed, and Ikiryo could have sworn she saw her light shine just a little brighter. "You're family."

Ikiryo returned it, more of that darkness pulling out of her as she held Fishy with Sunshine sitting cross-legged in front of her. Time blurred as they continued to pour out their hearts, Sakura petals drifted in the air, guided by the whispering winds carrying the promise of better days ahead.

CHAPTER 16

THE HEARTBREAKING TRUTH

A SHARP PAIN IN KOKORO'S STOMACH WOKE HER from her deep slumber, the growling itself so loud it nearly echoed across the house. She sat up, then immediately got a whiff of herself. She didn't smell completely terrible, but the time for a shower was long overdue, nonetheless.

Kokoro blinked and moved to the dresser, grabbing her clothes before heading to the bathroom. A short while later, she walked back into the room, refreshed. As she reached for the phone, a voice suddenly called from the door.

"Naoko? Are you up?"

A sudden fog of hesitation surrounded Kokoro. What about the plan they made? To pretend until he let them out? Should she just act like her outburst the night prior was just stress?

Kokoro glanced over at the mirror, at Naoko's face. She never could get used to seeing it. For one, it just wasn't her. On the other hand, it was a painful reminder. It didn't matter how well they faked their way to freedom. The truth would *always* hurt.

"May I come in?" Mr. Haneda asked again from behind the door.

"Of course," she said, albeit with reluctance.

The door slid open, Mr. Haneda entered with a gentle smile. "Ah. You're finally up."

Kokoro arched an eyebrow and glanced at the clock. It was almost four in the afternoon.

"Did I really sleep in this late?" she asked.

"More than that." Mr. Haneda frowned. "You've been up here since early last night."

"Wait…what?" she asked, blinking furiously. How? Just last night, she had finally told him the truth. How had it been that long?

Unless…

Her eyes widened. If not her, then who was in control during that time?

"We were getting worried. Every time I came up to check on you, you had barely moved. I was almost worried that you'd…" his voice trailed off.

"That I…what?"

"Never mind." He looked her square in the eye. "I know our conversation got a little intense, but even so." He hesitated. "If I upset you, I...I'm sorry. I know how hard it's been for you."

Kokoro's mind drew a blank. *What conversation?*

"I'm sorry, I..." She shook her head. "...what did we talk about again?"

"On Wednesday, when we made Onigiri. We...ah, talked," he said, staring at her.

"Oh. Sorry." Kokoro shook her head, her lip curled down. "My brain must be fried. Guess I just needed the rest."

"I...understand." Mr. Haneda nodded. "So, are you finally going to come down and join us? I prepared dinner."

"Sure." Kokoro smiled. "Do you mind if I take a few minutes first?"

"Of course." He walked back, then briefly stopped in the doorway, glancing back at her with apprehension. "Just don't take too long this time. Okay?"

"Okay," she replied with another smile. His tall shadow soon disappeared down the stairs; Kokoro quickly grabbed the phone from the dresser. Her eyes widened upon finding that she had no less than twenty missed calls from John.

She quickly dialed him back. It rang, seemingly forever. She paced the room, nibbling at her fingernails.

"Come on, come on. Damn it, John!" Kokoro grunted and tried again. This time, she got a response.

"Naoko! For Christ's sake, woman!" John's exasperated voice rang out from the speaker. "I've been trying to call you since yesterday!"

Kokoro blinked. "I'm…I'm sorry."

"Where were you? Did your dad take your phone, or…?"

"No, no, nothing like that." The harshness in John's voice made the hairs on her neck stand up. Something was wrong. "John? What happened? Is everything—"

"Shane and Claire," he said. "We were back at Shibuya Crossing. One of their goons spotted us, and…" He trailed off.

"And what?"

"They grabbed her, Naoko. They nabbed Sayuki."

The phone nearly slipped from her grasp as she tried to process the information. She didn't even remember collapsing on the ground, or nearly heaving up her guts. Shane and Claire, the damn cancers that had taken Naoko from them, now had the woman she loved.

"No, no, *no*," Kokoro said, her breaths quickening. It felt like she was reliving the past all over again. She was in hell. She had to be!

"You've got to get your dad in on this now," John said. "We can't be mucking about anymore!"

"Okay, okay." Kokoro nodded, inhaling slowly to control her breathing. "I'll go talk to him."

"Good. Call me back when you're done. In the meantime, I'll send him that plate to see if his guys can pull a location from it."

"Right. Will do." Kokoro hung up and threw on any piece of clothing she could find, not caring if it matched or not. Ikiryo's panicked voice echoed in the back of her mind.

"Did I just hear what I think I heard?"

"It appears so," Hideaki chimed in. Kokoro could feel him nearby, his calm analytical sense beginning to bleed into her. She was grateful for it.

"Shit. Shit, shit!" Ikiryo exclaimed, her panic undoing the effects of Hideaki's presence. "Kokoro…this is my fault. I'm so, so sorry—"

"This is nobody's fault but Shane and Claire's," Kokoro said, hoping to ease her guilt. After all, they needed focus. Uncontrolled emotion was a thing they couldn't afford. "Just back me when up I need it, okay?"

Kokoro couldn't see Ikiryo, but she felt her acknowledge with a weak nod. Hideaki did the same.

"What's the next step?"

"Like John said. Time to get Nao's dad involved," Kokoro explained, grabbing one of her hair ties. "Either way, we don't have time to waste. All hands on deck here."

"Right," Hideaki acknowledged before vanishing back into the inner world with Ikiryo. Kokoro quickly tied her hair into a loose ponytail, then rushed down the stairs where Mr. Haneda and mother were waiting.

"Naoko?" he asked, eyes widened. "What's the rush? Why—"

"They have her. They have Sayuki!" Kokoro said between breaths.

Mr. Haneda's eyes widened. "Who does?"

"Shane and Claire!" Kokoro said, her voice raised in a panic. "She and John were out, and…"

Kokoro's throat tightened, unable to finish the words. Thankfully, Mr. Haneda was already up the stairs. He came back down not a minute later with his gun and badge. His phone rang, and he opened the message and blinked.

"Why is John sending me a picture of you three?" he asked. "Is this just the last known photo of Sayuki, or…?"

"No. The license plate." Kokoro briefly grabbed the phone, zoomed in on it, and handed it back as she donned a hoodie. "That's the vehicle that Claire's using to get around and take girls. John sent it so you could trace it."

"Alright. I'll send it to my men at the station." Naoko's dad nodded, then stopped. "Wait. How do you know this vehicle is Claire's?"

Kokoro froze, then turned to face him. Her jaw clenched.

"John," she answered. "He's been keeping tabs on Shane and Claire. Sayuki was helping him and—"

Before she could finish, Mr. Haneda's hands were gripping her shoulders, his eyes widening. "Naoko, was this what you were doing those days when you were out and about? Trying to find Shane and Claire?"

Kokoro froze as his piercing gaze dug into her. She slowly nodded.

"Why would you endanger yourself like that, going after them like that?" His form appeared to grow bigger, the shadows on his face darkened. "Why—"

"Because of what they did to Naoko!" Kokoro exclaimed. No, she couldn't do this anymore. No more pretending, no more acting like someone she wasn't.

Mr. Haneda's brows creased, his jaw went rigid. His wife's previously dead eyes widened.

"Naoko," he hissed, his voice barely under control. "I think you need some *professional* help."

"I already told you. I'm not—"

"This isn't healthy for you!" His grip on her shoulders tightened, fingers practically digging into her skin. "Look, I'm glad you're trying to get better, but this 'Kokoro' thing must stop!"

"Don't you think I'd bring her back if I could?" Kokoro huffed, her breaths ragged. "Have her inhabit her own body instead of me?"

"Enough pretending! Come to your senses!" he growled. "You are my daughter!"

As his voice died down, Kokoro felt anger rise within her. Be it from Ikiryo or elsewhere, she didn't care. It was long past time for this conversation to happen.

"You daughter is gone, Itsuki!" she spat, breaking free from his grip, saying his name in the hopes her point would get across. "She's gone because of people like you!"

Mr. Haneda blinked, taken aback by her sudden boldness. He stood to his full height, closing his eyes. His wife took his side, rubbing his arm.

"Itsuki, you know what Dr. Maeda said…about her condition." She eyed Kokoro, her eyes glistening. "Naoko is gone. I didn't wanna believe it either but think about it. Ever since that day, she's been different."

A sudden, piercing silence hung between them. The air became crisper, making Kokoro even more aware of her rapidly thumping heart. Finally, Mr. Haneda opened his eyes and glared.

"So…you really aren't Naoko, are you?"

"No," Kokoro said. "I'm not."

"That must mean you're hiding her somewhere," he said, his voice calm, yet threatening. His brows furrowed, jaw clenched. "So…give her back."

Kokoro's eyes widened. Did he not listen?

"Itsuki!" his wife exclaimed. "What are you…?"

"It's just as Dr. Maeda said," he explained coldly, almost in a mockery of her. "These so-called 'alters' can't die, right? She has to be in there somewhere."

Kokoro shook her head. No, there was no way she could ever convince him. She couldn't waste any more time, not when Shane and Claire held Sayuki captive. She tried to move through them, but Mr. Haneda grabbed her arm and held her fast in an iron-clad grip.

"I said…" his eyes dilated as he spoke "…give my daughter back. Now!"

Kokoro screamed, her white hair flailing as she shoved him away. He released her and stared in blatant shock.

"Call me whatever you want, but I'm here, not her," Kokoro began. "I wish it was her in this damn body, living her life, going to school, but now? Now she can't. Between the arrest, the bullying, what…" her voice quivered, "…what they did to her."

Mr. Haneda frowned, the wrath in his eyes giving way to grief. "I…know what they did. I—"

"Now she's gone," Kokoro continued, her throat swollen, tears falling. "And not just gone but ripped from my very soul! She was my friend, my sister, and I *loved* her. When she struggled, I was there. When she tried to swallow pills, I took control and spit them out!"

Naoko's parents exchanged a horrified glance. They opened their mouths to speak, but Kokoro ignored them, continuing her tirade, though this wasn't fueled by Ikiryo or anyone else. This time, it was all her. "I *existed* for Naoko. To protect her. But that day, she saved me instead and I still don't know why." A tear fell down Kokoro's cheek, "But I am *done* blaming myself, because now I know the reason that she's gone is because of people like you!"

Mr. Haneda's eyes widened. With his eyes tightly shut, he sank to his knees, immobile, as time seemed to stretch on endlessly. Finally, he spoke back up.

"You're right."

Mr. Haneda's words chilled the already cold room. The heartbreaking truth was out, and it had finally been acknowledged. He planted his elbows and forehead to the floor: a deep, desperate prayer.

"I'm so sorry, Naoko," he whispered. "Please…come back."

Regret dug into Kokoro, her gut sinking. She could feel the reactions from the others, the shocked silence. It wasn't Mr.

Haneda's fault, not really. After all, he had done nothing but pour his heart and soul into rebuilding the relationship with his daughter. How dare she blame him? How could she say such hurtful words?

"I'm sorry." Kokoro moved forward and knelt next to him. "I didn't mean…"

"No." Mr. Haneda's tears slowly stopped. He held his hand up, as if to silence her, then sat up straight. "You're right. Naoko is gone. Everything I've been doing to make up for it?" He avoided her gaze. "Too little, too late. Now I'll never get to be the father that she deserved."

The moment he had spoken the words, Kokoro felt her heart sink. It was so painful seeing him like this, so broken. She didn't even want to think what Naoko would say if she saw him like that.

For a moment, Naoko's parents changed places. They were chasing each other around the kitchen, deep in the cake-throwing war she had started.

Before she could even think, the scenery shifted again to the day they were first taken by Shane and Claire. Mr. Haneda's car was parked, the passenger door open. Naoko was buried in his chest, happy that she had *finally* reconnected with her father.

The vision faded, replaced with the heartbreaking view of Mr. Haneda on the ground, in full acceptance of the truth. She looked in his downcast eyes to see his soul was just as fractured as hers.

"No," Kokoro finally said. "You're wrong about that."

"What?" Mr. Haneda looked up at her in surprise, blinking tears. "How?"

Kokoro inhaled, first phrasing the words in her head. "You say you'll never get to be the father she deserved, but you were. Remember her birthday, when—"

"—when we threw the cake around. Right." He smiled, if ever so slightly. "What about it?"

"I was there, but…so was Naoko." Kokoro said. "And the day you gave her a hug. That meant more to her than anything in the world. So don't lie anymore about not being a good father to Nao, okay? Trust me. You were, and she knew it. She was happy to have you as her dad."

Mr. Haneda's face contorted in agony as he clenched his fists and hunched over, clutching his chest and stomach. Mrs. Haneda embraced him tightly, and in response, Kokoro moved closer and joined, wrapping her arms around them both.

A few minutes of soul-shattering silence passed before she pulled away. Mr. Haneda took a moment to regain control of himself, sitting in Seiza pose and breathing deep.

"Thank you. I needed to hear that." He inhaled sharply, brows furrowing. "So, about your friend. They were taken by Shane and Claire, yes?"

She nodded quickly.

"Where are they?"

"John wasn't sure," Kokoro answered. "Although we had seen Claire around Shibuya Crossing. We think they were operating around there."

"Alright." Mr. Haneda nodded slowly, wiping the tears as he rose and made his way to the door, slipping on his shoes and trench coat. He inhaled sharply, his face hardening. "I'll notify the station and get every available unit out there looking. We'll find your friend, I promise."

"Wait!" Kokoro rose from the carpet as well. "I want to go, too."

"Nao—" He stopped just short of saying the name, closing his eyes and swallowing. "—I know Sayuki is your friend, but it's safer for you here."

"But—" Kokoro stopped. He stared with a rocklike intensity, his eyes unflinching and determined. She knew at that moment that his decision was final.

"I'm sorry," Naoko's dad said. "You may not be Naoko, but you're still all I have left of her." With one last sullen look, he ventured out into the white, shutting the door behind him.

Kokoro's lip twitched as she stood, fists curling. *No*, she decided. She wouldn't simply stand by, especially when her friend was in danger. With a huff, she ran back up the stairs, grabbing her thick jacket and boots from the closet and practically jumping back down to the front door.

"Kokoro?" a worried voice asked. "Where are you going?"

She paused, turning. Naoko's mother, Hana, was staring at her, eyes pleading.

She waited until Mr. Haneda had pulled out of the driveway, then began to systematically undo all four locks, feeling the cold air seep in as she opened the door. "I'm sorry, Mrs. Haneda. I have to go."

"But you know what he said. You're all we have left of her, we can't just—"

"Then try to stop me!" Kokoro snapped. She immediately regretted it, seeing Mrs. Haneda's face fall even further than before. The air between them thinned. She frowned, then slowly closed the door. "Sorry. I get it. You see Naoko's face when you look at me, but I'm not her."

"I know," Mrs. Haneda said. "It took me a while to come to terms with it, with Naoko being gone." She slowly reached for something on the shelf. "I can't stop you. But please, just listen first. I know someone who can help."

Kokoro blinked. "You do?"

Mrs. Haneda pulled down Naoko's toddler album, the same one she had looked at the day she had first taken control of the body. Naoko's mother moved from the shelf to the couch, Kokoro sitting next to her. She opened it to that picture of the old man and young boy, both dressed in traditional Kimono. The one on the left was familiar: short-cropped hair without the gray, yet instead of a hard line, a proud smile stretched from ear to ear. Kokoro's eyes widened.

"That's Naoko's dad, right?"

"It is," Mrs. Haneda confirmed, shifting her finger along the photo. "This is *his* father. Shinobu."

Something in Kokoro shifted upon seeing him. He was almost exactly like Mr. Haneda, yet there was something off about him. His eyes had the same sharp look, a hint of ruthlessness churning beneath the surface. From beneath the fabric of his loose kimono, she could see his tattoos. She blinked as it finally clicked *why* he had them.

"He's Yakuza?" Kokoro asked.

Mrs. Haneda nodded. "From the Akasaka-Daiichi clan. He was second in command."

Kokoro kept studying the picture. "But the clan leaders died in a fire. I thought nobody survived?"

Mrs. Haneda frowned, pulling the picture out and handing it to Kokoro. On the back was an address, with a note that read, 'Regardless of what happened between me and Itsuki, you and little Nao are still family. Don't hesitate to come find me should the need arise.'

Kokoro blinked as she pulled open the photo album. As she flipped through each one, she remembered something she noticed the day she had first taken control of the body.

"Why aren't there any baby photos of Naoko?"

Mrs. Haneda paused, inhaled deeply. "Your father and I…we had wanted a child for so long, but weren't able to conceive," she explained, almost reluctantly. "Naoko was rescued, then given to us to raise."

"Rescued?" Kokoro tensed, trying to process as the pieces slowly came together. "Naoko was adopted?"

Mrs. Haneda nodded, hands folded in her lap. Kokoro's lips curled, eyes darting from side to side in thought before settling back on her. "Were you ever going to tell her?"

"I…" Mrs. Haneda's lip quivered. "We wanted to, so many times. But we just couldn't. To us, it didn't matter who gave birth to her. Naoko was *our* little girl."

Kokoro's heart felt heavier. She inhaled slowly. "You said that Naoko was rescued, but from what?"

"It's…complicated," she said, gesturing to the photo with Mr. Haneda and his father. "This is a conversation better had with him."

"So, you want me to find him," Kokoro guessed, "this 'Shinobu.'"

"He has connections. If anyone can find your friend, he can," Mrs. Haneda explained. Her gaze fell, lips curled. "You may not be Naoko, but we still care about you. So, stay safe, please. For me."

Kokoro gripped the photo and tucked it in her jacket pocket. She leaned over and embraced Naoko's mother before releasing the hug with a gentle, reassuring smile. "I will."

"Good." Naoko's mother nodded solemnly. Kokoro rose from the couch, walked to the front door, slipping on her snow boots. She glanced back one last time, then pushed out into the cold. The winds immediately tore into her as she trudged her way through the snow-filled streets down to the station, and finally onto the train.

Kokoro sighed, then pulled out her phone to call John. The phone dialed for a few seconds before he picked up and she gave him the news.

"Wait, wait…we're going to find a Yakuza?" John asked, his voice imbued in static.

"Yep," Kokoro replied in a hushed tone as the train shifted around. "Nao…I mean, my grandfather."

John was silent for a good minute before he replied. "And he can help us?"

"Supposedly." Kokoro shrugged. "Either way, it's better than nothing."

"What about your dad?"

"Mr. Hane—" She stopped upon remembering that she was talking to John and not Sayuki. With a deep breath, she corrected herself. "—Father is looking too."

"And we can't help him?"

"He doesn't want me to. He wanted me to stay home."

"Why didn't you?"

"You know why."

Another silence at the end of the line as the train continued to roll onward. Finally, he spoke up again.

"Alright. You're scaring me, but we'll do this your way," John said, defeat and apprehension in his voice. "You got the address?"

"Hold on," Kokoro pulled the phone from her ear, sent it and put it back up. "Got it?"

"Got it," John confirmed. "See you there, Naoko."

"You too." Kokoro hung up on the call and sighed, staring out the window. The snow-capped buildings passed her by in a blur as the weakening sun faded into a cold, lifeless night.

The world is so much bleaker now. She frowned. It seemed like just yesterday that she and Naoko were always taking the train to school together, laughing, crying, or whatever shenanigans were involved. She missed those days, and her precious friend so dearly.

If only I had…

Kokoro shook her head. No, the time for self-pity was over. Now, she had to focus if she had any chance of saving Sayuki and others.

The train finally rolled into her stop. She rose and drifted out the doors with the others. The cold caught her breath as she pulled her hood over her ashen hair and walked down into the frozen night.

CHAPTER 17
THE GOKUDŌ'S SHADOW

"YOU SURE THIS IS IT, NAOKO?" JOHN ASKED. "Looks kinda dingy to me."

Kokoro was wondering the same thing. In front of them was a rundown bar that looked like it was older than anything else on the street. The vertical neon sign in front that read 'Shin's Tattoo and Pub' flickered, briefly illuminating the other sign below that read in clear, brute English, 'No foreigners!'

"I guess so." Kokoro shrugged and led the way, pushing the door. She stopped. The inside was much cleaner. Still old, but well-kept. Faded wood with markings burnt into it adorned the wall behind the bar itself. At the far end was a set of curtains, from behind which a faint buzzing could be heard. In two of the books sat a few disheveled-looking men in faded suits, tattooed head to toe. They continued to converse among themselves, yet their eyes still followed them as they entered the bar.

"Yep," John whispered behind her. "Definitely the right place, I think."

Before she could even reply, a large man emerged from behind the curtains. A large green dragon tattoo stretched from his neck into his partially unbuttoned dress shirt. His sturdy gaze came to rest on them, then solidified into a glare. Kokoro met his challenge, returning it.

"Uh, Naoko?" John asked from behind her. "What the hell are you doing?"

"Shinobu," Kokoro said to the man, interrupting John. "We're looking for Shinobu Haneda."

The tattooed man briefly assessed her, then chuckled, gesturing to the room behind him. He then walked away to the entrance, shoving past John, who recoiled.

"Bloody hell," John said, pulling back up next to her. "I don't like this."

Kokoro ignored him and kept moving, gently pushing aside the curtains. At the end of the back room was another man, who was cleaning a set of needles. He looked old, worn. His short, graying hair was unruly, the beginnings of a beard manifested across his jaw. He wore a dark blue dress shirt, sleeves rolled up, and a pair of faded dress pants complete with shoes. Like the others, he was partially covered in tattoos. The image of a lone wolf with a snake in its mouth adorned his left arm, with the inverted image on his right.

Once they had entered, the man paused. He partially turned in his chair, eyeing her with his peripherals as he held the tattooing needle aloft.

"You're too young, girl. You shouldn't be here. And you—" he gestured to John. "No foreigners. Can't you read the sign?"

"Wasn't my idea, sorry." John exchanged glances with Kokoro. "Just here with my friend. We—"

"Don't care." The man turned back around and continued to clean his needle. "Get out. Both of you."

"We need your—"

"Now," the man reiterated coldly.

John pursed his lips, turning to her. "This ain't worth it. Let's bail."

Kokoro refused to budge. She stepped forward. "I'm looking for Shinobu Haneda," she said firmly.

"Young woman…" His hands paused. "…where did you hear that name?"

They froze. Kokoro could have sworn the room was at least ten degrees colder.

"My mother," she said. "She sent me here to—"

The man suddenly spun and rose from his chair, his eyes narrowed. He slammed the needle down on his tray and inspected her. His eyebrow arched at the sight of Kokoro's ashen hair, but he continued to assess her until his gaze met hers.

"You look familiar," Shinobu noted, before his eyes narrowed. "How do you know my name?"

Kokoro paused, trying to parse the words together in her mind, before remembering the family photo. She fished it out of her pocket and held it out in front of him. He took it from her with hands that ever so slightly quivered. His hard gaze flicked to her as he held the photo aloft. "Where did you get this?"

"From my mother, Hana Haneda," Kokoro said, letting the words hang in the air.

Shinobu inspected the photo one last time, flipping it and reading the back. He removed his glasses, his eyes widened. "Naoko. Granddaughter. It's been so long."

Kokoro blinked. The others were dead silent as well, watching from within like a frightened rabbit in its burrow. The only exception was Sunshine, who was right there next to her in the inner world, Fishy secured in her grip.

"Ko," she said, tugging on her pants with urgency, "I know him."

"You do?" Careful not to let the words slip through the body's mouth, she leaned down. "How?"

"I'm not sure," Sunshine paused thoughtfully, then shook her head as she frowned at Kokoro. "I just remember him somehow."

Kokoro nodded and briefly caressed Sunshine's cheek. Shinobu and John were both staring at her, before the former spoke up.

"I'm sorry for the mess. I was not expecting visitors." Shinobu briefly gestured around the room. It was then Kokoro noticed a long, thin, wooden box with a sling propped up in the corner, with several paper seals at the tops and sides with warnings not to open. Shinobu hesitated on looking at it, then faced Kokoro. "I…heard about what happened, that they took you. I had hoped that you would never be forced into that life again, and yet…" He dipped his head.

At that moment, the familiar, eerie cries sounded. Next to her, Sunshine put Fishy on her shoulder and bounced him, muttering. Kokoro frowned, then turned her attention back to Naoko's grandfather.

"What do you mean, 'again?'"

"Your parents didn't tell you?" he asked. Kokoro shook her head.

"That I'm adopted?"

"Everything," Shinobu said, before hesitating. "I assumed your mother would have sent you here for that very reason."

Kokoro's eyes narrowed. There was something more to Naoko being adopted? A part of her deep within yearned to know, but she didn't have time, not with Sayuki in the clutches of Shane and Claire.

"No," Kokoro said. "The same people that took me now have my friend, Sayuki." She stepped closer. "Mother said you could help. That you had resources."

"Because I was a Gokudō?" Shinobu asked.

Kokoro nodded. Her plea hung in the air as she hoped the weight of her words would sink in. Shinobu's eyes softened as he gazed at her, setting the faded photo on his table. He rubbed his knees, eyeing the box before locking his hands together.

"I know it's a lot to ask of you," she said firmly, kneeling and taking the hands of Naoko's grandfather. "But Sayuki is so important to me, and I will do anything to save her." She demanded his gaze, staring deep into the turbulent recesses of his soul, hoping to find hope there. "Please."

Silence filled the room as Shinobu returned the stare. In his gaze, Kokoro saw something...familiar. His brows creased. "After all these years, I've never forgotten your eyes. They haunt my sleep."

Kokoro's lip curled. Shinobu clenched his fists, his brows furrowing.

"Alright." He broke the stare and rose, walking to the corner where the mysterious box was. From the side, he grabbed a long overcoat and donned it. He reached for the box, and picked up it, letting it sit in his hands for a moment as he closed his eyes and muttered something. After, he adjusted the strap and slung it over his shoulder. He made his way to the front of the room, passing the curtains and eventually the bar itself.

All the tattooed men stopped when they saw him. Their eyes widened, shifting from his mysterious box to him. Some of their expressions seemed...haunted. Almost reverent.

"I'm going to take care of something," Shinobu said as he regarded them all with a glance. "Don't destroy my bar while I'm gone."

The men rose and bowed. Shinobu returned it, and soon he, Kokoro, and John were out the door and into the snowfall. Hints of holiday lights from the main street adjacent to them bled through to the alleyways, though Naoko's grandfather seemed content to stick to the shadows, like a creature of the dark.

"So, the people that have your friend," Shinobu said, breaking the silence. "Tell me what you know."

"They're operating mainly in Shibuya, near the Crossing," John said, running up a little to keep his words in earshot of the old man. "The one called Claire Hanson is the one who is out and about luring them in, promising careers as models overseas and whatnot. From what I've heard, Shane handles the business deals with the gangs and tries to sell the girls off. Been feeding the info to Naoko's dad to take them down."

Eyes narrowing, Shinobu leaned in close to Kokoro and asked, "Who is this foreigner?"

"He saved me," Kokoro replied, nodding. "When they grabbed me, he saved me. Now he's doing it again for Sayuki."

Shinobu's gaze softened. "So, you trust him?"

"With every fiber of my being," Kokoro answered.

"I see." He nodded, glancing back at John. His brows creased, as if another thought were coming to him. "If Itsuki is still in the police force, then why do you need me?"

"The ones who snatched Sayuki are smart," John explained as they walked, tightening his jacket. "Mr. Haneda is out lookin' already, but with the traitor in the police force mucking about, we're worried they won't get to her in time." He pulled up his phone and scrolled through PULSE. "If what everyone is saying is true, then it seems like they're trying to leave Tokyo."

"Do you have a photo of the other foreigners?" Shinobu asked. "This 'Shane' and 'Claire?'"

"Oh. Er, yeah." John opened his photo app and moved next to Shinobu and showed him. "This one is Shane. No idea how he looks now. The next one is what Claire used to look like." He tapped the screen. "And here's what she looks like now. It's a little blurry, I know, but…"

"It will do. Just keep that close," Shinobu said. "We'll be there soon."

"Be where?" John asked.

"You'll see."

"Ah." John nodded, and exchanged a glance with Kokoro, shrugging. "Yes, sir."

Shinobu nodded, then turned to Kokoro. "You said your mother sent you?"

Kokoro nodded. "She seemed like she trusted you."

"Ah. Good daughter-in-law." A half-smile stretched across his lips as he said the words. Despite having only seen him scowl, it almost seemed unnatural on him. "She would call every few years, tell me about their life, how you were. She told me how you loved sunflowers when you were younger."

Next to her in the inner world, Sunshine beamed. Kokoro smiled, patted her on the shoulder, then faced the front once more.

"But she hasn't called me in years," Shinobu continued, "nor was I allowed to visit."

"Why is that?" Kokoro asked.

"Itsuki." The stiff wind strengthened by the shallow street picked up enough to send shivers through both Kokoro and John, though Shinobu appeared unbothered. "We never got along. He always hated having a 'Gokudō' for a father."

"Gokudō?" Kokoro blinked. "Why do you keep calling yourself that? Weren't you Yakuza?"

"To us, the term 'Yakuza' holds a weight laden with implications that resonate more as an insult. It's a word that seems to suggest we've intentionally embraced a losing hand in the game of life. However, we acknowledge the intensity and extremity of the path we tread." His gaze briefly met hers. "And so, some of us have chosen to identify as 'Gokudō'—a reflection of the utter dedication this path demands."

"I understand, I think." Kokoro nodded. "I'm guessing my father didn't exactly see it that way, though."

"Undoubtedly," Shinobu confirmed. "I'd even say it's probably why he joined the police force."

Kokoro paused. Suddenly, it made sense: Mr. Haneda's previous strictness toward Naoko. The 'standards.' Was it motivated by Shinobu the entire time?

"You mean he joined because he wanted to be different from you?"

"I don't blame him," Shinobu confirmed, though regret tinged his voice. "When he was ten, he ran away and was taken in by his grandfather." His eyes lowered. "At least he was raised by a better man."

"When was the last time you spoke with him?" Kokoro asked.

Shinobu stopped moving, his eyes meeting Kokoro's. He said nothing, yet she knew the answer was in the silence. Kokoro lowered her head, and the three kept walking. As they did, something heavy sounding clanked inside Shinobu's mysterious box. John stepped closer to it, his eyes narrowing.

"What's in there?" he asked.

"A family heirloom," Shinobu answered. "I…inherited it."

"Ah." John blinked. "Right."

Eventually, they reached another, thinner alleyway and turned into it, down a set of steps with an old door at the end. Lilac and sapphire neon cast a flickering light on the snow below, dueling the powerful shadows. Shinobu knocked, and within the minute, another tattooed man answered. Instead of bowing, they clasped hands and spoke, their voices so hushed that Kokoro wasn't able to make out any words.

The conversation stopped. Shinobu turned to John, motioning for his phone. He pulled it free from his jacket pocket, opened it, then paused on a photo he took with his father. Shaking his head, John swiped until he found the pictures of Shane and Claire, then gave it to him.

"Thank you," Shinobu said, passing it to the other man, who disappeared behind the door with it. A few minutes later, he emerged, saying a few words to Shinobu and nodding. As he handed the phone back, they clasped arms once more before the other man vanished into the shadows of the doorway.

"What did they say?" Kokoro asked.

Shinobu didn't immediately respond. Instead, he typed something into John's phone and handed it back to him. "Meet me there." He glanced at Kokoro. "If this works out, then we will find your friend soon."

Kokoro nodded, frowning slightly. With one last look, Shinobu disappeared into the room, the metal door slamming behind him. She turned, opening the address on her phone in maps and trudging through the thick layer of snow on the ground to her destination.

From the back, John finally broke his silence. "Pretty intense, that guy."

"No kidding." Kokoro thought back to their conversation at the bar, remembering the deep regret in his eyes. Beneath that rough exterior, there was something so familiar about him. What was it?

"Anyway," John began, shivering as he shoved his hands in his pockets, "how far is this meetin' place of yours?"

"About twenty minutes." Kokoro glanced at John. "You ready?"

"If you are," John replied.

With a nod, they pressed forth, further from the city lights into the frosty night.

"Hasn't it been an hour already?"

"More than that." Kokoro checked her phone for the third time in the last few minutes. Where was Shinobu? Surely, he hadn't changed his mind?

"Damn," John said, shivering. "It's cold out here. Are you sure your grandfather gave you the right address? Are you sure it's not in some nice, cozy café?"

Kokoro pursed her lips, tightened her jacket around her and checked the map on her phone, sighing. "According to this, yeah." The address wasn't really…anything. Just an old hole in the wall restaurant that looked like it hadn't seen a customer in practically a century. The alley seemed so isolated, barren. Even the hustle and bustle of the city felt like an afterthought; the silence seemed louder than anything else.

"Seems odd, doesn't it?" a voice said in the back of her mind. Kokoro allowed herself a moment to narrow it down, the speech pattern, the tone, the deepness. She smiled.

"Good to hear from you again, Hideaki. You guys were awfully quiet earlier."

"Apologies," he said. "We were just listening. Well, bar Sunshine, of course."

"I see," Kokoro replied inwardly, then paused. "So, Naoko's grandfather. What do you think?"

Silence. The sound of air sucked through bared teeth, followed by hurried words echoed from the inside.

"He kinda terrifies me," Ikiryo said.

"I concur. I'm not sure so enlisting his aid is such a good idea," Hideaki said. "While I'm certain he wouldn't harm us, there are still

299

so many unknowns. People like him don't pull their punches. He is Yakuza, after all."

"He's more than that!" a shrill voice protested, echoing. Sunshine's. "I know he's rough, but he's good!"

"How do you know?" Ikiryo asked. "We've only just met him."

That's true. Kokoro rubbed her wrist, frowning as she listened in. *We know little about him, other than him being Naoko's grandfather.*

"I'm not sure yet," Sunshine replied slowly, yet her delicate voice lost none of its confidence. "I just do."

Kokoro smiled. Why was that girl's optimism so contagious?

A shrill scream shook her from her thoughts. John whirled away from her, rising from the wall and stepping out. He turned to her.

"You hear that?"

"Yeah," Kokoro confirmed. "Sounded like it came from that way."

John shot her an apprehensive look. "Let's go."

Kokoro shrugged and set off toward the noise with John close at heel. She listened for more screams, or even the sounds of struggle, but none came. They walked until they turned the corner and found a young woman on the ground, hands bound behind her back, tied to a pipe protruding from the ground and walls. She rushed forward to help the girl, but stopped as the light passed her. Her blonde hair was tangled, dirty. Bruises and small cutes lined her cheeks and neck. Her head rotated slowly as her eyelids fluttered. Despite the injuries, the bitch's face was instantly recognizable.

"Claire…?" Kokoro caught her breath, stepping back as she eyed the bitch in disbelief. She felt Ikiryo's presence. From her radiated shock, though hints of vengeance bled through.

"Told you I would find her." Shinobu emerged from the shadows, his long coat resting on his shoulders. The coat obscured something in his left hand as the sleeves fluttered in the wind. At his feet lay the mysterious box, emptied of its contents.

"Damn, man," John said, his eyes wide as he warily inspected his former friend. Claire's swollen cheeks were smudged with blood that dripped from her split lips.

Kokoro assessed Claire once more. Despite the hatred that burned within, she shifted uncomfortably.

"I know, but…" Kokoro hesitated. "Isn't this a bit much?"

"You asked me to find Claire," Shinobu said, his voice unnaturally, eerily calm. "Here she is."

"He's right," Ikiryo echoed from within. Kokoro pulled back just enough to her next to the others, her fists clenched. "It's like we said. She has to pay."

Kokoro hesitated. Ikiryo's expression softened.

"Just five minutes," she pleaded. "That's all."

Kokoro allowed herself to drift back as Ikiryo rushed into control. She heard a thumping as the body's heart rate rose, blood rushing. Ikiryo grabbed Claire by the collar of her jacket and yanked her forward as far as she could.

"Do you remember us?" Ikiryo asked, an edge in her voice.

Claire looked around in a daze; her eyes came to rest on her former friend. "John. Long time no see, buddy."

"I ain't no buddy of yours, bitch," John snapped. "Especially not after what you did."

Claire managed a weak grin. "Like you're any better."

John jumped forward, bringing his face close to hers. "I ain't like you and Shane. I never was."

"Christ's sake, John." Claire laughed, blood seeping from her split lips. "Half the time you were too drunk to even notice. Otherwise, you were just too stupid."

John grit his teeth, then scoffed. Ikiryo scooted close so Claire could get a good look.

"You know John," she said. "But do you know who I am?"

Claire stared back, confused, her eyes half shut. Her throat rattled as she struggled to speak. Her mouth closed, and she shook her head.

Ikiryo's eyes narrowed in disbelief. "You seriously don't recognize me?"

"No…?" Claire groaned, wincing. "Should I?"

Ikiryo pulled her again, the chains that bound Claire to the pipe clanging. Rage filled her eyes, and yet Kokoro could also see pain just as prominent.

"You mean to tell me that after everything you did, you don't even know me?"

Claire didn't respond further. Ikiryo released her, fighting tears as she struggled to form further words. Kokoro moved closer to the front as Ikiryo collapsed into her embrace.

"I'm sorry," she said. "I thought I could, but…"

"It's okay," Kokoro said, pulling back and reassuring her. "Go to Void or Sunshine. I've got this."

Ikiryo nodded, then walked back to the others, her form disappearing as Kokoro slipped into control of the body, the cold chilling her. She inhaled sharply and looked the monster square in the eye.

"My name is Naoko Haneda," she hissed, before hesitating. It felt wrong saying those words, but to get to Sayuki, she would do whatever it took. "Ring a bell now?"

"Wait," Claire said, her eyes slowly widening. "Naoko, Naoko. That sounds familiar." She sighed and shook her head, a wry laugh escaping her bloodied lips. "Wow. It really is you, huh? Hard to recognize you with all those clothes on."

Kokoro grit her teeth, determined to resist her taunts. "Where is Sayuki?"

"Not good with names." Claire spat blood. "Well, except for you, of course. You were special."

Kokoro slammed her back and raised her fist. The confidence in Claire's face suddenly vanished, her eyes widening as she struggled to get away.

She's afraid of me? Kokoro paused as a loud click shook her from her thoughts, a shadow looming over both her and Claire. Shinobu was glaring at Claire and had taken a single step forward, yet it was enough that Kokoro could have sworn she smelled urine in the snow under Claire.

"Okay, okay!" Claire struggled against her restraints, shaking. "I'll talk! I-I'm sorry!"

Shinobu's eyes narrowed, but he withdrew as another almost indecipherable snapping sound was heard from the shadow of his overcoat. After that, Claire slammed her eyes shut in a pathetic attempt to regain control of her breathing.

"She will talk now," Shinobu said. "Right, Claire?"

Without hesitation, Claire shakily nodded, lips twitching.

"Good." Shinobu gestured to Kokoro. "Continue."

Kokoro didn't know whether to thank him or fear him. She shuddered, then faced Claire once more.

"Her name was Sayuki Sato. She was my friend, and you took her recently."

For a moment, Claire's brows furrowed as if she were about to retort something. A quick glance at Shinobu and her eyes were back on Kokoro, obedient. Submissive.

"I...uh..." Claire winced, her cheek twitching. "We don't go by names. We usually just refer to them by numbers, and—"

Kokoro heard the snow shift behind her. Claire's eyes shot open.

"B-But we take them all to the same place now! Right, right...by the docks."

"Be more specific," Shinobu said. "Or else it will just get worse."

"By the...erg, what's it called? Shib...Shib—"

"Shibaura-Futo?" Shinobu asked, brows raised.

"That's it! That's the one!" Claire exclaimed. "In an old warehouse!"

Shinobu paused for a moment. "On dock eight?"

"Yes!" Claire said, as if every word would somehow spare her a moment of pain. "T-they're leaving soon. Too much heat with the police, and Yakuza, and…"

"How much time?" Kokoro asked.

"I-I…" Claire stuttered with her words, her waxy face pale, though Kokoro couldn't tell if it was from the cold or the fear. "A day, maybe? J-Just depends on how fast they can pack up the girls."

"Then we've got to go now," Kokoro said, looking at John and Shinobu. "Come on. Let's—"

"W-w-wait! You're not just gonna leave me to freeze, are you?" Claire asked hysterically.

"I'm tempted." Kokoro's eyes narrowed. "Very tempted."

Claire groaned, shifting as she struggled against her binds. "I'm sorry, okay? I know I deserve this, after what I did to you." Her lips flapped as she shivered. "I admit, at first I was doing it for money. But-t-t then I had no choice."

"No choice?" Kokoro asked. A scoff escaped her lips as a cold puff. "Are you kidding me?"

"Please!" Claire begged. "Do whatever you want! Send me to jail, just…" Tears welled up in her eyes, yet didn't fall. The cold knew better; the bitch didn't deserve any sympathy. "Just don't let me die."

Kokoro's brows furrowed. How pathetic could she get? Despite intending to lash out, the anger in Kokoro collapsed beneath its own weight and faded to grief. Her eyes lowered.

"Damn it, Claire," Kokoro said, attempting to look her in the eyes, to get the message across. "You were supposed to be Naoko's friend."

"Please," Claire begged again, ignoring her words and avoiding Kokoro's gaze.

Silence. Next to her, John blinked, and Shinobu's eyes narrowed, though Kokoro didn't care at that moment; It needed to be said. Kokoro pursed her lips as Claire wept, the snow falling on her undoubtedly fake lashes.

"Fine," Kokoro growled, rising and staring down at her. "It's more than you deserve, but…"

Claire looked up hopefully.

"…I'll call the police to come pick you up," Kokoro continued. "You won't freeze, but you'll never see the light of day again."

At first, Claire's eyes quivered. Then laughed in relief. "T-Thank you. I—"

"—Not good enough."

Before Kokoro could even register it, Shinobu had strode forward to Claire, flinging aside the overcoat. A flash of silver later and there was a bowed, shimmering blade leveled at Claire's neck. The distance from the guard to the tip was about sixty centimeters, with professional designs etched into the backbone. The sheath he held in his left hand looked like it had been soaked in blood, with several haphazard scratches across it.

Kokoro froze, unable to take her eyes off the blade. Where had she seen it before?

"I said your pain would be short if you cooperated," Shinobu growled. "I never said you would live."

"No, no, no…" Claire desperately glanced over at Kokoro and John. "I was your friend! I'm begging you!" Her breaths became ragged, chest rising and falling rapidly. "Oh God, I don't wanna die! I don't wanna—"

She stopped. Shinobu had one hand on her quivering face. Her eyes widened in horror.

"Close your eyes," he commanded, removing his hand and standing to his full height as he stepped back.

Claire squeezed them shut, and the blade swung. A gasp escaped her lips, followed by a gurgle. Blood spurting from her neck, she fell sideways. Her body spasmed a few more times, then lay motionless, her face half hidden in the snow.

Kokoro blinked. It had all happened so fast it may as well have been a blur. Internally, she felt the sheer horror emanating from everyone; she could hear Ikiryo and Hideaki trying to comfort Sunshine, though their own breaths were labored. Kokoro shifted her focus back to the comparatively quiet outside, where the heavy snow covered the corpse of their former friend.

"Holy shit, mate," John said after the silence had hung in the frigid air, glancing warily at Shinobu. "What the hell was that for?"

"My swordsmanship is rusty. I needed the practice," Shinobu said, scoffing. "Besides, for what she did to my granddaughter…" he gestured to Claire's remains with the tip of his blade, "...she deserved it. And more."

Kokoro followed where the blade pointed. Did Claire deserve it? The way she died was too...brutal. Cold. Inhumane, even for her.

"Either way, it's over with," Shinobu said as he grabbed his coat and moved to wipe the blade with it but stopped. Instead, he wiped it against Claire's jacket, then snapped it back into its sheath. "Let's go."

And then he turned, walking out of the alley. John gave one last glance to his former friend, before shaking his head and following Shinobu. Kokoro stayed just a little longer, staring into those dead, glassy eyes, watching as the snowfall rapidly covered her, like vultures descending on a corpse. Kokoro clenched her jaw, then she too turned away, leaving the white silence to cover the blemish.

It always did.

CHAPTER 18

A WORLD OF MONSTERS

FOR THE ENTIRE TEN MINUTES Kokoro had walked behind Shinobu and John, she hadn't been able to get Claire's open throat out of her thoughts. She was undoubtedly a monster, though did it really warrant such brutality from another?

Kokoro shivered, though she wasn't sure if it was from a chill or the even colder thought that crossed her mind. Despite everything Claire had done, taking Naoko away, luring other girls to the same fate, Kokoro just couldn't help but feel like that crimson stain on the pristine snow was also on her hands. She was the one who led Shinobu to her, after all.

I may as well have killed her myself. Kokoro curled into herself, the air suddenly becoming far colder.

"I gotta ask, man," John said to Shinobu from the front as they walked. "I understood why you did her in like that, but ain't it a bit much?"

Shinobu stopped, glaring at him. "Don't tell me you're sympathizing with her?"

"No, it's just…" John paused, a puff escaping his lips. "Seems not long ago that she was my friend. At least, before I knew what she and Shane were up to. And then, seeing what you did, I…"

Shinobu stopped, gripping his blade tight as he eyed John, who recoiled slightly. "That girl you *think* you remember is not real," he said. "She never was."

"I know that," John said. "But still. The way you killed her doesn't make you much better than she was."

"I don't care."

John's jaw tightened, his body quivering. "You're touched in the head, you know that?"

Shinobu let out a derisive snort and pressed ahead. Brows furrowing, John dared to reach for his shoulder. In an instant, Shinobu reacted, forcefully slamming John against the wall and drawing his blade once more. The scarred sheath fell onto the snow below.

"Did you forget who I am?" Shinobu growled, brandishing the blade before him. John instinctively attempted to back away, but the sight of the sharp edge perilously close to his neck froze him in his tracks. His eyes widened in fear, and he ceased all resistance, anxiously holding his breath as the snow fell around them.

"If it makes you feel better, she died quickly," Shinobu said as he withdrew the blade. "More than she deserved."

John rubbed his neck as he finally released his breath. Shinobu let the tip of his blade fall as he retrieved the sheath from the ground and prepared to reunite the two. Kokoro's eyes followed the shimmering blade as it slid back into the sheath with an eerie grind.

The cries sounded again. Images of the dark place in the depths of Naoko's mind flashed: the run-down building, wallpaper in tatters, loud buzzing lights and a ceiling was so low that it seemed like it would collapse at any given moment. Kokoro's brows furrowed. What had that vision meant?

Unless. She froze. *What if it wasn't a vision, but a memory?*

Closing her eyes, Kokoro tried to wrack her brain for specifics, to pull something, anything, from the obscurity of it all: the rooms filled with the shattered statues of broken women, and finally the Oni that chased her throughout. What kind of place would have such horrible things?

No, no. She shook her head. *There's something else. Come on, think!*

"Kokoro?" Ikiryo asked from within. "T-The shadows…"

"The what?" Kokoro

"Please stop digging," Hideaki begged as well. "You're drawing them here!"

"No!" Sunshine said. "Let her do this. I need to know, too."

Kokoro nodded and continued to fight the fog that tried to deny her, willing herself back to that moment. The dark figures with luminescent tattoos and wicked grins that were about to kill her, until her savior had stepped in, ripping the shadows asunder in a flash of dazzling silver.

The blade. The truth hit Kokoro like a train, pieces all coming together. She released the memories, and subsequently heard sighs of relief from inside as the shadows faded, though the realization was still raw in her mind. *That's why the thing looks so familiar.*

As fate would have it, it was the same blade…and the same man who wielded it.

"It was you," Kokoro said suddenly. Both Shinobu and John stopped and spun to face her, with the latter arching an eyebrow.

"Kokoro?" John asked. "What are you…?"

"That place. The brothel." Kokoro ignored John and pushed past him, coming to stand in front of Shinobu. "It belonged to the Akasaka-Daiichi, didn't it?"

Shinobu hesitated, then nodded slowly.

"And the one who saved me from them was you," Kokoro concluded.

Naoko's grandfather returned the stare, yet there wasn't any hint of challenge in his eyes. Rather, there was that shame she had seen just beneath the surface of the scowl that masked it.

Kokoro's breath caught in her throat. So many questions hurled themselves at her all at once, that she wondered if it was the others. What was Naoko doing there in the first place? Why were the men after her? Instead, a different one escaped her lips.

"Why didn't you tell me?"

Shinobu's brows furrowed as he closed his eyes, his grip on the blade tightening. "Because that day is my greatest failure."

Kokoro blinked, confused. She felt a familiar presence close by in the inner world, and soon warmth flowed into her. She analyzed Shinobu again, seeing his downtrodden face, all the shame and years of regret flashing across his eyes.

"How?" Kokoro asked. "You saved me."

Shinobu's face softened, but the weight of regret still lingered. "It's not just because I saved you," he confessed. "It's because you were the *only* one I saved."

"The only one?" Kokoro remembered the haunting wails of the other women in the rooms that lined the hallway, yet only found husks that were broken beyond repair. She frowned. "What happened?"

Shinobu grimaced, then leaned against the brick wall. His brows furrowed.

"Twenty years ago," he began, "The Akasaka-Daiichi was one of the most powerful clans. From Hokkaido to Kagoshima, we ran much of Japan." His eyes lowered. "Back then, we were led by our Kumicho, Masaharu Akasaka. But he was so much more. My friend. My brother."

"What happened to him?" John asked.

"After Masaharu's death, his son, Akuji, took over, and the clan fell apart," Shinobu explained, his disgust palpable. "He started needless wars with other clans and turned the brothel into a den of horrors. Instead of voluntary prostitution, he enslaved foreign women and kidnapped fellow Japanese for his sick desires."

"You knew what he was doing?" Kokoro asked. "And you didn't stop him?"

"I *didn't* know," Shinobu clarified. "At least, not until I returned to the brothel from dealing with one of his 'distractions.' It was then I discovered the true extent of his wickedness, the way he had butchered the women." His jaw clenched. "I walked in on Akuji and his twisted partners about to kill a young girl that had been hiding in the brothel for months after her mother was slain by them." Shinobu's eyes met hers. "That girl, Naoko, was you."

Kokoro tensed. For a moment, she could almost see it as clearly as she could see everyone else in front of her; the skinny, long-haired man hovering over her, a twisted smile seared into his almost inhuman lips.

"And…after that?" she asked tentatively.

"To save you, I killed them all, starting with Akuji. I tried to save the other women too, but…" He slid down the wall, his hand's tightening around the blade's hilt, as if to keep from quivering. "The fire, the screams, they still haunt me." He met Kokoro's gaze, pain etched in his eyes. "I should have burned with them."

Kokoro's heart sank as she felt the weight of his torment as he continued, voice wavering. As clear as day, she could see the moment he had wanted to give in to the damning flames, though this time she could see his face; a soul broken by regret.

"Why, Naoko?" Shinobu asked. "Back then, why did you think I was worthy of life?"

Kokoro hesitated. She had experienced the memory, true, but it wasn't hers. Both the memory and cries belonged to whoever came before: a tragedy, nameless as she once had been.

She's still trapped in there. A part of us, maybe even the first.

Shaking her head, Kokoro snapped herself out of her thoughts and back to reality as she took a few deep breaths to contain herself.

All this time…she's been there alone. Poor girl. Kokoro's eyes shifted to Shinobu. *And he doesn't even know. About her, about Naoko. About any of it.*

Kokoro opened her mouth to speak but hesitated. The outside world partially faded as someone tugged her jacket. She looked down, seeing Sunshine with Fishy curled up in her arms, staring ahead through the body's eyes at Shinobu.

"May I?"

"Oh. Of course." Kokoro returned it, though she blinked in surprise. What was that girl up to?

Sunshine beamed, then pushed into control with Kokoro in tow. She knelt next to Shinobu and gripped his sleeve, demanding his eyes meet hers. The old man did so reluctantly.

"You think that because of what you've done in the past, that you weren't worth saving." Kokoro found herself saying, though the words were from Sunshine, coupled with an encouraging smile. "Everyone deserves a chance if they're willing to at least try, right? Especially you. So, thank you for saving me back then."

Shinobu froze for a moment, his sheathed blade gripped tight in his damaged hand. He exhaled sharply as the white silence fell, then rose, nodding to her.

"No," he said. "It is I who should thank you."

Kokoro blinked as Sunshine pulled back from the front. She stopped for a moment to regard her, a tear dripping down her cheek. "Thank you. I needed to say that."

"Oh. Of course." Kokoro watched as the young girl gripped Fishy tight in her arms, then walked back into the swirling mists. Her thoughts pondering the meaning behind Sunshine's words, Kokoro pressed back through to the real world, into control of the body as the air chilled her to the bone. The three began to walk in silence once more.

"So what now?" John asked. "We gonna go to this warehouse, or…?"

"I will handle it." Shinobu's face hardened once more, though not with the cold grief from before, but determination. "I just have to call in a favor first."

"A favor?" Kokoro asked, though her question was soon answered. They had arrived at another club like the first, though it was slightly more exposed, with two men guarding the glass doors covered to the brim with different advertisements. The men's eyes collectively widened at Shinobu, then they bowed.

"Like I said. A favor." Shinobu moved to enter the club. Kokoro and John tried to follow him, but the guards stepped in front of them.

"Hey, what gives?" John protested. "We're with him."

"Not anymore," Shinobu said. "Both of you, go home. I will take it from here."

"What?" Kokoro blinked. "No. I'm going with you."

"*No.*" Shinobu met her determined gaze, gripping his blade. "You think I'm gonna let you be endangered yet again?"

Kokoro's brows furrowed, her teeth clenched. Like son, like father.

"You don't have to protect me."

"Yes, I do," Shinobu said curtly. "Now, go. I'm sure your mother is worried sick."

Kokoro clenched her jaw, then tried to push forward, only to be rebuffed once more. "You really think I'm going to just stay home and worry about how everything will turn out? Sayuki is my friend—"

"—and she will be saved, as will the other girls." Shinobu turned to face her, rising to his full height. "I found Claire. What makes you think I can't find them?"

"It's not that, I…" Kokoro's cheeks flushed, "…I just…"

"Naoko," Shinobu said, placing a reassuring hand on her shoulder, gripping it tight. "Trust me on this. Please."

Reluctantly, Kokoro pulled back, though not without eyeing him. Shinobu returned it, though his previously determined gaze softened, like all he saw in her was the scared girl from the brothel. With one last nod to her and John, he opened the doors and disappeared into the hallway behind them.

Kokoro clenched her fists and stormed off around the same corner they had come from, John trailing not far behind her.

"I'm guessing you don't plan on going home?" he asked.

"Nope."

"Figured as much." John pulled out his phone. "Good thing I managed to type out what Claire had said. '*Shibaura-Futo. Old warehouse. Dock 8.*'" He tapped his screen twice, before he looked up and smiled. "There's also a station close by that stops there. You ready?"

"As I'll ever be," Kokoro said, returning the nod. She couldn't just sit back and do nothing while Sayuki and the other girls remained in danger. Together with John, she made her way to the closest station. The weight of the past and the revelations about Shinobu still weighed heavily on her mind, but she pushed them aside.

For now, it was time to save those missing girls and the woman she loved.

It wasn't long before they found the station and had boarded the train, though considering the weather, they were lucky it was still operating. She sat down and rubbed her arms, grateful to have a brief respite from the cold.

"Damn," John said, rubbing his hands together and breathing into them. He looked up to meet her eyes. "How you feeling? You ready for this?"

Kokoro frowned, glancing at the map on her phone as it slowly brought her ever closer to not just her friend, but presumably Shane and his goons as well. "Honestly, John, I'm feeling a bit scared. I'm worried that we'll be too late or…well. You know."

"Think I know the feeling," John replied. He placed his hand on her arm reassuringly. "Don't worry though. Whatever happens, I'll make sure both you and her get out."

Kokoro smiled. "You seemed to be really good at that."

"Hopefully luck holds for the third time." John chuckled, then stared out the window. "If I'm honest, I'm hoping to find Shane. Bastard lied to me all this time, so I figured it was time to settle the score, you know?"

"That makes two of us." Her grip on the pole tightened. "Either way, this has to end. No more girls being taken from their families, or…"

"Can't stop all of it, I'm afraid." John frowned. "Wish I could say otherwise, but that's just the world we live in. There will always be people like Shane and Claire, some even worse."

And there will always be those like Naoko.

"I know, but still." She sighed. Her mind drifted back to the argument between John and Naoko's grandfather. She glanced over at him, seeing that same mix of anger and grief trying to strangle his soul.

"Hey. You okay?"

"Yeah," John answered quickly. "Yeah. I'm just thinking about what Claire said, me not noticing what they were up to."

"It wasn't your fault," Kokoro argued, frowning. "You couldn't have—"

"—yeah, but what if I had?" John growled. "If I hadn't been so stupid, I could have stopped them from taking you! Or maybe even…" He stopped, gritting his teeth, "…maybe I could have stopped them from doing all that in the first place. Then maybe I wouldn't have had to see Claire get done in like that."

Kokoro's gaze fell. John noticed, then sighed.

"Sorry. I know what she did to you. But when I saw her there, it…" he hesitated, "…it was like seeing a monster wear my friend's skin, you know?"

"I understand," Kokoro said, managing a reassuring smile even though she truly didn't feel like giving one. "Believe me."

John nodded. His pocket vibrated, and he pulled his phone out to check it. He looked up. "We're almost there. You ready?"

Kokoro nodded and soon the train slid to a halt. She and John disembarked into the station, making their way down several flights of stairs back into the frigid air. They walked until they finally found what they were looking for. Dock eight was small compared with the ones around it, with a small container ship lined up alongside, several people hurriedly ferrying cargo onto it. She stopped, searching the buildings from afar.

Warehouse, warehouse…wait. Her eyes narrowed upon finding it. It was a partially rusted and inconspicuous old metal building, probably about thirty meters from the dock itself, with a few armed men patrolling nearby.

"There!" she said to John, pointing it out.

"Oh damn. Claire wasn't kidding when she said they were about to haul ass outta Japan. Doesn't look like we have long." He turned to her. "So, what now?"

Kokoro turned her attention back to the warehouse. The men with guns were shouting at the workers, urging them to hurry. The more she watched them, the harder her heart twisted in her chest. How long would Shinobu take? Why should they wait when Sayuki could be in any of those containers, trapped with the other poor girls? What if they were already on the ship?

The panic within her died slightly. She felt calm, yet focused. She analyzed every detail she could: guard locations, openings, whatever she could find to get them a way in.

"Hideaki," she said. "That you?"

"Sorry," Hideaki said. "I heard what you were thinking, and I borrowed your eyes for a moment to assess our chances."

"And?"

"Practically suicide," Hideaki said. "The guards are constantly moving, checking every corner. Those who aren't armed watch from above, radio in hand."

"So?" Ikiryo's voice rang out. "That's still our friend in there. We can't just sit here and do nothing."

"I agree, but let's not get ourselves killed," Hideaki replied. "As much as I want to save Sayuki and those missing girls, I want to live, too. When this is all over, I—" he stopped.

"You what?" Kokoro asked.

"—nothing." She heard Hideaki sigh. "If you're going to get in, getting past him is our first step." Her hand moved on its own, gesturing to the closest of the guards. "He patrols clockwise around that same set of shipping containers every two minutes, meaning we have to time ourselves opposite of him if we want to avoid detection."

"Okay," Kokoro said. "And after him?"

"It gets easier. The next one is stationary, facing outward from where the crew is loading the shipping containers. We just have to keep equal distance behind him and the workers."

"Out in the open?"

"That crane is right by that dock light and casts a large shadow," Hideaki pointed out. "Our clothing is dark enough to conceal us. I think."

"You think?" Kokoro hissed out loud, drawing a confused look from John. Her cheeks burned.

"It's our best chance," Hideaki said. "Go ahead and tell John. I want his thoughts as well."

Kokoro took a deep breath and quickly relayed their plan to him. John scoffed.

"Christ on a cross, Naoko, that's suicide," John said.

Kokoro heard the inevitable sigh from both Ikiryo and Hideaki. She gritted her teeth. She hated to admit it, but he was right. There really wasn't another way, unless…

She froze as an idea came to her. She fished around in her jacket pocket, pulling out the phone and dialing a contact. Soon enough, a surprised Mr. Haneda answered the phone.

"Hello?" he asked. "What's going on? Is everything—"

"I know where they are. Shibaura-Futo, in a worn-down warehouse by dock number eight." She pulled back, copied the address from the map program, and sent them to him in a message. "Please bring everyone you have. They're trying to leave soon."

"W-Wait. You're there?" Mr. Haneda asked frantically. "What the hell are you thinking?"

"Your father is coming too," she said, ignoring his protests. "Between the police and him, you guys can stop them, right?"

"My father...?" There was a brief silence on the other end of the line. "Of course, but—"

"Good," Kokoro said. She paused, inhaled sharply, turning away from John and whispering the last words. "I know you were Naoko's Dad, but..."

"...but what?"

"I've always thought of you as mine, too. I just wanted to thank you for that."

"Kokoro..." She could hear him barely able to control himself. "I..."

"I love you," she said, hanging up with a final click as she gripped the phone in her hand. After regaining control of her breathing, she turned to John, pressing the phone in his hand and removing her jackets until she was only in her hoodie, jeans and snow boots. "I'm gonna run across that field, screaming and running for my life. Use that opportunity to sneak in buy some time for my Dad to get here and free the girls, maybe find Sayuki if you can."

"Are you, crazy?" John asked. "They're going to shoot you on sight!"

"Maybe. Maybe not." She met his eyes, defiant. "They wouldn't dare harm the merchandise, right?"

It took all of two seconds for John to come up with a response to her idiotic plan. "Oh, hell no. No way you're—"

Kokoro quickly kissed him on the cheek and sprinted out into the opening as fast as she could, in plain view of all the guards and workers.

"Gotta get away," she screamed loudly, hoping to sell the idea. "I-I'm not going back!"

"Stop now or I'll put a bullet in your head!"

Kokoro froze, raising her hands and slowly turning around. There were at least five men clad in suits, an assortment of different guns pointed at her. Her eyes briefly flicked to the side, where she saw John stare at her, his eyes wide with horror.

"Go", she mouthed. "It's okay."

John frowned, his horrified gaze lowered. Reluctantly, he ran into the warehouse, off to find Sayuki. Kokoro sighed in relief, then turned her attention back to the guards who were closing in on her.

"Nice and easy," one of them said, walking forward and grabbing her by the arm. Kokoro didn't resist, but intentionally quivered, hoping to sell her charade. So far, it worked.

"P-Please don't hurt me," she said. "I'm sorry. I'll go back. I promise."

The guard scoffed, then pulled her along, a few of the others following behind her. The rest returned to their posts, patrolling the docks as they continued to load what she could only guess to be girls like her into the small cargo ship.

"Kokoro," Hideaki said, an edge in his voice. "This is a terrible idea."

"Ditto," Kokoro replied internally as they passed through the giant doors into the rusted warehouse. "But it worked. John got in."

"And it got us captured!" Ikiryo growled. "Way to go, idiot."

"I hate to be that guy, but I concur," Hideaki added. "Did you even think up an escape plan before you did that?"

"Yes," Kokoro said. Upon utterance of her lie, she felt immediate disdain from her head mates. She sighed. "Okay, no, but it'll be okay. The cops and Shinobu won't be far behind."

"For our sake, I hope so." She heard Ikiryo sigh. "What about Sayuki? Any sign of her yet?"

Kokoro immediately began looking around as the guard pushed her forward to the other side. The warehouse was filled with various boxes, some wood, some metal with holes drilled into them, presumably for breathing. The ones that were opened and emptied had foul smells emanating from them. She frowned.

That's probably where they keep them until they're ready to load them up.

"No sign of Sayuki yet." Kokoro inhaled, fighting to keep herself under control. "But still. How could someone do this to their fellow humans?"

"I ask myself that often," Hideaki replied, his voice somber. "My only conclusion is that those who would do these things have ceased to be human entirely. Unfortunately, we live in a world of monsters."

"Yeah." Kokoro scowled. "No kidding."

They continued to march her down the hallway, presumably toward one of the boxes, until a voice called out.

"Wait. Let me see that girl."

Kokoro tensed. The men obeyed as what she assumed to be their superior stepped in front of Kokoro and grabbed her by the chin, inspecting her.

"Where did you find her?"

"She was escaping," one of her captors said. "We caught her just in time. I—"

The superior ignored them and met her eyes. His brows furrowed.

"No, she isn't, you idiot. She's not an escapee." The man's brows furrowed. "She's an infiltrator. Think about it. How many girls with white hair have we had in the last six months?"

"Shit, you're right." The man holding her arm eyed her. "So, what should we do with her? Add her to the group anyway?"

"No. Just—" The leader stopped, patting his pocket and pulling out his phone. "Yeah? Wait, what?" He eyed Kokoro, then turned his gaze to the silhouette in the warehouse office window. "You want her up there with you?"

Kokoro's eyes widened. The man continued.

"Oh. Alright, then." The leader pocketed his phone, gesturing to her. "Take her up. Boss wants a chat with her."

They changed direction, pushing her down a different aisle and up a set of stairs to the warehouse office. The metal door swung open, revealing a simple, rusted office with dirty windows overlooking the warehouse itself. Off to the side were several girls, all dazed and drugged out of their mind. One of them caught Kokoro's eye.

"Sayuki," Kokoro whispered. Her friend was on the couch, eyes glassy, her eyelids occasionally twitching. Kokoro instantly felt her pulse quicken.

I swear, if they so much as laid a finger on her…

"Long time no see, love," a voice said.

Kokoro froze. Her gaze flicked to the back of the room, where the end of a cigarette lit in the darkness. Out of the shadows stepped Shane, long blonde hair slicked back, a small beard infesting his gaunt, misshapen jaw. He wore a loose velvet suit with an unbuttoned yellow dress shirt beneath it, his gold chains hanging from his neck. Worst of all were his sunken, bloodshot eyes, trained on Kokoro with a scowl to match.

"Welcome back."

CHAPTER 19
FACING THE DARK

"SHANE," Kokoro hissed.

"Hey now," Shane said, raising his hand with a cigar in it. "This is the first time we've even seen each other in a long time. Play nice this time and nothing bad will happen, eh?"

Shane moved to touch her arm, but Kokoro jerked back, only being stopped by the men that held her fast. Gritting his teeth, Shane scratched his arm, then his neck as he angled his head to look at her with bloodshot eyes.

"Well, fine. Be that way," Shane scoffed, wiping his twitching nose. "So down the business. What are you doing out 'ere?"

She clenched her jaw, arching her neck away from him. Behind her, she heard a soft voice call out.

"Kokoro…?"

Her eyes widened. She spun to see a groggy Sayuki pulling herself to a sitting position. She clutched her head, wincing.

Kokoro broke free from the guard's grip to sit next to her friend, bringing her into her arms. Sayuki's hand felt around for her arm, then gripped her sleeve. Brows furrowing, Kokoro glared at Shane.

"I swear, if you've—"

"Not much time for fun these days, especially not with all of Japan up my ass. Doesn't matter either way. Soon enough, she'll be on the boat out of here, as will you." Shane arched an eyebrow. "What's it to you, anyway? She your girlfriend or something?"

Kokoro's hate-filled stare hardened. Her protective grip on Sayuki tightened. Shane's eyes narrowed, his face twisted into a sneer.

"Ahh, I think I see now." Shane chuckled. "Tell you what. You play nice, be a good girl on the ride over the pond. Do that, and we can accommodate, give you two room to scissor and all that, long as you don't mind us watching. Whatdasay?"

The guards chuckled. Kokoro pulled Sayuki to her breast, brows furrowed before something caught her eye. In the far left corner of the room, something moved in the shadows, slowly, like a cat in the tall grass.

John. Her gaze shifted back to Shane. *Good. Just gotta keep Shane's attention on me.*

"Don't look so sour, love. It was a joke…mostly. Claire would have a laugh." Shane turned to one of his goons, nose wrinkling. "By the way, where is she? Less than an hour and we bail."

"Dead," Kokoro said. The venom in her words, she knew, was fueled by Ikiryo. "Gutted like the pig she is, bleeding out in a back alley somewhere."

"Think you're funny or something?" Shane's eyes narrowed. "Best watch that mouth, you hear? She's a bit loopy, but she's still my best mate."

"Your 'best mate' is buried under the snow in a back alley," Kokoro snapped.

Shane's lip twitched. He brought his face close to hers, brandishing his gun. "You better be lyin' right about now."

"I'm not," Ikiryo spat using Kokoro's lips. "The Yakuza got to her and opened her throat. I watched it happen myself."

The bastard's eyes widened in disbelief. He stepped back, his breaths becoming shallower. He glared at her.

"Oh, now you've gone and made it personal."

"Personal?" Kokoro asked. "Did you think about that before you trafficked me and dozens of other girls?"

"That's business," Shane hissed, his face twitching. "I told you before. I'm a goddamn businessman."

"No. You're a greedy, pathetic little boy." Ikiryo took full control from Kokoro and met him with a vicious glare. "A wannabe gangster who couldn't stand being in the shadow of his own father!"

Silence filled the room. The goons quickly exchanged glances before settling back on Shane, as if expecting something from him.

Shane's eyes darted between them, before settling his gaze back on Kokoro. He raised his gun and pointed it at her forehead.

"Know what? 'Bout had enough of this," he scoffed, wiping his nose. "Seeya."

Kokoro prepared to push Sayuki away and grit her teeth. A loud slam erupted from the warehouse below, followed by shouting.

"Police! Everyone get down on the ground now!"

Gunfire erupted. Shane's guards ducked, drawing their weapons before running out to join the firefight. Kokoro hadn't realized it, but she too was on the ground. The cracks of the soaring bullets multiplied tenfold as she froze, her thoughts swimming, her mind tearing herself apart as the outside world threatened to fade.

Come on, come on. Move!

The body didn't respond at first. Then she felt a comforting presence…no, more than one. She could sense everyone up in the front with her, pushing past the paralysis to seize control. With Sayuki in her arms, Kokoro began crawling toward the door.

"Where do you think you're going?"

Kokoro looked up to see Shane as he leveled the gun at her. Not two meters behind Shane was John, crouching in the shadows. She forced her gaze forward so as not to tip Shane off.

"You bitch." Shane's eyes flicked back down to her. "This was your doing, wasn't it?"

Kokoro glared up at him, defiant. Shane pressed the barrel of the gun to her forehead. The hammer cocked back.

John erupted from behind him, grabbing the gun and attempting to yank it away. The two struggled, slamming fists, knees, elbows, whatever they could into each other. Barely keeping his grip on the weapon, Shane broke free enough to jump through the window onto the fire escape.

"Go! I got him!" John commanded before stepping through the window. "Get her out of here!"

With a grunt, Kokoro helped Sayuki up and together they limped to the door. She glanced back, seeing John already beaten and bloodied, and contemplated going back to help him.

"Remember what we came for!" Hideaki said, his voice barely breaking through the chaos. "We have Sayuki. Get her to safety first!"

Kokoro nodded reluctantly and helped her friend out the door and down the steps, keeping low and out of the exchange of gunfire, ducking behind crates, piping, whatever she could find. The side entrance to the warehouse soon came into view, the flashes of police cars not far beyond it.

"Help!" she called. "My friend—"

Two police officers came to her, one with his pistol drawn. The second officer scooped up Sayuki and scurried back to their vehicles, turning the corner around a shipping container to a nearby ambulance. They placed Sayuki on a stretcher as a paramedic checked her vitals, placing an oxygen mask on her.

"What happened?" the paramedic asked.

"They drugged her, I think," Kokoro explained, rubbing her arms both out of nervousness and aversion to the cold.

"With what?"

"I'm not sure." Kokoro bit her lip, glancing at her friend. "She's gonna be okay, right? She—"

"Kokoro...?" Sayuki rasped.

"Sayuki?" Kokoro scooted closer to her, grabbing her hand. "Can you hear me? Are you okay? Did they—"

"Ma'am, please," the paramedic said. "She'll be okay, but right now, she needs space."

"But—"

"Please, just let us do our job," the woman said again, pushing her away. Kokoro reluctantly released Sayuki's hand as they rolled her away into the ambulance as the snow fell, the lights flashing, the world around her blurring as her heart thumped in her ears.

Why do I feel so damn helpless?

"She'll be okay," Hideaki said. "We got to her in time."

The noise from the sirens slowly faded. Hideaki, Ikiryo, Void, and Sunshine with Fishy in her arms all manifested around her. Void stepped forward to offer relief, but Kokoro waved him off.

"I hope so." Kokoro stared ahead, her vision tunneling and focused on the stretcher with Sayuki laid on it.

"Hey, this isn't like what happened with Naoko." Ikiryo placed a reassuring hand on her shoulder. Her grip tightened, her lip quivered. "We did it. We actually saved her."

Kokoro bit her lip and continued to stare. In the last moment before the ambulance doors shut, she could see Sayuki's eyes open, her gaze coming to rest on her. It was only when she smiled Kokoro knew everything was going to be okay.

"Yeah," she finally replied, allowing a smile of her own to reach her lips. "We did."

"Kokoro?"

Kokoro blinked. The urgent voices, the wailing sirens rang out, the gunfire from before had now completely stopped. There was someone else in front of her, dressed in a casual clothing with his badge pinned to his bulletproof vest. His aged eyes were trained on Kokoro.

"Mr. Haneda…?" She didn't even get the chance to finish her sentence. He was latched onto her, his grip tight.

"Kokoro," he began as he pulled back. "What were you thinking?"

"I'm sorry. I know it was stupid, I just…" She pursed her lips, avoiding his gaze. Despite the guilt that tore at her, his eyes held no anger, only relief.

"It's alright." Mr. Haneda sighed, turning toward the warehouse. "We have it under control. We caught the traitor at the station. The port is blockaded, and we have them pinned. The teams are clearing the warehouse as we speak."

Kokoro turned, seeing officers, paramedics and other escort groups of young women and captive goons. Her eyes widened as a thought came to her.

"Wait. Where's John?"

Mr. Haneda's brows furrowed. "John's here too?"

Kokoro nodded quickly.

"Damn it," he growled. "He'll be fine. We'll find him, alright?"

She tried to pull away but was grabbed by Mr. Haneda. "Please! I left him alone with Shane. I have to go help—"

One final gunshot rang out. Kokoro's eyes widened.

"No...no!" Kokoro used the confusion to break free from Mr. Haneda's grip, darting back toward the containers until she finally reached them. The stacked, snow-capped metal loomed and bent toward her, the distance between them lessened as she made her way through the maze.

"Come on, come on," she said. "Please don't be dead. Please—"

She stopped. Directly ahead was Shane, wiping blood from his bruised mug as John writhed at his feet, clutching his blood-soaked shoulder.

"Damn. Got me good there, John," he said, raising the gun to finish him. "Too bad for you. To think I once called you one of my best mates."

The body moved before Kokoro could even think, barreling into him.

"Leave him alone!" she screamed. "You won't take another friend from me!"

A loud crack filled the air. For a moment, Kokoro sat there, looming over Shane as the smoke sizzled from the barrel of his gun. Then a searing pain erupted within her, every nerve in her body burned. Her world spun as she collapsed backward, her blood seeping into the snow as Shane rose triumphantly.

"No, no..." she rasped, her heart thumping rapidly in her ear.

"Naoko?" John asked, grunting. His eyes trained on Shane, brows furrowing. "You piece of shit! I'll kill you for this!"

"We've been shot!" Hideaki said, his voice fading in and out like static. "Kokoro, stay focused. Just—"

"Kokoro!" Sunshine worriedly called out. "Please stay alive! The...oh no. It's getting dark in here!"

"Shit, shit!" she heard Ikiryo say. "Kokoro, we have to stay awake! Give me control!"

"It...hurts..." Kokoro wheezed. "I don't want you to..."

A sudden awareness took her. The fire in her gut that had faded returned with a passion, burning stronger than ever before. She cupped the wound and pressed, turning her attention back to Shane, her jaw clenching as her screams struggled to escape her lungs.

"Damn it," Shane said, rotating his arm and cracking his neck. "I really should bail, but what the hell. No way I'll get out now, thanks to you two, I imagine." He lifted the gun again, his eyes shifting between the two of them before settling on Kokoro. "I suppose I'll start with you."

Kokoro bared her teeth. Without warning, Shane's hand detached from its joint. Blood splattered the snow below in a flash of dazzling silver.

"Ah, shit!" He stomped the ground as he clutched the bleeding stump, screaming. "Damn it! Who...?"

A tall figure walked out from the dark. The shadows seemed to curl around him as if he were their master. Shinobu held his blade off to the side, his brows furrowed, eyes staring daggers into his victim.

"Shane Dreybuck," he said. "I've been looking for you."

Shane's eyes widened as he attempted to run the opposite way. He was blocked by two more heavily tattooed men. Shinobu smirked cruelly.

"As it would happen, so have they."

Shane's lip quivered as the three wolves closed in on their prey. Shinobu grabbed Shane by the back of his hair, forced him down, his right eye just a hair away from the edge of the blade.

"See this?" Shinobu asked. "Your friend Claire knew it, from base to tip. Little by little I fed her to it, but that's not enough. It wants more." His eyes narrowed. "It wants you, Shane."

Shinobu yanked Shane back, ripping a chunk of his hair out as he shoved him to the ground. Shane screamed and clutched his head.

"You know," the old man quipped. "I once knew a little shit just like you. Let's just say it did not end well for him, either."

Shane whimpered and continued to struggle. Shinobu pressed the blade closer against his neck, expertly drawing a line of blood from it, then ripped it away. Shane screamed louder.

"The things you have done to my granddaughter. The pain you put her through." Shinobu's glare hardened as he held the blade's tip in front of Shane, the blood dripping into the snow in front of him. "Her pain is over. Yours has only begun."

The two other men grabbed Shane by the arms and dragged him away into the dark. His ear-shattering screams pierced the night, until finally, there was nothing but the hair-raising silence. As Shinobu sheathed the blade, she could have sworn she heard Claire's screams, too.

"It's over?" Kokoro asked.

Shinobu nodded, the anger in his eyes fading. Kokoro exhaled slowly. Both relief and darkness flooded her like a tsunami.

"That's good," she said. "It's finally..."

John worriedly called her name as her peripherals darkened. The last thing she remembered was the vague sounds of sirens, shouting, and Mr. Haneda's voice softly begging her to hold on, before the shadows took her and everything was gone.

Kokoro was dreaming. Everything around her seemed abstract, formless, and yet solid. A swirling void that, for some reason, permitted her to exist among nothing. It was like the deepest sleep: restful, peaceful.

Kokoro.

She blinked. Was something calling her name?

Kokoro. Find her, please.

"Hey." She heard the snapping of fingers. "You awake?"

The swirling darkness vanished. In front of her was a familiar girl clad in rebellious black leather. Behind her was Sunshine, a worried look affixed to her face. To the right of her was Void, his expressionless figure standing perfectly still.

"Ikiryo," she said, shaking her head before giving her a gentle smile. "Good to see you."

Ikiryo sighed, then surprised her with a hug. "We thought we lost you for a minute, there. Hell, we thought we were gonna die, too."

"You mean we're not dead?" Kokoro asked, arching an eyebrow.

"We got out of surgery not too long ago," Sunshine replied from next to her, touching her chin. "Hideaki is up there, trying to listen in."

"To see if we're gonna live or not," Kokoro guessed with a frown. "I'm sorry, guys. I didn't mean to get us shot."

"It's okay," Sunshine said with a smile. "You were only trying to protect John. He is our friend, after all."

"Ditto," Ikiryo said before chuckling. "Besides, after watching what they did to Shane? Completely worth it, if you ask me."

Kokoro shuddered. Just as she was about to reply, the mists whipped together to form Hideaki, who clutched his abdomen and collapsed to the ground. Everyone instinctively moved to help him, but he waved them off, standing on his own.

"Everyone," he said, adjusting his glasses. "I have news."

Kokoro, Ikiryo, Sunshine and Void paused, waiting. Hideaki smiled.

"The surgery went well. We're going to be okay."

Cheers, shouts of excitement filled the air around them. Kokoro latched onto Hideaki, Ikiryo did a fist pump and Sunshine jumped up and down excitedly, Fishy still in her arms. Void didn't move, save for a brief nod.

"So that's it then. We're gonna live!"

"Not only that," Ikiryo added, "but we actually did it. We saved Sayuki and those other girls, too. We're heroes!"

Kokoro smiled as everyone continued to celebrate. Just then, a cry rang out. The shadows in the distance took on form, shaping themselves into a familiar building, the same one Shinobu had rescued Naoko from all those years ago.

The brothel.

"No," Kokoro said, turning her gaze toward that evil structure that had been haunting her since the day she came to be. "There's still one more we have to save."

The cheers from before fell into dead silence that was only broken when Ikiryo spoke up, apprehension in her voice.

"You want us to go in there?"

"Someone has to free her," Kokoro said. "She's been trapped there, probably long before any of us even existed. If you ask me, that's long enough."

Silence filled the air, only the haunting cries could be heard. The others shrunk away.

"I'm sorry," Ikiryo said, moving behind Hideaki. "I know I'm supposed to be brave, but…" she hesitated, "…not that place."

Kokoro sighed, then turned to Hideaki. "What about you? Are you with me?"

Hideaki stayed but, fists clenched, head dipped. "Ikiryo is right. I'd go with you to hell and back, but…"

"That *is* hell!" she hissed, attempting to make them look her in the eye, but they wouldn't relent. Sunshine stepped forward, shaking, but determined.

"Me and Fishy," she said. "We want to go."

Kokoro stood, unsure of what to say. She knelt in front of her and smiled gently. "Sunshine, I appreciate it. But this place? It's pretty dangerous. I don't want…"

Without warning, Sunshine, face hidden in her golden bangs, grabbed Kokoro by the collar and yanked her down to her level. The next thing she felt was the young girl's breath against her ear.

"Third floor," she whispered. "Make a right first thing, go down the hallway and make a left. Across the hallway with all the rooms, you'll see a door. That's where she is."

Kokoro's eyes widened. As the words seeped into her mind, she was pulled back into that memory from before, when Shinobu had picked her up and carried her away from the roaring fire. In the flames, there was that figure from before, the vague silhouette in the shape of a little girl that reached for its counterpart, crying for her as the doors shut, closing her in.

The burning brothel and the memory-Shinobu soon vanished, and suddenly Kokoro was viewing the half of the girl that *was* rescued from the outside. The darkness faded from her form, her hair lightening until it was blonde. She now wore a pair of jeans laced with different bead designs and a yellow T-shirt with sunflowers sewn in. Younger versions of Naoko's parents were next to her as she colored on a piece of paper, humming happily to herself as a warm light emanated from her.

"Naoko," memory-Mr. Haneda said, hugging her tight. "Our sunshine."

The Sunshine in the vision smiled, then froze. In the distance, she heard the cries of her long-lost counterpart. She stood, her eyes wide as she helplessly reached out, only to have the cries fade. Falling to her knees, her fists clenched tight to her chest, tears streamed down memory-Sunshine's face, grief pouring out from her soul onto her cheeks.

Kokoro pulled herself back from the memory as the present Sunshine stood, half-heartedly bouncing Fishy on her shoulder.

"That memory…" Kokoro began. "That was yours?"

Sunshine's young eyes met Kokoro's, eyes glistening as she fought to keep herself together. She nodded slowly.

"I didn't know." Kokoro frowned.

"Just…please. Whatever you do. Please save her." Sunshine dipped her head as she slowed. "She doesn't deserve to be alone anymore."

Her breaths ragged, Kokoro took a moment to process it. All this time, Sunshine had been here, even before the Naoko she knew existed. Teeth grit, Kokoro knelt down and embraced her.

"No matter what." Her grip on the young girl tightened. "I promise."

Sunshine returned the hug and nodded. Kokoro rose and spun to face the dark structure. The wails echoed across, and for a moment, she almost considered turning away.

No. Like Sunshine said. Kokoro clenched her fist, steeling herself. *She's been there long enough.*

With a deep breath, Kokoro broke into a run and slammed through the doors of the shadow brothel. A few of the venomous shadows whipped around, trying anything they could to stop her, but she would not be deterred.

Before she knew it, she was in, making an immediate right the way Sunshine had instructed. Down the first hallway, wallpaper was shedding, the buzzing lights flickered on the low ceiling. Kokoro inhaled sharply and moved again, breaching the last door on the left.

The door shut behind her, the dark lifted just enough to where she could see all the rooms from before, the petrified women trapped within them.

Kokoro stopped, assessing her surroundings. Something was wrong. It was far too quiet.

"There you are," a low, inhuman voice said. Kokoro spun to find one of the tattooed, shadowy figures looming over her, a wicked grin on its wide lips.

The blood rushed from her head as it grabbed her by her shoulders; she whipped around but couldn't escape its burning grip. From the darkness, more arrived, evil smiles and tattoos casting a sickening glow.

"No savior to help you this time," the shadow bragged. "Now, you're all ours. Oh, the things we've been waiting to do to you!" He flashed a set of wicked teeth along with a short blade. "Your little friend was right. Coming alone was a mistake."

"She's not alone!" a voice declared.

The shadow didn't even get to reply. He was immediately slammed by a familiar, red-haired young man, giving Kokoro the chance to slip his grasp. She stared at her counterpart in blatant shock.

"Hideaki?" she asked.

Hideaki rose, panting heavily. He pushed his glasses to the bridge of his nose with a confident smile.

"Not just me."

Kokoro spun, eyes wide. Two more of the shadows had been vanquished by Void, who simply punched through and absorbed them into nothing. Ikiryo erupted from behind him, bashing another with a crowbar she had found.

"Void! Ikiryo!" she exclaimed.

With a haughty smirk, Ikiryo continued to dash through the shadows with her makeshift weapon. "Better late than never, right?"

Relief flooded over Kokoro, washing the fear away that manifested in a laugh. A shrill, familiar voice called out.

"Kokoro, duck!"

Kokoro instinctively obeyed. The beast that was about to dig its claws into her recoiled as an orange blur collided with its face. It fell back and dissipated. Its killer came to rest in her arms.

"Fishy?" Kokoro asked, blinking. She turned to Sunshine, who had found a makeshift weapon of her own and was fending off the infinite waves of shadowy men with the others.

"Take him!" Sunshine shouted, pointing to her right. Kokoro followed with her eyes. They widened upon seeing it: the door that she had described earlier.

Behind it, Kokoro knew, was that poor little girl.

She worriedly glanced at the others. Hideaki was struggling against a fairly large Oni. Ikiryo barely held her weapon aloft, panting heavily. Void coldly assessed his innumerable foes.

"No," Kokoro said defiantly, moving to assist. "I'm not leaving them!"

"Go!" Hideaki said as he clashed with a demon. "We'll be fine!"

Teeth grit, Kokoro's eyes shifted between her friends and the door. At that moment, she thought about what would happen if she left them to fight the Oni alone. What would happen? Would they even survive?

Kokoro turned to Sunshine, whose wide, innocent eyes begged her to move on.

"Please," Sunshine mouthed. "You promised."

Regret tore at her insides like a rabid animal, but Kokoro gripped Fishy tight in her arms and bolted, avoiding Oni, shadows, and whatever tried its hardest to stop her from reaching the door. Her heart thumped in her chest, her lungs tightened so much she felt they might explode.

Just a little further.

With a cry, Kokoro summoned every bit of strength that remained in her and pushed through as she was enveloped by a bright light.

第二十章

CHAPTER 20
BREAKING FREE

THE LIGHT HAD VANISHED almost as soon as she was through. Kokoro was now in a dark room barely bigger than a broom closet. Bland concrete walls with faded strips of shredded wallpaper surrounded her as the light on the ceiling flickered. At the end of the room was a small platform, a mattress built into it, several torn blankets hung off the edge.

This is it? Kokoro looked around, taking in her new surroundings. Fishy, who had been relatively still, wriggled in her arms.

"What is it?" she asked. Fishy slipped from her grasp; she had to catch him to make sure he wouldn't fall to the ground. "Woah, easy buddy."

Something moved under the makeshift bed. Kokoro froze, watching as a young, dark-haired girl poked her head out of the shadows. Her wide eyes shook with fear yet brimmed with curiosity.

This is her. Kokoro's eyes widened. *The girl whose cries we've been hearing.*

The little girl froze, then tried to scuffle back under the bed.

"Wait!" Kokoro said, reaching out. She looked down at Fishy, whose wide eyes were focused intently on the young girl, like a puppy yearning to be reunited with its owner. She turned to the girl. "He's yours, isn't he?"

The girl nodded, slowly coming out from under the bed once more. She couldn't have been more than three or four. She was clad in a plain, dirty nightgown, as if she were hiding in every nook and cranny to avoid the Oni that sought to destroy her. Her hair was matted, her face covered in soot and filth. Hands shaking with trepidation, she reached out with one hand, while keeping the other tight to her chest. Kokoro offered Fishy to her.

"Go on," she said with a smile. "He's missed you too."

The girl stepped forward and took him into her left arm, her right hand held close to her chest. The koi appeared to snuggle into her, as she tucked him close, her eyes closing as she savored the moment. Kokoro felt every heartstring tearing in her chest. How long had this poor girl been here?

"My name is Kokoro," she told the girl. "What is your name?"

The girl looked up at her and shrugged. Kokoro frowned.

"Those monsters outside. They didn't hurt you, did they?"

The girl shook her head. Kokoro sighed, then froze once she noticed something in the little girl's other hand. It was a swirling dark, not unlike the ones that chased her, parts of it bleeding shadow from her clenched fist. From it, Kokoro could feel…everything. Every dark moment, every terrible memory, every instance of pain and horror that she had ever endured.

Kokoro frowned, then scooted closer, reaching to take it from her. The little girl recoiled.

"It's okay." Kokoro smiled reassuringly. "Let me help you."

The girl still refused, clenching the darkness even closer to her chest, backing away with tears in her eyes as she shook her head. Kokoro blinked in surprise.

Wouldn't she want to be rid of it? Unless…

Kokoro's heart shattered once the realization hit. The darkness wasn't holding the girl in its grasp, but rather, she was the one who had been trying to contain the worst of it at its core, to keep it from infecting everyone else as much as she could. To protect them.

Enough is enough. Kokoro's brows furrowed. *Its time for someone else to take that burden.*

Before the girl could react, Kokoro had sprung forward and snatched the darkness from her hand. The moment the venomous thing had contacted her palm, Kokoro's world nearly went dark. Shadows crept in from her peripherals, trying to consume her. She had never imagined that the pain she would endure could be so excruciating, so heavy. The chaos ravaged her all at once, a storm so unstable that she could barely hold a coherent thought.

No, no! Kokoro screamed as the worst memories forced their way in, invading, corrupting her soul: the wicked men chasing her at the brothel, the look of pure disgust and horror in the eyes of Naoko's parents as they discovered what she had done, then the pills she had tried to end her life with. The bullying. The isolation. Feeling tainted from the many hands and endless, greedy eyes.

And the darkness that promised an end to it all.

There is no point to any of it. The voices from the darkness, teasing and yet strangely alluring, echoed against the confines of her mind. *Death is freedom. Death is inevitable. Above all, Death is a mercy.*

Kokoro knelt, feeling the darkness dig into her like poison in her veins. It continued to burrow, dredging up any conceivable thing it could use against her. Again and again, she was forced to relieve the last smile Naoko had given before the shadowy hands had taken her to oblivion. The worst part was that it was all her fault; Kokoro should have been the one to fade. She was nothing but a fake, a copy meant to help her precious friend, and yet she couldn't even do that.

A failure. A nothing.

It hurts. It hurts so much.

Then end it.

I can't...I can't do it.

It's the only option.

I don't wanna die.

But you have to.

No. Please...

In this world, nothing beautiful survives. This trauma, this torment is all you are, and all you'll ever be. A broken husk; a shell of your former self.

Tears filled Kokoro's eyes, her lungs that had been trying so hard to breathe on the verge of failing. The shadows seemed to slow, a lull in the storm.

I am not your enemy. I just want this suffering to end. Don't you?

Her surroundings vanished to shadow and Kokoro knew it was over. The last sliver of herself was quickly fading, and she knew that too would fall to the inevitable nothingness. The endless eyes emerged from the dark, ready to claim their prize.

It's right. Kokoro's will faded as her thoughts slowed to a crawl, overtaken by the voices. *I just have to let go, then it will all stop.*

They stopped. A strange light fluttered over to her, settling into Kokoro's palm. Her eyes widened.

A butterfly?

The shadows retreated, if only a little. Kokoro blinked, staring down at the strange thing, its wings shimmering. In the butterfly,

Kokoro saw…something. She saw the day she had danced with Naoko down the street, or when they had looked out over the ocean from the Skytree. Next, there was the cake fight, then the time Naoko's dad had embraced her. Every happy moment any of them had ever bled into her soul, steadily purging the dark.

Kokoro caught her breath, a tear streaming down her cheek. Slowly, she stood, fighting the shadows as she gritted her teeth. This was no mere butterfly.

This was a reason to go on, the only one she needed.

"There's more than pain in this world," Kokoro uttered under her breath as she held the butterfly against her heart. "I will not give up. I *am* real, and I deserve to exist. I *can* be happy!" Her brows furrowed. "Above all, *I am not my pain.*"

The eyes among the shadows narrowed, then pushed forward in one last attempt to take her. Kokoro summoned every ounce of strength, every bit of hope in her soul, and let it out in a primal, existential scream.

"I AM NOT MY PAIN!"

Kokoro pushed out, and a light erupted, the dark whipping away in a flash. When it had faded, she and the young girl were somewhere else: a strange white room. Kokoro collapsed to her knees and into the girl's embrace.

"It's over," Kokoro said between ragged breaths, hugging her tight. "It hurt so much, but it's over now. We're gonna be okay."

The girl pulled back from the hug and looked up at her. A thought came to Kokoro, and despite her exhaustion, she chuckled. After that ordeal, it felt good to laugh.

"I don't know how you endured that all this time." Kokoro blinked her teary eyes in disbelief. "You're so brave, you know that?"

The girl smiled warmly, then turned to face where the strange white room ended. Ahead, at the end, was a field; the ethereal grass blew in rhythm as the girl led her through it, over a hill. The sky was so bright, so warm. She could see the shadows from before at the far edges, eyes always watching.

Kokoro's brows creased as she walked. She knew that haunting darkness would never truly go away, yet never again would it hold them like it had before, so long as they stayed strong.

At the top, Kokoro blinked at the sight that greeted her—a majestic Sakura tree, its snow-white petals swaying gracefully in the gentle wind. Near the tree's base, a young woman sat on a rock with dark hair cascading down her back. Her porcelain skin, marked with bruises and scratches, resembled a shattered piece of marble, yet glimmering veins of golden light coursed through the cracks, binding everything in place. It reminded her of Kintsugi: the mending of what life had broken.

Her eyes widened. *Is that really…?*

The young girl ran forward and embraced the figure on the rock, whose soft eyes slowly opened. She then turned to Kokoro, smiling.

"Kokoro," Naoko said. "I've missed you so much."

Heart skipping a beat, Kokoro froze. She stumbled forward, almost collapsing with each step. So many emotions battled within her she could barely form a coherent thought.

"You're…alive?"

Naoko's bright smile brought even more hope to Kokoro, though the slight downward curl of her lips betrayed it. The cracks in her skin seemed to magnify with her facial movements.

"I'm here," her friend replied.

"How?" Kokoro asked, frowning. "You were *gone*, Nao."

The surrounding air chilled. After all, such mention of tragedy was sure to bring the cold.

"I was," Naoko confirmed, her eyes downcast. "Or at least for a while. The next thing I knew, the shadows had taken me to that place. Eventually, I found her." She smiled, pulling the young girl from the brothel into her arms, holding her tight. Her eyes returned to Kokoro. "I saw her pain, the tragedy that made us. *All* of us." Naoko rested her head against the girl, brushing her hand through her hair, before releasing her.

Kokoro frowned, stepping forward and embracing Naoko. Her skin felt different, colder, with the promise of warmth only just below the surface.

Even so, her grip tightened. The only thing that mattered to her was that the one she cared about most in the entire world was *here*, in front of her. Naoko squeezed back, then pulled away with a gentle smile.

"What did they do to you, Nao?" Kokoro asked, assessing her friend as she pulled back. "You're falling apart."

"Don't think of it like that," Naoko said, brushing her fingers against the shattering skin on her cheek. "Despite everything that's happened, this is a good thing for me."

"How?" Kokoro shook her head. "They broke you, Nao."

"I'm not broken," Naoko replied, more of the shell falling away to reveal the light within. Her eyes met Kokoro's as a hopeful smile touched her lips. "I'm breaking free."

"Free…? What do you mean?" She shook her head as she gripped Naoko's hands. "You're coming back with me, right?" Without intending to, Kokoro's tightening grip caused Naoko's fingers to crumble partially, revealing even more light below it. Panic set in Kokoro's chest. "Nao, please. Don't leave me alone again."

Naoko gazed at her. She lifted her arms, cupping Kokoro's face in her palms.

"Ko," she began, her smile so gentle, "you were *never* alone."

Something caught Kokoro's peripherals; her head turned to her left, eyes widening. There, not far from there, were the others. Hideaki stood tall, confident, his eyes ablaze with curiosity. Ikiryo was next to him, tears streaming down her cheeks as she too beheld Naoko for the first time in forever. Next to her was Void, who stood still, yet his stars for eyes shined brighter at the mere sight of her.

Kokoro turned to see Sunshine approach the young girl from the brothel. At first, they simply stared, eyes quivering. Then Sunshine stepped forward and latched onto her.

"It's okay," Sunshine told her, a single tear streaming down her puffy cheeks. "I'm here, and I'm never leaving you again."

The girls embraced with Fishy the stuffed animal snug between them. Finally, after so long apart, they were reunited. Two halves of one whole.

"Pardon me, Naoko," Hideaki tentatively said. "That light that guided me to the others. That was you, wasn't it?"

"We live in a world where not even beautiful things survive," Naoko confirmed, nodding. "No one should have to go it alone."

Kokoro glanced at the others, fist clenched tight to her chest. From the group, Ikiryo stepped forward.

"Naoko," she said. "I'm not sure that you know me, but…"

"Actually, I do," Naoko replied with a smile. "It's good to see you again, Irkiryo."

Ikiryo blinked in utter shock. "You knew about me?"

"I've always had a feeling, but I wasn't sure, at least, not then," Naoko explained, her eyes slightly downcast. "It wasn't until the day I was taken that I saw you for the first time. I saw how terrified both you and Kokoro were. That's when I realized I had more than just her to protect."

Ikiryo's eyes shot wide open at the revelation. Her legs gave out beneath her, tears flowing freely from her eyes.

"Naoko…" she began, "*I'm so sorry.*"

"It's not your fault. It never was." Naoko smiled at her. Without warning, one of the shadows from the far edges moved closer. Kokoro's eyes widened.

"Naoko! Behind you! The—"

The looming shadow came to a halt, barely a meter away from Naoko, its single eye fixated on her with an accusing gaze. Without hesitation, she reached out and touched the side of what would have been its face. As her hand made contact, the eye closed, and tears trickled down. Naoko continued to brush her hand against it comfortingly until it gradually retreated and eventually vanished at the edge.

Kokoro blinked as Naoko faced them, revealing her radiant glow from beneath her cracked porcelain skin. It was at that moment that she realized the truth: the crumbling, cracking shell wasn't Naoko. It was nothing more than a shell, a cocoon to be shed. The *real* Naoko was underneath the surface, waiting to blossom.

"All these years, every one of you protected me in some way." Naoko glanced at each of them before her gaze finally rested on Kokoro. "I just wanted you all to know how grateful I am, how happy that you were all a part of me."

The ethereal wind picked up. The innumerable, luminescent white petals that had been floating in the air had flown around her and Kokoro. More of Naoko's shell fell apart until it was all gone. Out of her back stretched two butterfly wings, shimmering spectrums of powerful radiance. She pulled Kokoro forward, touching their foreheads together with a gentle smile.

"And just the same," Naoko continued, her body glowing brighter as her hands found Kokoro's face. "I'll always be a part of you."

"Naoko." Kokoro leaned forward and held on as she sobbed. "I love you."

As Naoko pulled her into her warm embrace, several memories flooded Kokoro's mind of their time together. From her awakening to the time they danced down the side of the Meguro, to their cake fight with her parents and finally, that time in the Tokyo

Skytree as they gazed across the cityscape to the ocean. Every moment that she shared with Naoko Haneda would always be a blessed memory for her, and yet that one last view of her beautiful smile was all she would ever need for as long as she lived.

"Let me be your angel this time. Okay?"

The luminescence that engulfed them soon spread like the sun across the morning sky, until all that was left was a comforting warmth, the promise that there would always be a bright tomorrow.

"Think she'll be okay?"

The soft murmurs of voices and the shrill beeps of the machine woke Kokoro from her slumber. Her vision slowly returned and with it, the pain in her side. The rest of the hospital room came into focus with each blink of her eyes. Seated at the opposite end of the room was Mr. Haneda, arms crossed, finger tapping. Across from him was Shinobu without his blade, elbows resting on his knees.

"I don't know," Mr. Haneda finally replied. "The doctor said the surgery went well, but…"

"She's strong," Shinobu began, nodding encouragement to his son, "and she's your daughter. Trust her to make it back home."

Mr. Haneda opened his mouth to reply but opted not to. Shinobu raised an eyebrow.

"Something wrong?"

Mr. Haneda sighed. "It's a long story. But the important thing is that she's here. She's alive." He smiled. "I couldn't be prouder."

Kokoro felt tears threaten to reach her cheeks, but she kept quiet. She wanted to hear more.

"You did good, Itsuki. Not just with her." Shinobu smiled. "You took a different path from your old man, an honorable one. At first, I couldn't understand. But now, seeing how far you've come. Your family." Shinobu lowered his gaze. "Not that I have any right to say it, but I'm proud of you, too."

"After what you did, saving my little girl?" Mr. Haneda smiled. "You have every right. Thank you, father." He rose and bowed deep.

Shinobu did the same, then chuckled wryly. "I knew this day would come. I assume they're waiting outside for me?"

"Unfortunately. I tried to wave them off, but it's hard when your father is on Japan's top ten most wanted list."

"Ten?" Shinobu asked, scoffing. "Not even top five?"

"Afraid not. But to be fair, they weren't looking very hard. Nobody wanted to jail the man that took down Akuji Akasaka." Mr. Haneda eyed his father with restrained regret. "Unfortunately for tonight, I could only negotiate a little time."

The old man sighed. "How long do I have?"

"Enough to say goodbye," Mr. Haneda replied.

Shinobu paused, then nodded in understanding, before looking up. "You know your grandfather's blade?"

"How could I forget that thing?" Mr. Haneda said before pausing. "Why?"

"I couldn't enter the hospital with it, so I surrendered it to your partner," Shinobu explained. "Does he still have it?"

"Probably." Mr. Haneda touched his chin thoughtfully. "Why?"

"Can you have him bring it up here?"

"I…" Mr. Haneda hesitated. "I don't know if…"

"I don't intend to fight anymore," Shinobu said, his eyes falling. "There's just…something I want to do before I'm taken away."

The room fell silent. Eventually, Mr. Haneda heeded his father's request. Within the hour, the strange blade was brought, albeit with a group of at least ten police officers. Mr. Haneda's partner reluctantly handed it to Shinobu, who closed his eyes and inhaled sharply, before bowing and offering it to his son. Blinking, Mr. Haneda took the blade.

"It's yours now. Although…" Shinobu grimaced. "I'm afraid it's nowhere near its former glory. I've disgraced it."

Mr. Haneda took a moment to inspect the sheath, then partially drew the blade itself. He positioned it so Shinobu could see his reflection in it.

"The shell is scarred, but…" Mr. Haneda smiled. "The inside is still pure. Just like you, Father."

For the first time since she had met him, Kokoro watched as a tear fell from Shinobu's eye. Father and son embraced. She smiled.

"Thank you, Itsuki," Shinobu said with a nod, before shuffling over to the bed. Kokoro closed her eyes, still pretending to be comatose as she felt his hand close around hers.

"It was good to see you again, granddaughter," he said, tightening his grip, like he knew it would be the last time. "Live well. Above all, be happy."

Kokoro couldn't stand it. She opened her eyes, struggling to even lift her head to see, but he was already at the door with two police officers.

Shinobu stopped. Just before he left the room, he turned and met her eyes with a smile. She knew he was thinking of that day, when he had pulled them from the flames of that brothel and made a happy life possible for her, for Naoko. For everyone.

Throat straining, Kokoro tried to call out, but to no avail. They shared one last stare before he was escorted out of the room into the dark of the hallway. She frowned.

"Kokoro?" a voice asked. Kokoro turned to see Mr. Haneda staring at her, eyes widened. He rushed to her side and embraced her. "You're awake! I..."

"I think I've been awake for a while," Kokoro said with a gentle smile.

Mr. Haneda paused, then pulled up a chair and sat down. "So you heard that?"

"Yep," she said. "I'm glad you two finally made peace."

Mr. Haneda glanced at the Katana in his hand, his eyes lowered. "I suppose. Although I really wish—"

"—that things didn't have to be that way?"

"Choices were made long ago, and that was the result, unfortunately." Mr. Haneda nodded sadly. "Such is life."

"I know." Kokoro's blinked. "Wait. Back at the warehouse." She froze. "Sayuki. John. What happened to them? Are they…?"

"John pulled through his surgery just fine," he said.

Kokoro sighed with relief, then froze. "And Sayuki?"

"On the third floor, awake in her room, waiting for news on you." He chuckled. "I'm glad she cares about you so much. It's good that she's your—"

"She's not just a friend," Kokoro blurted out.

Mr. Haneda arched an eyebrow. "She isn't?"

"No. She's the color in my world." Kokoro avoided his gaze. "I…I'm in love with her."

Kokoro let the silence hang in the air. She wasn't exactly sure why, but this moment felt critical. Her abdomen throbbed, both from her wound and from the butterflies that tingled beneath it.

"Oh." Mr. Haneda blinked in surprise. "Well…I suppose I should have figured that out by now." He smiled warmly. "She's a sweet girl. I'm glad she makes you happy."

"Thank you," Kokoro said, her cheeks flushing. She looked at him as another thought came to mind. "Say…what happened to all those girls?"

"Those that were there that night are all home safe and sound now." Mr. Haneda frowned. "Unfortunately, that was just a portion of the total that had gone missing over the last six months. It seems Shane and Claire shipped some off before any of us could do anything about it."

Frowning, Kokoro dipped her head. "So, we failed?"

"The girls you saved would beg to differ." Mr. Haneda sat up straight in his chair. "Unfortunately, this kind of thing happens despite our best efforts. We live—"

"—in a world that destroys beautiful things," Kokoro finished for him.

After a moment's silence, Mr. Haneda nodded. "Yes. But that doesn't mean we'll stop trying."

Kokoro nodded sadly, laying back on the pillow and closing her eyes. As she did, images of Naoko's cracked, smiling face flashed across. Her eyes shot back open, and she briskly sat up, ignoring the pain caused by it.

"By the way, I found her!"

Mr. Haneda blinked. "Found who?"

"Naoko." Kokoro blinked, remembering how she had faded into a strange light. The excitement that had brimmed before had died slightly. "I saw her one last time."

"One last time?" he asked, his face downcast. "So…she really is…?"

Kokoro paused as a strange feeling came to her. Logic would tell her that Naoko was gone, and yet that didn't quite feel true. She didn't feel that same grief she had before, but instead felt strangely…*complete*. Similar to how it was before, when Naoko was with her, but somehow…better?

"I'm not sure, but…" Kokoro bit her lip and nodded. "…I tried to bring her back with me. I really did."

After a long silence, Mr. Haneda sighed. "She's not suffering?"

"The opposite," Kokoro said, a sad smile on her lips. "She's free."

Mr. Haneda closed his eyes, muttering a few indiscernible words. Upon opening them, he gripped Kokoro's hand tight. "Good. That's all I've ever wanted for her."

Kokoro smiled. Mr. Haneda's eyes turned to her, flooded with both relief and sadness.

"I'm just glad I didn't lose you too," he said, nodding. "Daughter."

A flood of uncontrollable emotion enveloped Kokoro as she reached over to grip his hand tight.

"Thank you...*Father*," she said, though the word didn't seem like such a foreign concept anymore. The two of them sat in silence for the rest of the night, staring out the window as the snow fell. For once, instead of that terrible white silence, all Kokoro saw was beauty.

"Hey, mind giving me a hand with this?" John asked as he attempted to pull his suitcase from the back of the undersized trunk with his free arm, the other encased in a sling.

"Move over. Let a woman show you how it's done." Kokoro sighed, rolling up her sleeves to mock him before placing a firm grip on the handle. She gave a tug, but the damn thing wouldn't budge. "Or not."

Sayuki chuckled in the background as they continued to fight it, wigging, even shoving the small van back and forth. Finally, it gave, but not before taking them to the ground with it.

"Bloody hell," John said, standing and offering Kokoro his free arm. "Anyway, thanks for the help and the ride. We sure got here hella early."

Kokoro took his arm, rising to her feet. She frowned. "John, you know your flight leaves in like two hours, right?"

"Yeah, I know." John inhaled deeply, taking in his surroundings. "I gotta admit, though. I'll miss Tokyo." He turned to them and smiled. "And I'll miss both of you."

"You'll keep in touch, won't you?" Kokoro asked.

"It's a bit of a time difference, but yeah." He nodded. "On PULSE, right?"

Kokoro nodded, then opened the app to make sure his contact info was there but stopped. The profile photo was one Naoko had taken a year ago, with Shane, Claire, and John.

John noticed, and his eyes narrowed. "Don't bother. Delete it. We can take a new one."

She nodded but found herself unable to erase it completely. This photo was one of the few Naoko had ever taken of herself. No chance she would ever erase it.

But if I modified it…

Biting her lip, Kokoro opened the photo and edited out Shane and Claire, leaving only a cropped photo of Naoko and John. She smiled with satisfaction.

Yes. This feels right. Even if he doesn't know. He still deserves to have it.

Kokoro beamed and sent the photo to John. He opened his phone, first arching an eyebrow, then dismissing his curiosity with a smile.

"Thanks, Naoko. Now let's take some new ones, shall we?"

The three of them squished together, wrapping their arms around one another as they took more selfies, making a variety of silly faces. With every flash of the phone's camera, Kokoro knew it would be yet another happy memory for her. For all of them.

After they were done, Kokoro and Sayuki embraced John one last time. He pulled back and smiled, grabbing his suitcase before running off through the sliding doors of the airport. She averted her eyes and returned to the car, sliding into the passenger seat. With a wistful sigh, Kokoro shook the growing melancholy from her mind. Sad it was, today was also a good day. Ever since the white silence finally melted from Tokyo, she had been looking forward to it, to the month of April and the beauty it brought.

Sayuki entered the back of the taxi with her and soon they were down the road, back into the ever-thickening traffic that the big city wrought. The grand skyscrapers shimmered in the sunlight, reflecting each other like a hall of mirrors. The city of glass slowly gave way to more humble, low-rise buildings of concrete.

Kokoro's eyes widened as they finally reached the Meguro River. Countless cherry blossoms stretched above the concrete basin, casting a delicate pink hue over the scene below. The buildings obscured the fading sunlight; the lanterns that lined the river, along with the trees, had lit with anticipation of the festival.

The car rolled to a halt. Within seconds, Kokoro's feet were planted on the road, her eyes beholding the flurry of white and pink as the petals took flight in the gentle breeze. Crowds, more than half of them clad in kimono, shuffled along either side of the river.

With a deep breath, she closed off the world around her, letting her mind dance behind her eyelids. From her moments with John and Sayuki, to the time she and Naoko had jammed their way down the street. So many precious memories that she cherished, and yet…

Kokoro opened her eyes, watching the cherry blossom petals fall around her. With a sigh, she turned to Sayuki, her lip curled down.

"Something wrong?" Sayuki asked.

"No. Not wrong, just…" Kokoro frowned. "Just sad how things have to end."

"Don't think of it that way," Sayuki offered, eyes fixed on the blossoming trees. "Think of it as the beginning of something new."

"Something new, huh?" Kokoro asked with a smile. "Like what?"

A shiver ran up Kokoro's spine as she felt Sayuki's warm hand slip into hers. She looked into those beautiful brown eyes and could see every ounce of love and excitement she had been holding back.

Sayuki's soft lips curled into a gentle smile as some of the floating petals came to rest in her hair.

"Like us," she said, suddenly blushing and avoiding her gaze. "If that's okay."

Kokoro's cheeks flushed. For months now, the feelings between them had been slowly burning but growing stronger. Now, in this moment, was the perfect time for them to light their souls ablaze. She paused, waiting to hear any complaints from within. Instead, in her mind's eye, she could see their nods of approval, even from Ikiryo.

Turning back to Sayuki, Kokoro smiled, gripping her hand tight and pulling her closer and leaning in as her slowly darkening hair blew in the warm wind. "I do. More than anything, I do."

Sayuki's eyes widened as she struggled to say something, anything. Instead, her arms wrapped around her back, then her neck, and finally their lips collided. A rush of euphoria filled Kokoro in that moment. Every nerve in her body lit up like the crack of fireworks in the festival night sky.

They broke the kiss, yet not their interlocked hands. Together, they walked down the side of the Meguro, the cherry blossoms falling all around them.

"So," Sayuki said, brushing her hair out of her eyes, her cheeks still beet red. "Where to next?"

"Um…" Kokoro touched her chin, pondering it. The world was their oyster. Where should they go? Tokyo Tower? The gardens? Suddenly, she had an idea…a very romantic idea. "Say, why don't we go to the festival together? Wear our kimono, stay out and watch the fireworks until midnight? You know, that kind of thing." Kokoro turned to her and winked.

"Sure, but…" Sayuki blinked. "It is a school night for you, isn't it?"

With those words, all Kokoro's hopes and dreams for that night came crashing down. The events of the past year had put them so far behind. Because of extenuating circumstances, however, they were allowed the summer to play catch up. Needless to say, there was a lot.

"Oh," Kokoro said, frowning and running her hand through her hair. "I'm sorry."

Sayuki giggled. "How about a nice dinner instead?"

Kokoro smiled, planting a kiss on her cheek. "Works for me."

Sayuki blushed harder, then turned her eyes forward into the crowds. Inside her mind, she could feel Hideaki in the front with her. No doubt the word 'school' brought him there.

"I hate to be that person," Hideaki said, his faint voice growing. "But she has a point. We've only got a few classes left."

"Yeah!" Sunshine chimed in from somewhere. "Then we can pick flowers all day! Little Nao's been wanting to as well!"

A chuckle came to Kokoro as she imagined the young girl's blushing face next to Sunshine's. It was good to finally see the girl happy after being so strong all those years. "Is that what you want to do when you grow up?"

"Always," Sunshine said, her voice upbeat. "What about you, Ikiryo?"

"I don't care, as long as school's done," Ikiryo said. "I mean, maybe art? But I don't know how you guys would feel about it. We do share a body."

"True," Kokoro said before a thought came to her. "Say, Hideaki. Before, you said you wanted to live so you could do something, but you never said what it was."

There was a brief silence. Finally, she heard him draw in a breath.

"I wanted to be a doctor. A therapist, specifically," he finally said. "The way Dr. Maeda helped us… I don't know. It inspired me."

Kokoro couldn't help but smile.

"Besides," Hideaki continued. "It's all a pipe dream. Our situation certainly doesn't help. After all, Sunshine wants to pick flowers, Ikiryo wants to paint, you want to dance." He sighed. "How would we decide what we really wanted to do?"

Kokoro paused, considering his words. Then she smiled.

"Why not all of it?"

In the mind's eye, Kokoro could see them blinking in surprise.

"How so?" Hideaki asked.

"You think the way we are hinders us, but if you ask me, it couldn't be further from the truth," she explained. "We can do anything we put our mind to, just as long as we work together."

"Really?" Ikiryo asked. "You guys would really let me go and just paint?"

"We could make it work," she said with a smile. "Hideaki? How would you feel about it?"

At that moment, Kokoro could imagine him pushing his glasses to his nose. "Well, studies show that art is quite beneficial to mental health. It certainly wouldn't hurt."

Kokoro beamed, nodding. "Sunshine?"

"All good with me!" she said. "As long as you guys are happy. That's all that matters."

"Good," Kokoro said. "So, it's settled. Whatever we do, we do together. Agreed?"

"Agreed," Hideaki said.

"You got it," Ikiryo said.

Void said nothing but nodded.

"Yippee!" Sunshine said, jumping in the air with an ecstatic Little Nao and Fishy in her arms.

Kokoro beamed. Behind her, in the inner world, she could feel everyone not far behind. Hideaki, Ikiryo, Sunshine, Little Nao, Void, and Fishy. She could sense their pain, hear their tears, of loss, and of joy. They were as much a part of her as she was of them, and among the coldness of the world, they would always be one.

Together.

EPILOGUE

HOPE

DESPITE KNOWING THAT THE DAY WOULD ARRIVE, Kokoro still wasn't ready. It seemed like just yesterday that she was finishing the school year and spending time with Sayuki and her family. Now, she was packing her bags for a cross-country road trip to the university that Hideaki's genius had gotten them accepted to. There, they would specialize in Art Therapy and strive to help others like them.

Kokoro huffed as she finished cramming her suitcase in Sayuki's tiny van. Despite the bullet train being fairly cheap and quick, she accepted without a second thought. After all, what better way to move on to a new stage of life than taking the scenic route?

After bidding her parents goodbye with a somber hug, she entered the van and soon they were off. The residential areas faded to mid-rise buildings, then finally the skyscrapers. After that, it went in reverse until finally there was nothing but nature, the occasional town, and the long road ahead.

Just one stop to make first.

Finally, they arrived at the beach. The moment Sayuki had pulled into the parking spot, Kokoro flung open the car door, taking in the salty, damp ocean air.

Kokoro stumbled forward as she removed her sandals and waded into the cold water, the sun slowly rising on the horizon. The light purple sky turned to blue, then black, stretching on as the stars gradually faded to the day. She briefly turned back toward the direction of the city, thinking for a moment how *this* was the first time she had ever explored beyond Tokyo.

Kokoro stopped for a minute, brushing her nearly blackened hair with hints of white from her face. After so long, here she was, fulfilling their dream.

Without warning, two young children—Sunshine and Little Nao— rushed past her and sprinted into the surf. Within the minute, they were running and splashing, chasing Fishy as he ducked below and jumped above the waves.

Kokoro chuckled. To her right, Hideaki materialized.

"Guess we finally made it, huh?" she asked him.

"We did." Hideaki chuckled, removing his glasses, closing his eyes and spreading his arms. "This feels *amazing*."

"Damn straight," Ikiryo said, suddenly appearing to her left, sitting down in the shallow water. "I don't think I've felt this good in a long time, if ever."

Kokoro beamed. She looked ahead to see Void with Sunshine and Little Nao, splashing them as they giggled. Part of her wondered what Naoko would say. She frowned.

If only she could be here.

She paused, thinking back to the last time she had seen her precious friend as a realization dawned on her. Naoko was still a part of her, of each of them, watching over them and filling everyone with a peace not felt in ages. She was their light, the butterfly in their hearts. The frown on Kokoro's lips curled into a warm, fulfilled smile.

No, her friend wasn't gone. With them, *through* them, Naoko Haneda was more alive than ever.

"So," Kokoro began, pulling herself out of her train of thought. "What now? Was there anything you guys wanted to do while we're traveling?"

Hideaki and Ikiryo exchanged looks. Finally, he spoke up, "Well, to be honest, we were all going to head back in for a while."

Kokoro frowned. "You guys aren't coming with?"

"Well, we talked about it, and decided that we would let you and Sayuki enjoy the road trip." Ikiryo smiled. "But we'll be back just in time for classes. Promise."

"You'd better," Kokoro said, her lip curling slightly. "I'm still gonna miss you guys."

"Same here," Sunshine said, now suddenly in front of her with the others. Kokoro turned to each of them. How lucky was she to have such amazing people to help her through everything?

A tug of her pants interrupted her thoughts. Little Nao was staring up at her, arms raised. Kokoro lifted her to her shoulder, turning to the others once more. "So, I guess this is it, huh?"

"For now," Hideaki said, nodding. "But if you need us, you know we'll be here."

"What he said," Ikiryo added, smiling warmly.

Kokoro nodded and brought all of them into her embrace, closing her eyes. When she opened them, she was alone on the beach once more, staring out into the endless potential that was the ocean.

"Everything okay, Ko?" a voice behind her asked. Sayuki walked up, flipflops in hand, a concerned look on her face. She knew of the dream, what this moment meant to her.

Kokoro turned back, seeing the daybreak and with it, hope. The hope that despite everything they had gone through, the horror, the tragedy, the loss, that everything would be okay in the end. She faced Sayuki, a smile adorning her lips.

"Never been better."

Sayuki's concern quickly faded as she returned it. With a nod, she walked back to her car, giving Kokoro a few more minutes to soak in the warmth, the hope that came with the sunrise.

Because now, that hope was reality.

TYLER CRAIG NIXON was born in Tampa, FL, and served in the US Navy. He likes to experiment in many different genres of fiction, especially Sci-Fi/Fantasy. He is also the author of *Sky of Shadows* and its upcoming sequel, *A Broken World*. He currently lives in Lakeland with his wife, three dogs, and a cat.

@tylercnixonauthor

www.tylercnixonauthor.com

Author's Notes

It's hard to say where the idea for *Fractured Souls* came from. I can, however, say with certainty that it began back when I was in the Navy. It was undoubtedly inspired by works such as *Tokyo Ghoul* as well as my own struggles with mental health. It began first as a 3D comic, then a short story, and developed to the version you hopefully just finished.

The undoubtedly trickiest part of writing the book was Naoko's Dissociative Identity Disorder. As the story grew, I realized it was less about the multiple personalities and more about the darkness that trauma brings when it fractures a young soul. To protect its host from said trauma and function, the brain splits into parts. The person goes about their life, usually unaware of the others within. The only way to bridge this memory gap is through a process called "integration." It involves breaking the barriers between alters and facing the trauma with courage.

That brings me to the dedication at the beginning of the book. As the story grew, it became clear that, by its very nature, this wasn't just a book for me. By choosing to explore the topic of DID, I realized I was effectively representing the group. And thus, I did research. Lots of it. I watched a bunch of videos and testimonies on the subject. I read the stories of others, the things they had gone through, and the different ways their trauma manifested. I asked questions from a variety of people, ranging from those who had endured such traumas in their life to psychologists, and, of course, my beta readers. To everyone that helped me, I am eternally grateful.

And so, a year's worth of writing, researching, realizing an idea's stupid, scrapping and rewriting, it's finally here. I sincerely hope you enjoyed *Fractured Souls*, and I look forward to providing more stories in the future.

Acknowledgements

I want to express my deep gratitude to those who contributed to this book. Kirsty, my developmental editor, played a crucial role in refining the story while primary editor, Maddy, applied her grammar and prose expertise to whip the book into publishing shape.

Special thanks goes to my beta readers, including my wife, Chelcey, my sister, Meagan, "Bunni," a DID system, psychologist Nicole, and my friends/writing partners, Chuck and Yopparai.

I'd also like to give a shout out to one of my first ARC readers, "dbookishprincess," for enthusiastically wanting to read FS and bring this story to the masses.

Your early support and insights were instrumental in bringing *Fractured Souls* to its fullest potential. This is undoubtedly my most accomplished work, and it wouldn't have been possible without all of you!